ESSENTIAL NEW ZEALAND SHORT STORIES

ESSENTIAL NEW ZEALAND SHORT STORIES

SELECTED BY

OWEN MARSHALL

GODWIT

National Library of New Zealand Cataloguing-in-Publication Data

Essential New Zealand short stories / selected by Owen Marshall.
Includes bibliographical references.
ISBN: 1-86962-094-1
1. Short stories, New Zealand. I. Marshall, Owen, 1941–
NZ823.0108–dc 21

A GODWIT BOOK
published by
Random House New Zealand
18 Poland Road, Glenfield, Auckland, New Zealand
www.randomhouse.co.nz

First published 2002

ISBN 1 86962 094 1

Design: Inhouse Design
Layout: Kate Greenaway
Printed in China

CONTENTS

INTRODUCTION

Novelist J.G. Ballard, who began as a writer of short stories, is now pessimistic about their future. In an interview that appeared in the November 2001 issue of *Literary Review* he said, 'the short story seems, sadly, to be heading for extinction'. Such predictions have been regularly made for most literary genres, often with cogent supporting evidence, but somehow the literatures themselves will not so readily give up the ghost. Certainly short stories have a strong tradition in New Zealand writing and, despite the marketplace's preference for novels, they continue to be produced in large numbers, given prominence by well-established national competitions, featured in school and university courses and gathered into collections. They form a resilient genre with its own idiosyncratic pulse of literary energy. At one extreme it may be seen as the preserve of the literary purist, at the other the best opportunity for the aspiring novice. Whether writing short stories can provide a living is another matter entirely.

It has been argued that, for much of the 20th century, the short story was more characteristic of our New Zealand fiction than the novel, and more fully developed. That has changed. Witness not only the cumulative authority of Janet Frame, and the individual milestones of Maurice Gee's *Plumb* (1978), Keri Hulme's *the bone people* (1984) and Elizabeth Knox's *The Vintner's Luck* (1998), but also the considerable number of books that did not receive international exposure but whose strengths were recognised here. The novel's coming of age is to be celebrated. I do not see the novel and short story in some sort of artistic competition. They are equal, but distinct. They achieve different ends, or they achieve the same ends in different ways.

It is a truism that novels sell more readily than collections of short stories, and yet we live in an age of reduced attention spans, of sound bites and 10-second news items: a browsing age with an itch for novelty. People are pressed for time, we are told, with all manner of stimuli competing for their attention, yet doorstop novels are as popular as ever. Perhaps for an understanding of the short story's enigmatic contemporary role, we need to consider the literary form itself.

What is a short story? Most editors are too circumspect, or shrewd, to attempt an answer, and press on briskly to methods of selection, social context, delineation of literary trends and discussion of individual stories. But the question is a good one, and although I can give no answer, even to my own satisfaction, by wrestling with it we enlarge our appreciation of the form and of individual stories. In the end we are likely to favour definitions that agree with our own responses for, as Proust said, we read only what is within ourselves.

John Hadfield, in his introduction to *Modern Short Stories*, was dismissively pragmatic and unhelpful: 'A short story is a story that is not long; that would seem to be a sufficient, if inexact, rule of thumb by which to work.' Robert Louis Stevenson and his contemporaries often wrote stories of 30 or 40 pages and more, but today anything over 10,000 words is considered long, and many competitions and publications have limits of 5000 words, or less. But prescriptive length is surely a distraction, because the short story is not just a miniature novel. There is something unique in the short story; some characteristic, or sum of characteristics that, quite apart from word count, makes it a species within literature. But, if so, what is the gene that determines the genre?

What a difficult question that has proved to be. This is partly because, as soon as we move from an individual story to generalisations about literary form, there is a lack of critical precision. The genre itself falls to pieces in our hands: yarn, fantasy, fable, metafiction, romance, psychological realism – the short story, like the molecule, breaks down into smaller and smaller entities when under pressure.

In terms of what may be conveniently and clumsily termed the literary short story, however, the views of H.E. Bates and Frank O'Connor are both stimulating and helpful. For Bates, 'the short story is to fiction what the lyric is to poetry. In its finest mould the short story is, in fact, a prose poem.' American writer William Gass agrees: 'It is a poem grafted on to sturdier stock.' It does seem the economy the short story requires, inclines its practitioners to use poetic techniques of compression and figurative association. Think of such leading writers of short fiction as Anton Chekhov, James Joyce, John Cheever, V.S. Pritchett, William Trevor, Alice Munro, Grace Paley and Katherine Mansfield.

O'Connor identifies an ideological difference between the short story and the novel. For him, the short story arises from 'an attitude of mind that is attracted by submerged population groups', by which he means groups disenfranchised in various ways within their societies. It is easy to make a case that the short story has operated in this way within New Zealand fiction. We need look no further than Frank Sargeson and Janet Frame. The notion is intellectually beguiling, but difficult to demonstrate, yet I was interested to see, in his recent introduction to the collected stories of Canadian Alistair McLeod, that John McGahern supports O'Connor's view: 'I think of the novel as the most social of all the art forms, the most closely linked to an idea of society, a shared leisure, and a system of manners. The short story does not generally flourish in such a society but comes into its own like a song or prayer or superstition in poorer, more fragmented communities where individualism and tradition and family and localities and chance or luck are dominant.'

Poetry and disenfranchisement, then – perhaps in such ideas we see something of the special nature of the literary short story, but the art is a living, changing one and there will be as varied a range of successful stories as there are writers of unique consciousness. Fortunately we do not need agreement about form to enjoy individual stories, or to appreciate the significance of short fiction to our literature.

This anthology is a companion volume to *Essential New Zealand Poems* selected by Lauris Edmond and Bill Sewell. In his introduction Sewell said that their guiding principle of selection was immediate impact, and that they had a general readership in mind. Both considerations were important for me, but I also followed other guidelines. Some of these were of my own making, some were suggested by my publisher, all we agreed to own together.

An editor often seeks to side-step the best-known pieces, and highlight alternative work. This was not my brief here. I sought stories that have made their mark in New Zealand literature: stories that stand tall in the company of our very best short fiction, and are essential in that sense. Almost all of these are familiar and cherished. I also followed my own judgement, aware that what an editor considers perception may be seen by others as prejudice, or eccentricity.

I have long been interested in short stories, but before making this selection I read as widely as time allowed: I found also that some years of tutoring, and judging national competitions, were a useful challenge to my views of contemporary New Zealand writing and, I hope, prevented me from being too backward looking.

The collection is neither a historical survey of New Zealand short fiction, nor an attempt at a balanced presentation of literary concerns and constituencies. Any collection is of its time, and I have no doubt this one advantages those of our writers who have produced their best work in the last 20 years. I have been severe in selecting from early collections, and future editors will no doubt be equally discriminating concerning stories we presently hold dear.

I make a distinction between the selection of essential stories and the selection of the most popular, though I think the great majority in this anthology would survive both examinations. Roald Dahl, in his speech at the *Sunday Express* Book of the Year Prize in 1989, claimed the great writer was one who pleased the marketplace, and that the only purpose was to entertain. Laurie Lee interrupted him by shouting from the audience, 'Balls!' I'm with Laurie Lee, even though defining literary excellence is more difficult than assembling sales figures.

If artistic criteria are paramount, editorship, like politics, is the art of the possible, and practical constraints do have an effect. Not only did the gangway have to be lifted before all my choices could come aboard, but in at least one case the length of an individual story prevented its inclusion, though another by the same author is in the collection. Also, in fairness to the wealth of talent, even the very best of our writers are limited to a single work.

In the process of bringing these stories together I was struck by the increasing variety and richness of the genre during the 80 years spanned by the selection. It is largely to illustrate this development that the stories are arranged in order of publication. While the ley lines of Katherine Mansfield and Frank Sargeson are still discernible in the literary landscape, all manner of new magnetism is at work, and it is excitingly obvious when Maori writing, feminist writing, post-modernism or gay writing kicks in.

Has this development, as represented in this collection, resulted in a body of work that is more than superficially distinctive of New Zealand? Perhaps an overseas commentator is best placed to answer that question, but we would expect the response to be yes, and in my opinion it is. New Zealand short fiction is shaped not only by individual psyches, but by the creative tension between those forces that tend to create a uniquely local form, and those that promote wider commonality. Among the former are a more assured and relaxed sense of national identity; the accretion of a special social, cultural and political history; the acceptance, indeed validation, of a New Zealand variant of English, especially in the vernacular; the recent and vigorous Maori and Pacific voice in New Zealand writing; and the lack of overseas opportunities for our short fiction. Among the latter forces are our embrace of international communications; our susceptibility to dominant cultures; our enduring Pakeha links to a literature that originated in Europe; the burgeoning of an arts festival scene that regularly brings us influential overseas writers; and a brash global hi-tech youth culture.

There is another recent and significant influence at work within our literature – professional writing courses, pre-eminently those established by Bill Manhire at Victoria University of Wellington. It may be too soon to determine whether this development favours a focus on the distinctively local, or an increased awareness of overseas trends, but the collegial mode, academic stringency and links with publishers offered by such courses have certainly accelerated the progress of a growing number of writers.

Many of our best stories profit from the meeting of New Zealand and overseas influences, and are, as W.H. Auden hoped for his poetry, 'like some valley cheese, local, but prized elsewhere'.

The stories in this collection have voices of their own, and speak for themselves far more eloquently than any commentary I am capable of making. I have read and enjoyed them many times, and harbour the vain and selfish wish that I had written them all, rather than merely bringing them together for this group snapshot at the beginning of the 21st century. Although they have not been chosen as social documents, and the relationship between life in a given time and place and the art that arises from it is too subtle to be satisfactorily captured by the analogy of a mirror, a writer's consciousness is always informed by its social and physical environment, so the stories provide tangential, personalised glimpses of the journey we make as a nation.

My special thanks to the contributors and copyright holders who gave permission for work to be included, and to Jane Connor of Random House, who asked me to edit the book and supported me enthusiastically during the time needed for that to be accomplished.

Owen Marshall

KATHERINE MANSFIELD

When dear old Mrs Hay went back to town after staying with the Burnells she sent the children a doll's house. It was so big that the carter and Pat carried it into the courtyard, and there it stayed, propped up on two wooden boxes beside the feed-room door. No harm could come to it; it was summer. And perhaps the smell of paint would have gone off by the time it had to be taken in. For, really, the smell of paint coming from that doll's house ('Sweet of old Mrs Hay, of course; most sweet and generous!') – but the smell of paint was quite enough to make anyone seriously ill, in Aunt Beryl's opinion. Even before the sacking was taken off. And when it was . . .

There stood the doll's house, a dark, oily, spinach green, picked out with bright yellow. Its two solid little chimneys, glued on to the roof, were painted red and white, and the door, gleaming with yellow varnish, was like a little slab of toffee. Four windows, real windows, were divided into panes by a broad streak of green. There was actually a tiny porch, too, painted yellow, with big lumps of congealed paint hanging along the edge.

But perfect, perfect little house! Who could possibly mind the smell. It was part of the joy, part of the newness.

'Open it quickly, someone!'

The hook at the side was stuck fast. Pat prised it open with his penknife, and the whole house-front swung back, and – there you were, gazing at one and the same moment into the drawing-room and dining-room, the kitchen and two bedrooms. That is the way for a house to open! Why don't all houses open like that? How much more exciting than peering through the slit of a door into a mean little hall with a hat-stand and two umbrellas! That is – isn't it? – what you long to know about a house when you put your hand on the knocker. Perhaps it is the way God opens houses at the dead of night when He is taking a quiet turn with an angel . . .

'Oh-oh!' The Burnell children sounded as though they were in despair. It was too marvellous; it was too much for them. They had never seen anything like it in their lives. All the rooms were papered. There were pictures on the walls, painted on the paper, with gold frames complete. Red carpet covered all the floors except the kitchen; red plush chairs in the drawing-room, green in the dining-room; tables, beds with real bedclothes, a cradle, a stove, a dresser with tiny plates and one big jug. But what Kezia liked more than anything, what she liked frightfully, was the lamp. It stood in the middle of the dining-room table, an exquisite little amber lamp with a white globe. It was even filled all ready for lighting, though, of course, you couldn't light it. But there was something inside that looked like oil and moved when you shook it.

The father and mother dolls, who sprawled very stiff as though they had fainted in the drawing-room, and their two little children asleep upstairs, were really too big for the doll's house. They didn't look as though they belonged. But the lamp was perfect. It seemed to smile at Kezia, to say, 'I live here.' The lamp was real.

The Burnell children could hardly walk to school fast enough the next morning. They burned to tell everybody, to describe, to – well – to boast about their doll's house before the school bell rang.

'I'm to tell,' said Isabel, 'because I'm the eldest. And you two can join in after. But I'm to tell first.'

There was nothing to answer. Isabel was bossy, but she was always right, and Lottie and Kezia knew too well the powers that went with being eldest. They brushed through the thick buttercups at the road edge and said nothing.

'And I'm to choose who's to come and see it first. Mother said I might.'

For it had been arranged that while the doll's house stood in the courtyard they might ask the girls at school, two at a time, to come and look. Not to stay to tea, of course, or to come traipsing through the house. But just to stand quietly in the courtyard while Isabel pointed out the beauties, and Lottie and Kezia looked pleased . . .

But hurry as they might, by the time they had reached the tarred palings of the boys' playground the bell had begun to jangle. They only just had time to whip off their hats and fall into line before the roll was called. Never mind. Isabel tried to make up for it by looking very important and mysterious and by whispering behind her hand to the girls near her, 'Got something to tell you at playtime.'

Playtime came and Isabel was surrounded. The girls of her class nearly fought to put their arms round her, to walk away with her, to beam flatteringly, to be her special friend. She held quite a court under the huge pine trees at the side of the playground. Nudging, giggling together, the little girls pressed up close. And the only two who stayed outside the ring were the two who were always outside, the little Kelveys. They knew better than to come anywhere near the Burnells.

For the fact was, the school the Burnell children went to was not at all the kind of place their parents would have chosen if there had been any choice. But there was none. It was the only school for miles. And the consequence was all the children of the neighbourhood, the judge's little girls, the doctor's daughters, the store-keeper's children, the milkman's, were forced to mix together. Not to speak of there being an equal number of rude, rough little boys as well. But the line had to be drawn somewhere. It was drawn at the Kelveys. Many of the children, including the Burnells, were not allowed even to speak to them. They walked past the Kelveys with their heads in the air, and as they set the fashion in all matters of behaviour, the Kelveys were shunned by everybody. Even the teacher had a special voice for them, and a special smile for the other children when Lil Kelvey came up to her desk with a bunch of dreadfully common-looking flowers.

They were the daughters of a spry, hard-working little washerwoman, who went about from house to house by the day. This was awful enough. But where was Mr Kelvey? Nobody knew for certain. But everybody said he was in prison. So they were the daughters of a washerwoman and a gaolbird. Very nice company for other people's children! And they looked it. Why Mrs Kelvey made them so conspicuous was hard to understand.

The truth was they were dressed in 'bits' given to her by the people for whom she worked. Lil, for instance, who was a stout, plain child, with big freckles, came to school in a dress made from a green art-serge tablecloth of the Burnells', with red plush sleeves from the Logans' curtains. Her hat, perched on top of her high forehead, was a grown-up woman's hat, once the property of Miss Lecky, the postmistress. It was turned up at the back and trimmed with a large scarlet quill. What a little guy she looked! It was impossible not to laugh. And her little sister, our Else, wore a long white dress, rather like a nightgown, and a pair of little boy's boots. But whatever our Else wore she would have looked strange. She was a tiny wishbone of a child, with cropped hair and enormous solemn eyes – a little white owl. Nobody had ever seen her smile; she scarcely ever spoke. She went through life holding on to Lil, with a piece of Lil's skirt screwed up in her hand. Where Lil went, our Else followed. In the playground, on the road going to and from school, there was Lil marching in front and our Else holding on behind. Only when she wanted anything, or when she was out of breath, our Else gave Lil a tug, a twitch, and Lil stopped and turned round. The Kelveys never failed to understand each other.

Now they hovered at the edge; you couldn't stop them listening. When the little girls turned round and sneered, Lil, as usual, gave her silly, shameface smile, but our Else only looked.

And Isabel's voice, so very proud, went on telling. The carpet made a great sensation, but so did the beds with real bedclothes, and the stove with an oven door.

When she finished Kezia broke in. 'You've forgotten the lamp, Isabel.'

'Oh yes,' said Isabel, 'and there's a teeny little lamp, all made of yellow glass, with a white globe that stands on the dining-room table. You couldn't tell it from a real one.'

'The lamp's best of all,' cried Kezia. She thought Isabel wasn't making half enough of the little lamp. But nobody paid any attention. Isabel was choosing the two who were to come back with them that afternoon and see it. She chose Emmie Cole and Lena Logan. But when the others knew they were all to have a chance, they couldn't be nice enough to Isabel.

One by one they put their arms round Isabel's waist and walked her off. They had something to whisper to her, a secret. 'Isabel's *my* friend.'

Only the little Kelveys moved away forgotten; there was nothing more for them to hear.

Days passed, and as more children saw the doll's house, the fame of it spread. It became the one subject, the rage. The one question was, 'have you seen Burnells' doll's house? Oh, ain't it lovely!' 'Haven't you seen it? Oh, I say!'

Even the dinner hour was given up to talking about it. The little girls sat under the pines eating their thick mutton sandwiches and big slabs of johnny cake spread with butter. While always, as near as they could get, sat the Kelveys, our Else holding on to Lil, listening too, while they chewed their jam sandwiches out of a newspaper soaked with large red blobs.

'Mother,' said Kezia, 'can't I ask the Kelveys just once?'

'Certainly not, Kezia.'

'But why not?'

'Run away, Kezia; you know quite well why not.'

At last everybody had seen it except them. On that day the subject rather flagged. It was the dinner hour. The children stood together under the pine trees, and suddenly, as they looked at the Kelveys eating out of their paper, always by themselves, always listening, they wanted to be horrid to them. Emmie Cole started the whisper.

'Lil Kelvey's going to be a servant when she grows up.'

'O-oh, how awful!' said Isabel Burnell, and she made eyes at Emmie.

Emmie swallowed in a very meaningful way and nodded to Isabel as she'd seen her mother do on those occasions.

'It's true — it's true — it's true,' she said.

Then Lena Logan's little eyes snapped. 'Shall I ask her?' she whispered.

'Bet you don't,' said Jessie May.

'Pooh, I'm not frightened,' said Lena. Suddenly she gave a little squeal and danced in front of the other girls. 'Watch! Watch me! Watch me now!' said Lena. And sliding, gliding, dragging one foot, giggling behind her hand,

Lena went over to the Kelveys.

Lil looked up from her dinner. She wrapped the rest quickly away. Our Else stopped chewing. What was coming now?

'Is it true you're going to be a servant when you grow up, Lil Kelvey?' shrilled Lena.

Dead silence. But instead of answering, Lil only gave her silly, shamefaced smile. She didn't seem to mind the question at all. What a sell for Lena! The girls began to titter.

Lena couldn't stand that. She put her hands on her hips; she shot forward. 'Yah, yer father's in prison!' she hissed spitefully.

This was such a marvellous thing to have said that the little girls rushed away in a body, deeply, deeply excited, wild with joy. Someone found a long rope, and they began skipping. And never did they skip so high, run in and out so fast, or do such daring things as on that morning.

In the afternoon Pat called for the Burnell children with the buggy and they drove home. There were visitors. Isabel and Lottie, who liked visitors, went upstairs to change their pinafores. But Kezia thieved out at the back. Nobody was about; she began to swing on the big white gates of the courtyard. Presently, looking along the road, she saw two little dots. They grew bigger, they were coming towards her. Now she could see that one was in front and one close behind. Now she could see that they were the Kelveys. Kezia stopped swinging. She slipped off the gate as if she was going to run away. Then she hesitated. The Kelveys came nearer, and beside them walked their shadows, very long, stretching right across the road with their heads in the buttercups. Kezia clambered back on the gate; she had made up her mind; she swung out.

'Hullo,' she said to the passing Kelveys.

They were so astounded that they stopped. Lil gave her silly smile. Our Else stared.

'You can come and see our doll's house if you want to,' said Kezia, and she dragged one toe on the ground. But at that Lil turned red and shook her head quickly.

'Why not?' asked Kezia.

Lil gasped, then she said, 'Your ma told our ma you wasn't to speak to us.'

'Oh well,' said Kezia. She didn't know what to reply. 'It doesn't matter. You can come and see our doll's house all the same. Come on. Nobody's looking.'

But Lil shook her head still harder.

'Don't you want to?' asked Kezia.

Suddenly there was a twitch, a tug at Lil's skirt. She turned round. Our Else was looking at her with big, imploring eyes; she was frowning; she wanted to go. For a moment Lil looked at our Else very doubtfully. But then our Else twitched her skirt again. She started forward. Kezia led the way. Like two little stray cats they followed across the courtyard to where the doll's house stood. 'There it is,' said Kezia. There was a pause. Lil breathed loudly, almost snorted; our Else was still as stone.

'I'll open it for you,' said Kezia kindly. She undid the hook and they looked inside.

'There's the drawing-room and the dining-room, and that's the –'

'Kezia!'

Oh, what a start they gave!

'Kezia!'

It was Aunt Beryl's voice. They turned round. At the back door stood Aunt Beryl, staring as if she couldn't believe what she saw.

'How dare you ask the little Kelveys into the courtyard!' said her cold, furious voice. 'You know as well as I do, you're not allowed to talk to them. Run away, children, run away at once. And don't come back again,' said Aunt Beryl. And she stepped into the yard and shooed them out as if they were chickens.

'Off you go immediately!' she called, cold and proud.

They did not need telling twice. Burning with shame, shrinking together, Lil huddling along like her mother, our Else dazed, somehow they crossed the big courtyard and squeezed through the white gate.

'Wicked, disobedient little girl!' said Aunt Beryl bitterly to Kezia, and she slammed the doll's house to.

The afternoon had been awful. A letter had come from Willie Brent, a terrifying, threatening letter, saying if she did not meet him that evening in Pulman's Bush, he'd come to the front door and ask the reason why!

But now that she had frightened those little rats of Kelveys and given Kezia a good scolding, her heart felt lighter. That ghastly pressure was gone. She went back to the house humming.

When the Kelveys were well out of sight of Burnells', they sat down to rest on a big red drainpipe by the side of the road. Lil's cheeks still burning; she took off the hat with the quill and held it on her knee. Dreamily they looked over the hay paddocks, past the creek, to the group of wattles where Logan's cows stood waiting to be milked. What were their thoughts?

Presently our Else nudged up close to her sister. But now she had forgotten the cross lady. She put out a finger and stroked her sister's quill; she smiled her rare smile.

'I seen the little lamp,' she said softly.

Then both were silent once more.

FRANK SARGESON

When I was a boy at school our family lived some way along the
road from a tomato-grower who was supposed to be eccentric.
Among other things it was said that he didn't eat meat, neither
had he ever been known to smoke or drink. Neither, as I found
out for myself later on, did he use certain words or tell the usual
sort of stories. But a lack of the more obvious vices will make
people talk just as readily as the reverse, so I suppose it was only
natural for some such word as eccentric to be passed round the
neighbourhood.

He was a single man, this David Williams, and well on in years.
He was so dark in colouring that people said he had a touch of the
tar-brush, but if his name was anything to go by he probably got
his dark skin from Welsh blood. He was a sketch of a man to look
at, he walked pigeon-toed, and he was so thin his clothes seemed
to hang on a framework of sticks. When you talked to him he
laughed a lot, pushing his face in yours, and catching hold of your
arm. Over one of his eyes he had a dropping eyelid, and it didn't
fit in too well with the rest of him because it rather suggested
wickedness. He had his sister living with him, attending to the
house and helping with the outside work, and to look at she was
very much the same kind as her brother. Though, if anything, there
was even less of her.

On their place there was a tremendous lot to do. They had a
big glass-house for winter growing, and as soon as the warmer
weather came there'd be the outdoor work as well. One winter I
earned a few shillings by helping a milkman during my school
holidays, and driving along the road in the small hours of a frosty
morning we would see a light moving inside the glass-house. Some

mornings there would be two lights, and that meant Miss Williams was working with her brother. But no matter how early they started you'd see them working until well on into the evening, when they must have been too tired to do another stroke.

The Williams were grafters, everybody agreed about that. They never seemed to have any time for recreation, unless that was the name you could give to the time they put in on their flower beds and keeping the place tidy. They never went to socials or dances, they never even went to church, so nobody got to know them at all well. But they had people's respect for being such hard workers. Occasionally it would be said they were a pair of money-grubbers, living only to rake in the cash, but I think that would usually be said by somebody who wouldn't have minded being able to do the same thing. That is, if they were doing it. Nobody knew for certain.

Then after they had been on the place for a number of years Miss Williams became ill. She was taken to hospital and died after a few days. The funeral was a private one and her brother had her cremated, and a story got about that he afterwards took the ashes and threw them into the air to be scattered by the wind. I heard people talking about this and some said it was a horrible thing to do. They said it didn't show much respect for the dead. I remember my mother said that the thought of it was enough to give her the creeps.

Miss Williams' illness had happened round about Christmas time, when the outdoor tomatoes would soon be coming into bearing. Her brother was away for about a week after the funeral, the house was locked up and everything was neglected. Then it was noticed he was back again and he seemed to be just the same as ever, but he had about double the work to do. It was too much for him and one evening he came along the road to see my father. He wanted to know if I would like a job, and I think my father was a bit doubtful. He wasn't the sort of man to approve of queer fish, but I'd just left school and hadn't found anything to do, so finally it was all fixed up. I went over the next morning and began by following my boss about, watching until I got the hang of things, and after a week or so I began to develop into quite a capable lad. I couldn't keep up with the speed my boss worked at, but we got on all right together, and besides teaching me the work he told me all his theories. He was against the use of quick manures, he said, it meant that tomatoes grown that way didn't feed you properly, though what was a commercial grower to do? If he didn't do as the next man did he'd go broke. And he was against all the expensive and complicated business of spraying. He said it wouldn't be necessary if you had healthy plants that weren't forced. He didn't even approve of the poisonous spray for caterpillars, and as we worked along the rows he taught me to watch out for the moths' eggs, which you found underneath the leaves and on the flowers. It was quite a good method perhaps, but it took up a lot of time.

To begin with I'd go along the road home to my lunch at midday. But later on I'd stay and eat with my boss, he seemed to like my company and he got a butcher to call sometimes and leave a piece of sausage, though he never ate any himself. And it was mainly during our times of eating together that he began to tell me about how he had come to be a tomato-grower. Probably he said much that I was too young to understand, but it was all so different from what I was used to hearing in my own home, that I could always listen without feeling impatient. Also it fascinated me to watch him. He'd walk pigeon-toed across the kitchen to fill the tea-pot, or he'd bend his head back to look out at me from under his dropping eyelid.

He'd begun life in a draper's shop, he said, and for a number of years he'd liked the work quite well. He had the knack of arranging things so he was put on to dressing the window, and he did so well it wasn't long before he was able to get a job in a big store. He stayed there for years, finding the work quite to his liking, and getting more and more money, but at the same time he wasn't happy and he wasn't satisfied. Deep down he wasn't, he said. He'd begun to feel it was wrong of people to shut themselves away from the sun and fresh air by working in such places, except that you went home at night it was just as though you'd been put in gaol. As for people who worked inside cages behind the counters of banks, or sat all day going up and down in lifts – well, you might just as well live in a cage out at the zoo. And such ideas had kept coming into his head, until he decided he'd cut out all his pleasures and save hard so that he could set himself up in a new way of living. Why, he said, it had even meant he'd had to change his mind about getting married. Then later on when he'd got started he found out the life meant much harder work than he'd ever imagined. Yet he'd liked it all right, he said. He'd feel prouder over the sight of a good bunch of tomatoes, with the top ones just beginning to colour, than he'd ever felt over any window he'd dressed. And another thing, it was an education, because it had taught him things he never knew before.

If you grew something for sale, he found out, particularly if it was something that wouldn't keep, you mainly had to take just what people would pay for it, even though you might get a lot less than would pay for the work and expense it had cost you. And that was a different thing from what happened in the big store he had worked in, where you usually managed to buy at one price and sell at another that would always keep you on the right side. You didn't wait until you were offered a price, no, you mainly got the price you asked for. Well, the world was a funny place, he said, you'd strike people who'd grumble over the price of tomatoes when it hardly paid you for the work of picking them, yet if you'd asked these people to work for such little return they'd have properly hit the roof. And most of them you couldn't blame, because they could never have afforded to buy at a fair price. Well, well, he said, the world was all wrong, men couldn't be brothers to each other when they spent so much time worrying over the prices they were going to pay or get. It made you feel unhappy, but when you'd puzzled your brains you asked yourself what could you do? You could count yourself one of the lucky ones if you got plenty to eat and a good share of sunshine and fresh air, and didn't have to dress up to go to work. The only thing that worried him, he said, was that he hardly ever had enough spare time to read a book. And the joke of it was he'd thought when he started out he was going to have plenty.

All this and a lot more I mainly listened to during the half hours when we knocked off for lunch. A few things would sink in, and from time to time I'd be liable to fetch them up at home. Mr Williams says, I would begin, and sometimes I'd annoy my father by contradicting him with something my boss had said. I'm afraid my father was the sort of man who gets upset if people say things that aren't like what the newspapers say. One evening I heard him talking to my mother, telling her that I was under a bad influence, and that I'd better look around for another job. That was all I heard, but I knew my mother would be on my side. She was easy-going, and I knew she liked me to come home and tell her what I'd had for lunch, and what the inside of Mr Williams' house was like. It made her feel important to be able to tell people about how he did all his own cooking, washed and mended his clothes, and managed to keep everything tidy even to polishing the floors. What an eccentric man! Though I remember she hadn't got the word quite right and said *es*centric.

So in the meantime my father didn't interfere with my job, and it was lucky for my boss because the season was turning out a good one. Every day was a real scorcher. I lived with the strong tomato-smell always in my nose, and the hot smell of the earth that we were forever sprinkling with manure and drenching with water until it was soaked right through. I'd start early, stay late, and get paid extra, but we never seemed to be able to catch up with what had to be done. On top of the other work was the marketing, and tomatoes that were still warm from the sun hours after they'd been picked, seemed always to be layers deep on the floor of the packing shed. Like all good seasons it had benefited everybody's crops alike. It was one right out of the box, and my boss told me he'd never known so many tomatoes about at so cheap a price. Sauce factories that had contracted for whole crops had landed themselves in the cart, he said, deliveries were more than they knew what to do with, and they were buying dearer than they could have bought on the market. So the growers who had contracts were all right, but as for the rest of them, well, my boss reckoned a bad season of blight couldn't have been a worse blow than such plenty was.

Then one morning I turned up to work and got a surprise to find my boss hadn't even finished his breakfast. And instead of telling me what to get busy on he asked me inside. Have you had a good tuck-in? he said, and I said I'd had plenty. Go on, he said, I know what boys' appetites are like, and he made me sit down to a poached egg on toast. He sat there with his arms folded, and I'd never seen him taking it so easy. It's a silly game, this working so hard, he said, look what it did to my poor sister. With my mouth full I mumbled something, and he began to tell me about a growers' meeting that had been held the night before. He'd been along, he said, and they had a scheme for each man to dig a pit and throw away half his crop. But I'll guarantee they won't be able to trust each other enough to make that idea work. Besides, it would be a wicked shame. I got up to speak, he said, and the words wouldn't come. I just stood there like a fool with my mouth open, and the chairman told me to sit down. He told me this several times over, and he laughed as though it were a great joke.

When I'd finished eating he still didn't seem to be in any hurry. Instead of leaving the dishes until lunchtime he started on them right away, throwing me a tea-towel. Or don't you like women's work, my boy? he said, and laughed. Then he got me to wait while he swept the floor, and when we were finally out in the garden he just walked about saying that no man could help being happy in a garden on a day of such weather. A man in the garden, a woman in the house, and a child in the cradle, he said, that's what God put us on the earth to make come true. And then, just as if he hadn't said anything at all out of the ordinary, he told me what he wanted me to do. But don't work too hard, he said, and laughed. And if it had been anyone else but him I'd have thought he was slinging off.

He left me to go ahead and never came near me all morning, and I had no idea what he was doing. He should have been nailing up cases in the packing shed but I didn't hear him, though when he called me to lunch I noticed as I went past that the tomatoes we'd picked the afternoon before had all disappeared. He was drying his hands out on the verandah, and straight off he said, Come and tell me if I've made a good job. So we went down the length of the glass-house to the front of the section, and there, just inside the gate, he'd put all the tomatoes in a heap. Not just an ordinary heap though, he'd built them up into a sort of pyramid, the way you see them in the shop windows, only this one was a monster. He asked me if they looked nice, and I thought they certainly did. And it wasn't just because they made a pretty picture, each one a perfect specimen that showed a wonderful red polish in the sun. It was something more than that, I'd helped him do the work, and just to stand and look at the result gave me a wonderful feeling of being satisfied. Perhaps I'd never before understood what deep feelings you could have over things you'd made happen under your own hands. Perhaps I understood even more than that. I may have understood that the feeling had nothing to do with the money you could sell such things for. I'm not quite sure, but I know I had the feeling, and I knew my boss had it too, and that it was tremendously deep in him. And I think he knew about me as well, because instead of saying anything much he put his arm round my shoulders, and I wasn't at all keen about him doing this but I let him leave it there.

Once we were back up at the house he talked and acted just the same as usual, yet it turned out that day was the first of some very queer days for me. My boss would leave me to work on my own, while he spent most of his time sitting down at the gate in an old easy chair he took off the verandah. And besides leaving the heap of tomatoes there, he was all the time making it bigger with every fresh lot that we picked. One morning I turned up to work and struck him having an argument with our carrier. It was our main market day, and the carrier had made his call to pick up the cases we'd normally have been sending into town. My boss was saying he wasn't sending anything in, and the carrier was pointing to the heap and asking what the big idea was. I stood listening, and my boss just laughed and said, No, my friend, until the carrier got annoyed, and drove off after shaking my boss's hand from his arm, and telling him he was clean off his rocker.

Then stories about what was happening began to get around. Probably the carrier talked, but it wouldn't have made any difference if he hadn't, because anybody could look over the gate and see the heap, and my boss sitting in the old chair. More and more people began to stop and stare, and later on there'd sometimes be quite a crowd. I noticed people began to look at me in the street, and although I hadn't said a word at home, my father wanted to know what Mr Williams thought he was up to. I didn't know what to say so I didn't say anything, but I must have gone red because my mother suddenly changed the subject. Though when she got me on my own she asked me what Mr Williams was doing with that heap of tomatoes. I said I didn't know, and it wasn't exactly the truth, but I could never have explained, even if I'd wanted to try.

Then for a couple of days everybody had something else to talk about. The weather broke. All of a sudden there came a terrific gale that blew one way one day and the other the next, and in between there was a downpour that measured several inches in just a few hours. The wind lifted the roof off a house in our road, so it was no wonder my boss's tomatoes were all flattened out. The tea-tree sticks were dry and brittle from so much sun and the wobbling weight of the great top bunches was too much for them, they snapped off and the flax ties that held only meant a worse tangle. If it hadn't been for the rain the damage wouldn't have been so serious, but the sun came out hot again, and that sea of green tangle, lying thick on the wet ground, meant we had to go for our lives if we wanted to stop the blight from setting in. My boss never had time to sit in his chair for days. We'd both of us begin at daylight and work ourselves to a standstill, and after about a week it was certainly wonderful the way we managed to get things pretty straight again. Though of course a lot of damage had been done. All over the country it was the same and I read about it in the newspaper. Tomatoes were specially mentioned, and it was said that prices would go up.

Yet once things had been got straight my boss left me to work on my own again, while he went back to his chair, taking time off only to put more and more on the heap. Though by this time it had gone properly rotten inside, and was getting smaller if anything. Also it was smelling bad and bringing the flies around, and the sanitary inspector came and said it would have to be shifted into a hole and buried. And he didn't like it when my boss laughed and said it was a good smell, it meant that the earth was getting her own back again.

Nor was he our only visitor. They started driving up in their cars every day, looking as smart as if they'd just stepped out of bandboxes, and my boss would look a cut talking to them in his denims and sandshoes, and his shirt full of holes that he'd left off mending. There was a man from my boss's bank came, and a man from the markets, and a policeman along with one of our local doctors. But I never heard what they talked about, and I never said a thing to anybody, not even the Sunday morning when my mother came in from next door, and said they were taking Mr Williams to the hospital in an ambulance. They'd found him lying just inside the gate, she said, and he'd had a stroke.

I ran along the road and I was just in time to see my boss lying all tucked up on the stretcher. He couldn't move and he couldn't speak, and he didn't seem to be able to hear. The drooping lid was right down over that eye, but the other one was wide open. I got right in front of it, but he didn't seem as if he could see me.

GREVILLE TEXIDOR

The small sharp hills over-lapping like green waves converged on the train. The sun flashed out and the dead trees littering the hillside shone like white bones. Then it was raining again. The train stopped at a station and the carriages were suddenly empty. The passengers surged into the café, then hurried back with moist white sandwiches and tea. The station where Rex got down was only a long shed with an iron roof, standing alone in the middle of the green.

It was raining again, and there was no one about to tell him the way to Isaiah Chapman's place. He hailed a car that was passing along the road and the man driving said he would take him to Chapman's.

Old Chap as we call him is a cousin of mine, he told Rex. We're pretty near all related around here.

Rex asked about the farm.

Well, it's a pretty place, said the man. The park we call it. He has this hobby of growing fruit and other trees. It was clear the other dairy farmers thought it was a crazy hobby. It's behind the hills over there, he said. There's a shorter way through the paddocks.

The mountains in the distance that looked wild and grand under the rain were only hills when they got up to them. Little green calvaries topped with tall dead trees.

I suppose it doesn't pay, said Rex.

It doesn't. But Isaiah's an old man. You can't tell him anything. He's really more of an idealist than a farmer.

Then, remembering he was talking to Rex he looked a bit awkward and said, You'll be the new man, I suppose? Oh, well, I hope you'll like it here. Old Chap's a great Bible reader and all that, but a real good sort when you get to know him.

Rex was put down at the gate and waded through mud the half mile to the house. Mrs Chapman welcomed him at the back door and made him take off his shoes in the kitchen. She asked him if he had had a pleasant journey from Auckland and he said, Yes, very pleasant.

I expect you will find it very wet and muddy, she said, it's our normal winter state. But the spring flowers are coming on apace. Are you a flower lover, too?

Mr Chapman would be in soon, she said, and Rex would like a wash in the bathroom after his journey. That means they don't wash there themselves, thought Rex. It was cold in the bathroom. The solitary towel hanging beside the coffin-shaped bath was hard and thin. Round the walls stood bottles of petrified plums and jam, all neatly labelled with the name of the fruit and the date. There were several years of fruit and jam on the shelves.

Mrs Chapman was waiting outside in the passage to show him the way to his room. The room held the cold of a whole winter. The lino was shiny as ice. A framed printed card, hung near the dressing table, looked like the rules they have up in hotel bedrooms. Rex read, To A Pound Of Love Add A Liberal Measure Of Understanding And Mix. On the dressing table was a doily, and a shell with a ship painted on it that no one could ever mistake for an ashtray.

Facing the walnut double bed with its blue-white cover, two dreadfully enlarged Chapman ancestors in thick dark oval frames possessed the room. They had dark flaws in their faces like craters on the moon. Behind the glass a cheek-bone, a button on the man's coat, and the highlight on his hair stared blankly.

Rex began to unpack, looking for dry shoes. His brush and comb looked so uncomfortable beside the shell with the painted ship that he began to feel, not homesick for any particular place, but lonely and stranded. He reminded himself of other rooms he had slept in. This one would be no worse when it had been lived in. Someone must have slept in the bed once, and sat at the dressing table doing their hair, and looked through the window over the fields when it wasn't raining like this.

Rex opened a door which he thought was a cupboard, but it opened into a small sitting room which had the same clean but stale smell. This end of the house was a blind alley. There was a fluted fire place and a firescreen with birds on it, an upright piano, upholstered chairs and a round walnut table. Rex smiled over the things laid out on the table. The velvet album, the stereoscope, the Family Bible. These objects looked familiar, he had met them so often in books. They were always amusing. He tried to think of a funny formula for the room, but nothing crossed his mind but the Spanish slang-word *fatal*.

Thinking of Spain Rex saw the sun on the white wall of a house. Big black ants were busy about the cracks in the plaster. Pots of carnations basked by the wall. A fat red flower burst its sheath with a silent explosion.

The shadow under the fig tree is round like a pool. Dipping your hand in the shadow you feel its edge like water. Jim is sitting waiting under the fig tree where the plates and salads are set in the shade. The midday silence is full of life, and an exuberant smell of flowers and frying.

An old peasant sits down at the table, and cocking his head at Jim hands him a wine skin. Jim takes off his shirt, is standing up and throwing his head right back to catch the crimson trickle that floods his teeth. He raises the wine skin higher and higher. The wine falls in a thin bright arc.

Rex was lucky. He had had two years of living up to the hilt, then slipped out when the game was up. He hadn't said goodbye to his Spanish friends. Jim had been killed at Huesca.

Perhaps, Rex thought, his excitement over committees, his travels, his political work which had led him in the end to Spain, were only forms of escape from what he was feeling now in the Sunday smell of the sitting room.

He was young when it first got him. It was after dinner. The rain seemed to have set in and he had settled down with a book, when suddenly the sun came out in a watery way and he was told to go and play in the garden.

There was nothing in the garden but the long watery afternoon with Monday on its horizon. He walked down the path till he came to a jungle of trees and a high brick wall at the end. This was called 'down the garden'. Under the dripping wall was the puppy's grave, and an overturned flower-pot which Rex sat on when he cried about something. He didn't cry now. This wasn't something that had happened. It was there.

You're just a lump of misery, Master Rex, his nurse would say when he had the Sunday feeling. He grew out of it. It only came back in waiting rooms, and long dull dreams. But when it did he knew it was there all the time, and his interesting life was only painted over it.

The door of the sitting room creaked and a child came in. A plain little thing in a gym tunic.

Dinner is nearly ready, Mr Rex.

So you are Lila, said Rex, and the child came over to him.

Were you looking at the pictures? That's St Peter's at Rome on top.

I've seen that one, said Rex. It has a great wide space in front dotted with frozen fountains.

Oh, Mr Rex, could you play the piano then? Can you play a hymn? Our Lord Is Ever Present has a pretty tune.

I might have a try sometime.

Oh, do have a pop at it, Mr Rex.

But not now. I think they're calling you to lay the table.

Mr Chapman was small and bald, and wore a neat white beard. He shook hands with Rex and they all sat down to the meal. After piling the plates with pumpkin and potato, the old lady abruptly laid her hand on her forehead as a signal. They bent their heads in an attitude of prayer. During the next few minutes' silence Rex looked through his fingers at Lila, searching her dull face for a clue that would lead back to Jim.

Rex sat facing the clear blue eyes of the old man. He talked in a slow, high, gentle voice about the government and the weather. He seemed to be looking at Rex from a long way off. He said something about Spain. That it was through lack of faith that the Republicans had perished. But when Rex began to argue the point he was not listening. Rex thought at first that he was deaf, but he was not deaf. He was only out of focus.

Mrs Chapman kept urging Rex to have some more.

I hope our simple fare agrees with your taste, she said. Our neighbours don't bother to grow veges, but Isaiah has been on a sort of diet for years. You forget to eat while you're talking, she said to her husband.

I have sufficient for my needs, said Mr Chapman. Then turning to Rex, he began to denounce the forces of evil which he said were undermining the churches. Rex didn't know what the forces were. Whether it was the brewers or the Catholics or the Anglicans who were doing all the harm. When he appeared to have finished Rex tried to say a word about Jim. But the old chap had withdrawn again, and was absorbed in scraping the burnt edge off the pudding dish.

In the afternoon they went round the farm. The mud was so deep it oozed over the tops of the good boots Rex had been given in Spain. Rex had to see everything, Mr Chapman pointed out the places where he should have sown lupins to keep down the weeds, and telling him where things were, and where they used to be, and what might have to be done sometime.

Half his words were lost in the sudden gusts of wind that passed with a rattle of rain on the iron roofs like the sound of machine guns, leaving a dead stillness behind, and the rain quietly falling. Then the sun burst out with a startling feverish glare between the black clouds and the shivering green of the pastures.

Rex spoke of a plan that Jim had made for the farm. The old man stood very close to him while he was talking, as though he was waiting for something. Like a child who has run up with a treasure in his hand, and well-trained, waits quiet and expectant, until the people have finished their talk and will look at it. The old man waited, then with a meek insistent smile, he brought out what he had hoarded up to say.

They walked and walked through wet grass. Mr Chapman was amazingly active, and rosy as a child, but from time to time a wave of milky pallor flooded his face, like the first waves of death lapping over him and receding so gently that he was unaware.

You see yon trees, he said happily. I have seen them all grow.

He had started little gardens all over the place. Stopping at one of these forgotten gardens he said. That was Jim's garden. It's Lila's now, but she doesn't take care of it much.

The afternoon seemed endless. When they got back Mrs Chapman and Lila had changed into different dresses and they had tea, stewed apples and scones and home-baked bread. Mr Chapman was quiet now, he had talked himself out. Mrs Chapman was worried because she had made too much tea, and Rex had to have a third cup. The child would go to bed soon, and they would want to hear about Jim's death.

But when supper was over Mr Chapman began to turn the knob of the radio. There are several services on the air, he said. Managing the radio the old man was pathetic. He got first a waltz, then someone talking fast in a frightening voice, but at last the organ burst bitterly through. The Presbyterians. I believe, he said. He smiled like a conjurer. I hope that will be agreeable to you.

Rex longed to smoke to take the edge off it, but it was no good upsetting these left-behind old things the first night.

After the service ended Mr Chapman drew his chair to the table and began to write very slowly in a large book. Rex, passing behind him to get nearer the fire, read, 'August 28. Burnt bullock in three days.'

Mr Chapman read over what he had written and shut the book. Mrs Chapman counted stitches.

Shall I bring in a log or two? asked Mr Chapman.

I hardly think it's worth it, said Mrs Chapman, looking at Rex for assent.

I suppose you heard that Jim died very bravely. I sent back the few things he always carried with him. You got them all right?

Mrs Chapman nodded. Yes, thank you, we got the parcel. And then we got your letter saying you would be coming out to New Zealand just the same.

I didn't give you the details of his death in my letter. Rex seemed to be saying a lesson to the old things who happened to be Jim's parents. What was left of Jim seemed now to be lost between the three of them.

He had only been ten days up at the front. The front was changing all the time and we never knew where we were, but Jim and I were always together. On this day they asked for volunteers to go to some comrades with a machine gun a bit further up the road that went to Huesca. The road was impassable, but there was some cover beside it. We thought someone could get round with a mule load of stuff. They were out of munitions, you see. Jim passed an open vineyard, but when he was under the trees a stray bullet got him.

Rex got through the story he had told again and again. It was stale even before he had begun to tell it, because so many people had been killed that way.

The old man frowned, seemed to be groping for something. Mrs Chapman flushed and swallowed. Rex thought, They still don't really believe it.

Do I understand you to say that my son met his death as a soldier, a combatant?

Why certainly, said Rex. He was a good soldier. He died like a hero.

They sat in silence while a death ripple passed over the face of the old man.

It must have been a terrible shock to you, Rex said.

It is a terrible shock, said Mr Chapman.

You see we didn't know, said his wife. He went over to do relief work for the Quakers.

Of course. Anyone could have known it. Jim had even told him once about some sect his father belonged to. Why couldn't he have remembered? How easy it would have been to say their son was killed bringing in a wounded comrade. He might have been killed any day bringing children away from Madrid. The idiocy of implying that Jim was a fighter. Even his death of a hero had been an accident. Other people had been over there to the machine gun post and nothing had happened, till in the end it seemed pretty safe to go.

Done now. Couldn't be helped. He would leave in a day or two and find a job in Auckland, perhaps get back to Europe before the next war started. Thank God he'd hedged when he'd replied to the old man's letter offering him a job on the farm.

Well, I suppose it's time to turn in, he said.

You know the way to your room, said Mrs Chapman. There's an extra blanket under the mattress if you should need it.

She said goodnight and went out to the kitchen, where Rex could hear her fussing about preparing for breakfast.

Now that Rex had said goodnight and was standing up he wanted Mr Chapman to understand. It was easy now. The same as when you leave a house and have a last word over the fence, or when you go to bed and come back for something and stay for hours talking to the person you're supposed to have left.

If you had been there yourself I know you would understand, he said. At the front it was spiritually safe, but when you went on leave you'd find you couldn't sit in certain cafés because 'the others' were there. Jim thought it was mostly the fault of the foreigners who were coming and going, raising money and sympathy for Spain, and raising hell too. Political parties couldn't agree about what their adherents were dying for. Jim couldn't have stood any more without losing his faith.

I thought Jim stuck to the Quakers because they did the least harm. They were too busy saving children's lives. But as the war went on there was too much relief and advice. Jim said he wouldn't consider the children saved if the war was lost. One day he'd been to the centre with posters they'd asked him to get. Pictures of children playing and studying with underneath, Revolution In Education. They blacked out the R before they would use them. So Jim walked out and joined the Brigade.

If only Mr Chapman would sit still. He was busy again searching methodically among the papers on top of the bookshelf. He brought down a brown paper parcel, and coming quietly round the table while Rex talked laid it in front of him.

Some of Jim's books.

Perhaps some weeks before he had thought about the books and placed the parcel there where he could easily find it, to show Jim's friend. Though he seemed so vague the little plan, independent of anything that might intervene, had firmly stuck in his mind. So now Rex had to sit down at the table again and open the parcel, and turn the leaves of the books. The first page of an exercise book had written on it in curly writing:–

September 4th, 1915.   Padded
Purr

Whisker curley
Claws paws
Hungry rosy
Poetry
This is the weather the cuckoo loves
And so do I
Be careful always look first to right and then to left
People generally travel on camels when crossing
Dead said the frost
Buried and lost
The leaf buds are covered with tough leather flaps called scales
We must not bring razor blades to school because they are dangerous
Do unto others (I know the rest) This is called the Golden Rule . . .

Well, I think I'll turn in now, Rex said. I'll take the books if you don't mind.

Certainly, said Mr Chapman. We rise at six-thirty in winter. I hope you will find your room comfortable. We call it the guest room now. I thought you might find it more convenient later to sleep in a smaller room that opens onto the back verandah. It's very handy for the sheds and you wouldn't bring dirt into the house. That's a great consideration with Mrs Chapman you know. But there is time enough to make the change after you have started work and become familiar with our way of life. Mrs Chapman was insistent that you should have Jim's room at first. I suppose you saw his picture over the bed?

A. P. GASKELL

The football match at Carisbrook was over. Dusk was already falling, and during the last part of the game the flight of the ball and even the movements of the players had been hard to follow in the failing light. Now, looking across the field, I could see the crowd dimly massing around the gates. Here and there a small yellow flame flickered where a smoker was lighting up, and the whole crowd moved under a thin blue haze of tobacco-smoke. After all the cheering the place seemed very quiet, and from the street outside came the noise of cars starting up and whining off in low gear, and a tram screeching round the corner under the railway bridge. Overhead the sky was clear with a promise of frost. A few small boys ran with shrill cries under the goalposts; the rest of the field lay empty in the grey light, and the smell of mud came through the damp air. I shivered and glanced down at my steaming jersey.

'Well you'd better go and get changed,' said Betty. 'I don't want you to catch cold. You'll be playing Southern next Saturday now, won't you?'

'Yes,' I said. 'They were bound to win today. Beating Kaikorai puts us level with them.'

'Will you be too tired for the dance?'

'My old knee feels a bit sore but I'll ring you after tea. I must go and get changed now. So long.'

I trotted in under the stand. The lights were on, the unshaded bulbs threw a cheap yellow glare over the walls of the dressing-rooms, and up into the girders and struts above. My football boots clumped along the boards of the passageway. I stamped to get some of the mud off and pushed open the door chalked 'Varsity A'.

Inside the dressing-room there was a strong human smell of sweaty togs, muddy boots and warm bodies as the men came prancing back naked from the showers and stood on the seats drying themselves. The room was crowded. Togs and boots lay over the floor, clothes hung emptily from the pegs, and men were everywhere, shoving, jostling, reaching out their arms to dry themselves or climb into a shirt and taking up more room. Everyone was happy now that the strain was over, talking, yelling, singing, intent on their warmth and comfort and the clean feel of dry clothes. It was good to relax and know that we wouldn't have that feeling of before-the-game nervousness for another week. Next week it was going to be solid. The match against Southern was the Big Game.

'Shut that door,' roared Buck as I came in. 'Hello, it's Bennie. Did she think you played a nice game? Did she see my try? What did it look like from the stand?'

'They couldn't see it from the stand,' I said. 'They all thought you'd torn your pants when we gathered round you. Nobody knew it was a try.' I sat down and started picking at my muddy laces. My hands were too cold to grip them properly.

'Bloody liar,' said Buck amiably. 'It was a damn good try.'

He had a very powerful voice. 'Boy oh boy oh boy,' he chanted, 'won't I knock back those handles tonight. You wait till I tell old Harry about my try. He'll shout after every round.'

'What try?' said Mac, our captain. 'Hell, you aren't going to claim anything for that bit of a scuffle? You were a mile offside.' His head disappeared into his shirt and came grinning out the top. He put on his glasses and the grin seemed more complete.

'Like hell,' shouted Buck, dancing about on the seat and sawing the towel across his back. 'I took the ball off him and fell over. When they all got off me there I was over the line. A clear try.'

'Offside a mile. Rabbiting. You handled it on the ground. I was walking back for the free-kick,' said the boys. They all liked Buck.

'Free-kick be damned,' he roared. 'It was a good forward's try. Right out of the book. Plenty of guts and initiative.'

'Yes, a typical forward's try,' said Bob, our half-back. He was small and very sturdy and freckled. 'Big bullocking bastards always mauling each other about. Why can't you do something nice and clean-cut like the backs?'

'The backs? The pansies? I sweat my guts out getting the ball for you and then you canter along very prettily about ten yards and then drop it.' He struck a chesty attitude standing naked on the seat. 'Do I look like a pansy?'

'Not with that thing.'

Someone shied a ball at Buck and left a muddy mark on his backside. I went out to the shower. I could hear Buck's voice as I trotted along the passage. One of the Kaikorai men was still in the shower-room.

'How are you now?' he said.

'Pretty tired. It was a tough game.'

'We didn't want you to have it too easy. You jokers will be playing off with Southern now.'

'Yes. The big championship. Next Saturday.'

'Think you'll lick them?'

'Hope so. We'll give them a good go, especially if it's a dry ground.'

'Their forwards are good. Pack very low. Well, good luck.'

'Thanks.' I turned on the taps. There was still plenty of hot water left and it was great. Gosh I enjoyed it.

When I got back most of the boys were dressed and the coach was there talking to Mac. 'Shake it along Bennie,' said Bob, 'or we'll miss the beer. It's well after five now.'

'I'm practically there already,' I said. 'Don't rush me. Give me a smoke. Hell I feel good now.' I was in digs with Bob. 'What did the coach think of it?'

'He said you were lousy but the rest of us went well.'

I knew Bob was joking but I didn't like it much. I knew I wasn't particularly good and the coach was always on to me to put more vigour and initiative into my play. I was the heaviest man in the team and he would point out what the lighter forwards did and then what I did, and make me feel ashamed. If he thought I was lousy that meant I was in for a roasting at the next team-talk.

'He says you're to mark Jackie Hore on Saturday,' grinned Bob. 'You've got to dominate him.'

'I can easy fix Yackie,' I said. 'I bumped into him one game last season and he fell over. Fell right over from just a little bump. He's a softie.'

'Yes? Who was it broke your nose?'

'Aw, that was just his knee. Everybody's got hard knees.' I struggled into my shirt.

'Listen! Listen!' Mac was yelling above the din. After the uproar the silence sounded immense.

'Well boys,' said the coach. 'You know you're for it now. It's either you or the Southern for this season's champions, and next Saturday you'll have the honour of playing off with them. It's up to every one of you to keep fit. It's going to be a long hard game and I know I can rely on you boys to go on the field fit. I know Buck will leave the beer alone tonight.'

'What,' roared Buck, 'why do you think I go tearing round there for ninety minutes if it's not to get a thirst?'

'I knew you wouldn't mind,' said the coach, 'especially after they presented you with that try.'

'Another one,' said Buck in mock resignation. 'Another one. The best forward on the ground and I get nothing but abuse, I'll chuck the game and take on ping-pong.'

'Well boys, I'll see you on Wednesday at practice. I want you all out early. Will they all be out, Mac?'

'Anyone who can't?' said Mac. No answer.

'O.K. then. Goodnight boys. Anyone coming my way?'

They all began drifting off. Mac waited on Bob and me. The Southern match was just a nice distance ahead. I could get a thrill out of thinking of it but no nervousness yet. I felt good.

'Well Mac,' I said, 'how does the skipper feel about our chances? Our great public would like to know. Would you care to make a statement?' We often did these cross-talk acts.

'I think I may say with all due modesty that we are quietly confident,' said Mac. 'Tell our public that the same spirit of healthy rivalry that has spurred on our predecessors will again be found animating the bosoms of this year's team. Tell them that the game of Rugby fosters the team spirit and is the basis of our democracy. Tell them to play up and play the game. Tell them to go to hell.'

'Very prettily put,' I said. 'And now who else can we help?'

'A message for the expectant mothers,' urged Bob.

Mac was going well. 'Tell them we favour the quick heel,' he said. 'Never leave an opening for your opponent. God save Sir Truby King. For Christ's sake hurry up, Bennie.'

I was dumping my togs in the bag as the caretaker put his head round the door. 'You boys ready? I'm waiting to lock up.'

We went out with him. 'Think you can hold the Southern?' he asked. He called them Southeren.

'We'll give them a good go for it,' said Mac. He was our spokesman on occasions like these.

'They've got a fine team. You'll need all your luck to beat those forwards of theirs – man!'

'We're going to play fifteen backs and run them off the paddock,' said Bob.

'Are you now? Ay? Well I'll be watching you, but I'll no say which side I'll be barracking for. Goodnight.' He locked the gate after us.

It was quite dark now and all the street-lights were on. The air was keen and frosty. We went up under the railway bridge and stood in front of the lighted shops waiting for a tram. I was beginning to feel cold and stiff and tired now that the excitement was over.

'You know,' I said, 'football would be a good game if we could just play it on a Saturday.'

'Come up to date boy,' said Bob. 'This is Saturday. You remember yesterday? Well that was Friday. Today we've just beaten Kaikorai.'

'I bet he carries a calendar,' grinned Mac to me.

'No, fair go,' said Bob seriously. 'It's just general knowledge.'

'I mean it,' I said. 'It would be good if we could just play it on a Saturday. I've just been thinking, here we are just after slogging through one hard game and before we're off the ground even, everyone wants to play next week's game with us. Why can't they give us a spell?'

'I suppose they're greedy,' said Mac. 'They just get over one sensation and they're greedy for the next. They don't like having nothing to look forward to.'

'Hero worship too,' said Bob. 'They like to air their views in front of the well-known Varsity skipper. It makes them feel big. Or perhaps they think we don't bother about much else, we just live for football.'

'We will be for the next week,' I said. 'We'll be playing Southern all week and by the time Saturday comes we'll be so nervous we can't eat. It's one hell of a caper in a way. I'll be glad when the season's over and I can relax.'

'Did you get any knocks?'

'No worse than usual. The knee's pretty sore.'

The tram came along. It was good to sit down again. The conductor evidently recognised Mac. 'They'll make you run around next week,' he said. 'The Southern I mean. Be a good game.'

'How did they get on today?'

'Against Taieri? 46–3,' he said. 'How do you feel now?' He laughed and went to the back of the car. He came past us again later. '46–3,' he said again and winked.

The next Saturday morning, I woke early in the digs and looked out the window. The sky was right down on the hills and there was a thick drizzle. O hell. I stretched down under the blankets again and tried to go to sleep but the thought of the match kept me awake. It had been a tough week as we were getting close to exams and I'd had a good deal of swot to do but I felt very fit. We'd been for a run every night after finishing our swot, usually about midnight, and on Wednesday there had been a really hard practice. The coach kept us packing lower and lower, scrum after scrum, and kept us down there with the strain on for so long that my muscles were all quivering and Buck who locked with me was groaning under the pressure, and when we stood up I felt dizzy and queer little lights slid down across my vision. It felt a good scrum though, very compact. The line-outs afterwards were plain hell. And then of course, the team-talk on Friday night. We used to hold it in a lecture room in the School of Mines. All around us on the wall were wooden models of pieces of machinery and charts of mines and geological strata. They made you realise the earth is very big and old, and goes down a long way. The coach would stand on the platform and start on his old game of building us up to fighting pitch. He was an artist at it, he could mould us just the way he wanted us. He spoke for a while about the traditions of the Club and then about the honour of playing off for the championship. 'Tomorrow,' he said, 'we'll start off as usual by taking them on in the forwards. Here I am in the line-out. I look at my opposite number and I think, "You're a good man, but by Jesus I'm better. Today you've got no show".' His voice takes on a stirring note. He moves about on the platform suiting actions to his words. 'Into them! Dominate them! And every man when he sees where that ball goes, he thinks, "There's Buck in. I'm in too." Into them! And every man is thinking the same and we're all animated with the same spirit, we're going in to dominate them and we pack in tight and we're giving all our weight and strength and we're thinking together and working together and no one lets up. Dominate them.' And he goes on acting the part, words pouring out of him in that stirring tone and we watch him mesmerised, so that he takes us with him and we're there in the game, too, playing with him, working as a team. We leave the lecture room with a feeling of exaltation.

Then, on the other hand, there were the football notes in the paper. I know it was silly to take much notice of them, but I always read them. Referring to the Kaikorai game, the reporter said that I 'went a solid game but lacked the fire and dash that would make all the difference to his play'. The best thing I'd done, the movement where, to my mind, I had shown fire and dash was credited to Buck as 'one of his typical dashes'. Of course we are very much alike in build, but all the same I felt disappointed. The papers make people think that we are a sort of entertainment troupe, a public possession. Actually, I suppose we'd go on playing if there were no public; we'd relax and enjoy our football much more.

It's one hell of a caper really, I thought, stretching out under the sheets. I was lucky to have a girl like Betty who was keen on football. Some of the girls used to go very snooty when the blokes couldn't take them to the Friday night hops.

Well, this is the day. A few hours and it will be all over. This is it. It's funny how time comes round. For ages you talk of something and think of it and prepare for it, and it's still a long way off. You keep thinking how good it will be, and then suddenly, bang, it's there, you're doing it and it's not so enjoyable after all. I think football's like that, better before and after the game than in it.

Well, the day had come. I wasn't keen to get up and face it but anything was better than lying in bed and thinking a lot of rubbish. I put on my dressing-gown and slippers and padded round to Bob's room. He was still asleep. 'You won't look so peaceful in eight hours' time,' I said. 'They're queuing up at Carisbrook already.'

He raised his head from the pillow with a start. 'Eh?' He rubbed his eyes. 'What's wrong?'

'Jackie Hore just rang up to see how you are. He said their forwards are going to break very fast today, so he probably won't have an opportunity to ask you after the game because you'll be in hospital.'

He grinned. 'Then it's all bluff? I thought it was.'

'What?'

'About you forwards dominating them. I didn't think you could. I've never seen you do it yet. Just a bunch of big good-natured guys.'

'Not us,' I said. 'A pack of wolves just a-howling for prey. That's how we'll be today.'

Bob yawned and stretched his arms above his head. 'I must watch you. It would be interesting for a change. Have you eaten yet?'

So we went down for breakfast. Afterwards I cleaned my footy boots and packed my gear, and there was nothing to do but wait. I had no lectures on Saturday morning and I couldn't settle down to swot. The weather began to clear and a watery sun showed through the clouds so Bob and I went for a stroll. The town would be full of football talk and trams placarded, 'Big Game Today, Carisbrook 3 p.m., Varsity A v. Southern', so to get away from it we went down to Logan Park and climbed up above the quarry. It wasn't so cold in the sun and the harbour looked glassy. There was no-one about. We threw stones down into the quarry. It was good watching them. They dropped away from us, slowly getting smaller and smaller, then suddenly they struck the bottom and exploded shooting fragments out sideways, starlike.

At twelve we went back to the digs for an early lunch. I didn't feel very hungry, and while we were waiting for the food, Bob kept tapping his knife on the table. We caught the quarter past one tram out to the ground. It was better to watch the curtain-raiser than hang about the digs. The tram was packed and rows of cars were already making for the ground. Everybody looked very jolly and expectant. We saw Buck and Mac on the tram and that cheered us up a bit. It was good to realise that there were others who had to go through with it too. Buck didn't care a hoot about it all.

'Think you can win?' an old man said to him.

'Win?' Buck seized the old fellow's hand. 'Be the first to congratulate us on winning the championship. Get in early. Do it now. Be the very first.'

The old chap pulled his hand away looking a bit silly.

At Carisbrook we joined the crowd around the gates and pushed through to the players' entrance. I could see people nudging one another and nodding towards Mac. We showed our passes and went in along behind the stand and in underneath to the dressing-rooms. Most of the boys were early, there were other bags lying on the seats.

'Shall we go up for a while?' said Mac. We went out in front of the stand to see the final of the Junior Competition. The stand was packed and the bank opposite was dark with people. We stood about watching the boys playing with a sort of detached interest and then at half-time we went underneath to change. The strain was getting to me a little – I'd take things off and then forget where I'd put them. I had to undo my pants and look to see whether I'd put on my jockstrap. Most of the chaps were pretty quiet, but Buck kept going and we were pleased we had him to listen to. Mac was roaming round in his underpants looking for his glasses.

'Like to make a statement before the match?' I asked him.

He just looked at me. 'I can't find my bloody glasses. I suppose some bastard will tread on them.'

'Just a picture of quiet confidence,' said Bob. My face felt very tight when I tried to grin.

Soon the trainer came in and started to rub us down. The room was filled with the smell of eucalyptus and the rapid slap slap slap of his hands. It was a great feeling being done, he made us feel nice and loose and warm and free-moving. Then Jackie Hore, the Southern skipper, came in to toss and we looked at him. There he was, the man we had been talking about all week. He lost the toss and laughed. He looked a good deal smaller than I'd been imagining him. Of course we had played against him before, but the strain makes you think silly things. We felt better after he'd gone.

'He doesn't look so soft,' said Bob to me.

'Poor old Yackie. I'll try and bump into him again today and you just watch.'

'Never mind,' he said, 'unless you do it from the other side and straighten your nose up.'

I strapped up my weak knee and when the Vaseline came round plastered it on my face to prevent scratches. The coach came in and we packed a scrum for him.

'That looks all right,' he said. 'Well now, listen boys. Remember you're going out now as the Varsity boys have done for many years now to play off for the championship, and a lot of those old players are out there today watching to see how good you are. Don't let them down. Remember the first ten minutes in the forwards. Hard!' He punched his open hand. 'Go in there and dominate . . .' But the referee was in the room to inspect the boots and the coach's exhortation was lost in the movement.

'Righto boys. One minute to go,' said the ref.

We took off our coats and handed round chewing gum. Buck and I put on our ear-guards. Mac found the ball and we lined up in the passage. The Southern players were there already, skipping about and rubbing their hands. They felt the cold too.

The whistle blew, there was a glare of sunlight, and we were outside going out into the field, right out into the open. A roar from the crowd rolled all around enveloping us. A cold easterly breeze blew through our jerseys as we lined up for the photographers, squinting into the low sun. The Southern players looked broad and compact in their black and white jerseys. We gave three cheers and trotted out into the middle. The turf felt fine and springy. We spaced ourselves out. I took some deep breaths to get charged up with oxygen for the first ten minutes. A Southern player dug a hole with his heel and placed the ball.

'All right Southern? All right Varsity?' called the referee.

Both captains nodded. He blew the whistle. The Southern man ran up to kick.

'Thank Christ,' I thought. 'The game at last.'

DAN DAVIN

The band concert was over and three of us came out of the Regent into Dee Street with the rest of the crowd.

'I could swear she gave me the eye,' Sid said.

'I'll bet she did,' Wally said. 'One look'd be all she'd need, too. Who did, anyway?'

'That sheila with the black hat on that was in front of us about two seats away. You'd be too busy looking at the statue of the naked Greek dame to notice, I expect. Anyhow she was just in front of me when we were coming out and when I pushed the swing door open for her she turned round and gave me a real grin. Look, there she goes.'

He pointed the way we were going, and, sure enough, we could see a black hat bobbing along a bit in front where the crowd wasn't so thick.

'Come on, boys,' said Wally, 'here we go.'

'But, look here,' I said, 'I thought we were going to the Greek's.' All the same, I changed my pace to keep up with theirs.

'To hell with the Greek's. Who wants to be sitting down to eggs and chips when there's a chance of picking up a sheila, eh, Sid?'

Sid just grunted. You couldn't see the girl because of the crowd and he was staring straight down the footpath, towards where we'd last seen her. You wouldn't have needed to know him as well as I did to guess from the sour way his mouth was closed that he didn't fancy the shape things were taking much.

Wally was a tiger for the girls, and a good-looking joker, too. And old Sid hadn't had the same confidence in himself since the dentist made him have all his top teeth out. Wally didn't give him much chance to forget about it, either, calling him Gummy all the evening.

Not that there was anything in it for me, anyway. If there was only one girl I wouldn't be the chap who got her, that was certain. And, as a matter of fact, though I'd have been the last to say so, I'd have been scared stiff if there'd been the least danger of me being the one. I never really knew why I tagged along with them those Sunday evenings. I must have hoped some sort of miracle would happen, I suppose, and that some sheila or other would fall for me and put me into a position where one move had to follow the other in such a way that my mind'd be made up for me. At the same time I was terrified that just that would happen, knowing in advance that at close quarters with a girl I'd be like a cow with a musket. Anyhow, I needn't have worried. Nothing ever did happen and by this time I think I was getting to realise, only I wouldn't admit it, that nothing ever would.

That didn't stop me, though, from putting off going home till the last possible moment in case some sort of miracle turned up and when I finally left Wally or Sid at Rugby Park corner of a Saturday or Sunday night I'd trudge the rest of the way home in the rain or the moonlight, cursing myself and the town and everything in it and wondering what the hell was the matter with me, whether I was a different breed or what, and why it was always me that was left, and thinking that in some other country somewhere things mightn't be like that at all and people would see what I really was instead of what I'd always been.

So, with all that at the back of my mind, and Wally rampaging alongside with about as many afterthoughts as a dog has after a rabbit, and Sid on the other side getting down in the mouth already at the thought that Wally was going to pinch his girl, I didn't think much of the night's prospects. The upshot'd be that Wally would get her all right and I'd have to spend what was left of the evening at the Greek's trying to cheer Sid up by encouraging him to skite about all the girls that had fallen for him and pretending not to notice how much Wally going off with this one had got under his skin.

Well, after a bit the crowd got thinner and most of them started to cross over to where the last tram was waiting, towards the Majestic side. So we could see better what was in front of us. And there was the girl all right, about twenty yards ahead, all by herself into the bargain, and pacing along at a fair bat. Good legs she had, too.

'I reckon she knows we're following her,' Wally said. 'The trouble is, there's too many of us.'

'That's right, Wally.'

It was very sarcastic the way Sid said it but that didn't worry Wally.

'Go on, Sid,' he said, 'don't be a dog in the manger. A fair fight and let the best man win, eh?'

Of course, that was just the trouble, the way Sid looked at it. It's always the best man who says these things.

Anyhow, before Sid could think of an answer, or before he could think of something that wouldn't have given away he knew he hadn't a hope against Wally whatever kind of fight it was, the girl started to cross the road and so, us too, we changed course like a school of sprats and over the road after her, only about ten yards behind by this time.

She stepped up on to the footpath on the opposite side of the road, us tagging behind like three balloons on a string. She looked behind just then and saw us.

'Now's our chance,' Sid said, getting quite excited and nervous, I could tell.

Wally didn't say anything but he took advantage of his long legs and he was up on the pavement a good yard in front of us.

It was darker on the footpath because of the shop verandahs and because the nearest street-lamp was a good distance away. At first I couldn't see what was happening, owing to the notion I had that if I wore my glasses when we were out on the pick up on nights like this I'd spoil my chances, such as they were; but I felt both Wally and Sid check. And then I saw what it was. The girl had stepped into a shop doorway and there was a chap there waiting for her.

The girl and her bloke came out of the doorway and walked off towards the other end of Dee Street, her hanging on his arm and talking a blue steak and laughing the way we could tell the joke was on us. And the bloke looked back, once, as if he'd like to have come at us. But, seeing Wally and thinking he had the trumps anyway, I suppose, he turned round again and kept on going.

Well, I'm damned,' Wally said.

'Foiled again,' Sid said. But he didn't sound narked at all, really, and I knew by his voice he'd sooner have had it that way so that the laugh was on Wally instead of on himself as it would have been if things had gone differently.

I was pleased, too, for that matter, though I couldn't help envying that bloke a bit with a good-looking girl on his arm and a nice new blue overcoat and Borsalino and never a doubt in his head as to where he was going and what he'd do when he got there.

Still, envying him made it easier to pretend I meant it when I cursed the girl up hill and down dale like the others. For it wouldn't have done for me to show I was really relieved. It was sort of understood that even if I didn't mean business like Wally and Sid I had to go through the motions just the same. They really weren't bad blokes in a way, Wally and Sid, because they knew all the time I wasn't a serious competitor and yet they always treated me as if I was, thinking I'd be hurt if they didn't, I suppose.

And I would have been hurt, too. Somehow, if there hadn't been this kind of agreement about the way we were all to behave, I'd have had to drop the game altogether. I could tell that, because when, as happened sometimes, other blokes joined us who didn't know the rules or didn't care if there were any and they began to pull my leg, I always pushed off after a while. Which was what these other chaps wanted, I expect. 'The Wet Napkin', I heard one of them, Ginger Foyle it was, say once after I'd gone and he didn't think I could hear him, because I hadn't got my glasses on, perhaps.

No, Wally and Sid weren't like that, especially Wally. They knew I was all right once you got to know me and, besides, I used to be able to make them laugh when we were by ourselves and get them to see the funny side of things they'd never have noticed if it hadn't been for me.

Well, anyway, there we were left standing in the middle of Dee Street and all cursing our heads off in the same way.

'Nothing for it but to go over to the Greek's,' I said.

'Listen to him, will you, Sid,' Wally said. 'Him and his bloody Greek's.

And us all whetted up for a bite of something tastier than old Harry could ever put under our noses.'

I felt a fool immediately, because I might have known that was the wrong thing to say, the way they were feeling. Once Wally had got the idea of skirt into his head it wasn't easy to put him off. And Sid, for all I don't think he really liked Wally, would trail along with him all right, knowing that was his best chance. That was what fascinated him about Wally, he could always have what Wally didn't want. But it was what made him hate Wally's guts, too.

Besides, I suppose they felt I'd sort of broken the rules by not being keen enough and waiting a bit longer before giving up what we all knew was a bad job.

'Well, what'll we do now, Wally?' Sid said.

'Let's take a stroll as far as the Civic and back,' I chipped in, trying to establish myself again. 'You never know, we might pick up something.'

'That's more like it,' Wally said. And then, because he wasn't a bad bloke, a better chap in many ways than Sid would ever be, he added: 'After all, if there's nothing doing, we can always go over to have a feed at the Greek's later on.' Which showed he wasn't really fooled by what I'd said.

So away we went, down past the Majestic where Len Parry and Alec Haynes and all that bunch were as usual, pretending they were talking about who was going to win the Ranfurly Shield when all they were interested in really was the girls who kept scuttling by on their way back from the band concert. I took a look at the town clock on the other side as we went by and there it was, half-past ten already, one more Sunday evening just about over and nothing happening, only the same old thing. Already everyone who had anywhere to go was going there and soon the only people left in the streets would be chaps like us who couldn't think of anything better to do and soon we'd be gone home too and the streets would be empty and another night would be gone out of a man's life and him none the wiser one way or the other.

'Was that your cousin Marty I saw all by himself in the doorway next to that bloke who met the shelia, Ned?' Sid suddenly asked.

'I didn't notice.'

'It was him all right, poor bastard,' Wally said.

I pricked up my ears at that. My cousin Marty wasn't the sort of chap you talked about with that particular tone in your voice. He was rather a big shot in the eyes of our crowd. A good five or six years older than any of us, he must have been twenty-two or twenty-three, and he used to earn good money before the slump. A plasterer he was, by trade. But he'd been one of the first to be turned off when things got tough because, though he was good at his job, he had a terrible temper and was too handy with his fists. A big joker, he was, with reach and height, and they used to say that if only he'd do a bit more training there wasn't a pro in the business he couldn't have put on his back for the count. As it was he'd made quite a name for himself round the town as a fighter and once when I was at the barber's and got fed up with the way slick little Basset kept taking me for granted because I didn't know what was going to win the Gore Cup I'd managed to get in casually that Marty was my cousin and after that Basset could never do enough for me.

'What do you mean, "poor bastard"?' Sid was saying.

'Didn't you hear? The trouble with you, Sid, is you never hear anything now you've got your teeth out.'

'Come on, come on, know-all. What's it all about?'

'Yes, what was it, Wally?' I asked; for I could tell Wally was wishing he'd kept his mouth shut, knowing Marty was my cousin.

'Well, it's only what they're saying, Ned, and there mightn't be anything in it, though I have noticed Marty hasn't been about much lately. You know how you'd always see him and Dulcie Moore round together of a Saturday and Sunday night?'

'That's right,' Sid said, glad to get in on the inside again. 'I saw them coming out of the Rose Gardens about two in the morning the night of Ginger Foyle's keg-party and they were always at the Waikiwi dances together.'

'Well, they say he put her up the spout. And then he got some old dame who hangs out in Georgetown to fix her up. Of course, that's happening all the time all over the place, you know, and nobody ever thinks a thing about it as long as no one gets caught.' This was for me. 'But the trouble this time was that something went wrong and she got blood-poisoning or something, and now she's in hospital and they say the johns have been at her all the time beside her bed trying to find out who did it and who was the man. But so far she won't say and the odds are she won't pull through.'

'Jesus,' said Sid. 'I thought he looked a bit down in the mouth.'

'Wouldn't you be?'

'But, look here, Wally,' I said, 'who told you all this?'

'I heard Marty's crowd, Jim Fergus and all that lot, talking about it yesterday after the game. And when I was shaving in the bathroom this morning and they didn't know I was there, I heard Mum telling the old man about it. It was her that told that bit about her not being expected to live.'

We'd got as far as the Civic and turned back by this time and the crowd was getting very thin by now, everybody making for home, feeling much the way I'd been feeling, I expect, that they might as well be in bed as hanging round. Only I didn't feel like that any more. Things happened, sure enough, and even to people you knew, even to your own family, near enough.

Sid and Wally kept talking about it all the way back up Tay Street. It was queer the way they seemed to get a sort of pleasure out of discussing it. And what was queerer still was that I liked hearing them talk about it. It must have been partly how old we were and partly the town we lived in. You felt the place wasn't quite such a dead-alive hole, after all, and you felt you really were grown up when things like that, terrible things but things all the same, happened to people you even knew.

Anyhow, just as we got to the Bank corner, two girls came round it the opposite way and we almost banged into them. While we were dodging around them to let them pass and show what gentlemen we were they cut through between me and Wally and we could hear them giggling as they went on.

'Sorry,' Wally called back in an extra-polite voice I hardly recognised, he could put on the gyver so well when he wanted to.

'Don't mention it,' one of the girls said and giggled again.

We stopped at that and Sid made a great show of lighting cigarettes for us while we all had a good dekko back to see what the girls were up to.

'They've stopped in the doorway next the jewellers,' Wally said. 'Come on, Sid, here we go. We're home and dry.' He was so excited he forgot to pretend I was in on it, too.

The two of them cut back the way we'd come, like a couple of whippets at first and then as they got closer with a sort of elaborate stroll as if they might just as well be walking that way as any other. I followed after them, trying to catch up and yet not to catch up. I knew I ought to have gone away. There was no good just tagging on, being a nuisance. But I kept following, all the same.

'Hello,' Wally was saying as I came up to the doorway. 'Going anywhere?'

'What's that got to do with you?' the girl who had called back to us said.

'Well,' Sid said, 'it's getting late for girls to be out by themselves with all the roughs there are about this time of night and we thought you might like to have an escort on the way home.'

Sid could always talk well when it came to the pinch, especially if he had Wally with him. I of course couldn't say a thing, being as nervous as a cat, although I knew already that it didn't matter much what I did, me being only the spare part.

'You know what thought did,' the girl said.

'Come on, Isobel,' the other girl said. 'It's getting late.'

'Will you have a cigarette, Isobel?' Wally said. And he took out his case. It was the one he kept his tailor-mades in, not the one he used for home-rolled ones and butts. In that light you'd have taken it for silver.

'Don't mind if I do.'

'Come on, Isobel,' the other girl said again.

'Now, Jean, don't be an old fusspot. There's heaps of time really. Why don't you have a cigarette, too.'

'That's right,' Wally said, and so Jean took one from the case, a bit nervously, I thought.

'We don't even know your names, do we, Jean?' said Isobel when Sid had flourished his lighter for them. You could see them trying to get a look at us while the flame was there. But of course we had our backs to the street-lights and they couldn't have made out much what we looked like.

'That's easy,' Wally said then. 'I'll introduce us. My name's Wally Radford and this is my friend Sid, Sid Cable. And this is Ned.'

'He's a quiet one, isn't he?' Isobel gave Jean a nudge and giggled at me.

I tried to think of something very witty to say, the sort of thing that would have come to Wally or Sid in a flash. But I couldn't think of anything at all and I could feel myself blushing. I hated that Isobel then. It was always the good-looking ones that made me feel most of a fool. The other one, Jean, I didn't mind so much because I could tell by her way of giggling that she was nervous, too. She wasn't anything like such a good-looker, though.

There was a bit of a silence then. They were all waiting for me to say something. When I still didn't say anything I felt them all just give me up. Wally got into the doorway close to Isobel and tried to get his arm round her. She kept fending him off and looking at him and then at Jean in a way that said as plain as a pikestaff: Wait till afterwards when we can get away by ourselves.

Sid was talking a blue streak to Jean so as to give her a chance to get over her shyness, I suppose, and to shut me out of it and make me see I was being the gooseberry, in case I didn't see it already.

There was nothing to do but leave them to it. I was only holding Wally and Sid back from doing their stuff, hanging round like that.

'Well, I must be getting along,' I said.

'Why don't you come with us?' Jean said. Her voice sounded quite scared. But I could tell Sid wasn't going to get anywhere with her and I wasn't going to have her use me as an excuse to keep him off and then have him putting the blame on me next day.

'I'd like to,' I said, 'but I live up the other end of the town.'

'OK, Ned, good night,' Wally said in an offhand sort of way and Sid said good night too, in the friendly voice he always used when you were doing something he wanted you to do. That was one of the things Sid liked about me, that I always did the expected thing. It wasn't one of the things I liked about him.

So I set off by myself up towards the Bank corner again, feeling like a motherless foal, as the old man would have said. I thought I'd better give them plenty of time to get clear and so I decided I'd walk a few blocks up Dee Street and back again.

The town clock was pointing to nearly eleven by now. All the crowd that'd been in front of the Majestic was gone and Dee Street was as empty as the tomb except for a bobby standing in the library doorway over the other side, just in case there should be a row at the Greek's, I expect.

Seeing the Greek's lighted windows gave me the idea of going in for a feed, after all. But it was pretty late and I couldn't face going in there all by myself, with the blokes eyeing me and guessing what had happened. So I crossed Esk Street and went straight on up.

But it wasn't nearly so bad being by yourself when the whole street was empty like that and you didn't have to wonder what people were thinking about you. I quite liked striding along under the shop verandahs as if I were going nowhere in a hurry and listening to my heels hammer on the asphalt and seeing my reflection pass dark on the windows. It was better feeling miserable by yourself and not having to put up a show any more. Or else the kind of show you put up when there was no one but yourself to watch was more convincing.

'Hullo, Ned.'

I stopped in my tracks and looked round to see where the voice came from. Then I saw him. He was in the same doorway that the sheila had met her bloke in earlier on. He was standing there, all stiff like a sentry, and in that light you'd have thought his eyes were black they were so dark. A Spaniard, he might have been, with the long sideboards halfway down his cheeks and his straight, thin nose, that had never been broken for all the boxing he'd done.

'Hullo, Marty,' I said.

He didn't say any more, just went on looking at me. I didn't know quite what to do because it struck me it was probably only the suddenness of seeing someone he knew that had made him call out and probably he wished he hadn't now. Besides, knowing what I did, I felt uncomfortable.

I went up to him all the same, not knowing how to get away without it looking awkward and as if I'd heard about his trouble and was dodging off so as not to be seen with him.

'Have a cigarette,' I said and I produced a packet of ten Capstan.

'Thanks.'

I lit them for us both and when that was over there I was still stuck and unable to think of anything else to say. The only things that came into my head sounded quite hopeless compared with the things he must have on his mind.

'All the crowd gone home?' I said in the end, for lack of anything better.

'Suppose so,' he answered and took a puff of the cigarette. Then he added in a voice so savage that it gave me a real fright. 'Who the hell cares what they've done? Pack of bastards.'

I didn't say anything. I was trying to work out what he meant by that. Had they done the dirty on him and talked to the johns? Or was he just fed up with them?

He gave me a look just then, the first time he'd really looked at me since I stopped.

'You've heard all about it, I suppose?'

That stumped me properly. I didn't want him to get the idea the whole town was talking about him. Especially as that was what they were probably doing. I was scared of him, too. He'd be a bad bloke to say the wrong thing to.

'Heard about what?'

'You know.' He'd guessed by the time I took to answer. 'About Dulcie.'

There was no good pretending. 'Yes,' I said. 'How is she?'

He didn't answer but he kept on looking at me in the same queer way that he had been looking at me before. And then, as if he'd been sizing me up, he got down to what was on his mind.

'Look here, Ned,' he said. 'What about doing something for me?'

'All right,' I said. 'What do you want me to do?' My heart was in my boots because I didn't know much about the law but I felt sure this was going to be something against it.

'It's like this. I can't ring the hospital to see how she is because the johns are there and they keep asking me my name and they know my voice, too. What about you ringing for me?'

'All right, Marty,' I said. 'But what'll I say if they ask who I am? If I give my name they might come poking about home trying to find out what I know about it.'

'Say your name's Eddie Sharp. That's a friend of her young brother's and it'd be quite natural for him to ring. Will you do it?'

'I'll just see if I've got any pennies.'

We walked back towards the Post Office square. But the john was still in the library doorway and so I told Marty to go back to the place where I'd met him and wait for me there.

The john gave me that hard look that policemen give you but I went straight past him without giving a sign of how nervous I was. It was being so sorry for Marty that made me able to do it, I think.

'Southland Hospital,' a woman's voice answered when I'd got the number.

'I want to inquire about a patient, Miss Moore, Miss Dulcie Moore.'

'Will you hold on, please?'

There was a lot of clicking at the other end and I could hear whispering. Then a man's voice answered.

'The patient died an hour ago. Who is that speaking?'

I didn't answer. I just rang off and came out of the phone box.

How was I going to tell him, I kept asking myself as I went back past the john, hardly noticing him this time.

Marty was standing in the doorway, just as he had been the first time.

'How was she?'

There was nothing else I could do. I came out with it.

'She died an hour ago.'

He stood there without saying a thing, just looking at me and yet not seeing me. Then he took a deep breath and his chest came out and he stood even straighter.

'So that's how it is,' he said. 'She's dead.'

I didn't say anything. I just stood there, wishing I was anywhere else in the world.

'If only I'd known,' he said. 'Christ, man. I'd have married her a hundred times, kid and all.'

He stopped. His mind must have been going over and over this ground for days.

He gave a laugh suddenly, such a queer, savage sort of a laugh that I jumped.

'If it'd been twins, even,' he said.

I had enough sense not to think that I was meant to laugh at that one.

'And those bloody johns sitting by the bed.'

'Did she come to?' I asked.

'Yes, she was conscious a lot of the time. But she wouldn't talk, not Dulcie. Not her. She was all right, Dulcie.'

Then there was silence again. I didn't know what to do or say. It was getting late. They'd have locked the door at home and there'd be a rumpus if they knew what time it was when I came in. How queer it was: here I was in the middle of something that really mattered and worrying about what my mother would say if she heard me climbing in the window.

All the same I wanted to get home. And then I had to admit to myself it wasn't really that. It was that I wanted to get away from Marty. I think it must have been the first time I was ever with someone who felt as badly as he was feeling.

'I remember her,' I said. 'She was a stunner to look at.'

'Wasn't she?' Marty said. And the way he said it made the tears come into my eyes.

'Why don't you walk my way?' I asked him. If he did that I could be making towards home and at the same time wouldn't feel I was ratting on him.

'No, I'm not going home yet,' he said.

I shuffled from one foot to the other, wondering what to do next and a bit worried what he would do after I'd gone.

'We always used to meet here,' he said. 'In this doorway.'

'Oh,' I said. 'Well, look here, Marty, I've got to be getting home now.'

'That's all right.'

I tried to think of some way of saying how sorry I was. But there was no way of saying it.

'Good night, Ned,' he said, and then, as I began to walk away, he called out: 'Thanks for doing that for me.'

So that's how it is, I was saying to myself all the way home. That's the sort of thing that happens once the gloves are off. And by the time I'd got to the front gate and opened it with one hand on the latch to stop it clicking and sat on the front verandah to take my shoes off I think I'd taken it all into myself and begun to wake up to how we only kid ourselves we can tell the good things from the bad things when really they're so mixed up that half the time we're thinking one thing, feeling another, and doing something else altogether.

E. S. GRENFELL

Sunday afternoon, and in the cold bathroom the old man was shaving. Although it was fully an hour before sunset, he had pulled on the electric light, but finding it insufficient had stood a lighted candle on the shelf above the hand-basin.

He shaved laboriously, with trembling deliberation, the razor crackling slowly over his lean jaws. After every third stroke of the razor he wiped it carefully on a strip of newspaper. He was a tall, big-boned man; the mirror being too low he had to bend his knees slightly. Crouched in the wavering lemon light, his elbows upraised, he looked like some gaunt and dusty bird of prey. The jerky rhythm of his right arm was like the slow and painful flexing of a decrepit wing. But his left hand was still, spread fingers drawing the flaccid skin of his face tight against the crackling blade. From time to time he put his razor down to wipe the blurred mirror with a towel, or to twist doggedly but ineffectually at a bath tap which dripped, dripped, taunting his innate sense of orderliness.

Mumbling to himself about the tap he shaved on with finicking concentration until he had scraped the last fleck of lather from his face. When he had cleaned and dried his gear, he washed noisily in a full basin of cold water, vigorously, with great drowning gasps. Wet and freshly shaved, his skin had momentarily the gloss and tautness of health, in the weak candlelight. But with the drying of his face, and the snuffing of the candle, the illusion ended.

It was a grey cadaverous face with high sunken temples, the top lip long and pointed, cheek-bones flat and simian; a penny could have rested in the gaunt hollow beneath each foggy eye. A face redeemed from mere comic ugliness by the repose, the dignity of a contented old age.

Coughing dryly, the old man padded out to the kitchen where he poked up the range fire and drew the kettle over. And the time? Nearly four-fifteen, he saw, and in the glass of the pendulum clock caught a reflected glimpse of the sky beyond the window already smoky and reddening with frost.

He pulled on his boots and an old blue and black striped blazer and went out to the little shed at the end of the garden. In one corner stood two sacks of potatoes and his garden tools; opposite, a pile of forcing frames. Suspended under the ceiling on a strip of wire-netting hung last season's onion crop, and on the walls, besides a grass-catcher and empty paint tins and worn bicycle tyres, were two hopeful attempts at decoration – a large lithograph of Admirals Jellicoe and Beatty, and a weather-stained almanac depicting three kittens and two balls of wool in a wicker-work basket.

Along the wall nearest the doorway was a row of crude drawers with pieces of strap leather for handles. One by one, the old man pulled each drawer clear of the frame and carried it to the daylight, raking through each rusty, dusty collection of bolts, screws, split-pins with a long, patiently probing forefinger. A reddish dust began to fill the little shed. Near the end of the row he paused in his search to blow his nose vigorously, a loud, querulous toot into a blue spotted handkerchief. Then he went on with his search. The last two drawers contained larger articles – short lengths of bicycle chain, old dented door-knobs, round tobacco tins of parsnip and sunflower seeds.

Baffled, he stood on the asphalt outside the shed door, tugging at the lobe of his right ear. For some time he stood there patiently struggling with his failing memory. Then suddenly he turned, bustled back into the shed.

On a ledge above Admirals Jellicoe and Beatty was a pile of floor polish tins. In the second one he found a tangle of tiny expansion springs and three tap washers. The old man selected the shapeliest of the washers and going back to the house, to the bathroom, stuck it upright in the cake of soap in the hand-basin. Now, he told himself, I'm bound to see that in the morning.

At four-thirty he went outside to cover his chrysanthemums. The frost had flared even higher into the sky. One wall of the house, the east, was windowless, and snug under it grew the row of chrysanthemums, the drab limp leafage propped by manuka poles strong enough to support a sapling. The old man was thorough. Thoroughly now, he began to spread scrim over the protective framework, shuffling back and forth along the row to tuck under a protruding branch, or to ease the scrim away from a taller plant. Now and again he glanced up anxiously at the low pinkish sky as if he saw the frost suspended there like a raincloud, ready to fall at any moment. My own fault if they cop it, he thought. Messing about, wasting time.

His movements had a jerky urgency as he took a bucket from the wash-house and hurried out into the street, driven by the thought that somehow, somewhere that afternoon he had wasted valuable time.

The street wound along the ragged fringe of a small city, houses on only one side of it, and flanked on the south by a branch railway line – three trains a week and specials on Show Days. On the far side of the line were low swampy paddocks dotted with tussock; then a straggle of weather-board houses almost encircled by macrocarpas; beyond again, the sour, gently rising countryside.

The small corrugated iron shed on the far side of the line to which the old man made his way was used by surfacemen for the storage of tools, and occasionally a trolley. Behind the shed leaned a tumbledown wooden urinal, and a tap at which he began to fill the bucket. At the first clang of metal on metal, the horse cropping fifty yards away down the narrow railway paddock raised its head, stiffened its body expectantly, watching for the old man, gave a whinny of recognition when he emerged from behind the green rotting wall of the urinal.

For two months now the old man had been watering the horse. Its owner, a bottle-dealer, had temporarily retired from business. Plenty of easy money to be made just now, he said, without jogging round the streets in the cold. In the summer he'd probably get stuck into it again. She was a good little business.

A shiftless, mean-faced fellow, he snatched eagerly at the old man's offer to water the horse.

At first the horse had been none too sure of its new benefactor, had watched askance as he carried bucket after bucket over to the half-barrel, intimidated by the scarecrow figure, by the man's jerky flapping movements over the awkward fence and over the soft, uneven ground. A week later the horse was twenty yards nearer to the barrel, his rump towards the man, swinging his head in a wide arc as he cropped, all unconcern, all quivering alertness.

But now, two months later, the horse reached the barrel ahead of the old man who took some time to clamber through the sagging railway fence. Now, as the first bucketful of water curved down, he nudged gently, approvingly at the barrel with his nose – a habit which never failed to amuse and flatter the old man. He had worked in towns all his life and had handled nothing larger than a domestic cat. Seeing the horse accept him he was proud, as if he had tamed a fierce, intractable animal.

It took longer than usual to water the horse. The ground was frozen underneath, but the surface had thawed throughout the day and had not yet hardened again. A patch of sticky, slippery ground by the fence which skidded away underfoot like grease on concrete forced the old man – much against his will – to go carefully, to take time. Still, he managed to spare a minute to stand companionably beside the horse, listening to the greedy, crunching sound of it drinking. Then, like some huge regurgitating bird, he hawked twice and started off back to the house to change his clothes for his next job.

This was a dusty, dirty job, not warranting cleaner clothes, but it was a paid one and when he went to it he put on his second-best suit along with a sterner sense of responsibility. From April to September he tended the heating system of the neighbouring Presbyterian church, twice a Sunday, before each service. For this, the Deacons' Court paid him twenty-five pounds per season, to the satisfaction of both parties.

The house had chilled in his absence. Pulling down the kitchen blind his hand touched the window: it was like a sheet of ice. He put a heaped shovel of coal on the fire, and went into all the rooms in turn, shutting the windows against the creeping frost, peering around suspiciously for disorder before he left.

The rooms were scrupulously clean and tidy, the linoleums rich glossy reds and pale shining greens, plain, the patterns having long been polished away. Here and there the old man had spread sheets of newspaper. On his daily rounds of dusting, polishing, tittivating, he stepped carefully on the islands of newsprint. Sometimes he went in stockinged feet. In the bedrooms the covers had the stiff perfection of a showroom display. Made of cheap sateens they shone like polished sheets of coloured metal. And on the walls hung relics of the past life of his family – photos, hair-ribbons, a certificate which stated that Margaret A. Tollis had passed the League of Nations Examination for 1929, and in his own room, two of his late wife's hat-pins stuck behind the architrave of the wardrobe door.

The smallest and barest in the house, his own room had an iron bedstead, a tall, lowering chest-of-drawers, a small cane bedside table and on it a black-faced alarm clock, a spectacle case, a bottle of cough mixture and his two books – *Ben Hur* and *For the Term of His Natural Life*.

He changed hurriedly in the cold bedroom. His thin hairy thighs were wide apart; beneath the pink flannel undershirt they had the absurd, wide-spaced spindliness of a child's drawing. Wheezing and shivering he struggled into the brown tweed suit. Like all his suits it fitted him in three places – the shoulder blades, the elbows and the knees.

In the scullery, he knotted a scarf around his throat and spread the ends over his chest, buttoned his coat over them. A flat brown cap like a wilting mushroom, and he was ready.

On the way down the street he saw no one. It was the deadest hour, between tea and church. Silent on their withered lawns the houses were white-faced mausoleums. All seemed deserted, their occupants having perished from cold and boredom and loneliness. They had the merest, the most evanescent signs of life – a pale flag of smoke on a chimney, the glimmer of a fire in a front-room window like the flicker of interest in a dull apathetic eye. Darkness approaching, the frosty air had become tangible, congealed into a white, stinging haze. There were a few high, dim stars.

Only two blocks from his house, the church stood at a bleak cross-roads. Small and well-designed, its brick façade had been recently oiled and the coping white-washed. Bright in the gathering white haze it looked like a large freshly iced cake. Inside, it smelled faithfully and anciently of religion; the incense of varnished pews and dusty coco matting.

Groping in the fusty darkness of the back vestibule for the cellar key, the old man noticed a ribbon of light beneath the vestry door. Someone coughed, a chair scraped – his friend the parson pottering about. He thought: Well, it's his big day, he *ought* to be here on the job.

Still thinking of the parson and his soft, one-day-a-week job, he went round to the lee side of the building and opened the cellar door, switched on the light. The cellar was deep and very narrow, like a concrete slit-trench there underneath the church, but its atmosphere was warmish. Moisture glistened on the walls; at the far end the boiler squatted in a dark cavity. The old man had to go down on hands and knees to peer into the firebox, prostrate, it seemed, before a stern pot-bellied idol.

After he had raked the ashes away a small heap of live coals still remained from the morning's stoking, and on these he built a fierce bright fire with dry fruit-case timber; then adding coal eventually, shaping a little amphitheatre of fuel in the firebox with the careless assurance of an expert. His movements were clumsy but calculated; in the confined space the shovel struck repeatedly on concrete and metal, sending up a clangour of activity into the crisp air above.

Approaching, the young pastor grinned. Could be a smithy, he thought, descending. Or someone repairing a railway engine.

The old man was peering critically into the open firebox, studying his handiwork, the slowly expanding circle of low flame.

'Hello there!' said the parson and, when the old man jumped as always, continued as always with his weak ecclesiastical joke.

'One thing I know, Tolly,' he said, 'old Nick will get a first-class stoker when you pass on.' He was a humorous-minded, broad-minded young parson, very handsome, very self-confident.

The old man spoke his first words for that day. 'Should've been lit earlier,' he said, not turning. 'You'll want plenty of heat tonight.'

'I've got some red-hot stuff for them myself, Tolly,' the young parson laughed. 'They'll sweat all right.'

Straightening slowly, the old man turned a flushed, prim-lipped face to the parson. He liked the young man as a person; he deplored him as a parson. He thought the lad showed a lack of taste in his frivolous attitude to his job. Of course he himself held with the churches – they kept the nation from going off the rails. Look what happened to the Russians when they tried to do without churches – turned into a mob of worthless red-feds. All this although he didn't attend himself, not having the time. 'Look, the coal's got far too low,' he said. 'You'll have to get on to them. And keep at them or they'll put you off.'

'I'll make a note of that,' grinned the parson.

'You'd better ring tomorrow, first thing.'

'Yes sir,' said the young parson. 'I'll do that.' He backed meekly up the steps, nodding, his eyebrows assenting, his face boyishly and comically servile.

'And keep at them,' said Tolly sharply, to the disappearing legs.

After tea, Tollis had a letter to write. Remembering it at odd moments throughout the day he had felt quite important. A letter to write. Some business to attend to. He sat for a while after tea at the bare table, thinking out the letter and listening to the children's song service. Important and studious, he sat staring at a spot above the lintel of the scullery door, tapping fingers fumbling for the lively rhythm of the chorus, his mind fumbling for the words of the letter.

Then the service ending, the tinkling cymbals of the children's voices giving way to the sounding brass of the preacher, he switched off the radio and spread before him on the table a writing-pad, a bottle of ink, a pen, an extra blotter. Both the pad and the pen were new, specially bought for the occasion.

He knew exactly what he wanted to say to Margaret, wanted to thank her and yet to say firmly and definitely, 'no'. Because she was asking him to do the impossible. The more he thought of it, the more impossible he saw it to be. He saw the horse standing beside an empty barrel, the people sitting in a cold church, the chrysanthemums cut and blackened by the frost, the house going to rack and ruin. It was clearly impossible.

The pen was like a straw in his thick fingers. He puffed and writhed with the agony of transferring that crystal clear vision of impossibility from his mind to the devilishly thin paper with a devilishly sharp and wayward pen.

But crouched doggedly over the pad, his long nose tracing each spluttering stroke of the pen, after many blots and muttered damns he accomplished the letter.

Dear Margaret, he wrote, I now sit down to write these few lines in reply to your letter which got here Friday last. I am in quite good nick so dont worry. We have had a lot of frosts this winter three on end so far this week. Your new place must look very nice but you shouldn't have gone to the trouble of doing up a room for me as I have too much on my hands just now to come up there. As for me just playing bowls and billiards day in and day out all I ask is, can you see me? I dont know about getting a big price for the old place it wants a lot of doing up but as I was saying to Eric the other day, itll see me out. Your mums old school-mate Janey Andrews called in to see me the other week she was down on holiday just the same old six and eight but very deaf and failed a lot. Glad to hear that Arthur is doing so well and that you have got shifted into the new place but I wont be coming up in the meantime.

Love, he added, and meant it. He was fond of his children, but he mistrusted them. They were forever making some impossible proposal, 'all for his own good'. He had to be always on the alert.

Tollis folded the letter carefully into a stamped envelope and addressed it to his daughter in a town several hundreds of miles away. Seen in writing, a sprawling unfamiliar word, the town seemed even more remote to him. He could have been writing to the moon.

Anyway, she's got plenty to do without looking after me, he thought, going out with the letter, picturing her as a young bride absorbed in her own affairs and not as a middle-aged woman with time on her hands and affection to spare.

Outside, it was bright, icy moonlight and freezing hard. At the first sting of the bitter air he tucked his chin deeper into the thick knot of scarf. Frost glittered across the rooftops, and the smoke from neighbouring chimneys rose in white frozen columns. A crop of scarf, the drooping beak of his cap, the sharply out-thrust sleeves of his overcoat – he looked more than ever like some huge ungainly bird as he waded through the haze of frost across the crisp and crackling grass to his front gate.

Going down the street he whistled softly into the scarf; his echoing footsteps stalked him from behind the whitening hedges. Soon he had the snug feeling of lonely independence which these winter walks always gave him – the primitive joy of pitting his body against the cold and the wild weather, and emerging from the encounter invigorated and unscathed. In winter, too, there was little likelihood of meeting people with nothing better to do than to chatter.

The letter-box stood on the corner opposite the church. As he posted the letter he looked across to the church, noticed that the moonlight cast his shadow almost to the steps, and laughed gently remembering how the young parson had recently said, 'You ought to be ashamed of yourself, Tolly, never darkening a church door. But I'll have you a Deacon yet.' And 'Can you see me?' he had asked.

Then he stood transfixed by closer memories. His thoughts ran together like beads on a wire . . . the church, the young parson, the letter, that impossible proposal. 'Bowls,' he breathed softly over the wall of scarf, the word freezing into a little white feather of contempt.

He tugged the peak of his cap firmly down over his eyes and set off northwards with a brisk, stiff gait, an old contented man with no time to waste, heading for nowhere in particular.

MAURICE SHADBOLT

The night had come and almost gone again; now, when the rough sweep of his large hand gashed the mist of the carriage window, he was able to see, beyond steep yellow clay-cuttings crested with damp green bush, the brightening grey of the morning sky. His view was obscured for a moment as steam from the engine, shredding and spinning, gusted past the window. But he had seen enough: he sighed, stretched, yawned, and sat back in his seat.

The guard, his cap awry, picked his way through the swaying second-class carriage, carefully avoiding the pillows, heads and legs which jutted into the narrow, dirty aisle. He called the name of the next station, a one-minute stop. His voice in the dim, sleeping carriage was loud, without apology for intrusion. There was an angry mutter from one awakened passenger; but the rest, apart from the tall man stiff in his seat, stirred sleepily, adjusted their pillows, and slept again. The guard left the carriage, slamming the door after him: and once more there was only the sound of iron wheels racketing on uneven rails, and teacups and saucers rattling beneath the seats.

The tall man, who had sat sleepless through the travelling night, gashed the healed mist of the window again. But his view of the dawning sky was gone; in its place was a swift, gloomy blur of thick bush tangling close to the track. Weak spots of light flickered on his face: a face with a coarse, grainy quality; the spare flesh bleak and unhealthy. The features, though, were firm, the eyebrows dark and heavy, the eyes sharp blue, the nose slightly hooked, the lips dry and pale; there was a faint blackish stubble on his thin, pointed chin. He wore a tight black suit that had probably been too small even when it was purchased from a cheap ready-made store six years before; it was frayed at the cuffs and food-stained on the lapels. His thick, broken-nailed fingers and flattened thumbs had by degrees loosened his brown, imitation-silk tie: it hung askew, proclaiming its unfamiliarity with his sinewy neck. The top button of his shirt was undone, and the twisted collar grubby with travel.

He occupied a double seat, his back to the engine. He hesitated a moment before waking the woman and child who slept in the seat opposite.

The woman was upright, her head against the window: a woollen jersey packed between the window and her head served to cushion her from the monotonous violence of the train's motion. Her face was young and pale, verging on plumpness; it quivered with the movement, and her mouth had fallen open. The lapels of her shabby grey coat were drawn up to cover her white throat. Her figure was short and mannish, and her dumpy legs barely touched the floor. The child, cocooned in a faded tartan blanket, slept with his head against her thigh. He had the fresh, sexless face of a three-year-old; the features girlish and delicate, like those of the woman. A cream beret had slipped to the back of the head, releasing a small cascade of uncut crinkly blond hair, streaked with brown.

The man reached forward, finally, and touched the woman gently on the arm. She woke with a jerk, her eyes fluttering open: finding herself in the gloomy, jolting carriage, she was, for a moment, bewildered. Then she saw the man and smiled sleepily.

'Nearly there,' he said. 'We're nearly there.'

'There?' said the woman, vaguely. 'Already?'

'It's morning,' he said. 'Look out the window.'

'Ian,' the woman whispered. 'Ian wake up.'

The child woke and murmured. The woman stood, replaced the lapels of her coat, shook out wrinkles, and bent to the child. Uncovering him, she folded the blanket and put it away.

The train, hammering along a flat stretch of track now, had begun to slow. While she whispered placatingly, the woman fastened shoes on the child; the man removed luggage from the rack above their heads. There was a hoarse whistle: the train shuddered with a prolonged clashing of couplings, and was still.

The three descended from the stuffy warmth of the carriage into the chill of a sunless, misty morning; they were the only passengers to leave the train. His thick dark coat flapping obstinately about his legs, the man carried two heavy suitcases alongside the stationary, hissing carriages. The woman followed, carrying a small case in one hand, and guiding the slow child with the other. Their feet made crunching sounds on the raw gravel.

The station consisted of a square, broken patch of concrete, a set of hand-operated signals; and a dully reddish waiting-room, an uninhabited box of feeble yellow light. The buildings of the settlement around were dark and obscure in the mist.

'It's early yet,' the man observed, as he set down the suitcases in the waiting-room. 'We can wait here.'

The room smelt of soot and urine. They sat on hard wooden seats, the child's feet dangling above the filthy, paper-strewn floor. The woman blanketed the child and drew the coat-lapels over her throat again. The man sat hunched forward, his large veiny hands dangling fidgety between his knees: he looked at his hands, turning them over for inspection, as if seeking some answer there.

'It'll be all right this time,' he said at last. 'I know it will.'

The woman was silent.

'I got a good feeling about it,' he said, still looking at his hands.

The woman remained silent. The child was once again asleep against her thigh. The man became annoyed with looking at his hands, and suddenly thrust them deep into the pockets of his coat. He discovered, as if by accident, a tin of tobacco and began, laboriously, to make a thin cigarette.

The engine whistled: the shrill, imperious sound echoed and re-echoed against hills hidden in the mist. There was a renewed hissing and lurching, and a long line of unlit carriage windows streamed past the waiting-room.

A solitary railway employee, walking homeward, looked into the room. He was puffy-eyed; and under his railway uniform a pyjama-top showed. 'Anything I can do for you people?' he asked.

The man looked up. His eyes were sharp and hostile. 'We're just waiting here,' he said aggressively. 'No law against waiting, is there? That's what this place is here for, isn't it?'

The railwayman was startled. He blinked. 'Don't get me wrong, mate. Just wondering if I could help, that's all.'

'You can't,' the man said.

'Strike me dead,' the railwayman said. 'No need to bite me head off, mate.' He retreated, still astonished, and strode off; his feet crackled away into the quiet, grey morning. They were alone again.

'He was only trying to be helpful,' the woman suggested timidly. 'You could of been nicer to him.'

'Helpful?' The man laughed. 'Nicer?' He stopped laughing suddenly. 'I pick his sort a mile. Bloody snoopers everywhere.'

The woman shrank from him. The child stirred and murmured.

'Sorry,' the man said. He seemed dismayed. 'You're right. I don't know.' He shook his head. 'There wasn't no need for me to go crook like that. I'm just a bit jumpy about everything. I didn't sleep. I suppose he might of been all right.' He drew hard on his cigarette, but it had burnt out. He threw it away in disgust, then reached in his pocket, took out a soiled paper bag, and tore it open. There were three stale-looking refreshment room sandwiches inside. He offered them to the woman. 'You hungry?'

'We can wait a while,' she said. 'You eat.'

'I'm not hungry neither.'

The woman looked sick with tiredness: she touched his arm hesitantly. 'Where are we?' she asked softly. 'Do we have to go far?'

'This place here's a timber-milling outfit,' he said, pointing out the door to where mist still curtained the landscape. 'The mine's a couple of miles or so from here. There's a road down to the mine, and a railway track. Don't know how the locos run from here down to the mine. That's what we got to find out.'

'You could of asked that man then,' the woman pointed out cautiously. 'He could of told you how the locos run.'

The man sighed. 'I could of,' he agreed. 'I just wasn't thinking. When I seen him come along I was thinking of other things.'

The woman seemed altogether satisfied by his reply, by his admission that he had been wrong. It was an event of a rare kind, and she could afford satisfaction. He sat forward, looking out the door, thinking of his other things again.

The light outside was now quite bright. The mist, retreating from the settlement, fled up the sunlit flanks of the hills. In the waiting-room, the child slept against the woman, and the woman against the man; the man was awake. He at last reached for a sandwich and began to eat it slowly and thoughtfully. His movement woke the woman, then the child.

She took the child to a tap outside the waiting-room and washed his face with a dampened handkerchief. Then she set the beret squarely on his head and led him back into the room. She took a bottle from her case and poured some cream-flecked, sour-smelling milk into a peanut-butter jar that now saw service of a different kind. She gave the child the milk and a sandwich. There was one sandwich left. She looked at her husband, then at the child; and her hand darted out, as if of its own volition, and carried the sandwich quickly to her mouth. She ate almost guiltily.

The man stood. 'I'll find out what time a loco runs down to the mine,' he announced. He went out of the room, across the tracks, and into the settlement, walking with an abrupt, jerky strike. Presently he returned.

'There's a loco comes up about ten.' He said. 'It don't go back again till about one. That's five hours yet.'

'We can wait,' the woman said patiently; she fingered back her limp, wisping hair.

'Wait?' he said. 'I'm sick and tired of waiting. It drives you up the wall. We can walk to the mine. It's not far.'

'Walk?' the woman said faintly.

'All right?' he said briskly, but gave her no time to answer. He took up the two large suitcases. 'Let's go.'

They walked over the tracks and through the settlement. Along a single stony road, pooled with rainwater, there was a store and post office combined in an ungainly wooden building with unpainted weather boards; one or two early-morning loungers watched the three strangers go past. Further along there was a string of old houses, knotting at the end into a cluster of ramshackle single men's huts. The timber mill, which stood at the end of the settlement, was already alive with grinding, tearing noises.

'Hell-holes, them places,' the man observed.

'They couldn't be much worse than mines,' the woman said; but he didn't seem to hear.

An articulated timber-truck, unloaded and jerking, rumbled past, splattering them with mud. The man spat after it. 'Could of given us a lift,' he said.

'He mightn't of been going the same way as us,' the woman observed.

'How does he know till he's asked us?' he demanded. He spat again, at nothing in particular this time.

'Anyhow,' she said, 'there wouldn't of been room for the three of us in it. Not in the cab.' She was right in defending the driver; she knew she was right. But this time, she knew also, he would not admit it. So she added appeasingly, 'It doesn't matter much, does it? You said it wasn't far.'

'No. It's not far.'

They walked in silence. His pace, even with the two heavy suitcases weighing him, was too brisk for her and the child. Soon he was several yards ahead.

'Wait,' she called, her voice mild with an old despair.

He sat on his cases and waited. She expected irritation in his face, but found only concern. 'I'm sorry,' he said. 'I keep forgetting him.' He pointed to the child. 'Let's have a rest.'

The child's face was still sleepy, and bewildered; the woman sat him on her case. 'Where we going?' he said.

'I told you before, sonny,' the woman said, sighing. 'We're going to a new place.' She was tired of the question.

'Why?'

'Shush, Ian,' she said with annoyance. Then, repenting, she straightened the cream beret on the small head.

'Why?' the child repeated.

'Because,' she said, raising her eyes in appeal to the man. 'Because Daddy's taking us.'

'Why Daddy taking us?'

The woman didn't anwer: she didn't look at the man. He knelt beside the child; the child surveyed him gravely. 'We're going to a new place because it'll be a better place,' he said simply. 'That's why.'

The sun warmed the pale sky, lighting a landscape stripped and harsh. On the upper slopes of the hills, where here and there limestone outcrops stood gaunt against the sky, were long-dead trees, tangled and whitened, and giant ulcers of erosion scabbed with weeping crusts of clay and papa; on lower ground lank wire fences straggled about small, pine-sheltered farm houses. The pasture was a dead green colour, and loose-bellied cows grazed. The road unwound slowly, a thin strip of clay and bluish metal edged with ti-tree and gorse. They came, at length, to a crossroad, and a signpost which said: FERNDALE MINE 2 $\frac{1}{2}$ M.

'I thought you said it wasn't far,' the woman protested.

The man didn't argue. 'It was a bit further than I thought, that's all.'

'We should of waited. We should of waited for a loco.'

The man seemed to agree. 'I just wanted to get there. I just don't like hanging round.' He paused. 'I didn't think it'd of been so far. I'm sorry.'

She was placated; she nodded, as if she too well understood his impatience. 'I don't like hanging round neither,' she said. 'But we should of waited.'

They came to a rise. The man, walking ahead, crested the rise first. He stopped and set down his suitcases. 'There she is,' he said, pointing as the woman and child came up beside him.

The mining settlement discoloured the end of a tawny valley; the hills around were lacerated with black weals. Two groups of buildings made the settlement, one group large and dark and tightly gathered, the other small and white and more scattered. The large dark buildings belonged to the mine; the small white ones, a little distance removed, were the miners' homes. Above and beyond the valley were hills tall and blue and remote.

'What that?' the child said.

'That's where we're going,' replied the man. He said it almost with pride, sitting on a suitcase and rolling a cigarette. 'Might as well have a rest now,' he announced. 'It looks pretty good to me.'

Sitting beside him, the woman looked down the valley with a pensive expression. He touched her playfully under the chin, tilting up her face. 'What do you think, mother?' he said. 'Look good to you?'

'Any place,' she said. 'Any place looks good.'

'I think you'll like it here. I just got a feeling.'

'I'd like it anywhere. It doesn't matter where. Just as long as it's somewhere.' She continued to look pensively down the valley.

'I don't want to go,' the child said. 'I want to go back.'

'We can't go back,' said the woman, softly. 'We can't ever go back.' She didn't look away from the distant settlement.

'Why?'

She didn't seem to hear.

'Why?'

'Shut up,' she hissed suddenly, jerking her eyes to the child. Astonished, he began to whimper; she softened. 'Shush, Ian,' she whispered. 'We're going to a new place. A nice new place.' She pointed. 'See?'

But the child couldn't see; his eyes were filled with tears. 'My feet are hurty,' he complained.

The man picked up his suitcases. 'Let's go,' he said jubilantly. He set off with a jaunty stride, humming a tune.

The sun grew hot in an empty sky. A few hundred yards down the road they came to an old wooden bridge which spanned a clear, glittering stream. Upstream a little they could see a sandy place, like a miniature beach, strung around with toi-toi and flax, and shady with willows.

They made a halt on the bridge. 'It's a pretty place,' the woman murmured. 'A pretty place.'

'That'll be nice in summer,' said the man, pointing across the glittering water to the place of sand and shade. 'We could have picnics there. And swim. And eat our lunch under the willows.'

'Yes,' said the woman doubtfully. She had heard all this before. But there had never been picnics.

Their halts along the last circling stretch of road became more and more frequent. The child whimpered with hurting feet while the woman became tired and ill-tempered. The man, however, only seemed to increase his pace as they neared the settlement.

It was late in the morning when they came to it. The white miners' homes, so attractive from a distance, were now small square boxes, crudely built and ugly, crammed together as closely as houses in a city suburb; they looked as if huddled for protection in the bare valley under the burnt sky. Each had a black strip of garden and a green patch of lawn.

The man nodded towards one of the homes. No curtains showed in the window; no smoke wisped from the chimney. The lawn was long-grassed and unkempt, and weeds grew in the garden. 'That one's empty, he said. 'That might be the one we get.'

The woman looked at the place wistfully.

'Like it?' he said.

'There'll be a lot of work to do,' she said. 'I expect the inside's a mess. And the garden. But heaven couldn't be better.'

'I knew it was going to be good,' he said with satisfaction, spitting on his parched palm and gripping the suitcases again. 'I knew it was going to be pretty good here. I had a feeling we was going to like it.'

This too she had heard before. Reluctantly, she turned her eyes from the house, took the child's hand, and followed the man.

Beyond the store and post office they found the settlement's most imposing structure, the mine office; a squat grey building.

'Wait here,' directed the man. 'I don't think I'll be long.'

The woman and child sat outside while the man went into the office. She removed the child's shoes and massaged the small, blistered feet. 'We'll be all right soon,' she said.

'Why?'

'I know,' she answered, confidently.

The reception office was a small, gloomy room. Beyond a dark counter were two desks. At one a grey-haired woman sat typing. At the other was a clerk, a slight mousy man of about fifty. He had a shiny bald head with a slender periphery of silver hair; steel-rimmed glasses sat on a thin, bony nose. His face was dried-up and humourless. He worked in a limp black smoking jacket. Just beyond him was a door displaying the sign *Mine Manager*.

The clerk looked up from his papers, apparently to ascertain that the visitor was of not much account, and then bent to them again. His pen scratched briefly, and he rose without haste, fastidiously flicked a spot of dust from his papers, and minced slowly to the counter.

'Yes?' he said. 'Anything I can do for you?'

'I'm here about a job. I wrote a letter – '

'The name?'

'Morrison's the name. William Morrison.'

The clerk screwed on the top of his fountain pen; he began to twirl the pen slowly in his fingers. 'Ah, yes, Mister Morrison,' he said. 'I remember.' His expression was pained; the pen twirled.

'It's all right, isn't it?' the man said. 'You said in your letter – '

'There were two letters actually, Mister Morrison.'

'Two letters? I only got one. You said there was a job for me here.'

'It's apparent you couldn't have received our second letter. We only posted it two days or so ago. We hardly expected you would turn up here so soon. You see, there was some mistake.' The clerk smiled blandly.

'Mistake?' His voice trembled. "What do you mean a mistake?'

'About the job. An error in the office here. Really most unfortunate. What it amounts to is that there isn't really a job here for you at all.'

'But you said – '

'As I explained, Mister Morrison, there was a mistake. We tried to tell you in our second letter. Unfortunately you set off before that letter arrived.' The pen still twirled between nervous fingers. 'The whole thing is really most unfortunate.' He shook his head. 'I'm so sorry.'

The man's eyes flickered, and were suddenly sharp. He slammed his fist on the counter. 'Don't lie to me,' he snapped.

'Really, Mister Morrison. Please.' The clerk retreated from the counter; he gave a small, despairing shrug.

'I don't want none of your bloody lies.'

The grey-haired woman, startled, looked up from her typewriter. The clerk appeared to wither before the prospect of further violence of language. 'Please, Mister Morrison. Please. There's a lady present.'

'Tell me the truth,' the man demanded.

'I'm afraid I don't understand,' said the clerk weakly. 'I've explained all there is to explain.'

'Let me see the manager.' The man pointed to the door beyond the clerk's desk. 'Maybe he'll have some truth.' He went round the end of the counter, but the clerk blocked his way.

'He's a busy man. He wouldn't want to be disturbed. He really – '

Shoved aside, the clerk fell back against the woman with the typewriter. She gave a cry, and was just in time to prevent her typewriter crashing.

Without knocking, the man pushed open the door of the manager's office. This room was bright after the gloom of the other; too bright. He could not see at first. Sunlight fed through a long window in the opposite wall, silhouetting the desk and its occupant. The walls were cream-coloured, and there was now a thick green carpet beneath his feet. This room was not only brighter; it was luxurious by comparison. There were leather-covered chairs and light-varnished filing cabinets.

'My name's Morrison,' he announced.

He could see the occupant of the desk now, as he rose slowly to his feet, removing his thick tortoise-shell glasses. A short stocky man, moon-faced, in a pepper-and-salt suit; a gold watch-chain was looped across his waistcoat. He was a man with every appearance of assurance. He looked mildly puzzled.

'I beg your pardon?' he said.

'I said my name's Morrison. William Morrison. I want to know why I can't have a job here. After you people said I could have one. And I don't want none of your bloody lies.'

'A job?' the manager said. He resumed his seat and began, methodically, to clean his glasses with a white handkerchief.

'The job you people promised me. Now your bum boy out in the office tells me I can't have it. I want to know why.'

'Why?' the manager repeated. He seemed amused. 'You want to know why?' He coughed significantly, and added, 'There was a mistake. No doubt you've been told that.'

'I told you I don't want no lies. I'm sick of these kind of lies.'

The manager replaced his glasses and studied the man before him. The glasses seemed to give him added assurance.

'Well, Morrison,' he began casually, 'if you must know – '

The clerk put his head cautiously around the door. 'I tried to stop him coming in,' he started to apologize.

'Get out,' the man said. 'Leave us alone.'

The manager appeared to agree: he too irritably waved the clerk out. The head vanished and the door closed softly.

The manager straightened a file on his desk and closed it. 'Now,' he said slowly, fingering his lower lip. 'Your name is Morrison. William Morrison.'

'That's right. And I'm proud of it.'

'I daresay, Morrison. I daresay.' He slipped the file into a wire basket and drew out another one. The item he wanted was near the top of this file. He coughed before he spoke again. 'You're the Morrison who was gaoled for sedition three years ago, aren't you? You seem to get around quite a lot. And everywhere you've been there seems to have been trouble. Strange how trouble follows you around, isn't it?'

'I'm not ashamed of it. None of it. I've never caused no trouble. It's you people make the trouble. No, I'm not ashamed of nothing.'

The manager coughed with certain delicacy. 'That, of course, is no concern of mine, Morrison. My concern is that we don't have trouble here, or trouble-makers. Up till now we've been free of trouble. The management's on excellent terms with the men. We wouldn't like any change. We want to keep things pleasant here.'

'Keep them down, you mean. I know your kind. I suppose you run the union too, eh?'

'I don't want to hear speeches. Speech-making might be part of your business. Listening to them is not part of mine.'

'You won't get away with this. You can't victimise – '

'No one, to my knowledge, is being victimised. No one is being discharged from employment here. There was just a mistake, as I told you. In any case, I'm sure if I discussed this thing with the men they would certainly prefer to be without your company.'

'Or else,' the man said with sarcasm. 'I know your stunts.'

'They would,' the manager repeated, 'certainly prefer to be without your company.' With an expression of innocence, he held up his hands. 'The clerical error which led us to advise you that we had a job offering is, of course, most regrettable.' He laid his hands flat on the desk, as if to signify he was finished with the subject.

'Bloody lies.'

'If you persist in seeing things in that light, Morrison, then of course there is simply nothing I can do about it.'

'If everything's so sweet here, what are you scared of? Eh?' He didn't give the manager time for reply. 'You know as well as I do. This place is known right up and down the country as rotten, isn't it? That's why.'

'If it's as bad as you say,' said the manager calmly, 'why did you come here, Morrison? Why don't you,' he added deliberately, 'go to Russia?'

'You really want to know. Because I don't like the likes of you. Because I got a kid I want to bring up decent here. Because I'm not a Russian.'

'Just as well for you,' observed the manager. 'They'd shoot you.'

'And you.'

'I've a considerable amount of work to do today,' the manager said abruptly. 'I'm sure we could have a most interesting discussion some other time.'

'Like hell. Scared, aren't you? All your kind.'

'If you'll excuse me, Morrison.' The manager opened a new file. 'I have work to do.'

'Take a good look around you sometime.' The man pointed out the window. The colliery workings, the mine shaft, blackened sheds, rakes of coal-trucks shunting, were all visible against scarred hillside. 'One day that's not going to belong to you. Or any of your kind. One day this country will belong to the people who sweated into it.'

'Get out,' the manager said.

He strode out of the mine office into the street; a door slammed behind him. He went past the woman and child, as if he had not seen them. The woman ran after him and caught at his sleeve.

'Where are you going?' she said. 'It's all right, isn't it?'

He stopped to look at her; but his face was remote and expressionless. He hesitated, turned, and walked silently back to the suitcases. He lifted the sitting child aside, and took up the two large cases again.

'It's all right, isn't it?' the woman said, still plucking at his sleeve. He shook her away and began to walk. She picked up her small case, took the child's hand, and hurried after the man. 'Where we going?' she pleaded. 'It's all right, isn't it? There's nothing wrong? You got the job, didn't you?'

He stopped walking suddenly, and let the cases fall heavily. 'No,' he said. 'They knew. They found out.'

Her eyes trembled. 'But the letter,' she said. 'The letter. They said you could have – '

'They must of found out after they sent the letter.' He was not looking at the woman now. 'They said it was a mistake. All a mistake. Bloody liars.'

Her shoulders quivered; the child began to whimper in sympathy. The man took her by the arm. 'Stop it,' he said. 'Not here.' He looked up and down the deserted street, but there seemed, at that moment, no onlookers. 'Not here,' he repeated.

'Where we going?' she whispered. 'Now?'

He avoided the question. 'We'll wait,' he said. 'Until the men come up from the pit. The day needn't be wasted.'

The woman gave her attention to the child. 'Shush, Ian,' she said. 'He's hungry,' she appealed to the man.

He wasn't listening: he had taken a letter from his inside suit pocket and was shredding it. 'Liars,' he said, more quietly now.

A light breeze fluttered the torn paper from his hands; confettied, it whisked a little distance along the street and then lay still, like a thin paper-chase trail. 'Well?' he said at last. 'What are you waiting for? You can get something to eat from the store, can't you?'

In the late afternoon a low siren moaned: echoes circled the valley. Thick wire rope strained against turning winches: the cage from the pit screeched and rattled to the surface. Presently men emerged, dusty and blackened, in scarves and helmets, with eyes negro-white, through the colliery gate. They carried lamps and lunch-boxes and blinked against the bitter sunlight.

On one side of the gate they saw the short woman, drab and pale, with a child and some suitcases; on the other, the tall gaunt man in evangelical black. They were distributing leaflets with huge, exclamatory headings. The woman gave out her leaflets almost apologetically; the man was confident, entirely without apology, and called friendly slogans to the miners as they passed. 'The truth,' he said. 'Get the truth, comrades.'

Puzzled, most of the miners accepted the strange, rustling sheets of paper with urgent words; though some, as if fearing infection from a malady which they themselves could not properly define, side-stepped the outstretched hand, the humourless slogan, and hurried away. Some accepted only to repent, crumpling and discarding the leaflets as they walked with quickened steps towards the safety of their homes. One or two stopped to talk briefly with the gaunt man in black; one pressed money into his hand. And then they were gone, all of them, into their square ugly homes with strips of garden and patches of lawn: the streets were empty again.

The man, moving slowly now, gathered up the remaining leaflets and packed them into a suitcase glutted with pamphlets, books, and other leaflets.

'How are we going to get back to the station?' the woman said, as though waking from deep, dreamless sleep. 'Can we catch a loco?'

'Walk,' said the man. 'The way we came. There's no loco back now. It's too late in the day.'

'Walk?' the woman said.

They walked. The sinking sun coppered the land; the valley was still and quiet, dry and dead. The road had whitened, and their feet swirled pools of dust.

'Where we going?' the child said.

'Shush,' said the woman. 'Daddy's taking us.'

The sun sank; the valley was shadowed. In the east the clouds were pale and curdled; in the west they were gold and pink.

'Why?' said the child.

Dusk smoked, fine and blue, from the land. When they reached the rise in the road from which they had first seen into the valley, they paused and looked back. An island of weak lights had grown under the brightening evening stars. The child was tripping and crying.

'Why Daddy taking us?'

'Shush,' said the woman, patiently.

The man set down his suitcases and took up the child gently.

'He's tired,' he said. 'Poor kid.'

'Why?' the child said, stubbornly.

MAURICE DUGGAN

Miss Mary May Laverty drank her bitter and solitary drink (gin and angostura and lemonade, pink as a varnished nail) and looked out from the dark room through dark glass to the floor, the strewn floor of lights four storeys down, and out and away to night mountains and the candy stripes of the harbour lights. Mary May Laverty sighed. She screwed at a dull wisp of hair at her temple and pushed it for the millionth time behind her ear where it uncurled and fell listlessly forward again into the waiting twirl of thumb and forefinger. Light, reflected from somewhere, the sky? the stars?, gleamed faint in the burnished piano dark as a coffin, and on the keys. May Laverty played minor chords. She held the glass in her left hand. The wisp of hair curled forward and stayed.

Down at the street entrance Paul Mooney, aged nine years or ten, in his hand a violin aged not less than seventy years rocking in its case, inspected the faded card in the faded light: Miss Mary May Laverty, Violin and Pianoforte. Please ring. He knew it well. He rang long and listened (he could not hear the bell) then stepped back from the doorway into the street and looked up. A window shrilled, a voice called something lost in air, and something metallic hit the pavement, jangling. Paul Mooney took up the keys, picked out the bronze, opened the door, shut it, ascended the four spiralling flights in faded light and sourceless melody:

I hate to see that evening' sun . . .

A nameless tenant at the blues.

'Paul Mooney, you're late.'

'Yes, Miss Laverty. Mum said to say sorry but it's the electricity and dinner was late.'

May Laverty sniffed, twisted hair, let the boy advance into the now lighted room and shut the door.

He done left this town . . .

Very very far now and faint as he sprung his case and began tuning while May Laverty stared down on the lost lights dispersed, destroyed by the room's illumination. She moved backwards until she felt a chair behind her and dropped into it. She was more fatigued than drunk, she was sure. Tired to the middle of the marrow of her bones; the yellow bones of the blue Miss Laverty. She let her head settle back. The dark mohair bristled at the nape. She listened without any particular expression of face to the wailing tuning note and felt inside her something tautening in sympathy. (God send that nothing snaps, that's all.)

'Electricity,' she scoffed, sniffing. 'Last week it was the transport system, and the week before that you didn't come at all. No money, no apology, nothing. Who do you Mooneys think you are, that's what I'd like to know?'

'I don't know, Miss Laverty.'

'I've a good mind, Paul Mooney, to call your mother and see if you are playing tricks on me.'

'I'm not, Miss Laverty.'

'That's what you say. How am I to tell? It doesn't matter; but don't think I'm to be won with looks of innocence. I know what they're worth, angelic smiles. Play something, then. I'm not going to give you a full lesson every time you're late. I have to go out.'

'Shall I play the London thing, Miss Laverty?'

'The London thing,' May Laverty said wearily, 'is the Londonderry Air. It has nothing to do with London. Can't you get that clear? No, I'm sick of it. I can't have heard it less than a million times. Play what you like.'

Paul Mooney so clearly gave it thought, without result.

'Then play that thing, what is it, that I keep hearing in my head? It's been badgering me all day.' She hummed it. 'Yes, Saint Louis Blues. Play that.'

'I think it's what they're playing downstairs. I can't play that, Miss Laverty.'

'No, of course you can't. I was teasing. Give me the fiddle then. And turn off that big light and turn on the piano light. My eyes are burning.'

May Laverty leaned forward, wispy, the angle of her jaw sharpening as if to fury as she strained to hear. She placed the violin and waited with bow poised, inclined to the boy at the angle of an accent acute.

Up through the silent building it rose, tremulous, vague, continuing. May Laverty caught it up in the middle of a bar and thin, melancholy, faintly vibrating, the melody began to fill the room, slow and seeming to expand; seeming to press out to the bare walls and surge back.

'Turn out the light.'

She turned slightly, still playing, and the jewelled floor and beaconed sea glowed from darkness and on the night mountain one light, star or signal, burned and pulsed.

She played a long time, getting the tune sometimes mixed in her mind and straying off into Stormy Weather and coming back, marking her erratic journey with notes as thick as grief. The boy sat still and wondering in the dark, embarrassed by behaviour he found strange. He wished he might go. He too looked down. And when she stopped he could see her, dark against the dark window. And still there rose, oblivious to the violin, oblivious and constant, the sound like fine drawn wire coiling up:

If I'm feeling tomorrow like I feel today . . .

'Miss Laverty.'

'What is it? You don't like it, is that it?' The figure moved, the light went on. May Laverty had tears on her face, tears black as bruises and black-streaked runnels down either side of her nose. It didn't suggest grief to Paul Mooney.

'Can I go now, Miss Laverty?'

'I'll have to start all over again,' May Laverty said, and dabbed at her ruined eyes with toilet tissue. 'Oh damn it; damn everything. I'm sorry. Have you any money for me?'

'Miss Laverty, Mum said there was only a five-pound note and I'm to tell you I'll bring it next time and could you please write it down?'

'Why? I sent the account.'

'I think we lost it.'

May Laverty looked fiercely amused. She threw down the tissue and crossed quickly to the boy. He shrank away slightly as if expecting a blow. 'Only a five-pound note? That's lovely.' She found her purse and took out a card and wrote on the back of it and thrust it into the breast pocket of the boy's shirt. 'It wouldn't occur to your mother, of course, that I have to live too. *Only* a five-pound note – that's rich. Perhaps she fancies I live on air. I have to eat, don't I? Do I look like a canary?'

'No, Miss Laverty.'

'No, and what's more . . . Oh, what's the use? Run along. It's not fair to be slanging you. Make sure you shut the door after you.'

'You said you were going out, Miss Laverty.' The boy slackened strings and clipped shut the female case.

'You don't miss a thing, do you, Paul Mooney? I was going out to dinner on the money your mother didn't have the decency to send.'

'Won't you have dinner, then?'

May Laverty stared a long moment. 'Don't break your heart over that. I'll have dinner all right. Now run along; and shut that door or we'll have the bailiffs in like a draught.' She lit a cigarette and threw the match towards the empty grate, into a trash of cigarette butts and dead matches. She advanced and ruffled the short brush of the boy's hair. 'You've hair like a doormat,' May Laverty said. 'Like a pelt.'

'What's a bailiff, Miss Laverty?'

'That was a joke, Paul. It doesn't matter. Ask your mother.'

She let him out. Insistent, fine, the slow blues rose faint as a far crying through the quiet building. May Laverty went to the stairwell and bent over the rail and with her hands cupped about her mouth shouted with a surprising, shrill loudness: 'Shut it off, will you? Shut if off.' There was no more response than the echo which quickly ceased. Then the music welled up in volume, a yellow bar of light showed near the bottom of the shaft, and a voice shouted up, ringing: 'Go mind your own business.' May Laverty cocked a thoughtful miming eyebrow. In the silence, faint again, the melody continued.

'It gives me fits,' May Laverty said reasonably. 'To hear a tune being done to death like that, I mean. You'd think once, or even twice, but . . .'

'Goodbye, Miss Laverty.'

'You've got everything? Down you go then.' She tripped the light and the timing mechanism whirred like a secret beetle in the wall.

Unabashed, persisting, the thread of sound rose to meet the boy as he tiptoed down, fearful of rousing the ire of that rude tenant. May Laverty entered her room and slammed the door behind her: the latch was faulty and she was obliged to slam it a second time before it caught. She made herself another pink gin and turned off the light and sat staring again out and down and away. After a little while she began quietly to hum and then to sing:

I hate to see that evenin' sun . . .

Her voice was high, a breathy pipe.

'Oh damn,' she said. 'Damn it to hell.' And taking up her purse she made for the door, stumbling in the dark. She found the light and returned to drain the rest of her drink and went out then, plunging the room into darkness again, not waiting to repair the ravage to her smudged, bruised eyes.

On the landing of the first floor she paused. The music, she had to admit, was not loud enough for complaint; it squeezed out as she stood there, squeezed out with a bar of light under the door of Room 3. May Laverty remembered the force and brevity of that rejoinder and went quietly down. The time switch to the stair light was set mean and she was left in darkness with half a flight to go. In spiteful anger she pressed the switch again before she closed the door. The music which had followed her down was finally imprisoned, beyond hearing, behind that shut door where the light burned wastefully.

'Look at this, if you please,' Mrs Mooney said. She dropped May Laverty's card on the newspaper her husband was reading. 'A fine sort of thing.'

Mr Mooney stolidly read: 'Miss Mary May Laverty (lately Music Tutor at Haversham College): Violin and Pianoforte. Tuition for Beginners and Advanced Players. Telephone for appointment.'

'Where's Haversham College?' Mr Mooney asked.

'The other side,' Mrs Mooney said. 'Turn it over. I meant you to look at the other side.'

Mr Mooney turned the card and read: 'No tickee no shirtee. M.M.L.'

'In the matter of impudence,' Mrs Mooney said, 'I've never met anything to match. And from a teacher of music too. You might well ask where Haversham College is: I doubt she's ever been near it. Paul has been there for the last time, I can tell her that.'

'It's direct, certainly,' Mr Mooney said. He glanced at his wife's gaunt and inflamed face. 'I take it we owe her money.'

'After that sort of impudence I doubt that we owe her anything. There's no excuse for that.'

'I'm not suggesting there is. How much do we owe, Ella?'

'How should I know? I don't keep these things in my head. I suppose the account is lying about somewhere. I've had it out with Paul. She didn't even bother to give him a lesson at all tonight. She just sat him in the dark and played him some rubbishy popular song and then pushed him out.'

'In the dark? Is that right, Paul?'

'I think she was angry,' Paul Mooney said. He was distressed by his mother's anger and his sense of being disloyal. 'She said I was late last time, too. And the time before that I didn't go at all.'

'Is she right about that?'

'There were good reasons,' Mrs Mooney said. 'Her card is unforgivable and I don't see any profit in going into it any further. There's no shortage of music teachers.'

Mr Mooney turned the card. 'But she has the phone, Ella. Did someone ring her to say the boy would be late or that he was unable to come?'

'I don't know,' Paul Mooney said.

'That means no, I suppose. We've been rather inconsiderate too, Ella, by the look of it. I mean, if we're going to insist on such a standard . . .'

'We'll see about that,' Mrs Mooney said and snatched the card and went to the telephone. But May Laverty did not reply. It had the effect of short-circuiting Mrs Mooney's anger. For a moment she was nonplussed.

Mr Mooney shook out his paper. 'She has a right to expect payment, Ella. It could be a simple joke, you know.'

'Trust a man to side with a woman,' Mrs Mooney said curtly.

'I think we have to trust to that,' Mr Mooney said, a little amused.

'Just what she's a right to expect, we'll soon decide,' Mrs Mooney said. 'Paul, get your violin, if you please.'

'Now Ella. You're upsetting yourself unduly. It's a small matter.'

'Robert Mooney, sometimes I just don't understand you. If you think I am going to stand here and be insulted by . . .'

'All right. Have it your way. Get your violin, son. But tune it up before you bring it in here. I can't stand the sound of those things being wound up.'

The house in grief wailed long and uncertainly for Danny Boy, the violin calling like an aged and faltering tenor.

'Well, that wasn't all that bad,' Mr Mooney said. 'Though I would have preferred some other tune. What was the song this Miss – ah – Laverty played you?'

'I think, Saint Louis Blues.'

'Then what about playing that, now that you're here.'

'Robert Mooney.'

'What's wrong with it, Ella? It's old enough to be respectable, surely? I've always been fond of it.'

'I can't play it,' Paul Mooney said.

'I'm grateful for that, at least,' Mrs Mooney said. 'If you think we're paying out good money for the child to learn that sort of rubbish . . .'

Mr Mooney was again amused. 'But Ella, surely that's the whole point: we *aren't* paying out good money. That's what's got under the woman's skin.'

'I've no patience with you,' Mrs Mooney said.

'Then do what you want, between the two of you,' Mr Mooney said. 'The world isn't losing a Paganini, I suppose.' He took up the card and put it in his pocket and bent to his paper, oblivious to his wife's hard, colouring stare.

Of course, you could rely on it to ring when she was in the bath. Didn't it always? There were times when May Laverty suspected the telephone of being possessed of a malice not usually associated with bits of bakelite and metal or whatever it was. If she had a pound for every time she'd had to get out of the bath to answer the phone . . . She put on a towelling gown, dried her hands carefully (she had read somewhere that you could get a fatal shock if your hands were wet) and padded out. No hope of just letting it ring: she wasn't quite flush enough for that.

It was Mrs Mooney, mother of Paul Mooney, with a voice as chill as a sliding glacier. (Of course, that stupid card!)

Mrs Mooney clearly and coldly could not be expected to treat the matter as a joke. Her voice crackled to May Laverty down the defective wire. Mrs Mooney hardly thought from her son's report that the account could be treated seriously.

'It's serious all right,' May Laverty said. 'I never joke about money.' She managed to get a cigarette out of the packet and to light it with one hand.

Yes, quite; but didn't Miss Laverty see that it could hardly be thought part of the contract, if you called it that, simply to play the boy a hit-parade tune and send him packing.

'It hasn't been on the hit parade since you were a girl, Mrs Mooney.'

Was that intended as an insult? Mrs Mooney hoped that she herself had more dignity than to behave like a fishwife. She would like Miss Laverty to understand that her son would not be returning for further tuition. And, further, she, Mrs Mooney, would make a deduction from the stated amount and send Miss Laverty a cheque. There was one occasion, and Mrs Mooney regretted the lack of notification, when the boy had been unable to attend; and there was last night.

'Mrs Mooney, I'm sorry. I hadn't understood that you were so hard up. If you're as broke as that we'll just forget the whole thing. I'll make you a gift of the lessons.' May Laverty viciously considered the end of her cigarette.

Miss Laverty was being impudent. The telephone went dead.

May Laverty replaced the receiver with infinite gentleness and went back to the bathroom and lay in the lukewarm water and finished her cigarette. She did not enjoy it. Neither did she enjoy the coffee she made herself when she had dressed. She sat in the high window. There was a fog on the harbour and over the city. May Laverty sat rather glumly above it.

Later she made the four-flight journey down to the mail basket on the street door. The door to Room 3 was shut and the music silenced. There were some things yet that she could be thankful for. And there were two letters in the box. One was a sheet of numbers on pink paper which, searched later for the number of her ticket, showed May Laverty that she had not won the lottery this time either, nor even the most minor prize. The other letter contained a five-pound note from Mr Robert Mooney, pinned to a note asking her to accept this as some reimbursement for the trouble she had been put to over Paul's lateness and non-attendance. Mr Mooney had not yet seen the account, which would be met later. He took the opportunity, in a postscript, of expressing his purely personal preference for the Saint Louis Blues over and above the Londonderry Air which he referred to as Danny Boy. The letter was on business notepaper. Mooney and Masters, Public Accountants.

'Never say die,' May Laverty said, climbing the gloomy stairs.

In her room she made a note of the telephone number – she had a choice of three – on the scratch pad by the telephone. Mr Mooney must be thanked: the amount was far too much, of course, and May Laverty wondered at it. His tone was, at the least, so different from that of his wife that May Laverty wondered too what this might imply.

May Laverty stood among rings and brooches and wristlet watches in the doorway of the closed jeweller's shop and surveyed the street. There, that was surely him, standing as if on a hot brick on the corner and flushing red and green as the traffic lights changed. He looked as nervous as she felt, though she had only the back and side of him; but on the whole he was more presentable than she had imagined. Yes, all in all he represented something rather better than she had hoped. Didn't this, though, only serve to widen the gap. Hadn't he, she meant, all the more right if he looked like that, to hope on his side for something a little better than herself? Oh Lord: the long panel of mirroring glass too plainly gave the show away, too clearly told the familiar tale and kept too few secrets. Wasn't she all too raddled, all too much the blown and faded rose? She took up her courage and faced her image, prepared to be stern. (Was it what you called an assignation? No, surely that was too antique a suggestion. A blind date might better describe it. On the corner by the jeweller's in Cannon Street I'll be wearing my tweed, my apricot blouse, flowers, my cracked and batty smile; and my expiring perm. Mary May Laverty. Violin and Pianoforte. Please ring.) It had to be faced; no amount of pressing would take the baggy seat out of this skirt, nor the pouched elbows out of this jacket. She felt positively marsupial. Stand though she might, straight as a tent-pole, head alert and shoulders back, she still appeared to be crouched with elbows bent. Damn. True, her legs weren't bad, though you wouldn't venture more than that. And her face? May Laverty wryly contemplated it. Wide eyes, good forehead: take the best things first. But spreading out from the corners of her eyes, from the corners of her mouth, was a system of lines best to be compared with a railway siding or a shunting yard. Perhaps she exaggerated; but the mirror didn't flatter. Her mouth wasn't young; but then what would she be doing wearing the hopeful rosebud of a young girl?

'Miss Laverty?'

He'd made up his mind to approach. May Laverty took him in. A triangle of pocket handkerchief about the size of a postage stamp in his breast pocket; bald and not trying to conceal it; taller than she was with a kind, even an innocently mischievous expression of face; big, well-kept hands. Dark, groomed, good-humoured and rather at a loss, that was her impression. An Irish mug for all the rich trimmings.

'Mr Mooney, I presume.' She advanced her hand and laughed. The gods be thanked, her teeth were her own. 'Tell me immediately, have you an impulse to turn and run? Please say; now's the time.' She thought she sounded like a revivalist coaxing decisions, or just a little too much as though she hoped he *would* turn and run. The gin gave her confidence; but it was ebbing.

'Have *you* that impulse?' He faced her squarely. The street was empty of all but one or two people dawdling past lighted windows.

'Oh me?' May Laverty said. 'No, I've not.'

'No more have I.'

'Then what . . .?'

'I wondered, well, I wondered whether you'd be interested in a drink? There's a place I know down here; quite ordinary, of course, but not far to go.'

'An excellent idea,' May Laverty said with some relief.

The bar was noisy and rather crowded. He bought her a large pink gin, and gin and water for himself.

'I was sure you would drink whisky.'

'I'm not much of a drinking man, I'm afraid.'

'Look, there's something I want to say right off. I don't know whether *you're* used to this sort of thing. I mean I don't know what you think. Oh, I'm not pretending to be innocent. I just want things to be plain, so that we know where we stand.'

Robert Mooney was puzzled. 'I don't think I see. If you mean am I in the habit of, ah, this sort of thing – no, I'm not. I simply thought . . .'

'This is rather awful, isn't it? This place, I mean. I can't hear a word you're saying.'

'Perhaps if I got something to take away. Could we find somewhere, some place . . .?'

'There's my place,' May Laverty said frankly.

'Yes. Would that be in order?'

'I don't see why not.'

She noticed it immediately, before her hand found the light switch. The Saint Louis Blues was cascading in considerable volume down the dark stairs.

'No,' May Laverty said. 'It wasn't pre-arranged. We mustn't dawdle or we'll find ourselves in the dark.' The switch snapped and the timing mechanism took over, clicking. They passed Room 3, the crest of the wave, and the volume diminished as they climbed. 'You need a stout heart,' May Laverty said. 'I'm convinced, every now and again, that I'm no longer young enough to live at such a height; but the young ones don't seem to care for it either. So there you are.'

'You do need a stout heart,' Robert Mooney said, and his puffing suggested considerable distress.

The light held until they reached the high landing.

The room smelled a little of damp. Except for the piano it was poorly furnished. May Laverty fetched glasses and made drinks. Through their silent constraint ran the thread of music.

I'm gonna pack up and make my getaway . . .

'It tears at my nerves,' May Laverty said. 'Though I don't mind it at this moment. You find yourself actually holding your breath listening for it; and then you wonder if it hasn't stopped after all and you're imagining you can hear it.'

'No, I can hear it,' Robert Mooney said. He had recovered his breath. 'But I must have misunderstood. I thought Paul said *you* played it to him.'

'Oh that; yes, I did. When it goes on like that it's the first thing and the only thing that comes into your head when you're trying to think of what to play. I've complained; but it won't do any good. It will drive me up the wall if it goes on like that much longer.'

'Who is it?'

'I don't know. It's a man, that's all I know. The others have complained too. But they're scared to do anything because he's drinking in there and they think he might get violent.'

'Have you seen him?'

'No. We had some conversation. I told him to shut up and he told me to mind my own business; if you can call that a conversation. We were shouting up and down the stairs. He's been at it for days: something will have to break soon. Good luck.'

'Good luck,' Robert Mooney looked around. 'You must have a view.'

'Oh, I have,' May Laverty said with excitement. 'I have. It's the whole point. Look.'

She slid the curtains and put out the light and the moment their sight adjusted there, seemingly suspended in dark air, was a liner lighted in tiers and floodlit at funnel and mast, moving slowly across the dark glass, floating as fragile as tinsel above the broadcast yellow jewels of the city lights. Then the harbour lifted from darkness, striped with beacons and navigation lights, red, orange, yellow and green, and the liner or a tug or some incoming ship (who could know?) gave a long forlorn call. A bladder of a moon, partly deflated, hung over the night mountains; and far up were a few faint stars.

'I hardly understand my impulse,' Robert Mooney said in the dark. 'I don't think I was thinking of anything – ah – very much; to be honest.' He sounded embarrassed.

'But why should you? It was me who phoned.'

'Yes, but I suggested we might meet for a chat.'

'And I accepted, I agreed. What are you trying to say? You wish you hadn't is that it? Is that what you want to say?'

'Well, Miss Laverty, I'm a family man, and . . .'

'Oh look,' May Laverty said. 'The lights are going.'

The lighted liner, suggesting distance, luxury, something mournfully pleasant, sailed slowly out of the darkened pane, into the wall; and where it had been a ruby beacon flashed hard and brief, and after a full minute flashed in darkness again.

'It's all right, Mr Mooney,' May Laverty said. 'You may relax. I'm not after anything, you know; not your money or your life. And I could hardly help knowing you were a family man.'

'Well, I only meant that in a way I've no place to be here.'

'Then why did you come?'

'I don't know, to be truthful. It's pleasant; and you certainly do have a view.'

May Laverty drank and poured. 'You might ask why I let you come.'

'I don't think I . . .'

'I'll tell you, Mr Mooney. I'm not quite what I seem – picking men off street corners. I'm simply a rather broken-down teacher of music fed up to the teeth of my own company.' She spoke as if the fact were well known and needed no further comment. 'Let me put it another way, I'm not asking for anything more than a little human warmth.'

Robert Mooney stirred. 'Ah, that . . .'

The light came on full. May Laverty drew the curtains. They both winced at the brightness.

'Why? The other was pleasant,' Robert Mooney said.

'Because I've deceived myself too often, in the dark,' May Laverty said. Two coins of high colour burned in her cheeks. Her expression was one of remoteness, grimness. 'I'm like some bird perched over the city on a dark cliff. And that's not what I want to be at all.' She filled the glasses and went to her handbag and took out his five-pound note. 'Take it, please.'

'Why? I thought you'd agreed to accept. You thanked me for it. I don't want it back.'

'Nevertheless, you'll take it,' May Laverty said. 'I thanked you for it, certainly. I don't think I ever intended to keep it. There's no way I could. Take it, please.'

He took it from her fingers. 'I'm sorry about all this. I thought we might chat a little.'

May Laverty shook her head. 'How could we? You're too afraid.'

'Afraid? Of what?'

'Of me or what you think I am. You're afraid to be here. You suspect complications, scandals, and I don't know what. You said you've no place to be here; no right, I suppose you mean.'

'I wanted things clear. Anyway, the money has nothing to do with it.'

'But it has. It was a gesture I could appreciate even if I couldn't accept. Oh, this pride over money; its too sordid.'

'Why did we meet then?'

'Curiosity. I don't know. Curiosity is as good a motive as another. Perhaps gratitude on my part. What does it matter?'

'A little human warmth, was that what you said?' It embarrassed him to repeat it.

'Yes,' May Laverty said. 'You'd think it would be easy, wouldn't you?

You'd think it would be simple. Sometimes I wonder if there's anything harder.'

He rose and took up his hat and looked at her directly, for a second. She read relief in the steadiness of his gaze.

'You'll be all right?' he said. 'I mean, a straight out loan, if that would help . . .'

'There's too little security,' May Laverty said, and laughed with a high skirl of sound. 'No, I'm not grubbing for banknotes,' she said with some contempt. She went to the door and opened it. 'Goodnight,' she said. 'You'll find it's not so hard on the heart, going down. I'll wait and trip the light a second time in case you miss.'

If it weren't for powder and for store-bought hair . . .

'Goodbye, I'm sorry,' Robert Mooney put on his hat and went down, glancing up to meet her non-committal nod as he turned the first flange of the spiral. He dropped out of sight.

I hate to see that evenin' sun . . .

She tripped the light a second time. It clicked with a sound that echoed on the landing. When it went out she waited a long time, leaning on the stair rail in the dark, the door of her room swung shut behind her. Clear and full now it rose in the silence like the source and the refrain of all her elderly discontents. Her head was spinning: she felt dizzy. (Nothing. Just a song.)

The record must have ended. There was a break, so brief as hardly to be detected, and it began again.

May Laverty snapped on the light and went down the stairs. She stood at the door of Room 3 and loudly knocked on the painted panelling.

'What do you want?'

She'd expected to confront a violent and unshaven drunk, but if the man in the doorway was drunk he wasn't showing it. He was dressed in sweater and slacks; he was shaved; he was barefooted. The music welled out, beat past him and was magnified in the small walled space of the landing. On a table in the centre of the room May Laverty saw a bottle and a glass and a siphon of soda. An ashtray on the floor spilled cigarette butts. There was no sign of the wild or desperate carousal she had expected: the room was if anything tidier than her own.

'I said, what do you want?'

May Laverty continued to stand in silent indecision.

'Have you come to complain?'

'Would it do any good? To complain, I mean.'

He turned back into the room. The music stopped. He returned holding a record. 'You came at the right moment. Satisfied?'

'No, look,' May Laverty said seriously, frowning. 'I'm not complaining about the music. I admit it isn't even all that loud.'

'Just the one tune, eh?'

'Yes. I'll gladly let you have some records, if you want to go on.'

'No, it's finished. I hope never to hear it again. I've beat it to death.'

'Then what were you doing, punishing yourself or something?'

He swayed a little in the bright doorway, looking out at May Laverty. 'Were you wanting something else?'

'Why I . . . no,' May Laverty said. 'But I'm glad it's stopped. It was driving me up the wall.'

'Me too.'

May Laverty greeted it with a surprised and surprising giggle. She was more than a little drunk. Thumb and forefinger found the wayward wisp, twisted, tucked it behind her ear. She peered past him into the room.

'What are you looking for?' He stood there easily, watching May Laverty. He appeared to be amused.

'What was I looking . . . ? I beg your pardon,' May Laverty felt confused.

'It doesn't matter. I wondered what you were looking for, that's all.' He offered the record and she took it. 'Break it in half if you want. It's played to ribbons.'

'A little human warmth,' May Laverty said distinctly.

'What?'

'A little human warmth. I mean, you'd think there'd be nothing simpler, wouldn't you? You wouldn't think it too much to ask, a little human warmth. There was no reason to run; none at all. A little human warmth.'

In the doorway the man straightened. His features, slightly puffed, composed themselves into a frown of wonder. He gently and slowly shook his head and reaching behind him he found the door handle. 'What a hope,' he said. 'Lady, what a hope.'

Then the door shut and May Laverty was on the landing in the dark. She turned and began to climb the three flights to her room, carrying the record, steadying herself with a hand on the banister.

The unfamiliar and persisting sound which filled the stairwell was the sound of May Laverty's laughter: a neighing echo, a falsetto and quavering trumpet. It accompanied her on the steep ascent.

1963

DAVID BALLANTYNE

*I believe in one God the Father Almighty Maker of heaven and earth
and of all things visible and invisible light of light begotten not made
and was flesh Crucifixus etiam pro nobis . . .*

I sat staring at my grandfather. My grandfather was big and stout
and rosy-skinned, and he had a white, sharp-pointed moustache.
He had worked on ships, travelled round the world, worked in
snooty hotels and timber camps and, it seemed to me, just about
everywhere. My mother used to tell how he brought back from
the islands in the Pacific great clusters of bananas and heaps of
pineapples and oranges. That was in his younger days. Every night
now he ate spud and sausages, smacking his lips, going chup-
chup-chup, winking at me. Every night, too, he told yarns.

This night I was sitting across the table from him, my eyes
open wide. The radio on the sideboard was playing brass-band
music, I remember.

From the sink, my grandmother called: 'For goodness' sake
hurry up with that meal! If you got home at the right time, if you
didn't go gallivanting round the pubs, you wouldn't keep us so
late.'

And, as Grandad's fork went up with the last mouthful, his
plate was whisked from the table.

He winked at me. 'Doesn't give a man a chance, does she, Roy?'

I looked at him and I thought how he always reckoned I was
the best in the family because I stood guard for him outside the
pub on Saturday afternoons, watching for Grandma, and when
we were home I wouldn't tell where Grandad had been all
afternoon. Sometimes, though, I would not get the warning through

in time and Grandma would burst into the pub at full steam, grab Grandad and push him out into the alley, and we'd all hurry home.

'What was school like today, Roy?' Grandma shouted above the noise of the radio.

'Not bad, thanks,' I told her.

'Did you know your prayers?'

'Every one.'

'Truly, Roy?'

'Every one,' I said.

'Well, what's the first you say?'

'Oh, you know,' I said.

'Roy, what's the first prayer you say?'

'I believe in one God the Father Almighty Maker of heaven and earth and of all things visible and invisible – '

'The Creed!' shouted Grandma, delighted.

'You're a clever boy,' Grandad told me.

'He's got more brains that you, anyway,' Grandma said.

'You're right there,' Grandad said.

'I *haven't* got more brains than Grandad,' I told Grandma. 'He's got more – '

'Roy, don't contradict,' she said.

It was about half past seven the radio announced that a leopard had escaped from the zoo and everybody had better keep a pretty close lookout if they didn't want to run into danger.

I sat tight on my chair. Thinking of a leopard loose in the world scared me a bit, and I tried to forget about it because I didn't want anybody to guess how scared I was.

'You know, Roy, I'd hate to meet a leopard,' Grandad said. 'Unexpectedly, like.'

'You'd run a mile,' Grandma said.

'I wouldn't say that,' Grandad said. 'I don't believe I'd run.'

'You'd run, all right,' Grandma said.

'What *would* you do, Grandad?' I asked.

'I'd kill the beast, son.'

Grandma was placing the tea dishes in the sideboard. 'Just listen to him,' she said.

'I wouldn't be frightened,' Grandad said. He gazed at me. Then he said: 'Look, Roy, I'll go out after the beast. I'll go right this moment. Lend me your airgun and I'll shoot the leopard.'

Maybe he really would shoot the leopard, I thought. I had got the airgun for a birthday present, but my mother would not let me use it because she said such things were dangerous. I was sure she would let Grandad use it, though. I ran into the front bedroom where she was writing a letter to my father, who was away working in the country, and I got the airgun from the wardrobe and told her Grandad wanted it so that he could shoot a leopard. She followed me back to the kitchen.

I gave Grandad the airgun.

'Dad, you're not going out at this time of night, are you?' my mother said.

'Too right I am,' Grandad said. He was on his way to the door.

'You can't be!'

'I'm going out to shoot that damned leopard that's escaped from the zoo,' he said. 'It was on the radio.'

'Dad, come back!' my mother said as he reached the door.

Grandma was arranging ornaments on the mantelpiece. 'Let him go if he wants to,' she said.

Grandad went out, the airgun pointing downwards.

I sat in a chair by the stove. I stared through the grating at the ashes starred by red embers. I wished my mother had not been there so that I could have gone with Grandad. Everything was very quiet.

All things visible and invisible light of light begotten not made . . .

How many leopards had he killed by now?

But maybe the leopard would kill him. Maybe poor Grandad would never again eat spud and sausages, and there would be no more Saturday afternoons outside the pub, no more big oranges and Lucky Packets as rewards.

I could imagine man-eating leopards tearing my grandfather to bits.

'Hope nothing's happened to him . . . eh, Grandma?'

'You go to bed, Roy,' Grandma said.

'It's only eight o'clock,' I said.

'Well, stop talking about your grandfather,' she said. 'You're disturbing my sewing.'

'Can I go outside?'

'What on earth for?'

'Nothing.'

'What?'

'A little look. That's all, Grandma.'

'Well don't be too long.'

Outside in the still summer night there were slithering insect sounds, and crickets sang in the paddocks. Then a slight breeze rustled the passion-fruit vines. Corners held scents and shadows, over everything was a purple sky. But there was no sign anywhere of my grandfather.

I went back inside.

'Well?' asked my mother.

'Nothing,' I said.

'He'll be all right,' Grandma said.

She and my mother went outside at half past eight, and I followed them.

There was still no sign of Grandad. He was lost.

'I'll look up the road,' I said.

'Only to the corner then,' my mother said.

'Yes,' I said.

I ran very quickly for nearly a mile. When I reached the Royal, I felt my way down the dark alley and knocked on a door at the end. About five minutes after I knocked, the door opened and I blinked into light; I could see nothing for a smudgy blue cloud and I stared hard, trying to see through it.

'Have you seen my grandfather?' I asked the woman in the blue kimono.

'Have I seen your *what*?'

'My grandfather.'

Her face was very white, her lips very red. 'What does your grandfather look like, sonny?'

I believe in one God O Grandad a big man a stout man rosy skin snowy-white moustache sharp-pointed light of light begotten not made Crucifixus . . .

'And does he own a white-handled pocket-knife, sonny? Does he?'

She was kidding. I laughed.

She laughed, too.

'And what might your grandfather's name be?'

Her scent, or something, made me gasp.

'His name is Foley,' I said.

'An Irish name,' she said. 'I like Irish names. And what's *your* name?'

'Roy,' I said. 'Roy McKay. My father's a carpenter. My father's built some of the biggest freezing-works in New Zealand.'

'I'm very impressed, Roy,' she said.

'Do you know where my grandfather is?' I asked.

'I won't be a minute, Roy,' she said. 'I think I can help. Hooray for the Irish! And the Scots, of course.'

I had felt the change inside me from the first moment the cloud floated round me. Now the kimono lifted as she went down the passage, and I shuffled my feet while I waited. Then Grandad was there, smelling of booze, and I supported him down the alley to the street, and I remembered the leopard and asked Grandad what had happened to the airgun, and I couldn't understand his mumbling, and when I eased my grip he flopped to the gutter, just about asleep, just about.

'Hell, Roy, I'm tired, tired.'

'Where's the airgun, Grandad? What have you done with the airgun?'

'You get it, Roy. I'm very tired.'

So I went back along the alley, and once more she opened the door for me.

'Have you seen my airgun?' I asked, deep in scent.

'What would I be doing with your airgun, love?'

'Grandad was going to shoot a leopard, he borrowed my airgun, now he hasn't got it.'

'What did you say he was going to shoot, Roy?'

'A leopard.'

'Oh,' she said. 'Well, please come in, Roy.'

I followed her along the passage, and at the door to the room I took in everything: single bed against the left wall, a dresser, a small gasburner, table at the right side, window with pink curtains at the end, blue and yellow rug on the floor, two empty beer bottles on the table, some glasses, the bed mussed-up, the bed very small, the bed. No gun, though. She had hidden the gun.

'Come in, love,' she said. 'How old are you, love?'

'Ten,' I said.

'Double figures,' she smiled.

'Yes,' I said. I couldn't see the gun.

'You're a big boy for your age,' she said.

I thought of my skinny long legs and blushed.

'I bet you're smart at school,' she said.

'I'm not bad,' I said. In the fields near Saint Benedict's Convent I used to lie morning after morning, the bell ringing away the periods, the bell-tower sharp against the sky.

'Say something you've learned,' she said.

'A prayer?'

'Anything. A prayer would do.'

She lay on the bed. The kimono was open at the top, her skin was clear and pinky-white.

'This prayer is what we say every day,' I said.

'I'm listening, love,' she said.

Credo in unum deum Patrem omnipotentem factorem caeli et terrae visibilium et invisibilium. And in one Lord Jesus Christ the only begotten Son of God of God light of light true God of true God . . .

'We say it every morning,' I said.

'Good for you,' she said. 'Tell me about your grandfather, Roy.'

It was simple talking to her then. I told her how Grandad had worked on ships, how he used to bring fruit home from the islands in his younger days, how he loved eating spud and sausages, chup-chup-chup, and how he liked telling stories.

She lay curled up on the bed, like the women in pictures, red lips, white face, sometimes in the middle of a cloud.

Suddenly I had to go. 'I have to go now,' I told her.

She stood up hurriedly. She stood right in front of me, put her cupped hands over my cheeks, looked into my eyes. I did not want to see her breasts as she seemed to press them against me, but I could not look up once I had looked down. She had to push my head back, and I saw that she was smiling. I felt the softness of her skin through the kimono, and there was the warm and scenty smell of her body, and there were her hands stroking my face.

She embraced me.

I did not know what to do.

She let me go.

'Would you like some lemonade?' she asked.

'No thanks,' I said.

'Try some,' she said.

'No,' I said.

'I bet you're thirsty,' she said.

'No, I'm not.'

'I bet you are.'

She crossed to the dresser, and when she had poured the lemonade into a glass, the drink fizzing, I did feel like it and I drank it all. Then she got me some cookies and I ate these, too. I liked her and I did not want to leave this room. She was nice.

Remembering the airgun, though, I began squinting round the room.

'What's up, love?' she asked.

'I want my gun,' I told her.

'Persistent young devil, aren't you?' she said.

She looked under the bed, drawing up her kimono and staying bent over for several seconds. When she stood up she had the gun in her hand. She gave it to me.

'I thought Grandad lost it,' I said.

'Well, you've got it now.'

'Thank you very much.' I did not move.

'You'd better go now,' she said. 'Your mother would be angry if she knew you were here.'

'I like being here,' I said.

'Go home, Roy,' she said.

I went to the door, wanting to leave, yet not wanting to.

'Goodbye,' she said.

I said goodbye back and I never saw her again. Not in that room, her breasts against me, her warm woman smell, her hands upon my cheeks.

I found Grandad in the gutter.

'I've got the gun, Grandad. What about the leopard? You going to shoot the leopard?'

The street lamp shone shades of yellow and green on my grandfather. He must get to his feet, down the main road to home and bed. First support from the lamp-post, then on his feet, walking, staggering.

He said suddenly: 'Don't tell them.'

'You know I won't tell,' I said.

Crucifixus etiam pro nobis Grandad . . .

I knew there were no pellets in the gun, and I was glad it was unloaded because I had the idea it would be heavier if it were loaded.

Grandad, leaning on me, was enough of a weight.

A dog tore past us, barking at another dog. Both dogs crashed through a hedge into the paddock by the road. Then silence.

My grandfather stopped. He stood as though waiting for something to happen.

'What's the matter, Grandad?'

'I heard it, Roy.'

'Dogs, Grandad.'

'It's the leopard, Roy.'

'No, Grandad – '

'Give me that gun! I want to shoot the leopard.'

I handed over the gun and let him go. He crawled through the hole in the hedge, disappeared.

I looked up and down the street. Then I got on my hands and knees and followed my grandfather.

While I crawled, I remembered everything that had happened in the past hour. I tried to put that room from my mind. I tried to concentrate on the lemonade and the cookies. But it was no use; I kept remembering the kimono, the scent, the voice, the hands upon my cheeks.

I crawled on, and I knew where I was. I was near Saint Benedict's Convent, I had hidden in this grass.

Grandad sprang into the air. To his left was the outline of the convent bell-tower.

'Grandad!' I called.

He had the gun to his shoulder. He took aim, pulled the trigger. The click was loud.

'I got it!' he shouted. 'I got the leopard! I got it, I got it!'

I knew he wasn't really drunk. He was just trying to make me forget the room.

O. E. MIDDLETON

How beautifully named are the streets of our poverty! Piety, Pleasure, Parliament and Humanity Streets. All over the world, the poorest places with the richest names, until, one day, there is Paradise Street . . .

On the grey stone curbing opposite the Mission, a knot of seamen. Stiff-legged and slow, Magee is coming down the street. Lewin's sharp elbow works at our ribs.

'He's had another jab. See how pale he is!'

Magee declines to sit on hard stone. He leans against the corner railings and takes his time about unwrapping a brand-new packet of Woodbines.

'Have you heard the news, me boys?'

'What news is that?'

'About Her Royal Highness?'

Lewin has heard. It is written all over his avid face, across his cringing shoulders. Nothing pleases him more than to dole out hot dollops of gossip. He is our rumour-monger, our harbinger, our spy. But he shuts up and waits for the cigarettes to be dealt out.

'You mean about *her* coming down to Paradise Street to look over the Mission?'

Magee lights up carefully and hands over the match. We hold the flame right at the ends of our Woodbines so that only the tips catch fire. Oh the fine flavour, the perfume of the pale blue smoke when you have been without . . . !

'Sure that's it. All the beachies at Northend are talking about it. It's in the paper she's opening the new hostel, then going on a tour of the docks.'

Blackie pulls out the *Mail* which he carries folded small in his hip pocket and smoothes it out. We lean over it, breathing in each other's smells as we devour that fat print. *Duchess to open new club for Seamen*, it says. We are famished for more, but there is nothing about us. Not a miserable crumb about her coming down to the Mission.

'May I be struck dead if it's not the truth!'

'Ah don't speak so, Kevin boy!'

'. . . You'll see soon enough that it's right. Eleven o'clock tomorrow morning.'

'Who was it told you then, Kevin?'

'I keep my ears open . . .'

'It wouldn't have been that tall fruit up at the clinic?'

'No, it would not!'

'And how is the arm today, anyroad?'

'A little better, thank you.' Stiffly he straightens, shoves himself off the railings and coasts across to the Mission.

'He's got a bad one this time, it seems . . .' Our eyes linger on the open doorway, full of fellow-feeling.

Blackie says it is time for the tea-shop, but Lewin says he will stay at his post on the corner where he sometimes waylays affluent strangers.

Blackie is proud of his new find. Luckily for us, the dockers are very particular about their sandwiches. All the crusts are cut off and piled in wooden trays. If you are nice and civil, the girls who work in the tea-shop will let you help yourself to them.

The crusts are good and crisp. They fill our guts and our pockets to overflowing.

We pile the rest into a shoe-box for later.

Inside the café, the dockers munch their barbered bread, stamp their feet, swig huge mugs of tea and coffee. Oh the joyful noise of men with jobs! The din of their cheerful voices chivvying the girls, chaffing each other; the clumping of their well-booted feet, the scrape of benches, drift through the kitchen. Like sweet scraps of sound, they fall among us in the alley as we stow away the last crusts.

Blackie catches the eye of a bustling girl. 'Say, thanks, Mary! See you tomorrow if it's O.K. . . . ?'

She flashes us the dazzling, unseeing look of an angel – or a goddess. Even Blackie is subdued. Only Dougherty saves our wretched manhood.

'Sure we'd all come up here on our knees just for one sight of your darling face!'

The tinkle of laughter warms our backs as we pick our way among the dustbins.

'Oh the bliss of a full belly! And what wouldn't I give now for another of Magee's smokes . . . !'

'If he's not gone through them yet, there'll still be one more apiece when we get back.'

Once again we drag over the dreary miles of dock cobbles, climb cleated gangways, search shifty eyes for a glimmer of hope. The usual round and the same stale answers on every ship. 'All hands are hired through the Pool. Are you established members of the Pool?'

Why do they think we are tramping fifteen miles of dockside, when the other way, you have only to show your papers at the Pool office, and wait for a ship?

'Oh did you see that loaf?' Dougherty is making a mental meal as we come down the last gangway.

'. . . Sitting up there on top of the locker, and that Peggy too miserable even to offer us so much as a drop of tea!'

'The Limey bastard!' Blackie's spit on the cobbles speaks for Dougherty and me. Between our sweaty feet and the uneven stones there is a mockery of leather. Out of reach in every way, the dock train glides back on smooth rails. Clattering drays and rumbling lorries go by laden with bales and crates.

One dray grinds slowly past piled with boxes and cartons stamped with a black fern leaf.

'Say how would it be to try to speak to the Duchess?'

'About getting us a ship, you mean?'

'Why not? The interest of the Commonwealth, and all that . . .'

'You're crazy. You wouldn't get near her.'

'You'd have more show trying to put the bite on the Pope.'

Half-way home, we pass the ruin of the warehouse cellar, bared by bombs.

'See there! . . . And there!' It is Dougherty's ritual.

He is like someone catching lice on himself, or inspecting old wounds as he picks out the iron rings where slaves were tethered.

It is growing dusk as we strike the bottom of Paradise Street. The empty spaces left by the war are noisy with children and from his pitch near the tobacconist's the old man growls the names of the evening dailies. Lewin is waiting for us, hands in pockets, his triumph showing in a raggy whistle that puckers his face.

'What do you know, a geezer threw me a pound! Coffee will be served in the lounge . . . !'

In the last of the day, the bare brick and cold stone of the street soften to warm browns. As we converge on the Mission, Lewin getting his share of crusts and talk, a ripe melon falls from the sky and splits on the pavement. Fingers knead the flagstones among the scatter of seed and pulp as we draw near and the trunk and legs of this guy flutter in a way that is almost human.

'Hey! You below! Tell the office to phone the police!'

The square, white, undeniably human face of the detective looks down sternly from an open third-storey window.

Dougherty's eyes shoot sparks upwards: 'It's a priest and an ambulance, and not the police he's wanting, I'm thinking.' Mechanically, he crosses himself, looking down.

Why are the voices of the children suddenly still?

Through the door of the Mission, and from hiding places up and down the street, men hasten to view this insect squashed on the footpath.

'What was he doing?'

'How did it happen?'

'Caught in the act . . . ?'

'He won't do that again!'

Breathless, we escape from the press of eager bodies and stand, uneasy yet strangely renewed, on its fringe.

'I think *I'll* just . . .' Lewin, his wealth forgotten, bends over the gutter vomiting bread. Only Dougherty, calm and pale, stays to help the ambulance men.

Amid the dying talk which follows the ambulance, Lewin wipes his mouth, Dougherty makes another cross in the air.

'He'll not be signing on for any more trips . . .'

'Did you know him then . . . ?'

Two uniformed men are talking to the plainclothes man and the skipper of the Mission. All eyes, a thin child pushes her way among the legs and gazes at the smear of thick juice.

'Go on! Hop it, girly!'

Why is it not until we smell the harsh disinfectant, hear the wet sound of the janitor swabbing the flagstones, that Dougherty and I feel anything? Vanquished at last, we too bend over the gutter.

'Can't take it, uh, you guys?' jeers Blackie as we join the others in the Mission café. Even Lewin is perky again with coffee in his belly and a new fag in his face.

'Did you see his face?'

'His own mother wouldn't have recognised him!'

'Someone said he was from Dublin way, but what's it matter now? May he rest in peace, poor fellow.'

There is a glisten of sweat on Magee's brow, a sombre look in his eye.

'As like as not it was him took that fine razor of mine. But who can say what a man will do if he's pushed far enough?'

Slowly, we have drifted back into our haven. Some of us have on our best shore-going shirts, and those with a change of socks and underpants have put them on.

Before long, the Ladies' Welfare Committee will ask for volunteers to stack chairs and tables against the wall and the café will resound to the jolly laughter of decent, plain girls and to the twanging of the piano. But you never know your luck in a big ship, and where else can we go anyway?

'You staying for the social, Blackie?'

'Bet your life! Wouldn't miss the free tea-and-tabnabs. Besides, I kinda like homely girls . . .'

Of course we are all staying for the Mission social, to clasp clean girls and dance decently to the piano whose chords are already heavy with tomorrow's hymns.

The floor is clear, the pious, black-suited man with the stiff collar seats himself at the piano and already a couple of young officers have whisked away the only presentable girls. Magee is explaining to a motherly woman who bends over him that he is unable to dance since he strained his back, and Blackie carefully stubs out and pockets his fag and takes the floor with a hefty, bespectacled lass. Lewin leaves us with a leer and sidles up to a kindly looking committee-woman.

There is more than one kind-hearted tart in the town. The street outside is quiet now, but an odour of carbolic still hangs around the entrance. Certain of the flagstones gleam in the light from the street lamp. The words of an old sea-shanty begin to go around in my head and stars are twinkling through the dirty cloud above the street.

'Coming-ready-or-not!' calls a clear young voice from one of the empty spaces between the buildings.

The old man has left his pitch outside the tobacconist's. In his place, a trim young tart shows her wares to anyone who will look.

How long can you survive on an alien shore, fed only by hope and the company of fellow-exiles?

'Don't talk to me about the Commonwealth!' Blackie snarls at us on our bad days. 'If the god-damned Commonwealth meant anything we'd all be drawing the dole like every other mother-loving beachcomber in this God-forsaken, Limey hole!'

Young Maggie May mistakes my lingering look and follows me with sweet words.

At the bar, Clara is too busy to do more than buy us a drink between customers, and I am suddenly too tired or too fussy to wait till she's finished work.

Even the young fellow in the sea shanty had to go back to Paradise Street. Sooner or later, we all have to drift back there to our home, the Mission: beds 1/- in the dormitories and if you have another shilling you can walk into the dining-room and sit down to a hot meal and take as much bread from the common plate as your belly and your pockets can hold.

The Mission is a place to doss for the night; somewhere to meet your mates, swap news or stories; have a shave or a wash, rinse out your sweaty socks. It was built for us in the days of sail by God-fearing merchant-philanthropists of the town whose wealth came in ships from all over the Empire. We are grateful for the disinterested goodness of heart which built the Mission and for the upright men who run it. The marks we leave on the smooth walls of the lavatories, the shapes we draw and the words we write testify to our gratitude and manly joy.

Unbidden, we crowd into the upstairs lounge on Sunday mornings for the devotional service and offer prayers for our benefactors.

Sometimes, it is true, there is a misunderstanding, and a seaman who has skipped church finds someone else has been given his bed. The Mission is a popular place, especially in cold weather, and it is often hard for the skipper to decide which of us are the most deserving.

But to be one of the volunteers who bullock the piano up the stairs on Sunday morning, or at least to be seated with your red-backed hymn book in plenty of time, and so catch the skipper's eye as he counts heads, takes a great weight off the poor man's mind.

'Guess I'd better drift back, Clara.'

'Do you have to go right away?'

'There's a posh visitor coming down our way in the morning.'

'Go on . . . !'

'A duchess of something or other.'

'She can wait!'

A big West Indian drifts across to our table. His name is Daniel Defroe and he has just acquired some money and the itch to spend it.

'How are things, Johnny Kiwi?'

'Lousy as ever, Dan. How are the rats of Parliament Street?'

When he laughs it is like a ferocious black cat licking its chops and there is a sound from deep in his chest like the rustle of bamboo leaves.

'We're managing to keep them at bay, boy.'

Dan and some friends spent two years on the beach in London, living in cold, crowded basements in Cable Street. One terrible Winter, two of them managed to find work as builder's labourers, but Dan ended with pneumonia.

'How's the chest now?'

'Sound as a bell now, man. I'm eating like an old horse these days.'

He is working in the kitchen of a hotel and manages to stoke up his big boiler when the chefs have their backs turned. Why should I stand in his way if he wants to let off some perfectly good West Indian steam?

They are putting back the chairs and tables in the café. Blackie and his filly have vanished. Lewin still has the ear of the committee-woman and Dougherty has turned in. But Magee has saved me two slices of cold plum duff from supper. As we go up the stairs, he shares out another Woodbine.

'With luck there'll be another few bob from me Mum in the post Monday.' He has to pause on every landing, flexing his hams like an old horse with stringholt.

In the pale light of bare bulbs, the rows of black iron cots seem like racks. ('Seamen's carcasses stowed, 1/- per night. Please keep your streets tidy!')

At least, this way, we are snug and warm for a few hours, we who have come through the trials of the sea only to succumb to the ordeals of the shore . . .

'I wonder if they'll bring her ladyship up here?'

We have taken off our shoes and tied them to the bedrail by the laces. Magee has slipped his purse inside his underpants and our clothes are rolled under our heads or stuffed under the mattresses.

'Are you serious?'

A warm, familiar smell fills our nostrils. It is the odour of ill-fed, ill-washed bodies mingled with the sour smell of disappointment.

'The day I ship out of here,' Magee whispers in the dark, 'I'll get a sub from the old man and stand you boys a pint of Guinness each . . .'

'The day you ship out, Blackie and I will be well away . . .'

'No, the day I ship out of here . . .' Softly, obstinately his voice drones on full of hope, full of dreams.

When the bell goes at seven, daylight slanting through the narrow casements recalls us to our world and Blackie's immaculate cot.

'Come on now, all you lads! I want everyone up and spruce for our royal visitor.'

The skipper himself strides among us in his best dark suit laving his hands. Two window-cleaners who have followed him in begin washing the grime from the panes which filter light to us from the dark side of the street.

'Can you beat that! They're even washing the windows!'

Magee twists in his cot, making a face, and up and down the room, the racked sleepers squeak their cots, hawk, fart, cough and ease themselves awake.

Lewin leers at us from the other side as he pokes his legs into his pants.

'Come on, me loyal lads! Shake a leg!'

There are women on their knees scrubbing floors, polishing brasswork; men in shirt-sleeves dashing about, getting in each other's way.

Dougherty and I are the guests of Lewin and Magee at breakfast, and there is a great stowing away of bread in case Blackie comes back empty.

'Well, mates, Mrs Lewin's little boy Hector did a bit of all right for himself last night, anyway.'

It seems the committee-woman lent him ten shillings and promised to help him get a job as a waiter.

'Was that heifer of Blackie's the same one he had a fortnight ago?'

'No, a different one. That other one didn't come back.'

The desk clerk, the skipper, the old janitor and the extra helpers are still scuttling about. Magee makes a funny remark about them and bids us goodbye.

On the grey stone curbing opposite the Mission, the usual knot of loungers spreads itself in the thin sun. A red-haired donkeyman is having his say about the royal family. We have heard it all before, but it warms us, draws a few snickers of approval. Sunday in Paradise Street, and on top of it all, a royal visitor . . .

Somewhere off the coast, a small tanker ploughs for port with spirit from Aruba. The consul told us she is three men short, so we have looked her up in *Lloyd's Shipping News* . . .

A little dark steward from Manchester tells of an experience with royalty in one of the Cunard ships. It is an obscene story and the hard faces of the buildings opposite throw back our gusty laughter. Between my cracked shoes lies a granite pebble. It is rounded and hard and with a polish like smooth varnish. Without thinking, I pick it up and fret it against my trousers.

The stone begins to weigh heavy in my hand. It is as hard and unyielding as this shore. Although my ears follow the comical, jerky talk of the man from Manchester, my hand would like to hurl this stone against the dour face of this Northern city.

At the top of the street, a skinny figure swings into sight. Even this far off we can see the swagger in his rolling walk. Lewin has seen him and nudges Dougherty. Several pairs of envious eyes pilot him in as he catches sight of us and crosses over.

The talk has strayed from its starting-point and has settled around our favourite subject.

'Oh Boy!' Blackie lets out as he parks his lean nates on the kerb. A flourish as his hand goes into his shirt pocket, a flash of colour and bright cellophane and he is offering us real American cigarettes.

The stone falls back into the gutter, Lewin's trap drops open, Dougherty lets out a soft 'Mother of God!'

But for the moment, Blackie says not a word. With a half-smile he slits his eyes against the smoke, glances towards the far end of the street and cocks an ear to the talk.

It is almost time for the service. The skipper trots out of the Mission, polishing his knuckles in his palms. He looks up the street and down, takes off and polishes his glasses, puts them on again and bolts back into the Mission.

Reluctantly, we drift across to the dark side and through the door. Upstairs, a mournful-looking cadet is handing out the tattered books. Shamefacedly, we shuffle into the dark-panelled room, take our places on the benches. Pale as ever, Magee slips in and drops into the place we have saved for him.

Some of the hymns make us laugh. '. . . *Some poor wretched, struggling seaman, You may rescue, you may save,*' is one. The way the skipper stands up and sings it with his blue chin moving solemnly up and down has Blackie and me in fits. From what dizzy heights they look down on us, these self-righteous Victorian hymn-writers!

As usual, we end by singing '*For those in peril on the sea,*' and the skipper says, 'Let us pray' and bows his head. When he has scanned us carefully over the tops of his spectacles, he begins intoning the prayers.

' . . . And lead us not into temptation but deliver us from evil . . . '

'Amen!' we say fervently. It is the only part of the programme which has any real meaning for us.

As soon as the service is over, the skipper says we may remain seated until the arrival of our royal visitor. He looks at his watch and scurries downstairs and we let out gusty sighs and forced coughs as we shrug off the gloom and hand back our hymn-books.

From their dark frames on the dark walls, the stern fathers of the Mission look down on us. Their likenesses endure like the iron and coal of their era, the dark solid furniture they bequeathed us.

But what have they done with the poor sinner who tried to deliver himself from the third-floor window?

'Here she is! Here she is!' A chorus of awed whispering as charwomen and cleaners fly for their peepholes. Sounds of slamming car doors, of more hushed talk, then silence.

'They're coming up . . . !' Lewin's slantwise face listens for us, registering every sound from below. The pianist holds himself stiffly on his stool, squaring his narrow shoulders. Blackie has stopped breathing.

An old fellow we have not seen before, but who looks like the Mission's patron saint, bursts in and babbles, 'Her Royal Highness, The Duchess of – .'

In she comes like a barque in full sail. Tall, clean lines, fine clothes . . . What more can you say?

The red-haired, cockney donkeyman is the first to his feet; the small dark man from Manchester is only a split-second behind him.

A puff of wind to my left and right and Blackie and Dougherty are upright. Further along the bench, Magee gets slowly to his feet, a dark look on his face.

The donkeyman's back and red neck hide the duchess from me and me from her, but over the head of the little man from Manchester, the skipper sends me steely signals. Blackie begins to tug my arm in a half-hearted way, but soon stops.

The skipper's face is going red and his eyes seem watery behind his spectacles. By the time the piano has galloped through the national anthem, he is staring at the wall above my head.

Those who have handed in their names are being presented to the tall elegant woman who smiles simply and unaffectedly and touches their hands with the tips of her gloved fingers. There are three cadets in the queue and a young officer from one of the Canadian Pacific ships.

Blackie is full of sorrow. 'Oh boy, you're for the block for sure! They'll lock you up in the tower.'

Lewin is agog, though silent, but Magee leans across, his hand to his mouth:

''Tis what we all should have done. The best of luck to you, boy!'

'He's right! I'm a son-of-a-bitch to have let you down. If only we'd gone into a huddle about it beforehand . . . '

She is gone as suddenly as she came, so now we can enjoy another of Blackie's Virginias. More slamming of car doors and purring of muted engines and they have left the street.

The skipper reappears in the doorway of the lounge and gives us one of his watery smiles. 'Could I see you in my office, Mr Bellringer?'

Dark looks from Magee, Dougherty and Blackie. Lewin is neutral.

'You did what we all should have done. Don't let him bother you. He can only throw you out.'

How sweetly the flavour of certain moments lingers in a cigarette . . .

The skipper has recovered his self-possession and is gently laving his hands.

('Blessed are the meek, my friends!')

'Ah yes, ah, Mr Bellringer. I have no intention of asking you for an explanation for what was obviously a premeditated act of disrespect and disloyalty. It is my duty to see that beds go to the most deserving cases. As from now your bed is cancelled and you are no longer welcome here.'

He pushes over a slip of paper and a florin. The slip says, 'Refund on bed No. 33. Sun., Mon., 2/-.'

The others are waiting outside. Blackie, his hands deep in his pockets, kicks at the kerb with his scuffed, pointed shoes.

'That Bible-banging, psalm-singing old crawler!'

'There's one thing,' Dougherty remarks gently, 'you've no luggage to worry about.'

Blackie flourishes his packet. Solemnly we pluck out cigarettes, apply fire.

'We'll all go with you up to the new place. It's only a couple of miles. Their beds are dearer, but we can always have a whip-round.'

'If the old – hasn't been on the blower to the skipper up there . . .'

'The day I ship out of this place . . .' Magee mouths darkly at the street.

Blackie signs across to Lewin and we head out of the lower end of the street towards the dock café.

There are not so many crusts today because there are not so many dockers at work. But Blackie and the others insist they are not hungry. They make a fine parcel of the crusts and the bread we saved at breakfast, in the *Lloyd's Shipping News,* and Dougherty bears it before him as if it were the host.

'First thing in the morning, we'll go and see the consul. Is that a deal?'

Stiff-legged and slow, Magee drags at our side.

'Would you take a job now, Kevin, if it was offering?'

'Just as soon as I get over my strain, like . . .'

'This is the route the Rolls Royces took.'

'I'd sooner do it in one of them than in these . . .'

Through a hole in his pointed shoe, Blackie's yellow sole accuses us like an eye.

'. . . And to think there's a fine top-coat in Kelly's pawnshop you could have had the use of these cold nights.'

We are in the main drag. Lewin buys a copy of the *News of the World* and reads out the choice bits to us. There is a photograph of a fossil man who lived a million years ago. Blackie points out that he looks like the skipper of the Mission. There is another picture of a Greek shipping magnate on the beach at Cannes with a long-limbed film star. Her husband is suing for divorce and citing the Greek.

A millionaire has jumped from a skyscraper in New York and there are tens of thousand homeless after a tidal wave in Japan . . .

'Nothing about the geezer who did the swallow-dive out of the Mission!' Lewin raises his snout above the ink-smelling sheets.

'. . . May God have mercy on his soul,' one of us says mechanically.

'Happened too recent,' Blackie says flatly. 'Anyway, who wants to read about that? Why, it might have been one of us here now.'

But Lewin's face tells us he is not satisfied. He has been cheated of something he could have talked about, fondled, believed in. How can you be sure a thing happened until you read about it in the paper?

There is still an argument going on when I come out of the new swing doors.

'They only have cubicles here. They're 3/- each.'

'That old skunk at the Mission didn't reckon you could afford one of those or he'd have telephoned for sure.'

Cheerfully, Blackie counts out a florin, a sixpence and two hexagonal threepenny pieces. 'I've got a date with Priscilla in an hour. But Joe and I'll see you outside here at nine tomorrow.'

Dougherty passes me the bread. The package is still warm from his big Irish hand.

'See you in the morning then.' A surly nod and he swings away beside Blackie.

'Watch it, mate!' and Lewin has darted off too, his banner furled, his eyes not missing a face among the leisurely Sunday strollers.

Now there is only Magee.

'You might as well take these . . .' He is slipping a new packet of Woodbines into my pocket.

'No, Kevin. A couple's plenty . . .'

'Hush, man! There'll be word from me mum tomorrow for sure.'

'Anyway, I'll be seeing you.'

'Sure . . .'

'Maybe we'll all ship out together if the three of us miss the tanker . . .'

'Why not? You boys need someone to keep an eye on you, especially Blackie. Someone with experience.' He pronounces the word with the second syllable drawn out to emphasise its weight and meaning.

'Look after yourself . . . And thanks.'

There is nothing beautiful about the name of the street where they have built the new seamen's hostel. It is called Bond Street or Stock Street – something like that.

But the berths smell of linseed oil and new paint and their windows face the sun. When you pay your three shillings at the desk the clerk gives you a big clean towel and there is ample hot water in the shower and soap in the handbasins.

If it is only for one night, then all the more reason to make the most of it. Tomorrow, anything might happen – or nothing. Tomorrow they might give us the dole.

'. . . Oh yes, Mr Blackadder and Mr Bellringer. Your forms have come through now at last, I'm happy to say. Sorry about the delay and the little misunderstanding. Hope you have not been too much inconvenienced. Since you are British Subjects and have paid taxes in your own countries, you are of course entitled to full unemployment benefits here.' The little clerk at the Labour Exchange, who has always been so peevish and short with us because of our outlandish accents, beams at us full of respect and hands over two envelopes. Inside there are government cheques for £18 in back pay for each of us.

'If you will just sign here . . . and here, and call here every Thursday from now on with the regulars . . .'

. . . Or tomorrow might be another of those grimy, drizzly days when the early workers pull down the brims of their caps, huddle into their mufflers and coat collars and hurry along with their eyes on the greasy pavement. One of these days when exiles warm themselves with remembered sunshine, feed on a forgotten plenty. How many more treacherous tomorrows lie in wait for us before we exhaust our store of charms or join the ranks of the immune?

Is it possible that out of this already tainted tomorrow will come a small steel ship with deliverance for three? That there will be something to Lewin's advantage, mail for Magee . . .?

We are sitting in the crew's mess aft. Dougherty is on watch with a Swede.

'Boy, those fish-balls were good . . .'

'If I eat another hunk of bread and smør it'll be all I can do to stand . . .'

The messboy's discreet ropesoles pad patiently to and fro.

'They saved our lives, eh Kiwi, these Square-heads?'

'Amen!'

The messboy flits from his cubbyhole and stands beside the table, smiling with his pale Northern eyes.

'You like our food . . . Yess?'

'Yes!'

'That's good, no?'

'Good ship, good people!'

'Yess, I think so.'

Already Blackie is losing his haggard, hungry look. We like to sit in the mess long after the meal, talking and smoking American cigarettes, savouring our good fortune.

'I wonder if poor old Kevin's still going to the clinic?'

'And do you reckon Lewin was on with that committee-woman?'

'Not a doubt of it!'

'Say, did I ever tell you about Priscilla? Now there was a dame for you!'

The trouble is that once we are at sea again, we forget the mean faces, the false hearts, the ugly lives. And sometimes too, we forget the friends of our poverty in the streets with the beautiful names, and those others who have become immune.

When Mr Blackie took bad again that autumn both he and Mrs Blackie knew that it was for the last time. For many weeks neither spoke of it; but the understanding was in their eyes as they watched each other through the days and nights. It was a look, not of sadness or despair, but of quiet resignation tempered with something else, an unnamed expression that is seen only in the old and the very young.

Their acceptance was apparent in other ways, too. Mrs Blackie no longer complained to the neighbours that the old lazy-bones was running her off her feet. Instead she waited on him tirelessly, stretching their pension over chicken and out-of-season fruits to tempt his appetite; and she guarded him so possessively that she even resented the twice-weekly visits from the district nurse. Mr Blackie, on the other hand, settled into bed as gently as dust. He had never been a man to dwell in the past, not now he spoke a great deal of their earlier days and surprised Mrs Blackie by recalling things which she, who claimed the better memory, had forgotten. Seldom did he talk of the present, and never in these weeks did he mention the future.

Then, on the morning of the first frost of winter, while Mrs Blackie was filling his hot-water bottle, he sat up in bed, unaided, to see out the window. The inside of the glass was streaked with tears of condensation. Outside, the frost had made an oval frame of crystals through which he could see a row of houses and lawns laid out in front of them, like white carpets.

'The ground will be hard,' he said at last. 'Hard as nails.'

Mrs Blackie looked up quickly. 'Not yet,' she said.

'Pretty soon, I think.' His smile was apologetic.

She slapped the hot-water bottle into its cover and tested it against her cheek. 'Lie down or you'll get a chill,' she said.

Obediently, he dropped back against the pillow, but as she moved about him, putting the hot water bottle at his feet, straightening the quilt, he stared at the frozen patch of window.

'Amy, you'll get a double plot, won't you?' he said. 'I wouldn't rest easy thinking you were going to sleep by someone else.'

'What a thing to say!' The corner of her mouth twitched. 'As if I would.'

'It was your idea to buy single beds,' he said accusingly.

'Oh, Herb —' She looked at the window, away again. 'We'll have a double plot,' she said. For a second or two she hesitated by his bed, then she sat beside his feet, her hands placed one on top of the other in her lap, in a pose that she always adopted when she had something important to say. She cleared her throat.

'You know, I've been thinking on and off about the silk.'

'The silk?' He turned his head towards her.

'I want to use it for your laying out pyjamas.'

'No, Amy,' he said. 'Not the silk. That was your wedding present, the only thing I brought back with me.'

'What would I do with it now?' she said. When he didn't answer, she got up, opened the wardrobe door and took the camphorwood box from the shelf where she kept her hats. 'All these years and us not daring to take a scissors to it. We should use it sometime.'

'Not on me,' he said.

'I've been thinking about your pyjamas.' She fitted a key into the brass lock. 'It'd be just right.'

'A right waste, you mean,' he said. But there was no protest in his voice. In fact, it had lifted with a childish eagerness. He watched her hands as she opened the box and folded back layers of white tissue paper. Beneath them lay the blue of the silk. There was a reverent silence as she took it out and spread it under the light.

'Makes the whole room look different, doesn't it?' he said. 'I nearly forgot it looked like this.' His hands struggled free of the sheet and moved across the quilt. Gently, she picked up the blue material and poured it over his fingers.

'Aah,' he breathed, bringing it closer to his eyes. 'All the way from China.' He smiled. 'Not once did I let it out of me sight. You know that, Amy? There were those on board as would have pinched it quick as that. I kept it pinned round me middle.'

'You told me,' she said.

He rubbed the silk against the stubble of his chin. 'It's the birds that take your eye,' he said.

'At first,' said Mrs Blackie. She ran her finger over one of the peacocks that strutted in the foreground of a continuous landscape. They were proud birds, iridescent blue, with silver threads in their tails. 'I used to like them best, but after a while you see much more, just as fine only smaller.' She pushed her glasses on to the bridge of her nose and leaned over the silk, her finger guiding her eyes over islands where waterfalls hung, eternally suspended, between pagodas and dark blue conifers, over flat lakes and tiny fishing boats, over mountains where the mists never lifted, and back again to a haughty peacock caught with one foot suspended over a rock. 'It's a work of art like you never see in this country,' she said.

Mr Blackie inhaled the scent of camphorwood. 'Don't cut it, Amy. It's too good for an old blighter like me.' He was begging her to contradict him.

'I'll get the pattern tomorrow,' she said.

The next day, while the district nurse was giving him his injection, she went down to the store and looked through a pile of pattern books. Appropriately, she choose a mandarin style with a high collar and piped cuffs and pockets. But Mr Blackie, who had all his life worn striped flannel in the conventional design, looked with suspicion at the pyjama pattern and the young man who posed so easily and shamelessly on the front of the packet.

'It's the sort them teddy bear boys have,' he said.

'Nonsense,' said Mrs Blackie.

'That's exactly what they are,' he growled. 'You're not laying me out in a lot of new-fangled nonsense.'

Mrs Blackie put her hands on her hips. 'You'll not have any say in the matter,' she said.

'Won't I just? I'll get up and fight – see if I don't.'

The muscles at the corner of her mouth twitched uncontrollably. 'All right, Herb, if you're so set against it – '

But now, having won the argument, he was happy. 'Get away with you, Amy. I'll get used to the idea.' He threw his lips back against his gums. 'Matter of fact, I like them fine. It's that nurse that done it. Blunt needle again.' He looked at the pattern.

'When d'you start?'

'Well – '

'This afternoon?'

'I suppose I could pin the pattern out after lunch.'

'Do it in here,' he said. 'Bring in your machine and pins and things and set them up so I can watch.'

She stood taller and tucked in her chin. 'I'm not using the machine,' she said with pride. 'Every stitch is going to be done by hand. My eyes mightn't be as good as they were once, mark you, but there's not a person on this earth can say I've lost my touch with a needle.'

His eyes closed in thought. 'How long?'

'Eh?'

'Till it's finished.'

She turned the pattern over in her hands. 'Oh – about three or four weeks. That is – if I keep at it.'

'No,' he said. 'Too long.'

'Oh, Herb, you'd want a good job done, wouldn't you?' she pleaded.

'Amy – ' Almost imperceptibly, he shook his head on the pillow.

'I can do the main seams on the machine,' she said, lowering her voice.

'How long?'

'A week,' she whispered.

When she took down the silk that afternoon, he insisted on an extra pillow in spite of the warning he'd had from the doctor about lying flat with his legs propped higher than his head and shoulders.

She plumped up the pillow from her own bed and put it behind his neck; then she unrolled her tape measure along his body, legs, arms, around his chest.

'I'll have to take them in a bit,' she said, making inch-high black figures on a piece of cardboard. She took the tissue paper pattern into the kitchen to iron it flat. When she came back, he was waiting, wide-eyed with anticipation and brighter, she thought, than he'd been for many weeks.

As she laid the silk out on her bed and started pinning down the first of the pattern pieces, he described with painstaking attempts at accuracy, the boat trip home, the stop at Hong Kong, and the merchant who had sold him the silk. 'Most of his stuff was rubbish,' he said. 'You wouldn't look twice at it. This was the only decent thing he had and even then he done me. You got to argue with these devils. Beat him down, they told me. But there was others as wanted that silk and if I hadn't made up me mind there and then I'd have lost it.' He squinted at her hands. 'What are you doing now? You just put that bit down.'

'It wasn't right,' she said, through lips closed on pins. 'I have to match it – like wallpaper.'

She lifted the pattern pieces many times before she was satisfied. Then it was evening and he was so tired that his breathing had become laboured. He no longer talked. His eyes were watering from hours of concentration; the drops spilled over his red lids and soaked in the pillow.

'Go to sleep,' she said. 'Enough's enough for one day.'

'I'll see you cut it out first,' he said.

'Let's leave it till the morning,' she said, and they both sensed her reluctance to put the scissors to the silk.

'Tonight,' he said.

'I'll make the tea first.'

'After,' he said.

She took the scissors from her sewing drawer and wiped them on her apron. Together they felt the pain as the blades met cleanly almost without resistance, in that first cut. The silk would never again be the same. They were changing it, rearranging the pattern of fifty-odd years to form something new and unfamiliar. When she had cut out the first piece, she held it up, still pinned to the paper, and said, 'The back of the top.'

Then she laid it on the dressing table and went on as quickly as she dared, for she knew that he would not rest until she had finished.

One by one the garment pieces left the body of silk. With each touch of the blades, threads sprung apart; mountains were divided, peacocks split from head to tail; waterfalls fell on either side of fraying edges. Eventually, there was nothing on the bed but a few shining snippets. Mrs Blackie picked them up and put them back in the camphorwood box, and covered the pyjama pieces on the dressing table with a cloth. Then she removed the extra pillow from Mr Blackie's bed and laid his head back in a comfortable position before she went into the kitchen to make the tea.

He was very tired the next morning but refused to sleep while she was working with the silk. She invented a number of excuses for putting it aside and leaving the room. He would sleep then, but never for long. No more than half an hour would pass and he would be calling her. She would find him lying awake and impatient for her to resume sewing.

In that day and the next, she did all the machine work. It was a tedious task, for first she tacked each seam by hand, matching the patterns in the weave so that the join was barely noticeable. Mr Blackie silently supervised every stitch. At times she would see him studying the silk with an expression that she still held in her memory. It was the look he'd given her in their courting days. She felt a prick of jealousy, not because she thought that he cared more for the silk than he did for her, but because he saw something in it that she didn't share. She never asked him what it was. At her age a body did not question these things or demand explanations. She would bend her head lower and concentrate her energy and attention into the narrow seam beneath the needle.

On the Friday afternoon, four days after she'd started the pyjamas, she finished the buttonholes and sewed on the buttons. She'd deliberately hurried the last of the hand sewing. In the four days, Mr Blackie had become weaker, and she knew that the sooner the pyjamas were completed and put back in the camphorwood box out of sight, the sooner he would take an interest in food and have the rest he needed.

She snipped the last thread and put the needle in its case.

'That's it, Herb,' she said, showing him her work.

He tried to raise his head. 'Bring them over here,' he said.

'Well – what do you think?' As she brought the pyjamas closer, his eyes relaxed and he smiled.

'Try them on?' he said.

She shook her head. 'I got the measurements,' she said. 'They'll be the right fit.'

'Better make sure,' he said.

She hesitated but could find no reason for her reluctance.

'All right,' she said, switching on both bars of the electric heater and drawing it closer to his bed. 'Just to make sure I've got the buttons right.'

She peeled back the bedclothes, took off his thick pyjamas and put on the silk. She stepped back to look at him.

'Well, even if I do say so myself, there's no one could have done a better job. I could move the top button over a fraction, but apart from that they're a perfect fit.'

He grinned. 'Light, aren't they?' He looked down the length of his body and wriggled his toes. 'All the way from China. Never let it out of me sight. Know that, Amy?'

'Do you like them?' she said.

He sucked his lips in over his gums to hide his pleasure. 'All right. A bit on the tight side.'

'They are not, and you know it,' Mrs Blackie snapped. 'Never give a body a bit of credit, would you? Here, put your hands down and I'll change you before you get a chill.'

He tightened his arms across his chest. 'You made a right good job, Amy. Think I'll keep them on a bit.'

'No.' She picked up his thick pyjamas.

'Why not?'

'Because you can't,' she said. 'It – it's disrespectful. And the nurse will be here soon.'

'Oh, get away with you, Amy.' He was too weak to resist further but as she changed him, he still possessed the silk with his eyes. 'Wonder who made it?'

Although she shrugged his question away, it brought to her a definite picture of a Chinese woman seated in front of a loom surrounded by blue and silver silkworms. The woman was dressed from a page in a geographic magazine, and except for the Oriental line of her eyelids, she look liked Mrs Blackie.

'D'you suppose there's places like that!' Mr Blackie asked.

She snatched up the pyjamas and put them in the box.

'You're the one that's been there,' she said briskly. 'Now settle down and rest or you'll be had when the nurse arrives.'

The district nurse did not come that afternoon. Nor in the evening. It was at half-past three the following morning that her footsteps, echoed by the doctor's, sounded along the gravel path.

Mrs Blackie was in the kitchen, waiting. She sat straight-backed and dry-eyed, her hands placed one on top of the other in the lap of her dressing gown.

'Mrs Blackie. I'm sorry – '

She ignored the nurse and turned to the doctor. 'He didn't say goodbye,' she said with an accusing look. 'Just before I phoned. His hand was over the side of the bed. I touched it. It was cold.'

The doctor nodded.

'No sound of any kind,' she said. 'He was good as gold last night.'

Again, the doctor nodded. He put his hand, briefly, on her shoulder, then went into the bedroom. Within a minute he returned, fastening his leather bag and murmuring sympathy.

Mrs Blackie sat still, catching isolated words. Expected. Peacefully. Brave. They dropped upon her – neat, geometrical shapes that had no meaning.

'He didn't say goodbye.' She shook her head. 'Not a word.'

'But look, Mrs Blackie,' soothed the nurse. 'It was inevitable. You knew that. He couldn't have gone on – '

'I know, I know.' She turned away, irritated by their lack of under-standing. 'He just might have said goodbye. That's all.'

The doctor took a white tablet from a phial and tried to persuade her to swallow it. She pushed it away; refused, too, the cup of tea that the district nurse poured and set in front of her. When they picked up their bags and went towards the bedroom, she followed them.

'In a few minutes,' the doctor said. 'If you'll leave us – '

'I'm getting his pyjamas,' she said. 'There's a button needs changing. I can do it now.'

As soon as she entered the room, she glanced at Mr Blackie's bed and noted that the doctor had pulled up the sheet. Quickly, she lifted the camphorwood box, took a needle, cotton, scissors, her spectacle case, and went back to the kitchen. Through the half-closed door she heard the nurse's voice, 'Poor old thing,' and she knew, instinctively, that they were not talking about her.

She sat down at the table to thread the needle. Her eyes were clear but her hands were so numb that for a long time they refused to work together. At last, the thread knotted, she opened the camphorwood box. The beauty of the silk was always unexpected. As she spread the pyjamas out on the table, it warmed her, caught her up and comforted her with the first positive feeling she'd had that morning. The silk was real. It was brought to life by the electric light above the table, so that every fold of the woven landscape moved. Trees swayed towards rippling water and peacocks danced with white fire in their tails. Even the tiny bridges –

Mrs Blackie took off her glasses, wiped them, put them on again. She leaned forward and traced her thumbnail over one bridge, then another. And another. She turned over the pyjama coat and closely examined the back. It was there, on every bridge; something she hadn't noticed before. She got up, and from the drawer where she kept her tablecloths, she took out her magnifying glass.

As the bridge in the pattern of the silk grew, the figure which had been no larger than an ant became a man.

Mrs Blackie forgot about the button and the murmur of voices in the bedroom. She brought the magnifying glass nearer her eyes.

It was a man and he was standing with one arm outstretched, on the highest span between two islands. Mrs Blackie studied him for a long time, then she straightened up and smiled. Yes, he was waving. Or perhaps, she thought, he was beckoning to her.

PHILIP MINCHER

On the first day of barracks an instructor had made a fool of him over a Bren. He had been listening to the band practising on the other side of the field, and this young army chap had shown him up for inattention.

'What's the effective range of this weapon, cadet?'

Fainy had felt his face reddening. He had not actually known until then that he was a cadet, and he was not sure whether or not the soldier could make trouble for him. He had stood dumb with his throat thick and his eyes beginning to sting, and let the soldier bawl him out while everybody snickered.

That had been the first jarring note of his grammar school career: something beyond the initiation things and the hard frightening knot of the preliminary exams. What they referred to at the school as the first week's barracks had not turned out so nicely for the new boy. It was a school, he reasoned, like any other school. He wanted to do his best and stay out of trouble.

So that when a Mr Lewis came upon the scene, seeking new prospects for the trumpet band, Fainy remembered the nasty glint in the young army instructor's eyes and put up his hand.

Mr Lewis was a nervous untidy little man with long dry hair and insipid features. Fainy could tell at once that he would not be one of the popular masters. He was in charge of the trumpet band because he knew something about music, but he never took any drill or made a great deal of noise about anything. He had few volunteers: most were drawn more towards gunnery than music. He eyed Fainy hopefully.

'Which interests you, the trumpet or the drum?' he asked.

'The trumpet, sir.'

'Can you play?'

'No, sir.'

'But you have the general idea?'

Fainy felt that Mr Lewis wanted him to have the general idea, wanted it to be all right.

'I think so, sir.' He wanted very badly to be able to play the trumpet.

'Report to the drum major after lunch,' Mr Lewis said.

'Yes, sir. Thank you, sir.' Fainy thought now that he might have got himself into something. He remembered the eyes of the army instructor and shivered.

The drum major was a stocky, muscular sixth former named McCall. He was kind to Fainy without really appearing to see him, and passed him on to the trumpet sergeant, a tall, pouting youth named Clift who put a trumpet into Fainy's hands and forgot about him, looking over his head until he went away.

Fainy stood self-consciously among the grouped bandsmen, waiting to fall in. He held the trumpet awkwardly. It was the worse for wear, dented in the bell, with its braid shredded.

McCall gave the order to fall in. Fainy just found himself in the ranks, quickly placing the trumpet beneath his arm the way the others were holding theirs. The bass drummer hooked on his great bass drum and they dressed behind the side drummers, spacing with their sticks crossed to either side.

McCall held his mace, braided with the school colours. He walked seriously down the ranks. Fainy stood stiffly to attention among the motionless bandsmen. The drum major came abreast of him and stopped.

'Can you play that thing?' he asked.

He looked a good-natured young man and his eyes were smiling. But in spite of himself Fainy saw in his mind the cutting eyes of the army instructor, and he heard himself blurting out like a fool, 'No, sir.'

McCall smiled, and a ripple of mirth ran through the ranks. Fainy knew he had done it again. He wanted to die.

McCall passed on, then returned to face the band. It wasn't his fault, Fainy thought, his face red, his eyes stinging once more. He envied McCall his poise and his self-assurance. He kept his eyes on the drum major. He had to go through with it now whatever happened. McCall took up his place at the head of the band. Fainy tried to lose himself in what was happening, to be a part of the band and nothing more. Then McCall gave his order and it worked.

'Band – double flam, school tune, by the centre, quick . . . march!'

The drums began to beat and they were marching, and he was in fact a part of the band, feeling at last he was where he wanted to be. He felt himself caught up in the drum music, and he marched as he might well have marched a thousand times before.

The drum major marched with the mace in front of his band. They swung out of the school gates and Fainy could feel everybody watching. McCall signalled with the mace and blew his whistle, and as the bass drummer gave his double flam and the side drums rolled in introduction Fainy knew that the trumpets were going to play. Trumpet Sergeant Clift barked out the name of the tune.

They marched up the road away from the school, and Fainy felt himself inside the music, the drums rolling and the trumpets blaring, the whole band one single piece giving out its grand noise to the world. He saw, without staring, the people on the street stopping to watch. He carried the trumpet proudly beneath his arm, and he knew that he was going to learn to play it, and that he was always going to be a part of this magnificent noise.

It was a grand march. They marched round the block and into one of the back playing fields. Then they drilled for an hour. Towards the end Mr Lewis wandered across the field from the main school, a solitary figure crossing the green. They watched him come, and cruel remarks were passed. Fainy was not surprised: they hated him for his meekness.

After some preamble Mr Lewis and the trumpet sergeant took Fainy aside for an introduction to the instrument. He was nervous but he put his heart into it. He knew the others were listening, ready to make fun of him, but he could overcome that now. He tried with everything he could muster, as if his life depended on it. Clift played the notes with a casual perfection, then stood by with his constant disarming pout while Fainy struggled to follow him. Mr Lewis stood, willing him to play. Fainy felt that well enough. Mr Lewis wanted him to learn, perhaps he could sense how much it had come to mean to him. He put his soul into the test, and at last they decided he had the necessary potential. He marched from the field in the centre of the grand noise they made, not yet playing, but a part of it.

That was the start of it. The problems that followed were made to be overcome: the matter of somewhere to practise, for instance.

He had to be far enough away from the house not to activate his mother's migraines, yet a respectable distance from the nearest neighbour. His best possible site, the woodshed, was well within earshot of the man next door, a retired pork butcher named Sigley, who always managed an ungracious, easily audible comment at the first blast. But that could be overcome too. Mr Sigley had never marched inside the great brass wonder of a trumpet band, or he would have given up before he started.

Surprisingly, it was Mr Sigley's nasty comments that helped to bring Fainy closer to his brother Tom. One evening Fainy sat down to practise, and with the first note came Mr Sigley's sour remark; then, as he closed his mind and redoubled his concentration, there was Tom's voice cutting into the old butcher's with a well-worded counterblast. Fainy was startled. Tom's sentence was long and furious and a hair's breadth from libel. There was silence, and then Tom came into the shed:

'You play as long and loud as you want to, mate,' he said.

He was ten years older than Fainy, and a working man. He had never been much of a one for school, and at Fainy's age had been working out his own destiny in the engineering trade.

'That old pork chop doesn't worry me,' Fainy said, holding the instrument awkwardly.

'Yes he does,' Tom said with authority. 'I've got a better place.'

Fainy followed him in wonder across the yard to the other building, and into the secret world of the young man, his brother. Tom unlocked the door and switched on the light. The three stripped motorbikes gleamed before them.

Tom cleared pieces of machinery from a chair, and set it clumsily before the boy. 'You'll be able to concentrate better here,' he said.

'Gee, thanks, Tom.'

'I'll give you a key,' Tom said awkwardly. 'You just come in any time you want to get clear of old Porky . . . And watch out you don't touch anything or I'll knock your bloody head off.'

'Gee, Tom . . .'

Tom began to make his exit on the gruff note intended, then paused:

'Is it hard to play?'

'Not really. D'you want a try?'

'No,' Tom said flatly. Then − 'What's it feel like in the band − I mean, when everything's playing?'

'It's the best feeling in the world,' Fainy said truthfully. He felt the colour coming to his cheeks because he had spoken from the heart, but there was no sneer from Tom.

'Well, you do it then,' Tom said. 'Don't let anybody stop you.' He hesitated again. 'Your braid's pretty well shot.'

Fainy looked, knowing it was so.

'I could make you a new one,' Tom said.

'Boy, could you?'

'Sure. I can do braiding all right. That's one of the things Grandad taught me when I was younger than you.'

'And you still remember how to do it?'

'I remember all right. Grandad had a sail ticket, boy, and what he had to say was worth remembering. He taught me every knot in the book, and I could show you them all now.'

'He gave me *The Sea Wolf*,' Fainy said. 'He must have remembered those days. He must have been a young man when Jack London was alive.'

'I read *The Sea Wolf*,' Tom said.

'I've got some Joseph Conrad books,' Fainy said.

'I don't get any time for reading now,' Tom said, and went out.

But after that things were different between them. Fainy felt closer to Tom than he had ever been before. He felt how Tom tolerated him now, respected him where previously he had been prone to scorn.

He felt himself maturing. He settled into his studies, and he wasn't afraid any more of being caught out of line or of making a fool of himself. And all the while his love was the trumpet, and his secret was the grand, incredible thing that came about when the band played.

And although the other boys were keen enough, he felt that they didn't see it in the same way as he saw it. For Fainy it was as though something was brought to life when they played, something martial and magnificent that had come down to him through a thousand years, a spirit evoking the names of Waterloo and Balaclava and a million shows of splendour and feats of sword and lance he had never even heard of. This was the thing that was there in his head when they played.

And always in front of the band marched McCall, the drum major, with the school mace.

The mace was a magnificent thing of polished wood and chrome, with the school crest moulded into its head, and richly braided with the school colours. When you looked closely you knew that it had seen better days, but it was well balanced, and it was the focal point for band and spectators alike.

One day Mr Lewis released the news that the band was to appear in a parade. There was going to be a show in a month or so for a famous American general, and the band had been given the job of leading a unit of WAAFS on to the field. Everybody was excited, and they began to drill in earnest. The drum major too began to brush up on his mace work. For the first time Fainy saw him throw the mace in the air. They were marching across the field, playing their heads off, with McCall giving the mace everything he had, and then up it went, at the very peak of the music, up and up and over and down, and Fainy nearly died with apprehension as it came down and was taken mechanically, and spun again in McCall's hand.

After that McCall threw the mace at least once every time they trained, and they knew that he was going to throw it in the parade. In front of thousands, Fainy thought. Thousands!

Then one morning, drilling in the quadrangle, McCall threw the mace and missed. It hit the asphalt with a crash they could hear right through the music, and everybody stopped without the whistle and stood anxiously watching. It had fallen heavy end first, and the moulding about the head was shattered.

It was a blow to the whole band. The mace was its essence, the kernel of its concord. There was no mending it, although the tragedy might be disguised. But you couldn't throw an imperfect thing like that, not in front of thousands, and an American general to boot. The whole act would go sour without that big toss of the mace.

Mr Lewis was most concerned but offered no immediate hope. A new mace would have to be imported, he said. They didn't make them here. That was when an idea began to form itself in Fainy's head. Why couldn't they make them here?

That evening as usual he practised in the private sanctuary.

He had finished a tune and was draining the instrument of spittle when Tom came in with yet more pieces of machinery.

'Carry on, mate,' he said.

Fainy kept on with his draining.

'Needs a vacuum cleaner,' he said.

'Why not?' Tom said, appearing to consider it. He got busy at his work-bench. 'You must be pretty good at it by now.'

'I hope so,' Fainy said. 'We've got a big parade next month.'

'Big deal,' Tom said.

'McCall busted the mace today.'

'Oh, how?'

'He threw it up and missed, and busted it on the asphalt.'

'He's the one who should have practised,' Tom said.

'They can't get it fixed,' Fainy said. 'They say they don't make them here.'

'Tell them they don't know what they're talking about,' Tom said. 'And bring it home with you.'

His words rang in Fainy's ears like music.

So next day he was bold enough to approach McCall and tell him that the mace could be saved. It was a proud moment.

McCall pricked up his ears at the news.

'Does your brother do that kind of thing?'

'He's an engineer,' Fainy said proudly. 'If he can't do it nobody can.'

'All right,' McCall said. 'Take the mace home tonight then, Burridge.'

Fainy's heart swelled with pride. He took the mace reverently. It was all there, the very spirit of the band, locked in the wood and the braid and the damaged metal head of it.

He carried it proudly and delicately home to Tom, who received it with a different kind of interest. Fainy watched in fascination as he tapped it over. Tom measured and weighed and tested the mace with all the care and gravity of a surgeon preparing for a brain operation. He made a couple of realistic sketches and gave the mace back.

'Give me a week,' he said, and seemed to forget all about it.

'Is that all?' Fainy asked uncertainly. 'Shall I take it back?'

'Oh, yes,' Tom answered, closing the matter. Fainy felt it might be part of an act. Staking so much on his brother, he carried the mace back to school.

'He says about a week,' he told McCall.

'Can he fix it?'

'Oh, sure as eggs.'

He left McCall, feeling like a man on a tightrope. It was going to be a long week.

Every day he could feel all eyes in the band upon him. At home Tom went on with his 'I have spoken' act. Fainy thought seriously about prayer.

Then one evening Tom came into the sanctuary with a long object wrapped in old newspapers.

'See how this hits you,' he said, and got busy at his bench.

With trembling fingers Fainy stripped away the wrapping. It was a new mace, complete save for the braiding, resplendent in its polished wood and gleaming chrome-plated head and ferrule. Fainy wanted to shout. It all caught in his throat.

'Gee, Tom . . .'

'What d'you think?' Tom was going through with the act.

'Gee . . . but the whole thing!'

'Thought it was the best way,' Tom said. 'I'll braid it for you after tea.'

'But how'd you do it, the wood and all . . . and the crest and the lions?'

'It was nothing.' Tom indulged himself a little. 'Mate of mine turned the wood. I know a dame at art school and she modelled the lions and stuff and I got them cast. That's a furniture ferrule on the end. I made the dome piece out of a toilet float, screwed the castings on, and got it all chrome-plated. You feel the balance, mate. If he drops this one he doesn't know what he's doing.'

'Gee, Tom. I . . .'

'Is it okay?' Tom nearly gave himself away.

'Is it ever!' Fainy couldn't find the words. He was lost in the presence of the mace.

After tea Tom was true to his word and got busy with the braiding. He braided the mace with the school colours, naming with authority the various knots, passes, and tassels as they appeared. Fainy's head reeled with a myriad terms such as coach-whipping, Nelson braid, shroud knots, and six-pass turks' heads. As the mace grew in beauty there were things in his head as great and profound as the deep impenetrable thing he had about playing in the band. There were things now about his grandfather, who had sailed in ships as had Jack London and Joseph Conrad, and had lived as they had lived, and whose every word that he could remember would now be as precious as gold to him. And there were things too about his brother Tom, who had known their grandfather better, and had kept his words as sacred things, and was sure of his hands, and was a great craftsman, and had made the school mace for love.

When it was finished, the words wouldn't come; he was silent before its beauty. But he knew that Tom understood.

He all but burst with pride when he took the mace to McCall. He knocked on the bandroom door before morning school, and someone from the select hierarchy opened it. When they saw the parcel they let him in.

He thrust it into McCall's hands and waited as they all gathered round. The paper fell away and there it was.

'My God,' somebody said. Somebody else whistled. McCall held it up to catch the light, and they all gaped. Fainy felt their eyes as one by one they remembered he was there and turned to him.

He drank deep of their praises and fled. Most of all he would remember McCall's grateful acknowledgement and friendly hand on his shoulder: 'This parade's going to be one out of the box now, Burridge.'

All that week he was somebody in the band. Mr Lewis thanked him and asked that his compliments be passed on to Tom for such a fine job. The older boys seemed suddenly to be aware that he existed, and even Trumpet Sergeant Clift appeared not to look over his head so much when he spoke to him. McCall, who had always been kind, was exceptionally warm about the whole thing.

That was during the first week. Then it began to die off, and Fainy became himself once more – the third-former Burridge, with the oldest, brightest trumpet and the newest, cleanest braid. All interest focused once more on the mace alone.

It never occurred to Fainy that they had really seen the mace alone in the first place. It never struck him that the boys had no particular respect for Tom as an artisan, or that except in this one case they wouldn't have given twopence for his craftsmanship. When the affair settled down, the mace assumed its rightful proportions, and they trained for the big event as before. But for Fainy there was so much more that came out of the music when they played.

Finally the big day arrived.

It was a Saturday afternoon. Fainy was ready before time and sat needlessly polishing the gleaming trumpet. He felt there was something he wanted to say to Tom, but he wasn't sure about it. In the end he wandered uncertainly into the sanctuary.

Tom was busy at his work-bench, ringing a motorbike piston.

'All ready then, Tiger?' he said.

'I'm a bit early,' Fainy said.

'Better early than keep the general waiting,' Tom offered.

Fainy answered yes, and started to say what he wanted to tell Tom – how he felt about the mace and what Tom had done for him; but it wouldn't come. He stammered and stood there like a fool.

Tom bent over his work.

'Never mind about that,' he said, without looking up. 'You just go in there and blow their eyes out.'

He went out quickly knowing he was going to blow their eyes out all right.

He arrived early, the first bandsman at the rendezvous. They were to fall in at a small playing field a couple of blocks from the main park, and lead the WAAFS down the street and into their place in the show. Fainy stood anxiously waiting for the others.

They came at last, all excited but trying to play it cool. Finally they were all there except Barrett, one of the senior trumpeters. McCall was there with the mace, discussing the programme with the Waaf officers.

Barrett arrived at last. He had no trumpet. He spoke earnestly with Sergeant Clift. It seemed somebody had brought his trumpet into town for him, and there had been a mix-up, and it had been left in a car some place.

There was a hasty council of war. Fainy knew before they spoke to him what they were going to do.

He felt himself handing over his trumpet, hearing Clift's soft, brutal logic: 'Well, it *is* for the good of the band, Burridge . . .'

'That's all right,' Fainy heard himself saying. 'I don't mind.' He was afraid that his voice might crack, his eyes water and give him away.

Barrett accepted the trumpet apologetically: 'Sorry about that, Burridge . . .'

'That's all right,' Fainy said. He let go the trumpet, wondering how anybody could care so little. Just because he can play so well, he thought; to think that it ends there. He stood in a vacuum of shock, holding on to himself, coaxing himself to be brave.

It was time. McCall brought his band together and they fell in like professionals, dressing with precision behind the drummers; with their crossed sticks. Fainy stood without his trumpet, well in the middle of the middle-most rank. An idea came to him; he tried to drive it from his head, but it persisted. He felt that they would have stood him down entirely except for the space to be filled. He remembered Clift's cruel pouting logic: 'It *is* for the good of the band, Burridge . . .' Nobody need know of course. He wondered if he would be able to describe the show to Tom afterwards without actually lying.

They were ready. The WAAFS were ready and waiting. As McCall gave his order, the mace shone in his hand.

'Band – double flam, school tune, by the centre, quick . . . march!'

They marched out of the little playing field and on to the road. The drums played the school tune, and Fainy, truly in the centre of the band, thought of how the WAAFS were marching behind him. He saw without moving his head the people lining the streets. Then McCall gave his double flam and the side drums rolled, and as the trumpets began to play he felt himself encased in their music, so close to being a part of the thing they made it didn't really matter that he wasn't playing. He marched proud and erect, his eyes on the mace.

They marched up the road and through the main gates into the park. The field was a vast arena surrounded by a bubbling vibrant crowd. The distances appeared very great, and the troops already assembled seemed so far away. They marched out on to the field and the people began to applaud.

Fainy was a part of the music. It didn't matter any more about the trumpet. A million visions burst in his brain as they marched, splendid deeds and splendid names like Blenheim and Waterloo and Balaclava, and the march became the ultimate tune of glory, the epitome of a million battle hymns raised to the heavens.

They marched on before the cheering crowd. Then right in front of the grandstand McCall threw the mace.

Fainy saw it from the heart of the music. The mace soared – up and over, and up and over and down – and he heard the roar of the crowd while it was still in the air, as the metal gleamed in the sun and the tassels with the school colours flared, and his ears rang and his eyes stung and the back of his neck tingled with it, and the splendour of it stayed on as the mace returned correctly to McCall's hand, and he saw it still, on and on as they marched, etched into his soul for as long as he might live.

He was fourteen years old, and life was long, and the world was very wide. And the flashing splendour of the mace, flung high, with all the joy and flaunted pride of youth, soaring into the afternoon sun while all the world cheered, was the splendour of an instant that would never fade.

The train pulled into the station. For a moment there was confusion: a voice blaring over the loudspeaker system, people getting off the train, the bustling and shoving of the crowd on the platform.

And there was Dad, waiting for me. We hugged each other. We hadn't seen each other for a long time. Then we kissed. But I could tell something was wrong.

– Your Nanny Miro, he said. She's very sick.

Nanny Miro . . . among all my nannies, she was the one I loved most. Everybody used to say I was her favourite mokopuna, and that she loved me more than her own children who'd grown up and had kids of their own.

She lived down the road from us, right next to the meeting house in the big old homestead which everybody in the village called 'The Museum' because it housed the prized possessions of the whanau, the village family. Because she was rich and had a lot of land, we all used to wonder why Nanny Miro didn't buy a newer, more modern house. But Nanny didn't want to move. She liked her own house just as it was.

– Anyway, she used to say, what with all my haddit kids and their haddit kids and all this haddit whanau being broke all the time and coming to ask me for some money, how can I afford to buy a new house?

Nanny didn't really care about money though. Who needs it? she used to say. What you think I had all these kids for, ay? To look after me, I'm not dumb!

Then she would giggle to herself. But it wasn't true really, because her family would send all their kids to her place when they were broke and she looked after them! She liked her mokopunas, but not for too long. She'd ring up their parents and say:

– Hey! When you coming to pick up your hoha kids! They're wrecking the place!

Yet, always, when they left, she would have a little weep, and give them some money . . .

I used to like going to Nanny's place. For me it was a big treasure house, glistening with sports trophies and photographs, carvings and greenstone, and feather cloaks hanging from the walls.

Most times, a lot of women would be there playing cards with Nanny. Nanny loved all card games – five hundred, poker, canasta, pontoon, whist, euchre – you name it, she could play it.

The sitting room would be crowded with the kuias, all puffing clouds of smoke, dressed in their old clothes, laughing and gossiping about who was pregnant – and relishing all the juicy bits too!

I liked sitting and watching them. Mrs Heta would always be there, and when it came to cards she was both Nanny's best friend and worst enemy. And the two of them were the biggest cheats I ever saw.

Mrs Heta would cough and reach for a hanky while slyly slipping a card from beneath her dress. And she was always reneging in five hundred! But her greatest asset was her eyes, which were big and googly. One eye would look straight ahead, while the other swivelled around, having a look at the cards in the hands of the women sitting next to her.

– Eeee! You cheat! Nanny would say. You just keep your eyes to yourself, Maka tiko bum!

Mrs Heta would look at Nanny as if she were offended. Then she would sniff and say:

– You the cheat yourself, Miro Mananui. I saw you sneaking that ace from the bottom of the pack.

– How do you know I got an ace, Maka? Nanny would say. I know you! You dealt this hand, and you stuck that ace down there for yourself, you cheat! Well, ana! I got it now! So take that!

And she would slap down her hand.

– Sweet, ay? she would laugh. Good? Kapai lalelale? And she would sometimes wiggle her hips, making her victory sweeter.

– Eeee! Miro! Mrs Heta would say. Well, I got a good hand too!

And she would slap her hand down and bellow with laughter.

– Take that!

And always, they would squabble. I often wondered how they ever remained friends. The names they called each other!

Sometimes, I would go and see Nanny and she would be all alone, playing patience. If there was nobody to play with her, she'd always play patience. And still she cheated! I'd see her hands fumbling across the cards, turning up a jack or queen she needed, and then she'd laugh and say:

– I'm too good for this game!

She used to try to teach me some of the games, but I wasn't very interested, and I didn't yell and shout at her like the women did. She liked the bickering.

– Aue . . . she would sigh. Then she'd look at me and begin dealing out the cards in the only game I ever knew how to play.

And we would yell snap! all the afternoon . . .

Now, Nanny was sick.

I went to see her that afternoon after I'd dropped my suitcases at home. Nanny Tama, her husband, opened the door. We embraced and he began to weep on my shoulder.

– Your Nanny Miro, he whispered. She's . . . she's . . .

He couldn't say the words. He motioned me to her bedroom.

Nanny Miro was lying in bed. And she was so old looking. Her face was very grey, and she looked like a tiny wrinkled doll in that big bed. She was so thin now, and seemed all bones.

I walked into the room. She was asleep. I sat down on the bed beside her, and looked at her lovingly.

Even when I was a child, she must have been old. But I'd never realised it. She must have been over seventy now. Why do people you love grow old so suddenly?

The room had a strange, antiseptic smell. Underneath the bed was a big chamber pot, yellow with urine . . . and the pillow was flecked with small spots of blood where she had been coughing.

I shook her gently.

– Nanny . . . Nanny, wake up.

She moaned. A long, hoarse sigh grew on her lips. Her eyelids fluttered, and she looked at me with blank eyes . . . and then tears began to roll down her cheeks.

– Don't cry, Nanny, I said. Don't cry. I'm here.

But she wouldn't stop.

So I sat beside her on the bed and she lifted her hands to me.

– Haere mai, mokopuna. Haere mai. Mmm. Mmm.

And I bent within her arms and we pressed noses.

After a while, she calmed down. She seemed to be her own self.

– What a haddit mokopuna you are, she wept. It's only when I'm just about in my grave that you come to see me.

– I couldn't see you last time I was home, I explained. I was too busy.

– Yes, I know you fullas, she grumbled. It's only when I'm almost dead that you come for some money.

– I don't want your money, Nanny.

– What's wrong with my money! she said. Nothing's wrong with it! Don't you want any?

– Of course I do, I laughed. But I know you! I bet you lost it all on poker!

She giggled. Then she was my Nanny again. The Nanny I knew.

We talked for a long time. I told her about what I was doing in Wellington and all the pretty girls who were after me.

– You teka! She giggled. Who'd want to have you!

And she showed me all her injection needles and pills and told me how she'd wanted to come home from the hospital, so they'd let her.

– You know why I wanted to come home? she asked. I didn't like all those strange nurses looking at my bum when they gave me those injections. I was so sick, mokopuna, I couldn't even go to the lav, and I'd rather wet my own bed not their neat bed. That's why I come home.

Afterwards, I played the piano for Nanny. She used to like *Me He Manurere* so I played it for her, and I could hear her quavering voice singing in her room.

Me he manurere aue . . .

When I finally left Nanny I told her I would come back in the morning.

But that night, Nanny Tama rang up.

– Your Nanny Miro, she's dying.

We all rushed to Nanny's house. It was already crowded. All the old women were there. Nanny was lying very still. Then she looked up and whispered to Mrs Heta:

– Maka . . . Maka tiko bum . . . I want a game of cards . . .

A pack of cards was found. The old ladies sat around the bed, playing. Everybody else decided to play cards too, to keep Nanny company. The men played poker in the kitchen and sitting room. The kids played snap in the other bedrooms. The house overflowed with card players, even onto the lawn outside Nanny's window, where she could see . . .

The women laid the cards out on the bed. They dealt the first hand. They laughed and joked with Nanny, trying not to cry. And Mrs Heta kept saying to Nanny:

– Eee! You cheat, Miro. You cheat! And she made her googly eye reach far over to see Nanny's cards.

– You think you can see, ay, Maka tiko bum? Nanny coughed. You think you're going to win this hand, ay? Well, take that!

She slammed down a full house.

The other women goggled at the cards. Mrs Heta looked at her own cards. Then she smiled through her tears and yelled:

– Eee! You cheat, Miro! I got two aces in my hand already! Only four in the pack. So how come you got three aces in your hand?

Everybody laughed. Nanny and Mrs Heta started squabbling as they always did, pointing at each other and saying: You the cheat, not me! And Nanny Miro said: I saw you, Maka tiko bum. I saw you sneaking that card from under the blanket.

She began to laugh. Quietly. Her eyes streaming with tears.

And while she was laughing, she died.

Everybody was silent. Then Mrs Heta took the cards from Nanny's hands and kissed her.

    – You the cheat, Miro, she whispered. You the cheat yourself . . .

We buried Nanny on the hill with the rest of her family. During her tangi, Mrs Heta played patience with Nanny, spreading the cards across the casket.

    Later in the year, Mrs Heta, she died too. She was buried right next to Nanny, so that they could keep on playing cards . . .

    And I bet you they're still squabbling up there . . . .

    – Eee! You cheat, Miro . . .

    – You the cheat, Maka tiko bum. You, you the cheat . . .

MAURICE GEE

Mercy tied her father's scarf in a mean granny knot.

'Now remember, darling, if you want the little house just bang on the wall. We don't want any wets with the girls all here.' And Barbie, gentler, but not to be outdone, knelt and zipped up his slippers. 'You'll be lovely and warm in the sun, won't you? Just bang on the wall. No little accidents please. 'Bye, daddums.'

They left him in his rocking chair on the veranda and he rocked a little, pitying their innocence. He did not mean to pee in his pants today. He had other plans.

Presently the 'girls' came, driving their little cars; and they walked up the path in twos and threes, dumpy women or stringy, the lot, in Saturday clothes and coloured hair. They stopped for a little chat of course, politely, and sniffed behind their hands to see if he had behaved himself today. They were good-hearted women. Mercy and Barbie attracted such.

'Lucky you, Mr Pitt-Rimmer. Just loafing in the sun.'

He counted them. Ten. Three tables. There was Madge Ogden, a daughter of divorcees; and Pearl Edwards who taught mathematics at the Girls' High School; and Mary Rendt who had wanted to be a nun but had lost her faith and married a German Christian Scientist and lost that faith and her husband too; and the three Bailey girls, with not a husband amongst them, whose mother had broken their hearts by choosing to live in an old people's home; and Christine Hunt who had been caught shoplifting when she was a girl and lived it down and married the son of the mayor; and Jean Murray-Briggs, whose name annoyed him; and last the lesbians, though none of the other knew – Phyllis Wedderburn and Margaret Way. Charles Pitt-Rimmer, he knew. He winked at them and they blushed, but seemed a little pleased.

'Such lovely sun. We've only got old bridge.'

He gave them time to get warmed up. Mercy looked out once and wagged her finger, and Barbie once kissed him on the cheek.

They would forget him when they were well ahead. His daughters were the top pair in the district and he wished he could feel more pleased with them for it.

When the time came he stood up and walked along the veranda. He went down the path, down the steps, along the footpath to the park, and into the trees. It was twenty-nine minutes past two. He had run away twice before. Today he would outfox them. He would keep away from roads and butcher shops, where he had been caught twice before looking at roasts of beef. They would not think of searching on the hill.

Girls, he wrote in his mind, *There are other things than meat. Your father played chess.*

At nineteen minutes to three he reached the dairy. 'Here, you children, out of my way,' he said, and they stood aside with a quickness that pleased him. He did not mind that they giggled. That was proper in children.

'A bag of Turkish delight,' he said. He had planned it all morning and it came out with an English sound. 'And a packet of cigarettes.'

The woman behind the counter had a half-witted face, a nose that seemed to snuffle for scent like a dog's. She gave a smile and said, 'It's Mr Pitt-Rimmer, isn't it?'

'My name is not your concern. Turkish delight, and a packet of cigarettes.'

'Sit down, Mr Pitt-Rimmer. There's a chair right there. As soon as I've served these kiddies I'll ring Mrs Parsloe.'

'You will not ring Mrs Parsley. I wish to be served. Am I a customer or am I not? And are you in business? Answer me that.'

He was pleased to see confusion in her eyes. 'I'll have de Reszke.'

'Whosie?'

'De Reszke. You don't seem to know your business, madam. Do you make a living? I wonder at it.'

'There's nothing here called de Reszke.'

'Cigarettes. Cigarettes. Named after a great operatic tenor. Before your time, of course. I understand. It's all Bing Crosby today.'

The woman went suddenly to the telephone. 'You kiddies wait.' She started to dial.

'Very well,' cried Charles Pitt-Rimmer. 'You may ring Mrs Parsley. Tell her I'm striking out. I have my life. Tell her I'm smoking again. De Reszke. And eating Turkish delight.' He stopped at the door. 'And if she wishes to know where I am you may say that I've gone to the butcher's for a piece of German sausage.'

'Mrs Parsloe?' the woman said. 'It's the Regal dairy. Your father's here.'

He was very pleased with himself as he turned up the hill. Capablanca would have been proud of that move.

Girls, bridge is for simple folk. You must think ahead. I've never cared for German sausage.

He looked at his watch. It was thirteen minutes to three. Already he had beaten his old record. He pictured the little cars scuttling about Hardinge, driven in a dangerous manner by women with blue and pink hair. Barbie would be crying – he was sorry about that – and Mercy with her eye like a hanging judge's.

Girls, a man's a man for a' that.

He followed a path into the trees and climbed until he stood on the edge of the cliff with the wharves below him. Three minutes past three. He would have liked some Turkish delight. He had not had any since his last day in court, which was twenty-two years ago. His secretary used to bring in a paper bag full with his lunch. The gob-stopper he'd taken from the Regal dairy's counter would be no substitute. But he found that he enjoyed it once he'd torn the paper off. It tasted of raspberry, a flavour he'd forgotten.

He went to the safety fence and looked down. A girl had jumped down there on Boxing Day because her employer, a well-known man in Hardinge, had put her in the family way. She had lived for two hours but not said a word. He had heard Mercy and Barbie discussing it, in voices hushed but full of glee and dread. The man, Barbie said, was 'a weed in the garden of life' – which she'd pinched from her mother, who had also believed that such men should be hanged. Women had a poor understanding of certain needs.

The gob-stopper made him feel bilious. He put it in his pocket. Below him ships were tied up at the wharves, all piddling water out of their sides. One of them was a phosphate tub, moored at a wharf that he remembered now was Pitt-Rimmer Wharf. There had been those years on the Harbour Board – a tedious business. Jack Hunt had picked his nose behind the agenda. The Hunts had never been up to much, though they liked to believe that they were the bosses of Hardinge. He walked on and the cape came into sight, standing up like Chunuk Bair. He had no wish to be reminded of that. That had been a very great piece of nonsense.

Girls, you persist in reminding me . . .

A woman came towards him leading a tiny black dog in a tartan jacket.

'I don't care for dogs, madam. Keep him off.'

'Mr Pitt-Rimmer. Don't you remember me?'

'I've met many people. Fifteen thousand is my calculation.'

'But I'm Maisie Transome. Maisie Jack that was. You used to give me lollies.'

'Your mother was an excellent secretary. And a kindly soul. She had extraordinary bosoms.'

'Ooh, Mr Pitt-Rimmer, you're a rogue.'

'I don't care for animals sniffing about my feet.'

'Come here, Bruce. Where are your manners, darling? Mr Pitt-Rimmer, can I walk home with you? You shouldn't be out you know, dressed like that. Barbie told me you're being very naughty.'

'My daughter has more kindness than sense. She's a good woman but she's had a tragic life.'

'Who? Barbie?'

'She fell in love with a young man in my office. Parsley was his name. Mercy stole him away. "Mercy" was not my choice. I want that understood. My wife had a poor grip on reality. But Parsley – she married him and broke her sister's heart. Barbie never married. Parsley was not a good catch, mind you. She was well out of it. He played around as they say. There was a woman in my office called Rona Jack. Her marriage was unsatisfactory. Parsley used to visit there.'

'Oh Mr Pitt-Rimmer –'

'He died of course. They nursed him. My daughters are good girls.'

'But my parents had an ideal marriage. They were in love till the day they died.'

'Indeed. I congratulate them. You should not speak with strangers. The risks are very great. Good day to you.'

'But I'm taking you home, remember?'

'I wish to relieve myself.'

She did not follow him though her dog yapped in an impertinent way. The path led downhill and had many troublesome curves. His legs began to be sore. But a bank of nasturtiums pleased him and a smell of fennel. Fennel made him think of aniseed balls. He stopped at the memory. When sucked an aniseed ball turned white. And Turkish delight left sugar round the mouth.

Girls, when you were children I bought you sweets. Straps of liquorice. Be fair. Bags of sherbet. Bags of chocolate fudge.

The path ended by the Salvation Army Eventide Home. Two old men were sitting on a bench. 'A glorious morning, comrade,' one of them said.

'Glorious,' Charles Pitt-Rimmer agreed, smiling at his better knowledge.

It was twenty-nine minutes past three in the afternoon and his daughters were thoroughly bamboozled. He stopped by the reservoir and sat down on a bank. A boy was walking along a pipe, and a smaller boy rode up on a tricycle.

'Why are you wearing your dressing-gown?'

'Old men are allowed to.'

'Mummy makes me get dressed. Have you wet your pants?'

'I believe I have.'

'Couldn't you find a toilet? You could use ours.'

'The word is lavatory. You should not be frightened of calling things by their names.'

'Mummy said lavatory's not nice.'

'And you should not pay too much attention to women.'

Charles Pitt-Rimmer dozed for a moment. 'Poor Parsley. They made him eat his vegetables. Curly kale. A weed.'

'Mummy makes me eat my vegetables.'

'What do you have for pudding?'

His mind was lucid about food but cloudy about everything else. He was not quite sure where he was. 'My favourite is lemon meringue pie.' He felt in his pocket for the gob-stopper and gave it to the child who put it in his mouth at once, leaving only the stick poking out.

'You speak too much of your mother. The conspiracy starts at the cradle.'

The boy who had been walking on the pipe ran up to join them.

'Give us a lick, Tony. Come on.'

Charles Pitt-Rimmer went to sleep. He believed he was in a bath of lukewarm water that was turning cold about his legs. Soon he was wakened by a woman's voice.

'Let me see that. Give it to me at once. It's filthy. It's got a hair on it.'

She moved her arm violently and the boy on the tricycle cried. Charles did not know what was happening, but he saw that the woman was looking at him with hatred and was astonished at the ease with which people felt this emotion. Forty years of court work had not got him used to it.

'Beware, madam. It can get to be a habit.'

'You ought to be ashamed of yourself. And you' – she rounded on the older boy – 'I told you to look after him. Why can't you listen for once? Get into the wash house and wait till your father comes home.'

Now the older boy cried. They were an emotional family and seemed to be without reason, Charles decided. They vanished and he was relieved. He lay on the bank and tried to sleep, curled into a ball to defeat the cold. Where were his daughters? Where were the wretched women?

Girls, you're selfish creatures . . .

Again a woman woke him. This time it was Christine Hunt, with her hair like candy floss. He reached out for some.

'What are you doing? Oh! Mr Pitt-Rimmer. Let go.'

'Christine Perkins, you were lucky to get off with a fine. If you hadn't had me to conduct your defence you would have gone to prison.'

'Oh! Oh! My hair. You've ruined it.'

'Why did you choose such frilly things, Christine? If you remember, I told the court they were for your glory box? A clever touch. But you can tell me. I can be discreet.'

'You're a horrible man. Oh, look, you've wet your pyjamas. This is dreadful.'

'I understand, Christine. It's difficult to be poor. No nice frillies, eh? A girl likes frillies. But I always believed you married beneath you. Your father-in-law picks his nose.'

'My father-in-law has been dead for twenty years. And you've ruined our afternoon. You know that, don't you? It's a wonder to me how Mercy and Barbie keep going. They must be saints.'

'They're vegetarians. They struggle to ward off despair. I do my best.'

'Mr Pitt-Rimmer, I'm going to take you home. I am. Now come with me. Come on.'

She put out her hand and he was appalled at the size of it. It went right around his wrist, and her silver nails poked up from the underside. She was appalled too. She jerked away.

'Barbie will be the invalid when I'm dead,' said Charles Pitt-Rimmer.

Christine Hunt went away. 'I'm going to get your daughters. Don't you move.' Her little car scuttled off, and Charles lay curled up tightly.

Girls, it's time for my nap. You're selfish creatures . . .

'Oh daddums, daddums, why do you do these things?'

'Put down the rubber sheet, Barbie. No, spread it out, you ninny.'

They put him in the back seat and Barbie sat with him, rubbing his hands.

'You're so naughty, so naughty –'

'I've had enough,' Mercy cried. 'I'm going to put you in a home. You've made a fool of me for the last time. Wipe his mouth Barbie, can't you see?'

'You make it so hard for us, daddums. Oh, your hands are so cold.'

'I walked on the pipe, Mercy. If I'd fallen off you would never have been born.'

They washed him and put him to bed. He slept smiling for two hours, then rang his bell for tea. They propped him up with pillows, and Barbie sat with him while he ate.

'It's a special salad, daddums. One Mercy found. It's got avocados in it. Now drink your apple juice.'

She took away the tray and came back with his library book.

'Promise me you won't be naughty again. It makes us so sad.'

'What was the time when you caught me?'

'Four o'clock. You were gone for two hours. Oh daddums –'

'An hour and thirty-one minutes.' He grinned at her.

When she had gone he finished his book. He corrected one split infinitive and underlined two mentions of female breasts. Then he made his secret sign on page eighty-eight.

Barbie was doing the dishes and Mercy watching a television show full of American voices. On the final page, below a scene of love, Charles wrote a message:

My daughters are keeping me prisoner. Help! I have not had a piece of meat for twenty years . . .

Wilma told me of a talk she had with her mother one day. 'I'm sick of learning the violin off Mr Henderson. I want to learn the guitar off Mr Wood. He played the guitar for Josephine last night at the school social. It was beauty.'

From what I gathered, her mother answered, 'I didn't know Mr Wood played the guitar. I knew he played the piano and he drinks.'

Then Wilma said, 'He can play the guitar all right. Josephine said she never sang better. She reckoned it was Mr Wood that made her sing like she did. Gee, he can play all right. All the kids clapped like mad.'

Her mother rang my mother up and made an appointment. In the murky gloom of an October dusk Wilma kept her appointment.

The night before the band had played until five a.m. (so it might be better to say the morning before); one of the biggest sessions of spanking chords on the most beat-up piano I want to forget. I could light a lot of fires with that piano.

When the bell rang there was Wilma holding a guitar case. I was on the phone booking in another job for the band when she rang. I was half asleep and I was dressed in a pair of crumpled slacks, a pyjama jacket and I remember I was wearing carpet slippers with a great big hole in the toe of one of them. I had had a bath the day before so at least I was clean but I had forgotten to cut my toenails.

There was no one else in our big old house at the time so I had to go to the door myself. I rolled up my pyjama sleeves and put on an overcoat. The bell rang again but I still took time out to light a cigarette before I went to the door.

And there was Wilma. I was too tired to see what a cute-looking kid she was, but I remembered the moment I saw she was carrying a guitar case that my mother had booked in my first pupil. She saved me the trouble of trying to remember her name. She said, 'I'm Wilma so and so.'

'Come on in, Wilma.'

Wilma followed me down a long passage and I took her into a room with the oldest grand piano in the world in it. She was so interested in the big flat piano that she put her guitar case on the floor and she leaned over to look under the raised rosewood lid. I bent down and unsnapped the clips of the guitar case.

It was winter and in the Antipodes this can be the beginning of spring or it can be the heart of winter. It depended on the schools what sort of uniforms the girls wore. It was so cold this October that the pupils were in winter clothing and I guess the only thing I noticed were Wilma's worn and badly laddered black stockings and about an inch of flesh above them.

A hangover raises your blood pressure, your temperature, and makes you as sexy as a pedigree ram. While I was undoing the second clip on the case I tipped the whole damned case over because I was so busy looking up Wilma's legs.

My pyjama sleeves had become unrolled and were now showing around my wrists. My cigarette had fallen on to the top of the overturned guitar case. It was only half-smoked so I picked it up and had a drag. Wilma said, 'I've never seen a big piano like this before.'

I told her there were bigger pianos. I told her about table grands and concert grands. By this time she had stood up straight again so there wasn't any point in trying to see any further up her legs. Standing up must have taken a bit of the blood away from my head but I was still shaking a bit with a mixture of passion, self-control and alcoholic withdrawal.

'Look here, Wilma, how's about you hook out this cigar box of yours while I get myself a handkerchief.' I could tell she was looking at my pyjama sleeves.

I went down another long passage which led to the dining-room. The decanter on the sideboard was three-quarters full of whisky. I grabbed a seven ounce tumbler and poured myself a jolt that would have knocked a horse over; but all it did to me was make me drop my cigarette again with the first gulp. When I had drained the glass my stomach was hot and I counted up to ten to hold the booze down. I could feel my don't-give-a-damn attitude coming back. I picked up the cigarette which hadn't even scorched the Wilton. I pushed up my pyjama sleeves. Then I went back to Wilma.

Wilma said, 'I think it's out of tune. Mr Henderson was for ever telling me my violin was out of tune.'

That was when she told me about the conversation she had with her mother about leaving Mr Henderson. She gave it to me pretty nearly verbatim including the coda about me drinking. She grinned and I began to like her.

'Wilma,' I said, 'I'm sorry it's so cold in here. I'll put the heater on.'

To put the heater on in this music room was a fairly complicated business. It involved finding a long lead for one thing and a second jolt of whisky for another. After this I felt fine.

Just then someone started playing major scales in the next room so I knew my mother was home teaching one of her pupils. Although my mother loved me to distraction I had enough intuition to know she had a dreadful fear of me becoming an out-and-out waster. I was making good money in the band but no one knew better than she or myself that the bulk of it was going on booze. It hit me right in the guts when I remembered how happy she looked when she told me that I had my first guitar pupil. Mum's pupil was playing the scale of D major now so I decided I could have another jolt before it got played contrary motion. Back I went to Wilma.

The first thing I did was tune her guitar. If her violin was anything like her guitar it would have made Stradivarius turn cartwheels.

Then I made a tremendous effort. I tore some pages out of the back of an exercise book and taught Wilma the diagram system, four chords and a simple practice routine. I explained it all very carefully and she seemed to dig. She had good hands. While I was doing this my mother looked in and smiled at us both.

I said, 'Practise that, Wilma.' And then, Lord save us, I fell asleep. Wilma woke me up about half an hour later and said she would have to go.

I told her I had been playing the piano all night in a dance band.

'Wilma, I'm awfully sorry about this. I really am. Now, have you got your chords? Next week, Wilma, I'll be as fresh as a daisy.'

'That's all right, Mr Wood,' she said. She looked a bit cheesed off.

'I really am awfully sorry about dozing off, Wilma,' I said. 'You better not tell your folks about me dozing off like that. Crumbs, they'll think I'm a great teacher if you tell them that.'

And then Wilma did something I shall never ever forget. She crossed herself and made that age-old pretence of cutting her throat with a finger. I was so relieved that I made the first big blue of the day. I reached over and tried to kiss her but she ducked underneath my arm and walked out the door. I followed her down the hall and said, or rather croaked, 'Wilma,' but she didn't answer me so all I could do was let her out.

I felt ghastly. I was twenty-three years old and she was thirteen. Jail-bait and I was hooked. Nothing desperate had happened but she only had to blow it up a little to get me in real hot water. There was only one thing to do. I went back to the sideboard and poured myself a massive slug. Mum was still teaching in the front studio and I could have cut my throat.

Then the bell rang and I went down the long hall and opened the front door. There were two girls there. One was my blonde girlfriend who had been chasing me for eighteen months and the other was Wilma. I had no intention of marrying Dulcie because her family was downright common and she could swear like a bullock driver. I put on a big act. 'Come on in, girls. Dulcie, Wilma, come on in.'

Dulcie said, 'My God, do you have to wear an overcoat *inside* the house?' Neither of them had stepped inside yet. Maybe my breath was like a barbed wire fence.

Wilma said, 'Can I have my guitar please?'

'Shucks, Wilma, fancy forgetting your guitar. Come on, we'll get it now.

So, keeping as steady as I could, I set off back along the long hall. I went into the room where the grand piano was and there was the guitar propped against the keyboard. The case was on the floor beside the chair

I had fallen asleep on.

Wilma walked so softly that I didn't even know she was behind me. It wasn't until I turned around with the guitar and stooped down to put it back in its case that I saw her black stockinged legs about two feet in front of my glazed eyes.

The lid of the case was open towards me which meant I was doing everything back to front. I put the guitar down on the floor while I turned the case around. Wilma crouched down and her gym frock rode up. Now I could see five or more inches of bare leg above the black stockings and the tightest little pair of pants you ever saw in your life. They were like a snow-white handkerchief pulled into her crutch.

'Jesus,' I said huskily. 'You got nice legs, Wilma.'

'Thank you,' said Wilma primly.

I reached out and ran my hand up the inside of her left leg. She stood up quickly. I shut up the case and fastened the clips, just numb fumbling. She took the handle of the guitar case and picked it up and I lurched upright.

My blonde twenty-year-old girlfriend, Dulcie, was standing in the doorway. She said, 'I get the picture.'

Wilma couldn't get past Dulcie and she said, 'Can I leave, please? I'm late for tea.' It was quite dark outside now.

Dulcie was so mad she didn't budge. Wilma did the nicest thing since she crossed her heart and cut her throat. She squeezed past Dulcie, belting her to one side with the guitar case. Dulcie took a smack at her but she missed by nearly as much as I had done when I tried to kiss her.

'I'm going to put you up for carnal knowledge,' said Dulcie viciously. 'You dirty, lecherous, rotten bastard.'

The front door slammed. Wilma had found her way out.

'In your pyjamas and overcoat,' Dulcie said. 'You're nothing but a ratbag.'

Deep inside me I felt I was doomed, but the Scotch reasserted itself to give me enough bravado to say, 'What's wrong with this overcoat? You liked it well enough when you had your bare bum on it beside my car the other night.'

I fished out my packet of cigarettes and there was only one left. I went over to the heater to light it. I had one eye on Dulcie in case she belted me over the skull. Just as I had my smoke going nicely she made a threatening twitch in my direction but I stood up fast and she knew how well I could fight, so she spun around and walked away. As she went down the hall she called out. 'Ratbag.'

Poor old Mum came out of the front studio without knowing all the trouble there had been. Dulcie must have looked pretty grim but at least she had the good grace to say (or snarl), 'Good night, Mrs Wood.'

I didn't have to play for a dance that night so I went and got a new pack of smokes and headed for the sideboard.

I said I was off my tucker, which was nothing but the truth, and all I wanted to do was go to bed. Instead of undressing I just slumped down on the side of the bed and chain smoked.

Mum came into my bedroom and kissed me goodnight and said, 'Well you had your first little pupil today.' It would be an insult to the reader's intelligence to describe what went though my mind when she said that.

'Of course she'll tell,' I brooded and muttered. 'A kid like that. She won't be able to help it. I'll just have to deny everything. The police'll be here tomorrow. Even tonight. This'll kill Mum.'

My mind went over the same track so often I thought I was going nuts. When the front doorbell did ring, although my heart missed a couple of beats, it was a relief.

There was the outline of a big guy in the front porch.

'Mr Wood?'

'Too late to hush it up now,' the Scotch in me said, and I attempted a friendly smile.

'I'm Wilma's father.'

'C'mon in.' I opened the door wide and stood back. He came in. He was big sure enough; tall, broad and he had bushy eyebrows.

'You know what Wilma tells me?' he said. No smile.

I shook my head. It nearly fell off.

'She left her guitar behind after her lesson.'

'Holy smoke,' I said. 'I'll have a look.'

Sure enough the guitar was lying on the floor by the grand.

When I took it back to him, he said, 'Can you imagine a girl being so dumb she didn't know the difference between an empty case and a full one?'

I frowned, tucked my chin in on my Adam's apple and made a clicking noise with my tongue. 'Beats me.'

After we had said good night I did what those heroines in the old movies used to do. As soon as I had closed the door I put my back against it and leaned there with my eyes closed.

It was my big day for doing crazy things. Later on, in the dark, my bedroom, pyjamas, on my marrowbones, I offered up thanks to the mysterious Creator who, on reflection, by imbuing me with passion (and all of us, for that matter) and making us what we are, was the true culprit of the episode.

'Keep the dogs in.'

The man went around the cattle. Then he was indistinct in the dark.

The boy called the dogs in. He listened to the wires snap one by one.

'Come on,' called the man.

The boy felt his way over the logs and through the fern and rocks. He came up behind the cattle and drove them through the gap in the fence. The man tapped their backs with his crook as he counted them. They took a long time to go through. The man shouted for the dogs to shut up and stay behind.

'Hear the morepork?' asked the boy.

'Laughing owl,' said the man.

'Owl?'

'They live in the Park. Everything lives in the Park.'

They lugged the fence back across the opening.

An invisible owl laughed overhead.

On the other side of the fence the cattle were eating already.

'Will we have to pay?' asked the boy.

'Just listen to those birds,' said the man.

'Will we get the cattle back?' asked the boy.

'Twice as many again.'

'They won't die out there?'

'Die out there? In the Park? Goodness me, they're in seventh heaven!'

The boy stood with his hands between the barbs on the fence. Matai, miro and totara made a second storey of bush, while the tallest rimus were skyscrapers with smudgy balconies of orchid and fern. Supplejack hung like licorice.

'Listen to the woodhens,' said the boy.

'Yes,' said the man, 'those are woodhens.'

Several invisible owls flew and laughed high overhead.

'They're spooky,' said the boy.

'They like the dark,' said the man. 'That's all. Now help me with the fence.'

The boy bent down feeling about for the wire. He bumped against the man.

'Owls like dark nights,' said the man.

Together in the dark they could have been the same person.

A long-drawn cry, plaintive and clear, came from near or far.

'What's that?' cried the boy.

'A cuckoo,' said the man. 'It should have gone.'

'Gone?' said the boy.

'They come for summer,' said the man.

'Where do they go?' asked the boy.

'New Guinea,' said the man.

A woodhen drummed and then shrilled three times. Another bird went *chop-chop-chop*. The wire twanged and raunched as the man strained it.

'It's a concrete post,' said the boy.

'The Park's got everything! Roads. Water. Deer. Birds. Everything!'

The man tested the seven wires.

'Now they've got cattle!' He shook the fence. 'Let's go.'

Together they started back. The cattle went on tearing at the trees in the Park.

'They get rain when we never see a drop,' said the man.

'Those concrete posts must last a long time,' said the boy.

'At first there was no fence. For a long time there was no boundary fence. Now they've built a bloody fort!'

'Those concrete posts must be good for burning-off.'

' – we were part of that Park once, by Christ!'

'Our posts are all burnt.'

'Our posts are all right.'

The land fell away and it was downhill going with the ridges on either side. Now back over their shoulders in the west there was no moon.

'Follow the dogs,' said the man.

The boy felt his way along the track. The dislodged stones rolled a long time.

'This land isn't fit for goats!' The man swung his crook and slashed the scalloped limestone.

'Tell me about that stick – ' said the boy.

'Shepherd's crook.'

' – your shepherd's crook.'

'It was your grandfather's.'

'I know – '

'One day it will be yours.'

The boy did not lift his boots high and he kept his weight on his back foot until his front foot was safely down.

Possum paws scrabbled uselessly on limestone.

'Damn the dogs!'

'They're not even hungry,' said the boy.

'Those dogs are full as ticks! Stuffed full on heifers dead of starvation!' The man slashed the pup with the crook. 'Keep that cur behind you!'

The boy watched for the dogs and for the man's crook and he waited for the lightning.

'I should be able to follow the bloody track,' said the man. 'My first year out of school I rode out here every day. But the horse knew the way, and the path is not so good now.'

'Was it a bridle path?'

'It was madness. My father should never have bought this land.'

'I know.'

'He bought this godforsaken place to please my mother. That's why he bought it, and he never got rid of it.'

'Because of Gran?'

'He did what she wanted and that was that. Do you know, I got up before daylight every morning to ride out here. My first year out of school. I used to ride out with a married man who lived in the cottage – the hayshed was a cottage in those days. A single man camped out here, and when we got here we had breakfast.'

'Did he have a tent?'

'One of us would go ahead scrubbing. Slashing the undergrowth. The others cut the trees. We cut them up to three feet in diameter. We felled them all one way. When they were dry we burned the bush.'

'I know,' said the boy, and watched the man's crook.

'Nothing would stop the fires. They went up the bluffs and burnt the sky. Ash blew to Australia. Sparks landed on the house like brimstone. I spent whole nights on the roof. The women went to the city.'

The man stopped walking.

'We all should have gone – and never come back! Not for this! None of us should ever have come back!'

The pup's tail tapped the boy's leg. The boy's heart thudded like a dislodged stone. The bluffs walled up the dark.

'Aren't you had it?' said the man.

'No. Just hungry.'

'All for this!'

The man's hobnails struck fire in the dried-up creekbeds. Dead fuchsias lined the dried-up creeks like empty webs. The man's boots struck fire from the stones in the creekbeds. Woeful sheep jerked away.

The boy listened to how his grandfather should never have bought their land.

The boy listened to how his grandmother wanted to be queen of the mountains.

'She says she's queen of the mountains,' he said.

'Damn her!'

'Is she dippy?'

'She's old – '

' – her hands shake a lot.'

'She used to be clever with her hands. She spun a very old-fashioned way. She wound wool around a staff. She even spun flax from that staff.'

'When Mum was here, she had a spinning wheel.'

'She did.'

'It was spooky.'

'Women have always had those things.'

'I won't let my wife spin,' said the boy. 'If I have a wife.'

'You have no say,' said the man.

'I'll be a single man.'

'Yes, but someday you'll want a son.'

'You don't know.'

'Someone will want a son and you'll be the father.'

'If I have a son,' said the boy, and felt for the path behind his father.

'Don't ever be out here alone. There are enough bones in these holes. It's all right for me,' said the man. 'I know the way the gullies lie. I know the cliffs and the pot-holes.'

The lightning lit the stumps and burnt them black again.

'Damn the pot-holes!' cried the man, and slashed the limestone with his crook.

They came out on a spur and saw the glow of the city to the north-east but in between was a great pitblack pot-hole and the rest of the farm fell in the pit and they walked down into it and the night lay over the land like ash.

'You'd be nix if you were out here by yourself,' said the man.

'I'd find my way.'

'You'd wander around till kingdom come.'

'I've been this way before.'

'What way?'

'I've come this way in the dark before.'

'You must have dreamt it.'

White stumps populated the dark as though the man mustered them with his curses.

'I left school to fell this bush. She said I would be a man while the rest stayed boys.'

'How old were you?'

'We burned the bush and underneath it was stone. This land is all stone.' The man snorted. 'We're rich – rich in rock!' He spat. 'Rich as Pluto!'

'That shepherd's crook – '

'It was my father's. It's going to be yours.'

'Yes, I know – '

'Well?'

'It's a wonder it wasn't burnt – '

'Damn the crook!'

The boy kept the pup behind him and followed his father home. Their boots kicked the sides of the narrow sheeptracks cut into the granite between the stumps and the logs.

'How are you?' said the man.

'I'm all right.'

'You don't want a rest?'

'No. I'm all right.'

'How are your feet?'

'They're all right.'

'Give me the pack.'

'I can manage.'

The man's hobnails struck sparks. Each footfall was a furious description of sound.

They pushed through bidibid and briar and smelled the burning carcasses in the holding paddock at the bottom of the valley.

'When did you stop burning the bush?' asked the boy.

'When my father died.'

'I know how he died.'

'Damn you all!'

'Was he going to sell?'

'Was he damn well what?'

'Going to sell – '

'You can't sell land like this!'

The boy felt the night pressing on them. He thought of his grandfather's body, roped across his father's saddle like all the slabs of totara and rimu he had brought home over the years for the woodbox in the kitchen. He thought of the horse, how it knew the way, how it would falter and shy with the knowledge that it bore a dead man, and how its iron shoes would ring sparks from the stones in the dark. He thought of his grandfather trapped and suffocating in the billowing smoke of his own fire, collapsed, like a fallen tree, over his shiny crook. And he thought of the land, lustrous like priceless moonstone under the iron horseshoes, and then he thought of his mother who never came back from the city and his grandmother who did and another woman who somehow was all the women he knew put together, a daughter unavoidable as the night in which he followed, like a dog, the man and the memory of a man through the dark.

They had saved the surviving cattle and he could smell the man's sweat and he wanted to say that he liked being with him and helping him but he didn't say anything.

The dogs they had left chained up were barking. They went through the iron gates. The poplars stood black over shucked leaves. They passed the hayshed which had once been a cottage for a married man. The hydraulic ram creaked and clanked. They smelled the carbon from the gas-house.

Together they poked the unburned hooves and shins into the smouldering fires. The hair sparkled and died. The hides burned pungently. The man dragged palings from the cattle yards to stoke the blaze. The boy raked the earth around the fires to stop them spreading into the parched paddocks. The flames lit the man's beard like a libation of blood spilt and congealed on his chin.

'Don't get morbid!' he cried. 'Don't think about these beasts – they were skin and bone, they had to die. They'll make good ash. We'll dig this ground for spuds. Don't think about it. Think of the cattle in the Park – standing in water with leaves on their heads!' A decrescent moon of sparks hung from his flaying crook. He booted embers into the air. 'Damn the drought! Tie the dogs!'

The dogs strained at their chains and the boy felt their flying slaver.

The man's hobnails were lost and soundless on the lawn.

The boy smelled the mint and the rosemary outside the wash-house door.

The man hung his crook beside the copper and sat on the form and dropped his boots on to the floor.

He splashed his face with water. The water was loud and then soft as the soap lathered. He left soap behind his ears.

He left the water for the boy.

He took the food out of the oven and they ate quietly.

From his bedroom the boy heard the sprinklers on the lawn and the pup howling. Then he heard the man belting the pup and saying he'd kill him if he didn't bloody well lie down and shut up.

The dark was a cowhide of fire and mint and rosemary.

He heard invisible laughter.

Then gaslight from the hall fell across the boy's bed and he smelled the old woman in her white nightgown. Her shadow swaddled him, flew into the corner behind his bed and rose up like black wings high overhead.

'You can't leave land like this,' she said. 'If you leave it the bush comes back and you might as well never have been born. Now turn your pillow over and go to sleep.'

KERI HULME

You said, write it all down, write it out, put it in writing.

Well, I will try.

It is not easy.

After years of marking essays, one is inclined to mark oneself. Teaching a craft tends to make one overly sensitive and, thus, ill at ease when handling it. One becomes a critic rather than a practitioner.

However, I will try. I will take it as it comes.

I am neither young nor old. I suppose I had a sheltered childhood, and have led a sheltered life. For as long as I can remember, I wanted to engage in an academic career. I have been a lecturer for some years, with some success. My career has not been meteoric, but it hasn't been a failure. I have been out here for three months.

You said to mention the physical details as much as possible. There isn't that much to me, physically speaking.

I am not tall, I am not beautiful, but I am not ugly. I look puffed, like swollen dough, yet my nose is sharp and my fingers are long and thin. This is a family discrepancy, I mean trait.

It had been a usual kind of night, that is disturbed. Fogged. Anaesthetised.

I will try to make it *present*.

The day is bright.

At least, outside the day is bright. In here it's the same as it is at night, dark and stale and still.

The doorbell shrills a high continuing summons.

I have been trying to clean up, ever since I heard the car sound the horn. The horn was a challenge, the blare a knight crusading might have made, outside castle perilous.

The clamour stops.

I open the door.

Half a dozen of them, and M and K and C and D, bright in their summer clothes.

They importune,

'Come with us eh!'

and the children dart round, flashy and venomous as tropical fish.

I suppose I look furtive and sleepy-eyed, but they don't seem to notice. They chorus,

'It's a beaut day!' 'The weather's corker!' 'We'll have a neat time!' 'C'mon! C'mon!'

I cannot get used to the way they truncate, abuse, alter the language. 'What?'

'We're goin' to tha beach!'

They grin collectively, they all smile, they exude friendliness.

'It'll bring you out of your moodiness,' murmurs K. 'Chase away those blues eh?'

'Moodiness? Blues?' I disclaim them, but the demon children latch on the words and hurl them back at me, Moody blues! Moody Blues! Moody Blues! and their parents don't take any notice.

To stop it I say,

'I'll come, of course I'll come.'

They cheer loudly. 'Great!' they holler.

They are laughing at me of course.

The road twists, unreels in strange ways. There is a peculiar feel to it, as though it had only just decided to turn here itself and is surprised by the direction.

It arrives at an unexpected beach.

'Where is this?'

'Doctors' Point,' says C, smiling. 'The kids love it.'

I had dreaded crowds; noise; loud hilarious people straining for fun. But it is a bare beach, featureless, a dreary plain of sand. The wind tears at its skin.

I am afraid of the wind, and linger inside.

Everyone else surges out of the car.

They unwrap mysteries, parcels like stakes, parcels like heads. The children dance in rowdy circles and are sent to explore the sandhills for the sake of peace. Bottles are broached, fires coaxed. There is laughter and secret conversation.

It is cold, watching them.

This is the physical point: it is very cold, even though the sun is shining. I walk over to D.

'Can I help?'

He smiles, shaking his head. 'Have a glass,' he suggests.

He means, have a drink.

I try to sneer at his usage – he is a grammarian after all – but my head aches. The result must look like a lame, a timid smile. Another lie on my face.

I am tired of trying to give the lie to my face, to the mask Nature made of my face. I surge with torment inside, but to view?

Calmness. Composure. Plumply pallidly placid.

Do my eyes ever show agony? Life, even?

The dark is everywhere inside, the chase of shadows.

Nobody can see it by looking at me.

The sand on the beach is fine and white, like talcum powder. When I step on it, it squeals.

Unreal sand – for a moment I imagine I have fallen into a dream. I think there is nobody watching, so I accomplish experimental broadsides, producing crescendos of squeaks.

'It's the size and arrangement of the particles,' offers M.

She is crouched down by the sandhill to the left, ringed by avid-eyed children.

'O?'

She smiles softly. She looks down at the thing she is putting together. 'We're just going to put this kite up . . . do you want first go?'

The child horde is choiring, 'Me first! Me first! Me first!'

Shaking, I shake my head, No No No, walking away on the tormented sand.

The beach is littered with dead krill.

They appear to be the same kind here as at home, but I have never seen so many of them driven on to the beach before.

They are stranded everywhere, mounds of them heaped and ghostly, decayed to pale plastic shells.

Why have they died in this amount?

Possibly because the baleen whales kept the krill in check.

The factory ships destroyed the whales. 'A whale dies every twenty seconds.' And then there were no more whales left to die. Now the krill breed to superabundance, spread an insidious red tide through the sea.

This is possible, although I don't know whether it is correct. I haven't read newspapers, watched television, listened to vain talk for many months.

The sand is squealing hideously under my moving feet.

I try to walk stealthily, silently, tiptoeing, but the sand chitters triumphantly with every movement.

I sit down in defeat amidst the holocaust of krill.

I remember thinking in one of the northern cities, just after I had arrived there, 'Courtenay Place! What a ridiculous name! Place Place!' I chided myself immediately.

This is a new land, a new chance, a beginning. Ridicule has no place here.

I have a cousin called Courtenay.

He is presently unable to continue his research in genetics owing to nervous exhaustion. That, of course, is neither here nor there.

M has the kite aloft now.

It is a blue delta shape, batwinged. It looks like a cruel unnatural hawk as it sways on the end of its strings.

M pulls the left string. The kite dips. She pulls on the right string. The kite loops down to the sand, its white plastic tail whipping circles in the air.

The children are scrambling wildly round it. Their shrieks carry to me.

O why?

Is it triumph over the descent of the kite? Or have they found an ally? For the kite is a bird of prey . . .

I look at the sand, my eyes filling with tears.

Through the mist I see it is not stark white. That is a trick of the sun. It is really pale fawn, a dun colour. Though there is a mica-glitter, a light rash through it, that helps the sun's disguise.

One of the children comes trotting past.

She wears a garish t-shirt covered in scarlet and yellow blotches, and poisonous green shorts. Bare arms, bare legs, bare feet, all in defiance of the wind, the cold. She shies as she passes me, but turns to grin shyly. Small white needlepointed fangs.

My lips curl in reply. Suck off bloodimp.

Her smile wavers.

She trots away faster.

There were two things about the child; her whole air of sly friendship, defiant friendship, friendship that is not real, that snares, that entraps – that was one.

The other was the fact that she had a birthmark on her forehead, the port wine kind, and she seemed unconscious of this deformity. She did not hide it, or show herself ashamed.

I have thought about these things a lot. They troubled me: they trouble me still.

Then there is the uncomfortable feeling about the vividness and inappropriateness of her clothes.

Do people not feel the cold out here?

My dress was linen, plain, neat, covering. I felt ridiculous among the shorts and jeans and casual shirts of all of them.

But I am presently self-conscious about my clothes.

I had been sitting in my office with the door open, and I don't think they were aware of that.

D had said loudly,

'Holy Christ, have you seen her latest number? Sort of trimmed horse-blanket and the kind of necklace even my Aunt Gertrude wouldn't be seen dead in!'

Throbbing laughter from them all.

I closed my door very quietly.

I am tired of living a lie, the lie that is my life. Though it is better to appear dully normal. Better to be considered old fashioned and slightly eccentric because of my sane normality.

Let them be amused. Let them laugh. Let them sneer behind my back and smile falsely to my face.

It is far better that they do this than get a glimpse of the chaos within.

But I am tired of lying.

The girl child is a long way up the beach now.

Her curling floss of hair, her thick glasses, the stain on her head, all hidden.

Her garish clothes are easily visible however.

I have a theory about deformities. People are either fearful in the company of a monster, or they will worship it. Any other reaction is rare.

For instance, you are familiar with the giant stone Olmec heads?

Did you know the Olmecs worshipped were-jaguars? That their race was subject to a scourge of birth malformations, deformed children with warped skulls and squashed-in faces? Some of these mutations may have lived. Olmec heads seem to me to represent a deformed mutant with a protective head-covering. A were-jaguar born to a mortal woman. A fit subject for worship!

For my own part, I think all deformed monsters should be painlessly destroyed at birth.

The pain they cause to those who are closest to them is unbelievable.

The wind is blowing harder. To sit still is to shiver uncontrollably.

So I walk along the sea-edge.

There are pieces of krill, of crab and weed, swinging in oozy decay in the water's rim.

All that death . . . the sand feels unclean under my feet. It is unthinkable to rinse it in the sea. All the oil, all the mercury and phosphates and waste, and the brooding atomic foulness crated in leaking concrete: no wonder the sea is dying.

And I can see huddles of krill in scarlet encrustations round the bases of rocks in the sea. Doomed, because the tide is going out. Doomed to join the dead masses on shore. Some are already stranded on the sand, unmoving, cooking in their armour.

My eyes sting with tears again.

This is silly, silly.

Why cry for crustaceans? Why cry for an inevitable end? I mean, who cries for me?

The beach is narrowing. Rocks block the end. They look rotten, fractured dark-green rocks, knobs and specks and splinters of them, in higgledy-piggledy heaps.

But they have real shade and real shadows, and the wind is thwarted by them. Even the searacket is less. And they build in unsteady blocks, higher and higher. Vaults of them. A crooked cathedral.

The floor is fine damp sand. The sea has retreated from here. It feels peculiarly clean.

The walls are greenly wet, almost translucent, like chrysoprase.

The seanoise is muted. The air is still.

I love this kind of peace.

If I could shush the voices, shush the sounds, the last whimper, the talk and recriminations and my own drawnout anguish, still the noise of the badgering living, the crying of the dead; if I could make a cathedral of peace, a retreat in my head . . .

But I am aware that withdrawal is madness. You don't have to tell me that.

When I open my eyes, having rested a little in the cool of this cave, I see there are swarms of mussels on the wall. Crusts of them, blueblack and shiny as though varnished.

There is the occasional stranger mussel in their midst, pale green, like a wraith of a mussel. Pallid, obvious, vulnerable. There is never another palegreen mussel closeby for company.

The different, the abnormal the alien, the malformed.

Who – or what – selects a person for the torment of difference?

Do you know the sensation of pondering deeply on something – and suddenly falling into nothingness?

Something tickles the back of my neck.

A fly?

Suddenly they are everywhere, hordes of kelpflies, a monstrous swarm rising from the walls descending from the roof swirling in humming spirals everywhere. I batter my hands against the buzzing air.

I may have yelled.

K asks,

'All well?'

His voice is deep, concerned.

My breath catches in my throat.

'Of course.'

He smiles, a ready compassionate smile, a little too smooth to have come from the heart.

'Of course,' he answers.

He draws nearer.

'I've come to see the caves. And you?'

'I had come to see the caves.'

My voice is cool and steady, a pleasure to my ears.

'Good,' he says. 'They're a neat set of caves.'

He draws back again and disappears round the seaward end of the cave. I hadn't realised the cave went further. There is a conical thrusting rib of rock, at the far end a flying buttress carved by sea and wind. Beyond it is water, stirred by the tide.

I go forward. The seanoise beats on me, and the wind pierces my smile.

There is nothing but a shallow eddy of the incoming tide in the next cave.

In the third cave, K waits.

He grins from the rock he is perched on. He looks bulky and cramped on top of the rock.

'Well, do you like our caves?'

'Is this the last of them?' My voice is still cool, still steady, despite the ache and the waves in my head.

He waves a hand vaguely south.

'There's another one beyond, same sort of thing. Besides, you can't get to it now. Tide's too high.'

He bends his head, his smile lost. He doesn't appear surprised that I didn't answer his first question. The seanoise seems somehow louder however. Then,

'Are you all right?' he asks.

Do you know that inane joke, Are you all right? No, I'm half left? It skips through my mind but I say,

'Pardon?'

'You've seemed a little, ahh a little, *tense* these few weeks you've been with us. I've been wondering if something's wrong.'

It is the inevitable. The invitation to tell. To betray.

O, I know they must have gossiped back in the staff room. I know the year gap in my record must look peculiar. I have been prepared, almost, for this question ever since I arrived. But to have it put now, not in the clean bright confines of a university office, but in a shadowed cave with the sick and dangerous sea running close by!

I cannot see any way out.

I say my lie, quickly and finally:

'A very good friend of mind died in sad circumstances. It upset me a good deal. I was under a doctor's care for some time.' It doesn't work.

'And now?' asks K.

I am silent.

'And now?' asks K.

I press my hands together as hard as they can go.

'And, now?' he questions yet again.

I don't want to. I dontwanto, it blurts out, it's not me.

'O God I didn't mean to, it was puerperal insanity, she died by her own hand.' A small eternal silence. 'I mean, we had lived together happily for years, and then she had to go and have a baby. It was, it was, it wasn't born right. She killed it. Then she killed herself. They said it was puerperal insanity.' I am shaking again, my voice is shaking with my body. 'It was a long time ago, nearly two years, but it comes back to me. I am sorry. I try. I shall never get over it.'

The wind drips slowly, its voice moaning down to extinction.

The sea is conspiratorially silent.

His head stays bent. He remains on the rock, stolid and still.

He says at last,

'I am very sorry. We knew there was, ahh some tragedy, but we had no idea you see?'

'It is past.'

Only my hands are shaking now.

'You have had help?'

'Yes.'

'And you think you can get over it?'

'Yes.'

He climbs down from his rock and I step back. He will touch me in sympathy and I

but he says

calmly

'If you need someone to help, anyone to talk to, I am here. We are here,' softly, impulsively, compassionately. More compassionately than anything I have ever had said to me in my life.

Then he walks swiftly round the rocks into the other caves.

A wave rushes over my feet.

The tide is coming in fast.

It is nearly all lies of course.

I have been alone for most of my life.

And those nine months were horror afterwards.

Why do I tell this expedient set of lies? Why do I live a lie, portray a lie, many lies?

Because the chaos, the turbulence, the shadowhorror is too terrible a ruin and reality to inflict on anyone. To tell the truth about – NO!

If I explain with an acceptable melodrama, my frumpiness becomes an ally, my pallid composure a refuge. My alien self, a focus for pity and understanding.

UNDERSTANDING!!!

I rage. The rage shakes me harder, harder, harder, harderharderharder then convulsively to stillness.

If there had been a long period of peace and stillness after, nothing would have happened, you see.

The physical point to mention at this stage is, not only was I still very cold, but also I was so tense that if someone had dropped me I would have exploded.

There's a moon pale as gauze in the blue sky.

On the barbecue, the steaks drip fat. The fire smokes and sizzles and spits. Rustle and confusion as food and utensils are laid out. Clink of bottle to glass, and the laughter grows louder. The bloodstained paper that wrapped the meat lifts and shifts in the wind.

They talk casually, staff scandal and academic gossip. I am kindly included. The looks are discreet; the assumption, I will prefer pitying silence.

I am safe, for a while.

I nod, and I smile.

I know my nod is stiff, and my smile frosty and distant.

They are all sure they understand. The very air reeks of sympathy. It sifts through the talk like the burnt offering smell from the charred steak, which we are forced to inhale.

Why should I be so contemptuous?

They did their best, invited me out, invited me in. It's not their fault I don't fit.

And as for understanding . . . I don't understand.

I gave up understanding after the terrible gush of blood, after the final silence, after the weakening into darkness when all I could think was an internal gibberish.

The deed accomplished and my hands incarnadine have wreaked their mercy and all the sick sea shall fail now fail now fail now, this last pollution original sin and worst.

I gave up understanding after the wailing 'Owhydidyous?' had chanted themselves into quiet oblivion, after the slow slow settling back into a kind of normality. A normality of chaste lies. The mask face and the shadow chase of lies.

And I still don't understand.

I go for another walk on the beach after lunch, trying to feel warm, to feel at ease. I wander the high tide line of the beach, watching the sand, gazing at the sea debris. Snail shells. Giant cockles and clams — do they call them quahogs here? Bleached bones and things so worn by time and sea they could be anything. The broken husks of crabs.

And everywhere the krill.

The laughter of the others is very far away.

I look back once.

They are gathered in a group at the far end of the beach.

I cannot see what they are doing.

I turn back to my perusal of the dead and the broken.

It began as an uneasy feeling, as though something unfriendly was watching the back of my neck.

I couldn't understand why I should feel this disturbance.

When I looked up I understood.

It was the kite.

It is the kite, high above my head, a hard electric-blue intruder. A threat.

It sways easily on the end of its strings, as though it knows it could be free of them at will, free to hunt and kill.

Did not the kites feast on the flesh of the dead?

Did not the Parsees build the Towers of Silence to invite the kites to their feast?

The sand squeals risibly, a sharper tone than I have heard from it before. I glance down. The shadow sleeks by. The tail whips past my cheek.

I have crouched, my hands shielding my head before I am aware I have done so.

Before I can rationalise it, and think, 'It's all right, it's just the kite that's fallen.'

It had stopped so fast!

And already it is back in the sky. It swings back and forth in an ominous aerial jig.

I am pinned for a moment, still crouched, like rabbit under the scream of a hawk. Then I straighten slowly, my heart athud.

The kite above me wavers. Then it dives, striking the ground inches from my heels.

I look at the fallen thing, plastic and string. I look along the beach.

A child holds the distant ends of the strings, standing there gaudy as a toadstool, poisonous in its laughter.

The adults are laughing too, I know.

It is like being an automaton. I can approach them freely, smiling, can joke even, with equanimity.

Smiles all round, and a lot of heartiness and high laughter and backslapping.

They invite me to take the strings, and make a game of it. And I am still smiling as they scatter up the beach, all of them. The toadstool child as well.

They rush into kite territory, eager prey.

The sun has wheeled round a little. It is late afternoon.

The sky is still a striking blue, though black clouds lower over the rim of tamed and manbarren hills.

It is the lowering clouds that make me feel that this is an arena. I am minded of plays, of theatre. Of a starkly set opera involving gladiators and death.

The sky is painted blue.

The hills are fake.

The wind comes from a machine.

And we are protagonists in an ancient and misunderstood drama.

Yet now, holding the kite-strings, I am exultant. I didn't know I could still feel this alive. My blood has secret fires, and they are soaring, spiring through me. The kite has a voice, and it is speaking.

I can feel the sand sinking under my feet, the hem of my dress whipping the backs of my legs, and my teeth are so chilled the fillings in them ache. But these things are immaterial. They cannot dim my rising ecstasy.

I know the lethal bird above me is really insentient plastic, frail fibreglass rods, lengths of string.

I know that, and it doesn't matter. It isn't real knowledge.

The truth and beauty is: the vibrant strings are my hands and the way I now look, out of the kite's eyes.

Down there, they are dancing, M and K and D and C, and all their mocking children. They think it is their game.

I am laughing, I am laughing, laughter that has been absent for a year.

For all my life.

I am the beautiful killer. The strings are tingling sinews, and I am singing through the kite.

I know I can dive down through any one of their dancing brittle skulls.

We dip and soar and wheel and skim.

We drive them in a frantic scattering pack.

We sleek over their heads, and they dive screaming joy to the sand.

They applaud our skill wildly.

We whirl and we spiral. It is effortless. Coming near, speeding up and away amid all the gay retreating shrieks; sweeping down and brushing by with a smirking kiss of death.

With the forty-mile push of the wind, a fibreglass rod turns iron beak, and plastic and string make a griffin's skin.

And there she now runs giggling, the toadstool child. Hair an innocent halo, shining in the sun, and below it, the dark mark flaunted indecently . . . we swoop, and she shrieks with delighted laugher.

Ascend
   steady:
and we stoop.

Struck between the shoulder blades, she falls.

And then it is black night and we are breaking apart forever.

There are shouts and cries in the distance, and people running.

The dark clouds spill over, and the air is suddenly full of fine weeping mist.

I am numb now, so cold, so dulled.

They have grown strangely silent, along there, but I cannot let go the dead strings.

The silence grows with the fog, blotting out even the whimpering wind.

The sea is holding its breath.

The krill are dying, dying.

The hopelessness of the pallid mussels forever cloistered apart.

The endlessly crying sand.
And ah, my dark dark room . . .

Have I told you anything?
Has it meant anything to you?
Or is it all just writing?
All just words?

CHRIS ELSE

Big Jim Cook woke up. It was Saturday morning. The sunlight oozed through the slats of the venetians and trickled down like the lemon icing on one of the Old Sheila's sponges. Big Jim imagined it flowing slowly over the house, worming out of the sky from the nozzle of a cosmic icing bag softly squeezed. From out there, in the bright space of day, the world was just a fancy cake decorated with liquorice roads and sugar houses in bright pastel colours. Big Jim would have seen it clearly if he had closed his eyes, but he was awake and troubled, as furtive as one of the curled-up ants beneath the gnawed-out surfaces.

Behind him, in the soft Sleepyhead sprung foam warmth, the Old Sheila turned over and began to snore. Big Jim listened without anger or interest. Time was when he had thought her the best-looking little snorer in town but feelings had hardened into habit over the years. It wasn't her fault, just as it didn't seem to be his. They were both getting on, sagging a bit with the wrinkles coming, and somewhere between hired labour and the bar of the Whitby RSA Big Jim had bought himself a round white gut bristling with hairs like a side of raw pork. The Old Sheila had a right to snore. She did most of the work in the business these days, keeping the books and answering the phone while Big Jim stood around being the boss and watching other people sweat. Worked himself into a corner.

The sunlight trickled through the blind and over the window sill but it still hadn't dripped onto the La-z-boy, lay-back, padded chair beneath where his trousers and his checked shirt lay wrestling in a shadowy heap. The trousers had a head-lock on an arm or maybe the shirt was working a half nelson on the left leg, it was hard to tell. Neither had much advantage as far as Big Jim could see and both were waiting for him to stop looking so they could get down to it again. He stared and kept on staring. After a while, he had been staring so long he thought he might be dead.

The sound of a motor mower ripped through the wall from outside. Eight-thirty. The joker next door was shaving his lawn again. The Old Sheila snorted and twisted awake.

'Oh, Lord,' she said,' 'does he have to do that at this hour?'

'Looks like it.' His voice sounded too loud, booming like a coffin lid.

She grabbed the alarm clock and stared at it, heaved back with a yawn.

'What's wrong with you, then?' she demanded. 'You're usually up by now.'

'Don't feel like it.' And what did he feel like?

'Suit yourself.'

At breakfast, fresh as an ice cream in her pink housecoat, she served bacon and eggs and tea and toast. Big Jim watched Kevin stuffing his eighteen-year-old face and reflected on the mystery of having grown-up children. It seemed another reason for doing nothing. Viciously, he stabbed his bacon and eggs through the left eye.

'I reckon we ought to get one of those new wall-to-wall deep freezes,' the Old Sheila said, working over the plastic tomato with the sauce in it. Was that what she said?

'What for?' he asked.

'It'd be a lot more economical. Eat better for less.'

'We eat good enough now.'

'You are in a mood. I hope you're not going to spend the whole day moping.'

'I'll fix the bathroom tap and then go down the Raza.'

'Boozing,' Kevin said, his mouth full.

'And what'll you be up to?'

'Dunno. I might drag the bike round to Lenny's.'

'Bikes!' Big Jim echoed his son's tone deliberately. 'An idiot's game!'

'A bloody sight better for you than sitting round the Raza with a bunch of old twits what forgot to die in the war.'

'Don't you speak to your father like that!' the Old Sheila said, waving her knife.

'Well, it's true. He never even saw any fighting anyway. All he did was count socks in Malaya for a year.'

'That's no excuse!' the Old Sheila said.

Big Jim looked from one to the other. What were they arguing about? 'The kid's right,' he said. 'Everybody's right. That's the trouble.'

'He's not going down the RSA anyway,' the Old Sheila told Kevin as if Big Jim was somewhere else. 'Not first thing, he's not.'

'What is he doing, then?' Big Jim asked.

'Taking me to the Show.'

'What you want to go there for?' Kevin demanded.

'Why not?'

'It's full of fuddies looking at stuff they're never going to buy.'

'That's right. Like me and your father. I want to see them freezers.'

At the entrance, the turnstiles clicked like a pair of turbine pumps sucking in the air to keep the exhibition hall blown up to full pressure. Bits of the population were being dragged along in the draught. The Old Sheila in blue and beads was happy on her stack heels. Big Jim paid the money. Between the iron webbed roof and the concrete floor, partition walls rose up dividing the space into booths and stands. A model bathroom in pink and chrome presided over by a man in a neat striped suit. A cooking demonstrator red-faced, chef's hat, stainless steel voice whining soft instructions.

'What about these blinds?' the Old Sheila asked, pointing.

'We got blinds.'

'But those are the new ones, double-action, reverse pull nylon cords. I've seen them on telly.'

The young woman's smile fixed bright as they approached. Not long ago, yesterday even, Big Jim would have enjoyed looking at her and thinking about her body trapped in the tailored trouser-suit. Now it didn't seem to matter. Blinds with icing dripping through them squeezed by the cosmic cook in the chef's hat, soft instructions. Blind like a fried egg, split and bleeding yolk and tomato sauce. Kevin was right. A couple of fuddies, just looking.

The Old Sheila slipped the pamphlets into her bag. 'That freezer stand must be down here some place.' Down through the strings of people. Music blared from the amusement arcade. Across the aisle, above their heads, hung a great banner: 'Twelve o'clock Today. THE GREAT GOD GIVING LOVE SHOW. Live on Stage.' To the right, a thin man with a bald head was trying out a La-z-boy lay-back armchair while his wife looked on. Something to die in, maybe.

'Here we are,' the Old Sheila said, stepping up onto the stand amid the while enamel.

'Yes, madam, can I help you?'

'We want to look at the big one.'

'Ah, the new Freezemaster. Here we are. Eighteen cubic feet. Special section compound lid. Racks for easy handling.'

'That's nice.'

'And along this end we have the super quick freeze drop well.'

'For the gumboots,' Big Jim said.

'I beg your pardon, sir?'

'For the gumboots. I wear a lot of gumboots in my work.'

The young man's face tightened into a nervous smile beneath his black moustache. 'In the freezer, sir?'

'I don't wear 'em in the freezer. I keep 'em there.'

'Don't be a fool, Jim,' the Old Sheila said, nudging him.

The demonstrator laughed at the joke. His moustache quivered as if it was trying to polish his teeth.

'Frozen gumboots are the best thing in the world for tinea,' Big Jim said. 'You know what tinea is?'

'Er, no.' The smile came back.

'Athlete's foot. Big problem with gumboots.'

'Look,' the Old Sheila said, 'if you can't be serious, why don't you go throw coconuts or something. I want to talk to this man.'

'See you later.'

'Certainly, sir.'

Big Jim stood on a plywood corner and rolled himself a smoke. The coconuts didn't appeal but it was good to be shot of the responsibility of spending money. He couldn't cope with decisions, not today, not with the strange feeling of unreality which had scattered his waking thoughts even before he had got them together. Where was the man who had built a business out of nothing, working nine hours a day in clay trenches with a shovel until he could afford machines to do the job? He ought to be thinking of expanding instead of standing around on street corners. He ought to take an interest. In what? The question shrugged at him. He eased his belt around the only expansion he had done for a year and pulled morosely on his smoke. There must be something in the world a joker could do with himself. A child, its face buried in pink candy floss, stopped to stare at him until its mother dragged it away. I'm turning green, Big Jim thought, running his fingers round his unshaven jaw.

Down the corridor, between the blue spark of the welding demonstration and the insulation stand, there was a blare of music and a coloured roll of light. A knot of people was gathering. Big Jim sauntered towards them assailed by mute appeals for interest on both sides. Get your chain saws here, ladies and gentlemen! Every one a virgin, guaranteed! See the strongest lavatory bowl in the world! The tattooed bathmat! Daring bareback dishwashers perform death-defying feats! The crowd, thickening gently, moved on, ignoring such phrenetic claims, drawn to the dark squared doorway where the lights moved, blue, green, yellow, red, across the bodies packing in.

Big Jim peered round the lintel into the darkened hall. Dim figures moved together, jostling expectantly. Beams of colour flicked over their faces, momentarily distorting features with unfamiliar shadows. The lights came from a slow-moving wheel fitted with lamps which swung back and forth as they circled the dark centre, floating their random selection over the audience in a slow, hypnotic rhythm. Beside the wheel, illuminated by a single, white spot, stood a man in a dark suit and a bow tie. He held a book in one hand and he was leaning forward over the knob of a microphone.

'Jesus saves,' he crooned, in a healthy bass. 'Jesus saves and so do you.'

'What's it all about?' a voice whispered at Big Jim's side.

Another voice answered. 'Quiet. They'll start in a minute.'

'A load of rubbish, if you ask me.'

The man at the microphone tensed suddenly. He spread his arms and leaned back: 'And the Lord said, "Let there be light"!' A triumphant shout of joy and suddenly the stage was filled with brightness. The people gasped. There before them was a vast display of manufactured wealth: lawn mowers, refrigerators, stereograms, lounge suites, vacuum cleaners, washing machines, outboard motors, colour TV sets, all arrayed as if conjured forth by the compere's dramatic gesture. The great wheel, with its coloured beams, turned slowly, smearing the walls and the bodies below with dabs of soft pastel. Above it hung a huge banner which proclaimed in bold, black letters: 'THE GREAT GOD GIVING LOVE SHOW starring JUMPING JOHN THE BAPTIST by courtesy of GOLDEN WONDER CHICKEN, Tennessee, U.S.A.'

'Hi!' the man at the microphone breathed, sweeping the audience with his loving eye. 'A big, wide welcome to the Showgrounds here today. A big, wide welcome to all those who have the Faith, brothers and sisters. And if you don't have the Faith, then don't go away. We're going to show you the Power of God, here today. Oh, yes indeedy, the POWER OF GOD. For the Lord will lay his hand upon the Righteous and raise him up, but the Sinner will be cast down, even to the DEPTHS OF HELL.'

Big Jim, who had never had too much time for the Lord one way or the other, was not very impressed by this speech. He turned to go but, as he did so, his eye caught a face on the other side of the hall, a face briefly lit by a shaft of red light. It was Kevin, surely. Denim jacket and long dark hair, attention fixed on the slowly revolving wheel as if he was hypnotised. Big Jim changed his mind and began to edge his way through the crowd.

'This is the Lord's game,' Jumping John was saying, 'and the rules are simple. One easy question and if you get it right you can come before the altar and pray. One easy question and the light falls on you. Here we go now. The first question is . . . Who was the first president of the United States? Wait for the Light of God, brothers and sisters, wait for the light. Who was the first president of the United States?'

Big Jim squeezed through the press, apologising for the toes he crushed. Nobody seemed to notice him. Everyone's gaze was fixed on the lights which played their mesmeric rhythm over the waiting faces. Suddenly, the movement stopped.

'The red light, brothers and sisters. It's the red light. You there lady, with the glasses. That's right, ma'am. Who was the first president of the United States?'

'George Washington?'

'That is corrrrect! Come up before the altar, sister. Come up, come up. And while she comes, folks, we'll have another question.'

Kevin and his mate Lenny were standing close to the stage, their upturned faces stilled by tension. The lights stopped again. Another question was answered correctly. A collective sigh of satisfaction and envy swept up from the audience. Kevin shifted nervously and whispered something to Lenny. Big Jim touched his sleeve.

'Dad?' A startled look as if he'd been caught at the whisky bottle.

'Full of old fuddies, eh?'

'This is different, Dad. That trail bike, see?' He pointed to the gleam of chrome and paint on the stage. 'We're after that.'

'How do you reckon you're going to get it?'

'Answer the question and pray. If the lights pick you.'

'Pray?'

'That's what you have to do.'

And why not? Big Jim wondered. It made as much sense in his mind praying for a trail bike as for a clear conscience. You were just as unlikely to get the one as the other. He looked at his son's earnest face and remembered himself at eighteen, signing up for the regular army because he didn't know what else to do. A trail bike was an easy answer to a lot of problems and he could have wished he had a desire of his own to match it, some thing to lay his hand on and say, 'Right, I'm a happy man,' something to make sense of the sunlight through the blinds.

The air had gone strange, green as peppermint, soft like a bedspread. Big Jim was hardly aware of the change until Kevin nudged him.

A voice spoke: 'Where did Davy Crockett die, brother? That's all you've got to tell me. Where did Davy Crockett die?'

Big Jim turned his head and gazed into the green light which shone full in his face. The glare spread outwards from a cold, white-green centre. There was nothing else to see.

'Come now, brother,' the voice told him, beckoning him forward into the bright mystery. 'Where did Davy Crockett die?'

'Go on, Dad. The Alamo. The Alamo.' Kevin's excited voice was whispering at his shoulder.

'The Alamo,' Big Jim said like a megaphone.

'And you are right, brother! Come up, before the altar.'

The green light swung away, drifting once more in its endless probing. Big Jim stood bemused, wondering exactly what had happened.

'Go up on the stage,' Kevin said.

'What?'

'Get on the stage.'

'I'm not going up there.'

'Oh, come on, Dad. Think of that trail bike.'

'You can't sell out on us now, Mr Cook.' Lenny, pale and eager, appealed to him. And a man had to do something with his life.

Big Jim was the third in line after the woman with glasses and a small, bald man whose hands were shaking. There were people behind him too but he didn't know how many because the light at the side of the stage was dim. What time was it? It must be afternoon still but in the gloom of the hall he felt as if night had already fallen, as if he had jolted awake out of a dream he could not now remember, and was standing on the floor beside the bed wondering where the bathroom was. Except that there was no bed, only a gleaming line of appliances and gadgets in a flood of white light and the man in the dark suit holding the microphone. The lights had stopped scanning the audience now. The coloured beams cut straight down the hall through the darkness onto a screen at the far end where they turned slowly to the rotation of the wheel.

'Brothers and Sisters! Here are the sinners!' Jumping John the Baptist pointed to the line of waiting people. 'They have eaten of the tree of knowledge, folks. They have come before the altar seeking grace and forgiveness and God's Gifts. How will the Lord God receive them? You don't know, brothers and sisters, and I don't know. Only the Lord God can see into their hearts and tell if they are truly repentant.' He turned and beckoned to the woman with glasses. 'Come up, sister. Come up and pray.' The woman stepped forward.

'What's your name, sister?'

'Doris.'

'Well, Doris, and what do you do then?'

'I'm a housewife.'

'Aha. And what do you want to pray for? Which of God's gifts have you got your eye on, eh?'

'I'd like the washing machine.'

'The Mighty Tub Double Action Fully Automatic Condor? That's number nine. Okay, Doris, we'll see how pure your heart is.' He pointed down the hall to the turning circle of lights. 'There's the wheel of God, sister. Pray your prayer for number nine and we'll see if the Lord will answer.'

The woman stood staring down the hall. The Wheel of God turned. Slowly, a number defined within the circle. It was seventeen.

'Oh, ho, ho,' Jumping John crowed, hovering over the woman, his face twisted in a satanic grin of triumph. 'Your sins have found you out, sister. God gives a no-no. You're unclean, sister. Your soul is a mass of weeping sores, ulcerated with sin. How dare you come before the Lord in a state like that?' The woman began to cry, still staring at the far wall. 'Tears won't help you either. You're bound for hell, sister. Unless you go back and repent for another time.' He turned to the audience. 'Where's she going, folks? She's going to Hell. Where there are no Mighty Tub Double Action Fully Automatic Condors and you have to wash your clothes in stinking mud. Begone, sinner.'

The woman turned away and walked back to where the waiting contestants were standing. Her face was folded in a grimace of pain, puzzlement, and disbelief. The man with the shaking hands looked up at Big Jim.

'I'm not going on there,' he said.

'Why not? You got something to be ashamed of?'

'Plenty. Haven't you?'

'I never thought about it,' Big Jim told him.

'You're next, then. You can have my turn if you're so sure of yourself.'

Sure of himself? Big Jim wasn't sure of anything today.

'Come up, come up and pray, brother,' Jumping John was saying. There seemed no reason not to.

'What's your name, brother?'

'Jim Cook.'

'Uhuh. And what do you do, Jim?'

'Drainage contractor.'

'Make a good living, do you?'

'Fair enough.'

'To him that hath shall be given!' Jumping John announced. 'You've picked out a blessing, of course.'

'Yes. I'm after that trail bike. My boy wants it.'

'Number forty-seven for you, brother Jim. Number forty-seven for your boy.'

The lights turned, red, yellow, green, blue, slowly at first and then faster and faster until they blurred into a brown-grey-white glowing ring. Big Jim stared. His mind was as blank as a dawn breakfast. He did not feel the audience below him or the grinning compere by his side. He could no more think of God than he could of the trail bike or the number he had been given. Somewhere in the depths of memory was the vague image of an eighteen-year-old on his first parade, wondering what the hell he had got himself into. He could picture the Old Sheila pursing her lips like a cash bag full of good sense because he was making a fool of himself again. Forty-seven came up in the middle of the circle.

'Hallelujah, brother!' Jumping John shouted and there was a burst of cheering and clapping from the audience. 'Hallelujah for a sinner saved! Your prayers are answered, brother Jim, and because the Lord finds favour you can try again. Three prayers for the Faithful, Jim boy. Three prayers. What's it to be this time?'

'My wife has her eye on that freezer over there.'

'Selfless again! Your number is now five. Five, brothers and sisters.

Five for the sinner who came back to the fold. Pray with him, folks. Bow your heads before the power of Almighty God.'

The wheel turned. What did it matter if he made a fool of himself? He had been doing that ever since he had outgrown his ambition. In the days when he had shovelled clay for a living he had had some sense of purpose. Now he was fit only to stand on a stage and raffle his desires in public. Number five came up in the centre of the wheel. The crowd cheered and hooted. Jumping John the Baptist leapt high into the air and screamed delight. An angel stepped out of the darkness behind him. Her wings were silver, sparkling with rainbow sheen. Her long gold dress rippled softly as she walked and she smiled with all the mystical assurance of a photograph. Smiling, with perfect painted lips, she took Big Jim's hand.

'Your Guardian Angel,' Jumping John said. 'She's here to help you with the Star Prize. Pray for the Star, brother Jim. Pray this one for the Holy Ghost.'

Big Jim stared at the long white fingers which had gripped his own. The nails were delicate and painted red. He wondered what he was supposed to do with them. The angel had blue eyes and blonde hair. Her face held a slightly peeved expression as if she wished she was back in Heaven. She didn't seem too interested in a drainage contractor who was pushing middle age and forty round the waist. She didn't seem delighted when a star came up in the Wheel of God.

There was a burst of organ music and a choir began to sing the Hallelujah Chorus. A spotlit, golden throne descended from the roof in a blaze of glory. Jumping John the Baptist could hardly make himself heard.

'Paradise, brothers and sisters! Paradise by courtesy of Air New Zealand and the Tourist Hotel Corporation. A year's holiday in every part of the country with free travel and accommodation and fifty dollars a day spending money. Thus is the Lord's Anointed raised in benediction for the Glory of God and the Wonder of Mankind.'

The angel led him to the throne. They sat together side by side. As the choir sang and the audience cheered, they rose into the heavens. The angel's wing got caught in the pulley but Big Jim untangled it. He looked down as the world receded below him.

JANET FRAME

In the summer days when the lizards come out and the old ewes, a rare generation, a gift of the sun, gloat at us from the television screen, and the country, skull in hand, recites To kill or not to kill, and tomatoes and grapes ripen in places unused to such lingering light and warmth, then the people of Stratford, unlike the 'too happy happy tree' of the poem, do remember the 'drear-nighted' winter. They order coal and firewood, they mend leaks in the spouting and roof, they plant winter savoys, swedes, a last row of parsnips.

The country is not as rich as it used to be. The furniture in the furniture store spills out on the footpath and stays unsold. The seven varieties of curtain rail with their seven matching fittings stay on display, useless extras in the new education of discernment and necessity. The dazzling bathroom ware, the chrome and fur and imitation marble are no longer coveted and bought. For some, though, the time is not just a denial of gluttony, of the filling of that worthy space in the heart and the imagination with assorted satisfied cravings. Some have lost their jobs, their life-work, a process described by one factory-manager as 'shedding'.

'Yes, we have been shedding some of our workers.'

'Too happy happy tree'?

The leaves fall as if from other places, only they fall here. They are brittle in the sun. Shedding, severing, pruning. God's country, the garden of Eden and the conscientious gardeners.

Some find work again. Some who have never had work advertise in the local newspaper. There was that advertisement which appeared every day for two weeks, full of the hope of youth, sweet and sad with unreal assumptions about the world.

'Sixteen-year-old girl with one thousand hours training at hairdressing college seeks work.' The *one thousand hours* was in big dark print. It made the reader gasp as if with a sudden visitation of years so numerous they could scarcely be imagined, as if the young girl had undergone, like an operation, a temporal insertion which made her in some way older and more experienced than anyone else. And there was the air of pride with which she flaunted her thousand hours. She was pleading, using her richness of time as her bargain. In another age she might have recorded such time in her Book of Hours.

And then there was the boy, just left school. 'Boy, sixteen, would like to join pop group as vocalist fulltime' – the guileless advertisement of a dream. Did anyone answer either advertisement? Sometimes I imagine they did (I too have unreal assumptions about the world), that the young girl has found a place in the local Salon Paris, next to the Manhattan Takeaway, where she is looked at with admiration and awe (one thousand hours!) and I think that somewhere, maybe, say, in Hamilton (which is to other cities what round numbers are to numbers burdened by decimal points), there's a pop group with a new young vocalist fulltime, appearing, perhaps, on *Opportunity Knocks*, the group playing their instruments, the young man running up and down the stairs, being sexy with his microphone and singing in the agony style.

But my real story is just an incident, a passing glance at insulation and one of those who were pruned, shed, severed, and in the curious mixture of political metaphor, irrationally rationalised, with a sinking lid fitted over his sinking heart. I don't know his name. I only know he lost his job and he couldn't get other work and he was a man used to working with never a thought of finding himself jobless. Like the others he had ambled among the seven varieties of curtain rail and matching fittings, and the fancy suites with showwood arms and turned legs, and the second circular saw. He was into wrought iron, too, and there was a wishing well in his garden and his wife had leaflets about a swimming-pool. And somewhere, at the back of his mind, he had an internal stairway to the basement rumpus. Then one day, suddenly, although there had been rumours, he was pruned from the dollar-flowering tree.

He tried to get other work but there was nothing. Then he thought of spending his remaining money on a franchise to sell insulation. It was a promising district with the winters wet and cold and frosty. The price of electricity had gone up, the government was giving interest-free loans – why, everyone would be insulating. At first, having had a number of leaflets printed, he was content to distribute them in letter boxes, his two school-age children helping. His friends were sympathetic and optimistic. They too said, Everyone will be wanting insulation. And after this drought you can bet on a cold winter. Another thing, there was snow on Egmont at Christmas, and that's a sign.

He sat at home waiting for the orders to come in. None came. He tried random telephoning, still with no success. Finally, he decided to sell from door to door.

'I'm going from door to door,' he told his wife.

She was young and able. She had lost her job in the local clothing factory, and was thinking of buying a knitting-machine and taking orders. On TV when they demonstrated knitting-machines the knitter (it was always a she, with the he demonstrating) simply moved her hands to and fro as if casting a magic spell and the machine did the rest. To and fro, to and fro, a fair-isle sweater knitted in five hours, and fair-isle was coming back, people said. Many of her friends had knitting-machines, in the front room, near the window, to catch the light, where, in her mother's day, the piano always stood, and when she walked by her friends' houses she could see them sitting in the light moving their hands magically to and fro, making fair-isle and bulky knit, intently reading the pattern.

'Yes, door to door.'

The words horrified her. Not in her family, surely! Not door to door. Her father, a builder, had once said that if a man had to go door to door to advertise his work there was something wrong with it.

'If you're reputable,' he said, 'you don't advertise. People just come to you through word of mouth, through your own work standing up to the test.' Well, it wasn't like that now, she knew. Even Smart and Rogers had a full-page advertisement in the latest edition of the local paper. All the same, door to door!

'Oh no,' she said plaintively.

'It can't be helped. I have to look for custom.'

He put on his work clothes, a red checkered shirt, jeans, and he carried a bundle of leaflets, and even before he had finished both sides of one street he was tired and he had begun to look worried and shabby.

This is how I perceived him when he came to my door. I saw a man in his thirties wearing a work-used shirt and jeans yet himself looking the picture of disuse, that is, severed, shed, rationalised, with a great lid sinking over his life, putting out the flame.

'I thought you might like to insulate your house,' he said, thrusting a leaflet into my hand.

I was angry. Interrupted in my work, brought to the door for nothing! Why, the electrician had said my house was well insulated with its double ceiling. Besides, I'd had experience of that stuff they blow into the ceiling and every time there's a wind it all comes out making snowfall in the garden, drifting over to the neighbours too.

'No, I'm not interested,' I said.

'I tried that loose-fill stuff once and it snowed everywhere, every time the wind blew.'

'There's a government loan, you know.'

'I'm really not interested,' I said.

'But it's new. New. Improved.'

'Can't afford it, anyway.'

'Read about it, then, and let me know.'

'Sorry,' I said.

My voice was brisk and dismissing. He looked as if he were about to plead with me, then he changed his mind. He pointed to the red print stamped on the leaflet. There was pride in his pointing, like that of the girl with the thousand hours.

'That's my name and phone number, if you change your mind.'

'Thank you, but I don't think I will.'

He walked away and I shut the door quickly. Insulation, I said to myself with no special meaning or tone. How lovely the summer is, how cosy this house is. The people here before me had carpets that will last for ever, the ceiling is double, there are no cracks in the corners, that is, unless the place decides to shift again on its shaky foundations. How well insulated I am! How solid the resistance of this house against the searching penetrating winds of Stratford. The hunted safe from the hunter, the fleeing from the pursuer. The harmed from the harmer.

'How well insulated I am!'

That night I had a curious ridiculous dream. I dreamed of a land like a vast forest 'in green felicity' where the leaves had started to fall, not by nature, for the forest was evergreen, but under the influence of a season that came to the land from within it and had scarcely been recognised, and certainly not ruled against. Now how could that have been? At first I thought I was trapped in a legend of far away and long ago, for the characters of long ago were there. I could see a beggar walking among the fallen leaves. He was the beggar of other times and other countries, and yet he was not, he was new, and he was ashamed. I saw a cottage in the forest and a young woman at the window combing her hair and – a young man with a – lute? No, a guitar – surely that was the prince? – and with the guitar plugged in to nowhere he began to play and sing and as he sang he sparkled – why, it was Doug Dazzle – and he was singing,

> One thousand hours of cut and set
> my showwood arms will hold you yet
> baby baby insulate,
> apprentice and certificate
> God of nations at thy feet
> in our bonus bonds we meet
> lest we forget lest we forget
> *one thousand hours of cut and set . . .*

The girl at the window listened and smiled and then she turned to the knitting-machine by the window and began to play it as if from a 90 per cent worsted, 10 per cent acrylic score. I could see the light falling on her hands as they moved to and fro, to and fro in a leisurely saraband fair-isle. Then the beggar appeared. He was carrying a sack that had torn and was leaking insulation, faster and faster, until it became a blizzard, vermiculite falling like snow, endlessly, burying everything, the trees and their shed leaves, the cottage, the beggar, the prince, and the princess of the thousand hours.

The next morning I found the leaflet and telephoned the number on it.

'I'd like to be insulated,' I said.

The man was clearly delighted.

'I'll come at once and measure.'

We both knew we were playing a game, he trying to sell what he didn't possess, and I imagining I could ever install it, to deaden the world. All the same, he measured the house and he put in the loose-fill insulation, and following the Stratford custom, although it was summer, I ordered my firewood against that other 'drear-nighted' winter.

There was a man who came into the tearooms at Rai Valley and gave her a look that shook her in the depths of her stomach. She was terrified. She hoped that Mavis would serve him, but Mavis was unloading the oven so Nonny stood and looked at the side of his head. Something soft and heavy had forced one temple out. When she came back with his tray he looked at her again. All the time she was wiping he stared. Then he winked and slipped a cigarette into her hand.

'My home town's Shannon,' he said. 'How do you like it here?'

'It's O.K.' Nonny was paralysed with the cigarette.

'You can put your hands around those hot loaves in winter.'

'Yes.'

He winked again.

'Here . . . what do you think of this?'

He pulled a round pink tin from his suit and squeezed it open. There was ointment with a little skin.

'What is it?'

'For all your little aches,' he said, and raised it to her nose.

Nonny reared back. He laughed and left it on the table. She saw him drive away in a patchy van with a handwritten notice on the window.

Another day Mavis said, 'There's a man asking for you.'

Nonny was alarmed. It could only be a policeman or last year's schoolteacher. She blundered out and he was there again, trying his eyes on her.

'How have you been?'

'All right.' Nonny wanted to back off but she could not feel the floor with her legs.

'I haven't been by,' he said. 'I couldn't afford petrol. But I've got enough for a cuppa.'

He dug into enormous desolate pockets and his face became confused, like a dog that has been poorly clipped.

Nonny felt like a child in socks with cold legs. It was very clear: she could say anything to this dogman.

'How old are you?' she asked.

'Twenty-eight,' he lied.

'I'm sixteen.'

'That's a nice age,' the man said. 'I'm Clive Barrow.' He held out a big roughened hand and they shook. 'I'm getting another job.' He was schoolboyish. 'I've bought a milk round.'

Nonny made a noise.

'I haven't paid for it yet,' he admitted. 'And I'm delivering papers in the afternoon.'

Nonny imagined him with stark knees pedalling through winter streets.

'You'll be busy then.' She had never talked like this to a man before.

'It'll keep me occupied,' he said.

Close up, his face was pieces poorly put together. Never again did she get the feeling in the pit of her stomach. But she could get weak at the memory of it.

As he was going he dug into his pockets again and gave her a tube. She took it unwillingly.

'It's for your cat. In case it gets sick eyes.'

'I haven't got a cat,' Nonny said. Her mother had a spaniel that smelt like old washing and was not allowed past the door.

'Well, you can get one now.'

Later she sat on the tube and a puddle of ointment spoilt her skirt.

He knocked on the door three months later.

'Good morning.' He wanted to take her hands. 'What about a picnic at Pelorus Bridge?'

'I don't know . . .' Nonny had forgotten who he was. Her mother was puffing behind.

'Who's this man?'

'Good morning, Mam,' Clive Barrow smiled.

'Clive's got the milk run in Nelson,' Nonny remembered.

'We don't want milk from Nelson!'

'Clive's an old friend who used to drop in at the tearooms. He's going to take me for a little ride in his car.' Nonny surprised herself. It seemed important that she go out with this man.

He came closer – his teeth growing yellow towards the gums – and Nonny had the weight advantage over her mother.

'We should be off to church today,' the old lady said peevishly.

'They had it last week, Mum.' The minister came fortnightly from Havelock.

'Don't be long then,' her mother grumbled.

Nonny changed then bolted out, but Clive was not going to hurry. He smiled at the flower beds as he sauntered to the gate. His Morris Eight would not start. Nonny was sure her mother would lean out and claw her back.

'Let's push it!'

They pushed it for a hundred yards, then two youths nudged the snout of their De Soto into the back and the little car jerked into life.

'I've got some bread,' Clive announced when they were sitting above the river.

The loaf looked lonely on the stones. He tore a hole in it and handed her the gaping remainder. It was ready for the chooks.

'Have you any butter?'

'No butter,' Clive said.

Nonny nibbled, then put her bit on the stones. Clive made bread balls and flicked them towards the water.

'It's cold,' Nonny said.

'We could make a fire.' Clive Barrow smacked his head.

'We could make toast!'

'We could,' Nonny agreed.

'Have you any matches?'

'No.'

There were noises of people behind, so Clive went to borrow matches.

Nonny knew that she should gather wood, but she could not stop looking at the swirling water. There was only a cardigan and a dress between her and the naked air, and she wished she had stayed home and made date scones for lunch. She sank into a daze and when she aroused herself she thought he had been away for an hour. She wandered down mossy paths and over endless rocks until she found him lying under another car – she recognised his socks and his heels worn to one side. He was shouting to a man who had his face in the engine. Nonny stood on one foot, then slowly on another, then went back and sat in the Morris Eight.

Later she returned. Clive was pulling the starter over and over, and Nonny felt the air whistle down into her stomach then spread out like empty hands. She stood in front of the car and waved at Clive Barrow. He stared at her; she was frightened. Then he looked again and winked. Nonny waited, then she went out to the road and walked the four miles home.

'I don't want you going out with that fellow.' Her mother sucked her gums angrily over the heater. 'He's got the ugliest nose I've seen on a man. He should have it removed.'

Nonny's head spun, and she felt as if flesh had fallen off her in pounds.

'Don't worry, we'll probably never see him again.'

She fried three eggs, tomatoes, onions and bread, then helped herself to cold mutton and potatoes from the refrigerator.

'Besides,' the old lady grumbled, spooning an egg, 'he's old enough to be your father.'

Nonny received a post card from the West Coast two months later.

'I'm doing big business in greenstone,' wrote a stumbling hand. 'Yours everloving, Clive.'

She forgot about him. There were a few youths in their V8s who came into the tearooms and drank from their saucers, and when she wiped down they would grab the cloth. Then one night in summer there was a tap at the window. Nonny was so bored that she forgot to be scared.

'Gidday,' Clive Barrow said. 'It's a beautiful night.'

The air smelt soft and Nonny had been restless for nights, while things grew feverishly beyond the walls.

'Come to the flicks with me in Nelson,' Clive Barrow whispered.

'It'll be half-time already.'

'Let's go to the pub at Canvastown.'

'No,' Nonny said. Pubs had red interiors.

'Let's get some fish and chips then.'

Nonny could always find a space in her body that needed filling.

'The back door squeaks . . .'

'Come out the window.'

She changed into her cotton dress with trees on it, and when she got on to the sill her shoulders jammed.

'I'm stuck,' she breathed.

He dug his hands into her armpits so that she howled with laughter, and her skirt ripped as she fell on top of him. They lay stilly in the garden, then tiptoed down to the gate. A truck was parked down the road, and when she sat down a spring rose into her bottom. Clive Barrow pushed a board beneath her.

'Look.' She shoved her knees through the tear in her dress.

He grabbed her knees and jiggled them.

'Yummy. They feel like peaches.'

They drove to Havelock and she spread the fish and chips out to warm her knees. Clive parked on a dirt wharf, and the moon glared across the mudflats.

'Have you ever eaten a swan?'

'Never,' Nonny replied. It would be like eating a pile of feathers.

She sucked air to cool the chips and her fingers got burnt. She glanced at him bolting slabs of fish; there was a mouth with green lips, and eyes and nose gone away into the tip of his head. He rummaged in her lap and sometimes dropped a chip on the floor.

'Oops!' he said. Nonny had bare feet and she giggled.

'Oh, I'm thirsty!' She could have danced across the mudflats and lapped the fringe of water beyond.

'Ah . . . I have just the thing.'

Clive Barrow dived down the side of the seat and held up a bottle in the moonlight. The beer was warm, as if it had been cooking on the engine.

There were two more bottles. He gave her a toffee bar that tasted like a pocket. Nonny could not find her mouth to put it in.

'You'll have to excuse me.'

'Do you need a hand?' he asked.

'No thank you.' Nonny sat suddenly on the ground.

The moon was attacking through the tear in her dress. She peered closely at the craters opening on her thighs. Clive Barrow came round and lifted her on to a coat.

'Your eyes have gone,' she complained, and held up her hand to his brilliant face. 'I'm cold.'

He lay on top of her and started chewing her fingers.

Six weeks later she slipped down behind the counter. Mavis pulled her up and dusted her chest and made her sweet tea. Nonny went home. There were lots more off-colour days, but Nonny was evasive about them. She crept along to the district nurse, but the old lady was in a hurry and gave her aspirin. She was dizzy over lunch one day, and Mavis said, 'You're pregnant.'

'Am I?'

'How long is it since your period?'

Nonny had forgotten. She went home and thought hard, and did not tell her mother.

'What will you do?' Mavis asked.

'Have a baby,' Nonny said, tight-lipped.

Still she did not tell her mother, but she sometimes hoped Clive Barrow would turn up.

There was scrabbling at her window one night in April.

'How have you been?' he asked enthusiastically.

'Sick.'

'I'm very sorry to hear that.' He seemed about to heave himself into the room.

'I'm pregnant.'

Clive Barrow slid back.

'Oh.' There was a gap: all the night lay between them.

'We need to have a talk.'

'Yes we must . . . I'll drop by tomorrow,' he said.

He turned up a week later. Nonny's nausea had lessened. She was feeling thicker than ever. Clive Barrow grasped her hands so the tea on the tray slopped.

'I've been thinking about you!' Nonny felt she could look and look into his eyes and never find the centre. 'I've got a new job. Guess where?'

'I can't.'

'Shannon,' he cried. 'Come with me!'

So that's where I'm going to end up, she thought.

'Mum would never let me.'

'We can get married in the church I was baptised in . . .' He trailed off.

'You're broke, aren't you?'

'We could get married in the registry office and leave the do until later,' he said.

Nonny was relieved about the church: white made her look fatter than ever. But she was sad about the cake.

'Where will we live?' she asked.

'I've found a beaut house a couple of miles from town.'

All that week she wanted to burst out to her mother, but something stopped her. She wrote a note, and when she went out the squeaky door for the last time she was swallowing madly. But when the Rai Valley school loomed past, then the pig farm where she threw potatoes as a child, a grunt started deep inside: some sort of fish was forcing its way up her chest. She howled so hard that Clive Barrow had to open all the windows, and when he finally drove the truck into the bowels of the Picton ferry he sat white-faced with his hands over his ears.

But later he took her up to smell the pungency of the sea.

'Once I cried for a whole day.' He laughed bleakly. 'If I think about it too much I could cry again.' Nonny was alarmed. 'My dad never came back from the war.'

'Oh,' Nonny sniffed. 'I'm sorry.'

'He wasn't killed. He had to stay on and clean up. He was an important person.'

Nonny was impressed.

'Then he had to stay on in the desert and teach the Arabs target practice. When he'd finished they sent him to England to work in the war office. My mum got letters from him once a month. Then he went to the Korean War and won a medal. I was twelve and I told all the kids at school. They thought that was smart. But one of them came up the next day and said I was a liar, that I didn't have a dad and there was nothing in the paper about a New Zealander winning a medal. I got my hands around that kid's throat and I wouldn't let go. Then I tore home. My mum was out and I turned her room upside down. There was nothing there that could've come from a man. No photos, no letters, no clothes. When she came home I screamed at her so loudly that she got frightened and she said that once I had a dad, but she didn't know who he was. She thought he might've been an American sailor. Or an Australian. That's when I started crying.'

Nonny stood with her cheek against his rough coat which smelt of petrol and tobacco.

'What happened to your dad?' he said.

Nonny paused, she had told nobody about her father.

'He's in a home in Nelson. Mum took me to see him one day. I thought he was the caretaker. He's been there for twelve years.'

'Why?'

'He was silly in the head.'

There was a sheep living in the house, and the wash-house wall had disappeared. The first day Clive was kicked by a cow, and at the end of the week he cracked the tractor engine by pouring freezing water into its boiling innards. By the time Nonny was ready to give birth Clive had tried two other jobs and they were living in an army hut in Shannon.

For two days she laboured. She felt like a fruit pressing out a distorted seed, but when the baby finally came he was tiny, with a closed face and dark hair like the down of a chicken. Nonny expected her body to be full of caves, but when she reached a mirror she saw only a stocky elderly girl with a rumpled skin. And when the baby stared up with his dark unblinking eyes and the beginnings of a moustache, Nonny thought instantly of a print framed in glass in the lounge at Rai Valley. It was the only painting in her life: a dark man with liquid eyes. She made Clive send a telegram to her mother: 'Jesus born today. Six pounds. Your loving daughter, Nonny.'

'What about Des?' Clive suggested angrily. 'Or Robinson? I've got an uncle called Robinson.'

Each morning he left early to work on the roads, and Nonny would whip around the oblong room and wash out some nappies. She fed Jesus with mashed bananas and sugar and he quickly lost his silken look; his shapely ankles thickened. Clive went hunting the big money at the freezing works, so that he was often away for days at a time. At eleven o'clock each day Nonny would take Jesus down to the bakery and buy cream cakes. Or custard squares. Clive got a job fencing, and mats of thorns spread over his body. More than ever it seemed difficult for him to see out of his face, so that when she discovered him watching her she was alarmed.

'That's it,' he said thickly, 'you just live for bread. All that starch.'

'You eat it yourself!'

He would cover slabs of bread with a tide of butter, then spread out lumps of jam.

'I burn it. You just store it.'

Nonny felt like a block. She imagined somebody coming with a mallet and making her shorter.

She locked the door and ate more, glancing over her shoulder at each mouthful. She would wake each morning feeling full up to her throat. But with her mouth still hungry. She would fry herself pancakes then lie down with bounding indigestion. One morning Jesus made a porridge island on the table and she threw a cup at him. He ducked and the cup broke a window.

'We've got to get out of this dump,' she told Clive Barrow. 'We've been here five years.'

'Four and a half.'

'What can you do in a one-roomed house all day?'

'Eat,' he said truthfully.

'Let's cash in the benefit and buy our own place.'

Clive was silent.

'Nobody would give us the rest of the money,' he said slowly. 'I can't hold down a job.'

'*Why* can't you!'

'Well, there's a job for me *somewhere*. I've just got to find it.' Then he added wistfully, 'I always wanted to fly aeroplanes.'

'You never told me that before.'

'I never had the education for it.'

'Don't worry,' she sympathised, 'I always gave the wrong change at the tearooms.'

Hi face was gaunt and obscure, and his stomach was growing remarkably. But he brightened.

'I've applied for a job as a railway yardman. If I stick it out I might end up as station master at Shannon. Then we'll get a house provided.'

Nonny sniffed.

But he got the job and went to Palmerston North on an early train each morning. He came home in a black waistcoat, boots, and serge trousers. He wore his brown fedora in the house.

'This is it!' This is my job!'

He never missed a day, and they put a down-payment on a three-roomed house. They moved in one weekend, and Nonny met Lucy. They had seen each other at the bakery for years, and now they were neighbours. They made each other cups of tea on alternate mornings.

Clive took Nonny to the pictures one Friday, and then Nonny climbed giggling into his side of the bed. She could still feel the warm smudge of the cinema upon her. And the night cooling her cheeks.

'You haven't laid a hand on me for months,' she said. 'Not since . . .' She could not remember when.

Clive rolled his eyes and crept gingerly beside her.

'It's the new job and the house . . . All this excitement.'

He drew away from her hand with an intake of breath.

'What's wrong?'

'My stomach gets tender occasionally.'

She drew back the covers and revealed him uneasily extended.

'Where does it hurt?' she demanded.

He skirted the side of his belly nervously. The flesh looked tight: Nonny could feel a subtle pressure behind it. His torso and legs were shrinking. Her excitement had gone.

'How do you wear your trousers over it?'

'I button them under my chest.'

'It's been there a long time, hasn't it?' she said angrily.

'When the jobs got bad, it got worse.'

'You've got to go to a doctor.'

'There's no need.' Clive covered himself.

'If you don't I'll leave. You'll have to look after Jesus!'

So he went, and she knew the day the tests came through.

'There's a bus at work,' he said. 'One of the repair gangs used to go out in it. I want to buy it.'

'What did the doctor say?' she shouted.

'Not much. I've got to take it easy. He gave me some pills to ease the pain.'

She wanted to smash plates. She wanted to hit his nose. Instead she gobbled hot bread. Later he came back dolefully.

'We could make it into a travelling home. We could go around the country doing odd jobs.'

'You're mad,' she shouted. 'We'd never do that together.'

He drove the bus home one night. It was green and blind, and Nonny said:

'You're going to sell it. You're not keeping that heap of junk while I have to do all the washing by hand.'

'I want it. I *need* it.'

She had not heard him speak like that before. She glared at him, but he took the bus down to the back fence and put a lock on the door. He ripped out all the battered seating and glued newspapers at the windows.

'What are you doing that for?' she asked suspiciously.

'I'm going to do a paint job on the inside.'

But he never did. Instead he hammered tremendously and shifted things in when she wasn't looking. Then he spent a night in it.

Nonny panicked.

'Are you going to sleep in it from now on?'

'Not when it's chilly.' They were already into summer.

'Perhaps we *should* go on holiday in it.'

'No thank you,' he muttered.

She found it unlocked one evening when he had gone to borrow a tool.

In the murk she saw a bed spring, an unconnected sink, a primus, his old bike, a radio, and a television frame propped up on a table. There was a smell of warm newspaper and tea leaves. Nonny hastened away, feeling that she had been intruding in another's house.

Clive stopped eating his dinners.

'I can't help it,' he explained. 'I always feel full nowadays.'

He began taking a bowl of bread and milk down to the bus; easing out of the door each night like an old swollen rabbit.

'Start getting out and about, my dear,' Lucy advised. 'Now that Jesus has gone to school.'

But Nonny was short and fourteen stone; it was easier to make cake mixture and eat it raw.

She was drawn down the section one evening, and without thinking she lay down under the bus. There was a noise from above, a kind of fragmented plumbing, and she half-followed it with her mind while her body pressed on the warm oil-smelling earth. Her face was suddenly alive with the feeling of him a few inches above. Dust fell on her eye-lids as he slurped his milk and sang a song that went up and down and was very flat, but sounded most like: 'Hoon, hoon, hoon . . .'

She went down the next evening and wriggled her shoulders into the cup of dead grass. She realised that the remote plumbing was his stomach; he could play it, and sometimes terrible smells crept down. And when he started singing songs his mother had taught him, her eyes moistened.

And so I go to fight a foreign foe although I know I'll be sometimes missed by the girls I've kissed. Goodbye . . .

One morning she had to belt on the bus door.

'Are you sick? It's past nine.'

He wound a window down and prised his eyes up.

'I've got a month's sick leave.' Later he said, 'I'm taking the bus out for a few days.'

'What about me and Jesus?' Nonny screamed.

'You've been left before.'

'Lucy's taking me to *Hair* on Friday. Why don't you come?'

'Why would I like to go to that?'

Why indeed, Nonny wondered, but raced on.

'There's no wheels on the bus . . .'

'I'll just put them on again.'

'What will you eat?'

'I'll just throw in some bread.'

But he made a big pot of soup for himself and generously let her throw bits in. He put his arm over her shoulder, and in the morning he kissed her forehead. It took him hours to start the bus and she went back to bed and dropped crumbs down her chest.

On Friday she took out her purple suit and Lucy came over in her sprayed leather jacket. Nonny smelt like the cupboard her clothes had hung in.

'He's gone then?' Lucy peered sharply down into the drizzle.

'Just for a few days. To give the bus a run.'

Towards Wellington the sky was black. Nonny wanted to tear the suit from her body and sink in beside the range. But Lucy had sharp spots of rain on her cheeks and her legs were thrust into thin electric shoes. They would buy oysters and chips coming home.

Beyond Levin they were caught up in a quick line of cars.

'This won't let up until we hit the motorway,' Lucy said triumphantly.

On the other side of Otaki they saw the green bus pulled over nearly into the ditch. Nonny squawked, and Lucy pulled up cursing.

Some of the newspaper had been scraped off the windows, and the door was locked. Nonny clambered on to the running board and made out the sink and the rumpled bed. She called desolately into the countryside, but there was only the hissing of the cars. Lucy revved.

'Come on! We don't want to be late.'

The slow cars lumbered past and Lucy chased them dangerously. Nonny was confused: she did not want to go forward or back.

Ten miles on an elderly man in a gaberdine coat was thumbing uselessly at cars. He had a sugar sack over his shoulder and thin hair in his eyes.

'He's got another think coming!' Lucy said, swerving onwards.

Nonny gave a cry and jerked around. But Clive had not seen them.

'He's dying,' she wailed. 'He's only got a little time left!'

Lucy shot her a hasty look of disbelief.

'Who says?'

'I know it! Way down inside I know it . . .'

She craned back further, but he was gone; there was only the spray of the cars speeding behind.

After all she and Ana wore shoes to the pictures now, and hers had the toes and heels out, and she'd been promised stockings for the winter. 'I might get me some earrings,' she said to Ana, as though earrings grew on trees.

They'd spent most of the afternoon getting themselves ready for the pictures, heating the irons on the stove and going over the skirts and blouses – pressing and steaming, reheating and pressing. Then they'd taken the basins outside and washed their hair, and now they sat on the stile waiting for it to dry. 'And I might get me a haircut,' Ana said. Charlotte drew in her breath, 'Ana, we wouldn't be allowed.'

'Yes, well. I might get me a haircut anyway – and I'm putting mine up for tonight.'

'So am I.'

'Let's go and try it now. See if it suits us. You do mine and I'll do yours.'

In front of the bedroom mirror with clips and elastic. Charlotte pulling the wire brush through her hair. Pounding the brush on to her scalp, dragging it down through the layers of thick tangles. Scraping up now, and out, up and out. Until the room is filled with flying streamers of Charlotte's hair.

Ana spread the circle of elastic on her fingers and worked carefully, putting the ends of Charlotte's hair into the band. She let the band close, then tied a ribbon tightly over the band and pulled the bundle of hair up and under at the back of Charlotte's shoulders. A clip above each ear to hold the hair in place. Finished.

Charlotte looked into the mirror smoothing and patting. Not

bad. Not too bad. As long as the elastic would stay, as long as the clips would hold.

Ana was hovering, 'It suits you. It does. It suits you.' 'Ye-es. Not bad. Not too bad.' Charlotte could see Macky and Denny Boy peeping round the open door at her but she couldn't be bothered with them, not with her hair done up, and it suiting her. She arched her eyebrows and stroked her hair, 'Get those kids, Ana,' she sighed. 'Get those nosey brats out.'

'Get out,' said Ana, making a face and slamming the door. 'We don't want any kids hanging round – Yes, it suits you, Charlotte.'

'It's okay. Course when I get dressed up. With the skirt . . . and shoes . . . I'll do yours now. Then we'll go over to Linda's and do hers and tonight we'll wear some old boots on to the road to keep our shoes clean.'

'Are those kids still hanging around?'

Ana opened the door. 'They've gone,' she said.

The boys had wanted it to be a cowboy one but it was going to be a sloppy one after all, with kissing and people singing – La la la . . .

'La la la,' Macky sang with one hand on his heart and the other extended to his love Denny Boy. 'La la la, will you marry me?'

'No,' Denny Boy sang. 'No I won't, my darling.'

'Thank you. La la la . . .'

'Anyway,' said Denny Boy, flopping down on to his stomach, 'we mightn't be going yet.'

'We'll go. We'll get there.'

'Aunty Connie won't give us any money. I just walked over her scrubbed floor – by accident. Just by accident.'

'What did she do?'

'Picked up her mop. So I took off. She's in a bad mood. For nothing.'

'We better not ask her for any.'

'No . . .'

'What about Uncle Harry?'

'He's too mingy.'

'We could hoe his garden for him, and chop his morning wood.'

'Boy we'd be working all day.'

'And he mightn't give us anything. He might be broke.'

'And we might work all day for nothing.'

'Let's go and see Aunty Myra then.'

'Okay, she might.'

'But she mightn't.'

'But she might.'

And there was Aunty scratching her borders with the rake and all her ducks scrummaging into the loose soil at her feet. Wonder what sort of mood she's in.

'Tena koe, Denny Boy.' Talking Maori ay? Must be in a good mood – not like that Aunty Connie.

'Hello Aunty.'

'Tena koe, e hoa. Kei te pehea korua?'

'Kei te pai, Aunty.' Talk Maori back to her.

'Yeh. Kei te pai, Aunty.' That'll keep her in a good mood.

'Kai pai.'

'We came over to see you.'

'To see how you're getting on with your flowers.'

'And your ducks.'

'Kai pai ano. Kei whea o korua hoa?'

'Down the beach.' Hope that's right.

'Yes down the beach. And Charlotte and Ana are do-dahing themselves up for the pictures.'

'The pictures tonight.'

'Ah.'

'It's a good one.'

'Yes real good.'

'Kei te haere korua?'

'Not him. Not me, but all those others are going. Everyone else.'

'But him and me, we can't go.'

'Na te aha?'

'Because . . . because . . . Aunty Connie's in a bad mood. For nothing.'

'Yes just for nothing.'

'Kare aku moni, e tama ma.'

And that's easy enough to understand, she's bloody well broke. Shit what a waste of a good mood . . .

'Well . . .'

'Well . . . we have to go, Aunty. I hope your flowers are all right.'

'And your ducks.'

'Haere ra e hoa ma.'

Uncle Harry was hoeing up the dirt round his kumara plants. They could see him from the willows at the back of his place.

'All that and he might be broke, like Aunty Myra.'

'Wait a bit longer. When he gets to the last two rows we'll go and help.'

'If he's broke we'll have to try to get Aunty Connie in a good mood.'

'That's too hard.'

'Mmm. Worse than hoeing up Uncle's kumara.'

'All this trouble and it's only a sloppy love one.'

'Yes. La la la . . .'

'Shut up, he'll hear.'

'Anyway he's nearly finished. Let's go and help.'

'Hello, Uncle. We came to help you hoe up your kumara.'

'Hello, boys. Good on you. Get another hoe from the shed and one of you can have this one. I'll sit down and have a smoke. You two can be the workers and I'll be the boss.'

He sat down and began shredding tobacco along his paper as the boys started to mound the dirt up under the vines.

'That's the way, boys. Heap them up. When we dig them there'll be plenty for you to take home.' Well it wasn't a bag of kumara they wanted.

'Plenty of potatoes too.' Or spuds.

'Those others are playing down the beach, Uncle.'

'Yes they're lazy.'

'Just playing. But Macky and I, we like to come and help you with your garden.'

'Instead of playing.'

'That's good boys. Keep it up. Careful of those vines.'

'After this we'll chop your morning wood for you.'

'That's the way. Good on you, mates.'

'. . . Uncle?'

'Ay?'

'You know what Charlotte and them are doing?'

'No.'

'Looking at their ugly selves in the mirror.'

'And ironing their clothes ay?'

'They think they're bea-utiful like ladies in the pictures.'

'And their hair is all done up funny like rags.'

'And they got banjo feet and gumboot lips, but they think they look beautiful, la la la . . .'

'Hey, Uncle.'

'Ay?'

'You know why Charlotte and them are ironing their clothes and washing their hair?'

'No.'

'They're going to the pictures.'

'Ah the pictures. What's on tonight?'

'Well it's a good one . . . a cowboy one.'

'Yes, a good cowboy one, Uncle . . . All those lazy kids are going.'

'All of them, ay?'

'Yes, all.'

'Well, boys, you've done a good job there.'

What was the matter with Uncle Harry? Wasn't he listening? They'd hoed up two rows of kumara and now they were lopping the dry bush heads off the manuka and tying it into a bundle to start his stove in the morning. They'd told Uncle that all those lazy kids were going to the pictures but he wasn't listening.

'Good, good. Put your hoes away in the shed now, and stick our axe in the block.' Was he deaf or something?

'Got any more jobs, Uncle?'

'No that's all, boys.' Deaf all right. No ears. All that hoeing, all that chopping. And old Uncle No Ears going up his steps and in his door . . .

'See you later, Uncle.' Deaf Ears.

'OK, boys. Hey don't you want these?'

Up on to the verandah, pecking the coins from Uncle's big dried paua of a hand. Running, shouting. Shouting . . .

'Thank you, Uncle.'

'Thank you.'

'La la la.'

'La la la.'

Lizzie was coughing again. Mereana ran with her down the track past the garden, Lizzie's eyes bulging like two turnips, her chook hand clawed over her mouth. Running into the dunny and banging the door. Then the coughing. Mereana kept watch outside because they wouldn't let Lizzie go to the pictures tonight if they knew she had her cough.

And from where Mereana waited, she could hear the cough gurgling and rumbling up Lizzie's throat then barking out of her mouth as though Lizzie was a dog. Then after a while the gurgling and rumbling and barking stopped and she could hear Lizzie spitting down the dunny hole.

Coming out now with the bottom half of her face all white and stretched and her pop eyes watery and pink. 'Come down the beach,' Lizzie gasped at her. 'So they won't hear.'

Down through the lupins with the black pods busting, which was nothing really, only a sound. Lying on the beach stones and licking them for salt. Lizzie gurgling and squeaking, and Lizzie was nothing but an old crumpled bit of paper there beside her. What if Lizzie died right now?

'Lizzie, Lizzie! There'll be a lot of kissing I bet.'

'Mmm. Plenty . . . of kissing.'

'And she'll have lovely dresses, Lizzie.'

'Yes . . .'

'The men will fight over her. Ay?'

'Mmm.'

'But the best one will marry her.'

'Mmm. At . . . the end.'

'And they'll have a long long kiss.'

'At the end.'

Bending over the sea now. Her neck stretched and lumpy like a sock full of stones. Spitting on the water. 'Don't cough, Lizzie,' Mereana called. 'Don't. They'll hear you. They'll make you stay home.'

Oh but it wasn't that. Not the staying home. The cough was too big. Bigger than the sea – bigger than the sky. Now standing up, pulling a big breath in, 'Yes . . . I bet she has . . . lovely dresses.' And another long breath. In. 'There'll be a long long kiss . . . at the end . . . I bet.'

At the gate where the road began, Charlotte, Ana and Linda took off their old shoes and hid them in the lupins, then carefully slid their feet into the good shoes and smoothed the skirts, patted the hair. Ahead of them the others were running along the sea wall yelling. Leaping down on to the sand, running back up to the wall, but they were only kids. They didn't want kids hanging round. Mereana and Lizzie dawdling along behind them and that Lizzie barking her head off. 'We'll sit up the back,' Charlotte said, 'so we won't have *kids* hanging round.'

Not that the others wanted to anyway. Charlotte, Ana and Linda stank and had canoes for shoes and rags for hair. What's more, Charlotte and them, they had hairs under their arms and they were growing tits as well, just like cows. Along the top of the sea wall, flying now, and landing in sand. Cold. Sand goes dead at night time, up the wall again. Bits of shell everywhere, winking, on the road getting blacker every minute.

And waiting. At the store waiting. Lollies and a drink, then up the verandah poles, swinging and sliding – except for stinky Charlotte and them. Not Lizzie and Mereana either, Lizzie coughing like an old goat and baby Mereana nearly crying. Then . . .

'Here it comes.'

'Here it comes.'

Two eyes rounding the corner, bowling downhill. Jack had his foot down tonight.

Slowing down, Stopping.

'At last.'

'Yes. At last.'

Money in the tin. Smart the way Jack flicks you the ticket.

But Charlotte, Ana and Linda were waiting till last. What was the hurry? Damn kids. Always in a hurry. Always pushing. Always in the way. Well . . . well . . . Might as well get in.

'Might as well get in you two.'

'Might as well.'

'Go on then.'

'No you.'

'You first.'

'Go *on*.'

Up the steps. Gum rolling, eyes down. Wondering who's staring. All those big eyes in the bus must stare – or were they? Have a look, look away. They knew it, people were staring.

'All looking pretty tonight, aincha?' Jack yelled.

Bloody Jack. And now that Ana. That Ana had started giggling. Charlotte and Linda were wild with her. No wonder everyone was staring. No wonder . . . And look at Linda. Now Linda was going to. Sneaking along the bus with her hand up over her mouth, snorting behind her hand. Gee they made Charlotte wild those two – and Jack. Everyone staring.

Now Linda was looking at her with cow's eyes, rolling her fat eyes at her and cackling like a chook. Then oh! Oh shame. She, Charlotte, could feel all the little dribbles of laughter gathering in her throat – climbing, pushing . . . Pushing. She threw herself on to the seat between Ana and Linda as the sounds fizzed and exploded behind her hand.

The boys who had sat behind the girls at the pictures got off the home bus at the store and followed the girls along the beach road. They were tossing bits of shell into the girls' hair and shoving each other. The girls were giggling and telling each other secrets. Those kids were going to get a good hiding too, running up and down the sea wall. Shouting, 'Give them a kiss.'

'Kiss.'

'Kiss, kiss.'

'Kiss, kiss, kiss.'

Making sure to keep out of Charlotte's way because she wasn't really a beautiful lady you know. You had to watch Charlotte for the left hook and the leg trip, yes.

Ack, those big boys were dumb following Charlotte and them. Whistling between their teeth and chucking things.

'Give them a kiss.'

'A kiss.'

'La la la.'

But no. No kiss. The boys had stopped now that they had come to the end of the road, and they were calling out to the girls.

But Charlotte, Ana and Linda weren't answering. They had remembered something and were walking ahead, not talking, not turning, not looking down . . .

Their hair suited them.

Their skirts suited them.

They had shoes to wear to the pictures.

They might be getting earrings.

And stockings.

And haircuts.

And they'd just remembered.

And now Macky and Denny Boy had remembered too. 'Hey, you girls. What about your old boots you hid in the lupins?'

'Your old pakaru boots.'

Then away for their lives over the dark paddocks, through the thistles and plops. Lucky they had a head start. Up over the stile and jump the creek. Lucky they could see in the dark, those smartheads would never get them now – across the yard and in. Canoes for shoes. Rags for hair. Not till tomorrow. They'd kill them tomorrow.

But that's tomorrow.

Yes.

MICHAEL MORRISSEY

Late on Christmas Day Jack Kerouac was hitching through Putaruru with a Maori driving a 1967 Falcon Ute. The town was so quiet – even the Takeaways were closed – that Jack said, 'Are they making a film here?'

'Not in Putaruru,' said the Maori laughing. 'They made an ad here once.'

'They did!'

'Yeah,' nodded the Maori, 'about the end of the world,' his body shaking so violently Jack Kerouac could hear the forty-five cents in his pocket begin to jingle.

'The world isn't going to end,' said Jack Kerouac, 'even though it feels like it.'

'Hang-over?' asked the Maori.

Jack Kerouac stared forlornly at the empty street. 'Any girls in Putaruru?'

'Lots of them,' said the Maori, 'but not this time of year.'

'I'm looking for a grave,' Jack Kerouac said.

'On Christmas Day? – you got it wrong, Pakeha – that's the day he got born – he got buried at Easter.'

'His name's James K. Baxter. I heard he died around these parts.'

'Not in Putaruru,' said the Maori. 'Never heard of him.'

'He wrote a lot of poetry before he died.'

'But not much after he died, eh?' the Maori laughed again.

'I don't think death should stop us doing anything,' said Jack Kerouac.

'There's no red lights on Christmas.' The Maori roared through an amber one. 'What are you doing for a feed?'

'Bottle of Coke, takeaway – that's all I need.' Jack Kerouac looked down at the holes in his blue canvas crêpe shoes.

'You look thin, Pakeha,' the Maori grunted, 'haven't you got anyone to look after you?'

'Course I have,' said Jack Kerouac, 'but mémêre isn't here.'

'Who's mémêre? A racehorse?' The Maori shook with laughter.

'My mother,' Jack Kerouac's voice froze over.

'O.K.,' said the Maori, 'but you listen to me, Pakeha. I got chicken, eggs, plenty of kai – and lots of beer – how about a feed?'

'I've got to find Baxter first,' said Jack Kerouac.

'He won't feed you though, will he?'

'He'll feed me,' Jack Kerouac flicked his hair, 'he'll feed me.'

The Maori dropped Jack in Taupo.

Jack went into a Takeaway and ordered a Giantburger without the pineapple.

The girl behind the counter was six feet four inches tall and wore unrimmed glasses. As she bent over the vats of bubbling fat her glasses misted over.

Jack Kerouac wondered if she would look beautiful without her glasses.

He imagined her naked with just the glasses on.

Then he took the glasses off.

The muscles of his imagination had to flex, for it was hard work picturing *large* girls naked.

While waiting he noticed the machine in the corner. Walking over, Jack Kerouac peered into the cloudy glass. He saw three plateaus, heaped with ten-cent pieces, grinding slowly back and forth. The stated object was to drop a coin so as to successfully overload the first plateau, thereby nudging a further coin on to the next plateau and so on. The end result was an avalanche of ten-cent pieces.

Jack dropped a ten-cent piece in.

The plateau moved but nothing happened.

Jack Kerouac dropped in a second coin.

Again, no jackpot.

'Honey,' he said to the giant with fogged glasses. 'I need some change.'

'I could do with one myself,' she smiled down at Jack.

'Don't get fresh with me, honey,' snapped Jack Kerouac, 'remember what happened to Primo Carnera.'

'Who?'

'You don't have to worry – he won't come back.'

The girl gave him five more ten-cent pieces.

Jack dropped the coins in one by one without causing a single avalanche.

Then he noticed a sign which read. 'DO NOT TILT OR BANG THE MACHINE.'

'Yippie,' cried Jack Kerouac, banging the machine with his fist.

The lights went out and a bell started ringing.

The giant looked at him through her fogged glasses.

Jack Kerouac felt nervous. He had been beaten up in New York but this was Taupo. He'd heard they were killers in small towns. They blew your head off first and asked your name afterwards. He heard a car outside. Two cops came through the door.

The larger, younger cop looked questioningly at Jack.

Jack wished Neal Cassady was here.

'How are the Russians tonight?' the cops asked.

How are the Russians tonight. Jack Kerouac was terrified. They must think I'm a Communist, he thought. They must be a special squad. They would bundle him into a helicopter and give him a joyride over Tarawera. He would say, 'You can't do this to me, I'm Jack Kerouac. Wait till I tell Neal Cassady.' But that wouldn't cut any ice. They would slide open the door of the helicopter and shove him out. 'Merry Christmas Jack!' On the way down he would think about mémère and his little cat Tyke and feel sad. When he hit the Tarawera she would open her giant belly and Jack would go out like a letter on Caesar's Palace.

But nothing happened.

The cops talked to the giant, got their Whoppaburgers and left.

Jack played for the jackpot again with no luck.

Then a young guy dressed in patched jeans and jandals came reeling in. The whites of his eyes were poultice-yellow. He began telling the giant how he had ton-upped down the wrong side of the road at midnight, tyres ribboning and how when the cops had stopped him, he had laid them out cold as frozen hams . . .

Jack put in another ten-cent piece.

Poultice-eyes came over. 'You want to get rich, mate?'

Jack Kerouac nodded.

'Here's what you do.'

Poultice-eyes banged the machine with his fist.

There was a hard clinking sound that reminded Jack of the subways of New York, then several coins came sliding down the chute.

'That's the way you do it, mate,' said Poultice-eyes, collecting the coins.

'Say,' Jack Kerouac flicked back his hair, 'that's my money you've got there.'

'You want to make something of it?'

'No – I just want a few coins back.'

'Get lost pal!'

'I am lost,' said Jack Kerouac, 'I'm looking for Baxter.'

'Who?'

'Baxter.'

'Never heard of him.'

'Have you heard of Jerusalem?'

Poultice-eyes had, but he told Jack Kerouac that there was a lot more action in Taupo.

He reckoned they should have a drink.

They went to the nearest pub and got drunk.

Later on, the giant with fogged glasses joined them.

She took off her glasses and started singing dirty songs, her voice a razzy contralto that made Jack Kerouac's knees tremble.

Afterwards, reeling over the streets of Taupo – no cops in sight – they all lurched back to her flat and made love.

Jack was in the middle.

'This isn't helping me find Baxter's grave,' Jack Kerouac told the mirror next morning.

The mirror winked right back.

Poultice-eyes dropped Jack in the heart of a green nowhere.

By midday he was sitting beside a river.

Not far away he noticed a girl dressed in white overalls. On her hips she carried a bunch of keys, the kind that janitors used to carry.

She did not turn when Jack Kerouac sat down beside her but simply went on staring down into the slowly turning river as though she was totally Nirvana-ed and in a private ecstasy to which no one else was invited.

No one spoke.

But Jack Kerouac was sure their silence was warming up.

He began picking daisies and trying to slit their stems to make a chain, but he had bitten his nails down trying to hitch through Hamilton.

'How are your fingernails?' he said at last to the girl.

'Why do you want to know?' She frosted him with her eyes.

'I want to join these fuckers up.'

'They look all right to me,' said the girl.

'Yeah, everything's all right,' said Jack Kerouac softly. He lay back and tickled his throat with one of the unchained daisies. Turning his head he looked at the girl with such vast, dark desolation that even her private river-turning ecstasy was broken into. She seemed to soften a little, her legs bending at the knee.

'I guess those keys unlock many doors,' Jack Kerouac was imagining the girl without her overalls, naked, the big metal keys swinging from her hips.

Yes,' she said.

'And what's through those doors?'

Rising to her feet and zipping up her overalls the girl led Jack Kerouac to a large white house, half hidden behind trees, ferns and vines. It was cool inside the house, where there were big iron pots and grandfather clocks and little laced cradles devoid of living children.

'Ghost town?' asked Jack Kerouac.

'No,' the girl laughed, her throat was full of muscles.

'God, your neck is beautiful,' said Jack, 'it's full of −'

'The house is well over a hundred years old,' the girl went on.

'Yeah, I know that feeling,' Jack Kerouac said. 'But I'm on fire now. You feel me.'

The girl wheeled at the dark wooden staircase. 'Where are you from?'

'The world − Lowell − but that's not important now. It's where I'm going that's what counts. I'm looking for a grave of a man who never died. He wrote a lot of poetry. His name was Baxter.'

'He could be in the cemetery up the river. I'll drive you there.'

They left the house, got into her car and snaked off down the winding metal road. The ride was full of terror. The road hung over a sheer drop to the river. The girl, driving as though eager to test her theory of reincarnation, told Jack how she had never been inside a city longer than a day. 'So how do you like New Zealand?' she asked nearly skidding the car over a two hundred foot drop.

'I just came through Putaruru,' said Jack Kerouac. 'They were making a film there about the end of the world − I couldn't get a hamburger, no Coke, nothing − so I went on down to Tokoroa and ordered a thickshake and felt sad.'

'Why did you feel sad?'

'I thought about Christmas and Gerard and when I tried to hitch back from Bixby Canyon and couldn't get a ride on Highway No.1, and how I got known as the Buddha who was the Great Quitter − I thought about all that and got sad.'

'Wasn't Buddha always smiling?' the girl asked.

'Yeah, you're right,' said Jack Kerouac, 'but when he was me he cried.'

The girl shot him a Tantric look.

'Why don't we stop the car,' Jack said.

The girl stopped the car on the edge of a cliff and kissed him.

She had a stronger tongue than Jack's so when they parted he felt as though the top of his head had been hit with a tyre mallet from the inside.

Then they got out of the car, lay in the warm grass over the river and made love.

Jack was underneath.

Coming into Jerusalem from the Raetihi side Jack Kerouac didn't get the picturesque view. In the middle of the dusty narrow road was a huge sow.

As Jack climbed out of the car, the sow snorted.

'Okay mother,' Jack Kerouac murmured. 'I know you're a big one.'

He made a mental note that there were no takeaways in Jerusalem. Looking upward he saw the small white wooden church high on the hill. He began walking toward it. As there was no direct path he walked in a zigzag, seemed to get lost, even though he never lost sight of the church. Passing two sheep he got on to a track that led into undergrowth, lost sight of the church, came round to the road again. The sow was about three feet away. She charged. Jack Kerouac vaulted a barbed wire fence and ran straight up towards the church. Again a hedge blocked his way. He wondered what to do next.

'Looking for someone,' said a female voice.

Glancing up Jack saw a woman entirely dressed in white.

'Sister Magdalene,' she said. 'Would you like a cup of tea?'

Jack Kerouac smiled, raising his hand to his brow to shade out the sun that dazzled behind her.

Sister Magdalene took Jack Kerouac inside the convent and gave him a cup of tea, a lamb roast with five different kinds of vegetable, a plate of blood plums, a slice of apple and blackberry pie covering one hundred and ten degrees, then another cup of tea and a dozen date-impregnated scones.

He was scared that the nun was going to ask him if he was Catholic. But she didn't.

'I know what you've come for,' she said.

'You're wise,' said Jack.

The nun looked so satisfied Jack started to feel uncomfortable.

'Okay,' he said, rising to his feet, 'where is he?'

'Don't worry,' Sister Magdalene said, 'he isn't far away.'

She took Jack outside and pointed him in the direction of the cemetery.

'He's beyond the graveyard. You go back down there where you came, and come up the path.'

'There's a huge pig down there,' said Jack Kerouac.

'Don't worry,' said Sister Magdalene, 'she hasn't killed anyone yet.'

'Mam, you gave a condemned man the best meal he could have.'

Jack Kerouac went down the path, walking past the sow so coolly the pig took no notice, then up a winding path to where James K. Baxter was buried. Passing car corpses, rusted and overgrown with apple trees, Jack picked an apple and bit into it. It was sour.

He heard a noise behind him.

It was the sow, following him.

'Get along, old mother,' said Jack Kerouac softly.

The sow snorted.

'Okay, watchpig, you come too.'

At the top of the path there was a tethered black goat and a house. On the verandah a group of Maoris sat motionless in the evening twilight. The air was so still that an unbroken pencil of smoke rose from the chimney and went ramrod straight into the pale indigo sky.

The Maoris watched Jack Kerouac as he walked up toward their house. No one spoke.

Reaching the top of the path, Jack Kerouac saw the solitary gravestone with the single word HEMI written on it.

A dog came over from the verandah and barked at him.

'Watch out,' one of the Maoris called, 'he might take a bite.'

'I taste of blackberry pie and blood plums,' said Jack Kerouac patting the dog's head.

'He wasn't recognised till he died,' said the Maori. 'We lectured together, Hemi and I – you see that stone? – we pulled it out of the river, carried it up here – hand-carved the name out – there was no charge.'

The Maori continued to talk about James K. Baxter as Jack Kerouac sat down in the grass beside the headstone, lay back and looked up at the darkening sky.

From his pocket he drew out *The Rock Woman* and began reading aloud some of the poems.

Jack Kerouac felt something tug at his eye.

It was a tear.

'Merry Christmas,' he said, and once more bit into one of the sour apples, the tears from both eyes running down into a white stream that shone silver in the last rays of the sun as it flowed into the black heart of the Wanganui River.

'Merry Christmas, Jim.'

IAN WEDDE

The Gringos, a former rock and roll band of the nineteen fifties, seldom met these days. When they did it was by accident. Though none of them now played professionally they'd all kept their gear, with the exception of Nigel who'd sold his kit after the band's break-up because he'd felt stupid playing the drums by himself especially when his wife was listening.

But he still had his suit and since his attachment to performing days had increased over the years he'd also guarded those potent accessories: two pairs of blue suede ripple soles, a couple of chunky rings set with huge fake rubies, some velvet Mississippi string ties.

He was pretty sure the other Gringos had hung on to their clobber too. In their heyday they'd had a band suit: a midnight blue three-quarter length jacket shot with silver lurex, shoulders padded right out, wide scarlet silk lapels plunging to a single button at navel level, a scarlet Edwardian waistcoat with a rich paisley pattern, pegleg pants with a zipper on the inside of each ankle, blue silk shirts with a foam of blue lace on the front and scarlet piping on the cuffs. The Gringos had been good enough to afford this number and they'd played anywhere there was a hop between Christchurch and Invercargill, though Dunedin was their base and summer at Caroline Bay in Timaru what really took care of the brass.

There, they'd got the cops out more than once as local bodgies and yahoos packed dances to pick fights with kids on holiday at Caroline Bay. Of course The Gringos got the blame, or rock and roll did. But they played four summers anyway. In those days there was no bullshit. The lead guitar's pickup went straight into the amp and the metallic music came straight back out again. The two saxophones blew right in the faces of rock and rolling kids. The Gringos' bass went electric long before that was common, but he still marched it up and down, solid and even, that split-second ahead of the beat, the notes sliding out from under the guitar's syncopation.

From time to time they used a second guitar, but they found it complicated the music too much. Then there was Nigel with his basic kit: snare, foot-bass, hihat, one tomtom to the side, and one cymbal, a pair of seldom-used danceband brushes, and a rack of hickory clubs. The rim of the snare was battered, the paint and chrome flaking off down the side. But he wasn't just a walloper. If Pete had the knack of keeping his marching bass just an eyelid-bat ahead of the beat, Nigel had an equally necessary talent for staying that split-second behind: this was what gave the music its truculence: 'shootin' the agate'.

After the old rock and rollers stopped being heard – those endlessly interchangeable pros who blasted away behind Chuck Berry and Bo Diddley and Elvis Presley – Nigel thought the only rock drummer who got close was Charlie Watts of the Rolling Stones. But he didn't listen to much 'modern' rock music. After The Gringos stopped playing there didn't seem to be much point in listening either. And after about two and half minutes of any rock track he listened to these days he kept hearing a coda asking to be played, some final chop, a chord that would stamp down like a shoe on a cigarette butt. But the music went on. *Nah nah nah*, like jazz. He didn't like jazz, never had. Years back a friend had tried to get him to listen to Charlie Parker.

'That's bullshit, mate. The bastard doesn't know shit from clay.'

It was Chuck Berry from the start and it was still Chuck Berry as far as he was concerned when the band broke up. A few years later he'd listened in disbelief as a new English group called The Beatles sang 'Roll Over Beethoven'. The music had been ironed out a bit, he could hear how the equipment had changed, but it was the old Chuck Berry number all right.

Only it wasn't the same. Why he felt like this he didn't know. When he thought about it he decided it was because he wasn't playing any more. When he talked to the band they said the same. Also Lorraine didn't like rock and roll any more. She said it was all right when you were a kid, but . . .

But *he* could remember her dancing back then in 1959.

It had occurred to him that The Gringos lasted only a short professional time: '56 to '59. It was a thought whose meaning he couldn't catch. The *real* time was more than four years. Here he was in '73, he had one kid who'd be leaving school soon, and two more as well, he had a house up Brockville and an okay job with Cooke Howlison, it was fifteen years since The Gringos had played 'Maybellene', the last song they played as a band, Chuck Berry's first hit, their homage to Chuck. But *then* was still the most important time in his life.

'It was okay when we were kids,' said Lorraine.

And his son, who was fourteen, said he liked the old records but it made him laugh to think of his dad playing in a rock and roll band at Caroline Bay in Timaru.

'I can't imagine it.' Ha ha.

All the same the boy would skite to his friends. Sometimes a bunch of them would turn up, look at Nigel, and listen to some of his collection: 'Maybellene', 'Johnny B. Goode', 'Sweet Little Sixteen', 'Memphis'. Then he'd play them Little Richard, Elvis, and even Muddy Waters. The records were scratchy and worn. Down in the basement rumpus room of his house he longed to put on his gear and show them what it had been like. They stood around, amused, *listening*. He played his collector's item, a recording of Chuck Berry from the film *Jazz on a Summer's Day* at the 1958 Newport Jazz Festival, a performance of 'Sweet Little Sixteen' with Jack Teagarden's trombone blasting in behind. It made him sweat. He wanted to say, 'It took over, see?' They jigged awkwardly, shifting their feet. Then he'd play 'Rock and Roll Music' or 'Roll Over Beethoven', knowing what was going to happen, and sure enough one of the kids would always say, 'But that's a Beatles' song . . .'

When he went back upstairs with his records carefully under his arm they'd put on Osibisa or The Moody Blues or Grand Funk Railroad or for fucksake Simon and Garwhatsit. It was rubbish. He'd hear the *clok* of pool balls on the miniature table and from time to time the fizz of aerosol freshair as they doused their cigarette smoke with Pine Fragrance.

At fifteen he'd been a chippy's apprentice and smoking a packet of cigarettes a day. He couldn't afford it. But like everything else it had to be done with style. You spent hours practising, letting the smoke dribble from your lips and back again up your nostrils. You practised lighting matches inside the open half of a matchbox. Kidstuff . . .

It was no coincidence that The Gringos all had similar jobs. Nigel was a warehouseman. So were two of the others. The other two were clerks. They were all married. They all lived in suburbs near Dunedin. So it was natural they all got home on a certain day and saw a photograph of Chuck Berry on the front page of the evening paper, and all reached to ring each other up for the first time in months or in some cases years. It took a while before any of them was able to get through the scramble of lines. And then, as if by telepathy, there was nothing to say.

'D'ja . . .'

'Yeah it's . . .'

'When I got home . . .'

No sooner had Nigel hung up, heart thumping, than the phone rang again.

'Hey, d'ja . . .'

'Yeah Chuck . . .'

'Inna paper . . .'

'Fuck me dead . . .'

They met in the pub. What had happened? Where had the time gone? They went over a half-forgotten litany of names and dates and places. They remembered songs. They swallowed tears.

The day before the concert Nigel gave in to a nagging temptation. In the bedroom he took a large box down from the top of the wardrobe and from it he carefully lifted out The Suit. It was wrapped in tissue and then polythene and had been impregnated with thymol crystals. The Shirt was there too. He hadn't got it all out for so long he'd forgotten the texture and feel of the heavy cloth. It was perfectly preserved. He held the jacket up by the shoulders. He felt furtive and exalted. Quickly he buttoned himself into The Shirt with its chemical smell and its frenzy of lace. The neck button wouldn't do up. No matter, he'd . . .

Sitting on the edge of the bed he undid the inside zips of the trousers and stepped in pointing his toes like a dancer. In spite of their generous forward pleats he couldn't get the trousers past the tops of his thighs. They'd have to be altered.

Spreading his legs to hold the pants up as far as they'd gone, he grunted into The Jacket. Though cut to drape full and free, tapering not to the waist but to a point below his backside, The Jacket crushed his armpits and wouldn't button. Lorraine could let it out for sure.

Keeping his legs straddled, his arms held out from his trunk by the crushing jacket, he pushed his feet in the Blue Suedes. They fitted.

He shuffled sideways to the wardrobe mirror. There he saw a fat-faced man of forty with a shit-eating smile, whose hair, still black, had receded from his temples along the path the comb still took it, straight back. The fat man's hornrim glasses had slipped a little down his nose. He was standing with his trousers half up like someone caught having a nasty in a bus shelter. Between the straining buttons of a lacy blue shirt came tufts of black chest hair. The man's arms were held out sideways. The bottoms of his trousers were concertina'd against the insteps of blue shoes whose scarlet laces trailed on the floor.

Skip the waistcoat.

'Jesus Christ . . .'

But he stood outside the town hall with a dry mouth and a pounding happy heart. The other Gringos were there too with their wives. That made ten altogether. They felt like a club. It was a cold spring evening. The rest of the crowd was mostly young. The Gringos felt conspicuous but proud. They exchanged derisive glances as the crowd whooped it up. Some of *them* had got dressed nineteen fifties style: there were kids of nineteen and twenty with makeshift duck's-arse hairstyles and there was even one beautiful girl wearing pedal pushers, a sweater and a pony tail, and bright red lipstick. Nigel's eyes wandered her way. He wondered if she could rock and roll. It was certainly news to him that Chuck Berry was still appreciated or was being appreciated again. Lots of these kids were only a few years older than his own son! What did they know about the old style?

'The old style . . .': he caught at the phrase as it sidled though his mind. Then they were going in. He was still examining the phrase as they took their seats. The ten of them sat in a row. All around was the racket of a young excited audience. But no dance floor. A *town hall*. Like for concerts, the symphony orchestra.

He was still thinking 'the old style' when the backing group came on: guitar, bass, drums, electric piano. They powered straight into some standards beginning with 'Johnny B. Goode' and going without a pause into Little Richard's 'Awopbopaloobop'. It was deafening. The amps were six feet high. There was wire all over the stage. The bass player kept getting off licks like cracks of thunder which jabbed at Nigel's ears. He could *feel* it in his guts. The guitarist and singer had beanpole legs. He banged his knees together as he sang and play. He appeared to be chewing at the microphone. You couldn't really hear what he said. The audience sat somewhat sullenly.

Then there was a pause. There were groups chanting 'Chuck Chuck Chuck!' It just wasn't like rock and roll. The Kiwi backing group came on again and began tuning up. They looked scared. The phrase 'old style' was still whining away in Nigel's ears which he felt had been damaged by the preceding hour of noise. He watched the drummer up there as he straightened out his kit. He had about twice as much gear as Nigel had ever played with. For a start he had two tomtoms mounted on the foot-bass and another to the side as well. Then he had a total of four cymbals including a sizzle and not counting the hihat. What for? You didn't need it. Nigel admitted the joker was quick and fancy. But he couldn't play rock and roll. He was whipping the music along like a jockey taking his nag away in the home straight but what you wanted to get into rock and roll was slouch, you had to shoot the agate. You had to feel the slug of it like the sexy split-second between the thud of a girl's heart and the squirm of the artery in her neck, her breath gasping as she swings back under your arm, catching her flying hand as she goes past again, then rocking back in close. Or it was like not letting a fuck accelerate away with you before the lights changed, yeah . . .

This thought struck him as original. Leaning sideways to confide it to another Gringo he missed Chuck Berry's entry. When he heard the crowd go mad he looked up and saw a lean wolfish Negro wearing a check shirt and narrow peglegs grinning back over his shoulder as he slung his guitar and moved across to the electric piano to tune. This he did with such care and absorption, moving from member to member of the backing group, that the audience thought it was a put-on and began to howl.

But The Gringos knew better. Nigel was sweating but he sat like a boulder. The wolfish man struck a few elegant licks off his guitar. The sound was simple and familiar. The amps had been turned right down but he waved to turn them down further.

Then he cracked off a couple more licks with a bit more velocity behind them, grinned, rode rubber legs to the front of the stage and all at once was into 'Reelin' and Rockin'' while The Gringos sat petrified in their seats three-quarters of the way back from the stage of the town hall with all around them a howling audience of kids not much older than their own.

At one point as Chuck lolloped into 'Too Pooped to Pop' a group in front of The Gringos struggled out into the aisle with a banner which read 'We love you Chuck'. They ponced round the front of the stage with it and back down the next aisle. Chuck Berry acknowledged this gesture with an ironical double-take. But the music rode on. He swung his gat arm knocking the steely chords off the instrument as though brushing lint from a coat. He rode one heel across stage, the other leg stretched out in front. He did a pretty good splits and never stopped playing. Lowering the guitar between his legs he shot wads of sound into the audience which was by now dancing wildly in the aisles, not rock and roll, just . . .

But The Gringos sat without moving, as though turned to stone. They didn't miss a thing. They noted the glances Chuck shot at the electric piano player who couldn't rock the instrument. Nigel noted with satisfaction the looks Chuck sent from time to time in the direction of the drummer who was sweating blood. The bass player had been briefed. He marched it up and down.

And Chuck Berry, lean as a knife, lazy as calm water, mean as a wolf, sang and strutted and rubber-legged and licked away at that guitar whose pickup went straight into the amp while the music came straight back out again, no bullshit, metallic, 'in the old style', as though Chuck could never get old, as though rock and roll could never die, and The Gringos sat there with their wives while their Suits stayed at home with the real Gringos folded up inside somehow with the thymol crystals.

Oh Maybellene
Why can't you be true?

sang Chuck Berry. The Gringos had been a good rock and roll band for four years and that had been a lifetime. It was fifteen years since they'd played 'Maybellene' for the last time at Caroline Bay in Timaru in the summer of '59, and that had been even longer.

BUB BRIDGER

When Topaz found she was pregnant she went straight down to the pie-cart and told Mr Wheeler.

'Mr Wheeler,' she said, 'you've knocked me up!'

Mr Wheeler dropped the bottle of milk he was holding and it went everywhere.

'Not now, Topaz,' he whispered, 'not here – I've got customers.'

'Where then?' asked Topaz.

Mr Wheeler looked at the customers, who were watching them curiously, then he looked down.

'I'll have to clean up this floor,' he said.

'I don't give a stuff about the floor, Mr Wheeler,' Topaz said, 'I want to talk about what's up with me!'

'Please,' begged Mr Wheeler, 'please Topaz, I'll come round tonight. Ten o'clock – soon as Arnold gets here to take over.'

'Ring Arnold now!' ordered Topaz. 'Tell him to come down now.'

'I can't – not with all these customers here. *Please* Topaz.'

'All right then,' Topaz nodded, 'but you better be there Mr Wheeler. Tonight! Ten o'clock sharp!'

Topaz caught the bus back to her bed-sitter. All the way her stomach rumbled with hunger. As soon as she got inside she opened a tin of baked beans, but the smell made her throw them into the waste bucket. She put her head down on the sink and cried.

'Baked beans are me favourite, what the hell's happening to me?'

She put her head right under the cold tap and let the water run all over her face. It took her breath away, but it made her feel much better. She took her head out of the sink.

'That bastard!' she said, wiping her face on the tea towel. 'He'll be sweating right now and he'll sweat worse before I'm finished with him!'

She crossed the room and switched on the bedside lamp. In the long mirror by the bed she looked at herself, running her hands down her breasts and smoothing her flat little belly. She flopped on the bed and began to cry again. In the middle of her tears she saw the new love comic she had bought on the way to the doctor's surgery. She stopped crying and reached for it.

When she heard the doorbell, Topaz looked up in surprise. Then she remembered. The clock said 10.15. She put the comic under her pillow and looked in the mirror again.

'I shoulda done me face,' she said. She reached among a hoard of perfume bottles and chose one, splashing it about her throat and wrists. When she opened the door Mr Wheeler fell inside, grey-faced and trembling.

'Whatsa matter?' asked Topaz. 'You got the flu or suppm?'

'I'm upset, naturally,' said Mr Wheeler.

'Serves ya right,' said Topaz. 'I'm two months gone, the doctor said.'

'Are you sure?' Mr Wheeler whispered.

'*Sure*?' hissed Topaz. 'Watcha mean sure? The doctor! He's sure!'

'I don't know what to do,' cried Mr Wheeler. 'I'm in despair, Topaz. Me and Phyllis –'

'I'm not innarested in anya that, Mr Wheeler. You been after me since I started at that pie-cart! Well, you got me now – right in the shit! An' you can get me out!' Topaz didn't really think he could.

'Look at me body,' she cried. 'It'll be ruined. What joker'll ever look at me again!'

'Don't cry.' Mr Wheeler patted her.

'Will she divorce ya?' asked Topaz.

'What?'

Mr Wheeler reeled as though she had struck him.

'She might, when she hears about this,' said Topaz.

'Topaz, I been married to Phyllis for 16 years.'

'Ya shoulda thought about that before then, shouldn'ya?'

Mr Wheeler glared helplessly about the room, then he sagged against the sink.

'Could I make a cuppa tea?' he begged.

'Suit yasself.' She turned her head away and stared at the wall.

Mr Wheeler set about making the tea; whistling tunelessly under his breath.

'You want a cup?' he asked.

'No – it'll make me sick,' said Topaz. 'Y'know what? I got bloody morning sickness and it's night-time! Wouldn' that turn ya right off?'

It turned Mr Wheeler so far off that he swallowed his tea in one gulp and put his cup down quickly.

'I'll have to go, Topaz,' he said. 'I swear I'll talk to Phyllis as soon as I get home. Phyllis'll know what to do.'

All the way home he wondered how he'd tell Phyllis and what Phyllis would do to him. Panic jumped about inside him like a mad frog.

When he told her, Phyllis was so quiet he thought she might be in shock.

'Phyllis? Phyl?' The frog in his chest dived into his belly and leapt about in the tea he had gulped. 'Oh my god,' he whispered, 'all this is too much for me – I feel ill . . .'

'So you ought,' said Phyllis at last, 'you dirty old man.'

'What will I do?' he pleaded. 'Please Phyl! I need guidance!'

'You need a swift chop in the balls Bob, that's what you need.' But her tone was resigned. 'This Pearl –'

'Topaz,' he said.

'Where'd she get a name like that?'

'Her real name's Doreen but she doesn't like it.'

'Poor little bugger,' said Phyllis.

He grabbed desperately for a bit of the sympathy in her voice. 'Phyl – oh Phyl –' he reached for her hand.

'Don't touch me, Bob,' said Phyllis quietly. 'If you touch me I swear I'll chop you.'

He dropped his hands and clasped them against his stomach to quiet the frog. He began to rock back and forth, making small moaning sounds.

'Shut up!' said Phyllis sharply. 'You sound like a dog.' He shut up. But he clutched his stomach tighter and rocked harder.

She watched him thoughtfully, probing her tongue under her bottom dentures. It wasn't a pretty sight, but it was a familiar one and he felt a little better for it. But only briefly. Phyllis suddenly withdrew her tongue and the dentures popped back in to place.

'Do you want to marry her?'

'No! No! No!' he screamed, leaping from his chair.

Phyllis laughed.

'Oh Bob! She can't be that bad, surely.'

He slumped back into the chair.

'Okay –' said Phyllis, 'you'd better go to bed – I'll talk to you tomorrow.'

'What're you going to do, Phyl?' he asked timidly.

'Go down to the pie-cart and have a talk with Arnold.'

On the way, Phyllis bought gin and tonic. She liked Arnold. He was her friend. He had worked for Bob for years. She got out of the car waving the bottle of gin at him. 'Close up Arn,' she said. 'We're going to get drunk!'

Arnold finished his orders and slammed down the awnings.

'Nice to see you, Phyl,' he beamed. 'What are we celebrating?' And then he saw the worry in her face. 'Phyl?'

'Arn – that girl who works here – that Pearl –'

'Topaz,' said Arnold.

'Oh yes,' nodded Phyllis. 'She's going to have a baby, Arn. Bob's baby.'

Arnold's mouth fell open.

'Yes – I know –' Phyllis sighed. 'Pour us a couple of stiff ones, love.'

'What'll happen now, Phyl?' asked Arnold, sloshing gin into pie-cart cups.

'I was thinking of giving him to her.'

'Christ Phyl!' He held out her drink with a shaking hand.

'What's she like, Arn?'

'Phyllis,' Arnold replied carefully, 'Topaz looks like peaches but she's a bunch of razor blades.'

'Well,' said Phyllis downing her gin, 'that's probably what he needs – she could sharpen him up a bit.'

Arnold spread his hands. 'I don't know Phyl – I don't know. I wouldn't wish Topaz on old Bob . . . What about you? Do you love him?'

Phyllis smiled warily. 'Love, Arn? After 16 years with Bob I don't know what the word means anymore. Habit now, I think. Might have been different if we'd had kids . . .' She looked up at him suddenly. 'I couldn't get pregnant in 16 years. She manages it in three months. It's a funny world Arn, a bloody funny world . . .'

'Have another gin,' said Arnold gently.

When they'd finished the bottle, Arnold put her car keys in the till and sent her home in a taxi.

'You'll know what to do, Phyl,' he said warmly. 'I got faith in you.'

And blind drunk in the back of the cab Phyllis did know what to do.

Bob Wheeler didn't go to bed. He sat at the kitchen table drinking whisky and talking to the cat. The fourth whisky put his frog to sleep and he got brave.

'Listen Vera,' he said, 'Phyl better watch her step – I been a good husband to her. We got a nice house and she's got her own car. I take her to Taupo every year. I let her go to the Melbourne Cup in 1983 – and that cost me. I never mucked around all that much – a bit of bumble-fumble here and there, but what man hasn't?'

He poured another whisky. 'And I'll tell you another thing – she thinks the sun shines out of Arnold, but the only reason he wasn't in like a big hungry Labrador was because he's got a fast-eyed meter maid who keeps her tabs on him day and night!' He leaned down and stroked Vera's back. She smiled up at him then went back to sleep. 'You're a good friend, Vera,' he said.

He poured another drink and then it occurred to him that she might be thirsty. He brought milk and a saucer but the milk slopped all over the floor as he poured and it reminded him of the accident at the pie–cart and Topaz's bombshell. Straight away his frog woke up. He began to cry. He gave Vera a great kick and she leapt screaming through the open window.

'That serves you right, you bitch!' he sobbed. He got a mop and swished it about the floor. Vera poked her head back through the window and saw the milk. She eyed him warily and then she jumped down and began licking. He was filled with remorse. He got down on his knees and apologised. 'It's the state I'm in, Vera,' he said. Vera forgave him and went on lapping up the milk. He put the mop carefully down and passed out beside it.

Topaz went to bed without any tea because of the night-time morning sickness. She read two sentences of her love comic and fell fast asleep with her mouth open, snoring softly, in rhythmic little snorts. She looked like an angel.

In the morning Phyllis went to the kitchen for tea and aspirin. One eye was half open and the other quite shut so the top of her head wouldn't fly off. She fell over her husband and the mop. Once again Vera made a startled spring for the window. Phyllis held her head on and opened both eyes. Her husband didn't move. She closed her eyes again. Then she got up with an effort and swayed to the cupboard to feel for the aspirin. Behind the pain, her mind shrank to a hard little stone of dislike and it banished the last of her pity for him. She swallowed three aspirins and put the kettle on.

Topaz woke with an appetite. She poured milk on a bowl of Bixiewheats and ate while the toast cooked for poached eggs. She was halfway through a finishing-off piece of sponge when she saw the tin of baked beans upside down in the waste bucket. For a few moments she stared at it, then her mouth fell open in a shrill howl and bits of passionfruit sponge flew all over the table. She huddled whimpering in the chair for a while, but she was still hungry so she cut another piece of cake. She bit into it and felt better straight away. The phone rang.

'Hullo,' said Topaz, swallowing a massive bite.

'Hullo dear,' said Phyllis, 'this is Mrs Wheeler.'

Topaz almost dropped the phone. Then she rallied, 'Izzat so?' she countered.

'Now don't get upset, Pearl,' said Phyllis kindly. 'I want to help – I'd like to come round for a chat.'

'I'm not Pearl, I'm Topaz,' said Topaz. 'And how can you help? How can anybody help?' Her voice rose to a wail.

'Dear –'

'Don't "Dear" me!' spat Topaz. 'That bastard! Where's he?'

'Pissed as a fart on the kitchen floor!' said Phyllis coldly.

Topaz gulped with sudden respect.

'I'll be round in half an hour,' promised Phyllis.

Topaz put the dishes in the sink and cleaned up the cake crumbs. She washed her face and put on purple harem pants and a lolly-pink shirt. When she opened the door to Phyllis she looked like a flower. Phyllis gaped.

'You're beautiful!' she gasped. 'My god! What the hell were you doing – letting Bob Wheeler?'

Topaz shrugged. 'Ya better come in,' she offered reluctantly.

Phyllis sailed into the bedsitter. There were big posters of pop stars on the walls and a shelf stacked with love comics. And perfume. Bottles of it, crammed on the dressing table.

Topaz saw Phyllis's eyes pop. 'They're presents,' she said. 'From Mr Wheeler.'

Phyllis looked at all the French labels.

''E gave me perfume and clothes and that.' Topaz smoothed her purple pants. 'I like nice things.'

'I can see that,' Phyllis nodded. 'If Bob Wheeler spent as much on your back as he did on those bottles, you're not doing too badly, are you?'

'Watcha mean?' prickled Topaz.

Phyllis laughed. 'Yeah, so what?' she said, 'I've come here to try and help, love, not to pick on you. Do you want this baby?'

'Would you?' shrilled Topaz. 'If you was 16? Would you want a kid? What'll I do with a kid?'

'Do you want an abortion?' Phyllis had to ask.

'*No*! I can't do that! I can't! That's a mortal sin!'

Phyllis smiled warmly. 'Well then dear . . .'

When Phyllis got home Bob was in the bath trying to ease the pain and stiffness of nine hours on the kitchen vinyl. She opened the door and walked right in. She was smiling. He lay there in the bath staring up at her. He felt a terrible fear and his little frog quietly died.

'It's all settled,' she said. 'I've fixed everything.' Her smile was dreadful.

'Phyl!' he screamed, trying to sit up. But his frog came back to life and he turned into a toad which leapt to his throat and tried to choke him. He fell back into the bath.

'What's the matter?' Phyllis beamed.

'Tell me what's going to happen, Phyl?' he whispered.

'Oh yeah, of course! She's coming here. Tomorrow. Young Pearl. She's going to live with us. For as long as she likes. And when the baby comes I'm having it. You'll have to move into the back room. I want that big sunny one for her.'

'*My bedroom*?' he choked.

'Not any more – it's Pearl's.'

'Topaz,' he whispered, 'her name's Topaz. Oh Christ!'

Phyllis couldn't hear him. She was bustling into the big room, intent on removing all traces of him, singing like a bird.

FIONA FARRELL

. . . this afternoon, sitting under a silver birch in early summer, I decide I shall write about three things I do not understand: a man, a motorbike, and an aeroplane. Why? It will be a challenge (think of Ibsen with Nora at his elbow in her blue dress, Hardy and his secret red-lipped Tess). It will be an adventure. No guidebook, only a smattering of the lingo, up and over the border into foreign territory . . .

I'll begin with two boys. Those square-faced, white-haired boys with pink cheeks who went to country schools and wore cut-down trousers and striped handknitted jerseys. A barn, grey wooden slabs pulling this way and that, letting in zigzag streaks of dust-laden light. Harrow, dray, wire in exploding coils, bags, some full, some empty and flung down. Straw tumbling, nest for mice and rats and the narrow grey farm cats. And behind the harrow, leaning against the wall, a Harley Davidson 989cc motorcycle.

'That's Jim's bike,' says one white-haired boy who is Graham to the other who is Eddie. Jim is in France. Jim is with the Royal Flying Corps. Jim is 'Anzac Atkins'.

'We got a letter today, from Jim,' says Graham.
    'Oh,' says Eddie, sitting astride the bike, leaning forward nyerrowwmm into the long invisible straight.
    'He shot down a Hun four weeks ago.'
    'Mmmm,' says Eddie.
    'The newspapers call the Flying Corps the 'Knights of the Air'.'
    'My uncle's in France,' says Eddie, taking a fast corner.

'What's he do?' says Graham. 'It's my turn. Get off.'

'He's a sapper,' and Eddie climbs down slowly.

'What's a sapper do?'

'I think he blows up things.'

(You couldn't compete with a Knight of the Air.)

Another afternoon, rain beating on the barn roof, dripping on to the straw and the sacks, trickling along a muddy furrow in the floor.

'His plane's called Annie,' says Graham. 'After our cousin.'

Curious. Annie is small and sharp with freckles. 'What did he want to go and call it after her for?'

Graham shrugs. 'It's painted brown, his plane. But all the German planes are different colours, like in a circus so that's what they call them, the circus. They're red and yellow and black and all colours.' Eddie sits on a sack picking at bits of chaff and red, black and yellow splinters scatter in a grey French sky.

Under Graham's bed and well hidden, knees tucked up away from brothers and sisters. There's an applebox filled with treasure, his plane collection cut carefully from magazines '. . . and that's a Sopwith Scout . . . and this is a Fokker Eindecker EIII . . . a Handley Page 0/400 but it's not a real fighter they just use it to drop bombs . . . a Le Rhône Nieuport Scout . . . an SE5. And this is a Sopwith Camel' which was the best because it had two guns and could climb high and it was the fastest.

'What does Jim fly?'

'A Sopwith Camel, of course.'

Of course.

It was a thin black metal cross, punctured by two neat holes. Graham brought it to school in a toffee tin lined with cotton wool. It had been torn by Jim off one of those bright little planes.

'He's bagged six. This was off the sixth.'

'Are those bullet holes?' tracing the rough metal edge with your little finger.

'Yep.'

The uncle who is a sapper is in hospital in Kent. You couldn't compete with a Knight of the Air.

. . . Sopwith Scout . . . umm, Fokker Eindecker EIII . . . Albatross . . . SE5 no Handley Page 0/400 . . . Nieuport Scout and Sopwith Camel, the fastest and the best . . .

'Just think of it, Graham (the handwriting thick, black and sloping) we taxi out in the early morning, the whole flight, and wait wingtip to wingtip, till we get the order. Then it's open throttles and off we go with a whoop and roar you can probably hear all the way back at home. We head out towards the lines, keeping a sharp lookout all the time. The Hun is very cheeky and very clever. He'll wait up in the eye of the sun where he can't be seen then swoop down like a hawk on a mouse – so you must always watch and keep your wits about you.

'We give chase to any Huns we meet, rattling away at them and they go like stink. Then back to base when we've cleared the sky, stunting and spinning. Our chaps are A1 Hun-getters. We have a hit roll in the mess and the list grows daily. P.S. I have a little dog, a terrier cross. I call him Bert because I found him on the road near Bertangles. He is a scallywag, but good company and he keeps my toes warm on these cold French mornings . . .'

'Those cold French mornings.' So clear. You lift up though mist and cloud into autumn sunlight. At 13,000 feet it's cold and ice forms round your nose and mouth under your mask. The plane you've named after your cousin shudders under your hand and you climb up over the lines through puffs of smoke, white for ours, black for theirs, watch for gunfire flash, count, change course, zigzag towards the enemy, sunlight on wings and wind driving full in your face . . . No. Nothing could compare with it, being a Knight of the Air.

Nyerrowwwmmmm. Dadadadadat.

Mrs Everitt is small and round and soft as a bun. She has to stretch to reach the top of the board, so Eddie stays behind sometimes to help her dust off words and sums to leave a clear black space for the morning. That's when they talk. That's when he tells her about the bike. That's where the experiment takes shape.

It was one Saturday. Graham was away but Eddie had gone over to play and while he waited there was this bike, Jim's bike, a Harley Davidson 989cc. Really fast.

He'd ridden it up and down the road and no, Graham's mother didn't seem to notice or mind, so he was looking at it and suddenly he thought why couldn't it fly? Because it would be simple if you put some poles on the sides and tied a sheet or something over the top, if you got up enough speed. (The mountain clear and white overhead, the paddock stretching away toward the house.)

'And how would you steer it, Eddie?'

'With a kite, Mrs Everitt. You just put the kite on the back, then you sit on the seat and lean on the handlebars with your chest like this,' (leaning over a chair while Mrs Everitt prints carefully 'Today is Thursday, March 3, 1918' on the board) 'and it goes wherever you want.'

So he made the wings from bamboo and sheet and flew the Harley Davidson round the paddock first, just to try it out. Mrs Everitt said, 'That's very interesting, Eddie.'

A week later the Harley Davidson flew round Egmont. Eddie rode alone, leaning against the handlebars, bending this way and that, sunlight on bamboo and sheet and the Tasman wind full in his face. He recalled quite clearly how the bike had at first bumped over rabbit holes and gorse as they raced down the paddock and then the clean lift into the air. There was no question. No doubt. Mrs Everitt wrote Qq Qq Qq in a row and said, 'You're a very clever boy, Eddie. That must have been thrilling.' And it was.

Nyerrowwwmmmm. Dadadadadat.

And that could be the end of the story. But I like him, this boy. I like especially the way his thin little-boy legs press firm against the triple comforts of metal and power and speed. I like the way he bends forward, eyes streaming in the wind. So I shall put him aside, keeping just the corner of one eye upon him. And I shall think more about Jim . . .

Jim is a tougher assignment. See him as Eddie sees him first that summer, at the welcome home. He sees Anzac Atkins with thirteen Huns torn and burning somewhere in the air about him. And he sees a tall man with Graham's white hair and wary eyes who dances carefully heel toe one two three with all the girls and sharp-faced Annie. Eddie slick as a new pup drinks his lemonade with the other boys by the door and twists the button in his hand: it is a button from the uniform of Anzac Atkins who is also it seems just Jim and for which he has contributed two Indian rupees and a fossilised shark's tooth to Graham's toffee tin.

Jim says little, but the whole district hears him often enough for the two months he is home. The Harley Davidson roars into life up and down the road to town a dozen times a day at least, skidding into corners and a great streamer of dust rising. Jim rides like the devil, as though all the Huns in the world were screaming down out of the eye of the sun after him. Bent low over the bike in goggles and flying jacket, coaxing every stroke from the engine. Then silence and Jim is away again, to a resettlement farm up the Papaoiea valley. The road is suddenly quiet and the bike is back in the barn.

The Papaoiea valley. It closed around Jim as though a door had shut. No more letters to Graham, just odd scraps from grown-up conversation. It was rough country, heavy scrub, steep. Jim had driven some stock up the track in 1920 and he was 'trying to make a go of it', they said. Then he'd married, not Annie after all, but 'a girl from Stratford'. They had two kids. And in 1925 they came back down the track. No stock. No farm. No money.

Beaten. She moved back into town near her parents' place with the kids, and he kept right on going. He did some fencing here, scrub-cutting there. Droving. He was over on the east coast for a bit. Then up north. Just once he came home.

The boy Eddie has grown, well past playing on the Harley. He has discovered capitalism, and is earning money rabbit-shooting. The skins don't fetch much but it is easy enough to get them, the rabbits that year practically lining up to be potted. He goes out with Graham and returns with a sack stiff with blood and dirt over one arm. So here they are one July afternoon coming down the gully behind Atkin's place, sacks full, mimicking the easy stride of older men. The gully is dark, thick with overgrown pines and poroporo and near the house they hear it, a howl and a sudden smash. Graham drops his sack and is up the gully and scrambling through the rank green leaves and Eddie is two seconds behind. There's a caravan behind the wash house, completely dark. No movement. They walk round it, not breaking a single twig. Open the door. The van gasps smoke, booze, body reek. The crash they'd heard was a bottle hitting the stove, glass shattered and whisky dribbling to the floor. Jim sits on the bed, smoking. He doesn't look up as they come in so they stand, a little foolish, uncertain, and watch while the Knight of the Air struggles to light a cigarette, striking matches with stiff fingers. Who had waited wingtip to wingtip in the early morning, who had headed out across the lines, spun and looped and zigzagged through detonating anti-aircraft fire and expected death to knife down on him clean from the sun. Whisky drip drip drips from the stove.

'You all right?' says Graham.

'Eh?' says Jim, cupping the cigarette like a flower.

'You all right?'

'A1,' says Jim.

Graham takes some kindling and makes up the fire in the stove while Jim sits. As they leave he turns, rolls over on to the bed and drags a blanket round him, lying like a long grey bag someone had flung in a corner.

'We'd better get these skinned before dark,' says Graham, and they talk loudly about decent football boots, a watch and a bike as the light goes.

And the story could end there, but I can't let him creep away like that. He must pull up out of it and through to clear air again. Let's say Jim teamed up with an old Air Corps mate, that they began flying, making deliveries, offering rides, stunting up and down the country. You read about him in the papers. He'd work from a park or a paddock, take people up for rides at 10/- a time, spin them round the town for a bit, loop the loop if they looked like they could take it; he'd buzz the church, the main street and upside-down over the showgrounds to finish – all the evasive tactics he'd learned during the war. And let's say that one afternoon Graham comes over to Eddie's place. They see each other less often now. Graham has left school and works for his father who believes in getting his money's worth but it's pay just the same, so Graham runs a bike and sometimes Eddie in cap and shorts sees him at the station in the morning, waiting for some delivery, nonchalantly astride his Indian, feet planted in the gravel. It's a barrier. But Graham has come to say that Jim plans to fly under the Awanui bridge that afternoon as part of the aerial display.

'You're kidding,' says Eddie, and Graham says no, his father thinks Jim is going to kill himself and Eddie says he's probably right.

'Come on,' says Graham. 'Let's watch him try.' So they ride Graham's bike into town.

And let's say the showgrounds by the river are packed. They stand shoulder to shoulder with the crowd peering up into the sun. The faintest buzzing at first above the murmur of voices, then there they are, the aeronauts, swooping over the clock tower. The crowd sighs watching them skim the trees and grandstand, two little grey Moths looping, twisting, tumbling and rolling. Gusts of applause blow up from the crowd and the planes zigzag above it. The showgrounds overlook the bridge on the Main North Road. From where the crowd stands the arch looks impossibly narrow, but at last one of the planes circles and lands, and Jim draws back alone up the river. The crowd, in the words of the local paper, goes quiet. The noise of the engine drums up the river, closer, louder, a flash of sunlight on wing and it's all over. The little plane is through the arch as neat as a pin and gaining height quickly before the river narrows at the gorge. Graham takes off his jacket and swings it over his head. The crowd, one voice now, roars. They have watched death slide through the eye of the needle. So they yell and cheer and (as the paper said) give Jim a hero's welcome.

'Come on, young Eddie,' says the Knight of the Air late that afternoon. 'Hop in. Give yourself a thrill.' So Eddie hops and feels the plane bouncing over the rough turf before lifting as a swan does, easy after much flailing, into unimpeded air. Through the ear piece he hears Jim call from behind 'Hang on' and the plane lifts. A roll. Eddie's body sags against the narrow straps while the flat plate of the earth turns over his head. Then up again and it switches into sharp focus. Trees, hill, buildings, the mountain. You have never seen them so clear before. You will never see them so clear again. You are God on the seventh day, beating slowly over a new earth.

Two weeks later, Jim tried the bridge stunt near Auckland. He hit the river at 110 mph, bounced and flipped for a quarter of a mile and smashed into rocks.

And the story could end there.

But I want to return to the barn, to the Harley Davidson draped with a sack or two behind the tractor. When Eddie drags it away from the wall chaff flies in the sunlight zigzagging through the cracks. He wipes the dust from the seat, tears cobwebs from the wheels, and pulls it heavy against his side out into the afternoon. Behind the barn the track falls away down the hill towards the creek, rutted and channelled by the winter's heavy rain. He steadies the bike and puts a leg over the saddle settling into its wide leather curve. Egmont stands over them, so white it slices the air. He looks up testing the wind, hearing sheep and trees and the creek and pushes off. The bike lurches over the ruts at first and he swings his legs taking giant strides to drive her down, hold her straight. As the track steepens she gathers speed. Egmont shudders and the bike thuds so on flat tyres and rough ground that he can hear nothing but his body shaking apart and wind drumming in his ears as the Harley Davidson, earthbound, careers down the hill and over the bridge teetering from side to side through pothole and puddle until on the flat it leaps under his hand and they fall. Into a sudden smooth quiet so total he could have slipped under the mountain. Or perhaps they'd begun to fly.

CRAIG HARRISON

He sat back in the chair and the summer sounds of the garden began to fade. The sun warmed him harmlessly through the ultra-vi screening agent exuding from his pores with a faint herbal scent. It was illegal to sunbathe without taking a melanoma-cancer suppressant tablet.

His watch bleeped on the Newsfax frequency. *Damn*, he thought. He got up and went indoors. Charrie was watching video. A chain-slaughter epic.

'The microwave's set for eighteen thirty,' she said.

'I know.' He tapped his wrist. 'Newsfax. I'll take it through here.'

He went into the dining room and waved his hand over the wall console, thinking: was there ever a time when she used to say, *dinner in about an hour*? Had she ever said that?

The word processor came to life, showing Newsfax UK IntelSat Code A1. He felt a tremor of alarm. Bad news from England. After a short pause, he pressed the relay button. He could see his reflection in the screen, and he kept staring at his reflection as the message shot its blocks of glowing words across the surface, cancelling his transparency. Then he began to read.

His mother had died. All the facts were outlined. The NHS Death Register Database, centralised in Cardiff, noted termination of life functions at 0427 GMT, Cause of Death Bronchopneumonia comp. Cardiovasc occl., Social Security Number 30759438-ZKW3, NHS Code number Medics Database Access Number, and so on rattled silent across the screen.

Then, in green letters: INPUT MEMORY FUNCTION? The machine asked.

He pressed the MF button to input and the message was stored.

'What was it?' Charrie asked, turning as he entered.

'IntelSat from England.' He sighed. 'My mother.'

She got up and came to him, her face creasing in concern.

'Oh, Denny,' she said, and they embraced. Over her shoulder there were images of a chainsaw descending onto a naked girl. Then blood decorating a room.

'Send an Intel to Edith,' Charrie murmured; 'we can afford a hologram.'

'She doesn't understand them,' he said.

'She'll be expecting something, though.'

'Yes. All right.'

He went back to the console and pushed his credit disk into the bank database slot. Yes, they had credit for a hologram. He punched the Intel message to his aunt in Manchester; request person-to-person hologram, suggest 1200 GMT. Charrie came from the kitchen.

'I've reprogrammed the microwave,' she said.

'Do you want to come along?' he asked. She shook her head.

'No. Better if it's just you.' There was a pause. Then she said:

'Doctor Steinbach has a video series on grief therapy. On Ceefax. Or they have interface encounter sessions at the Resource Centre. Josie did one as part of her Thanatology degree. She said it's very enriching.'

It did not take him a very great effort to shake his head.

2230: Waiting for the IntelSat feedback from England, he switched on the news.

. . . said in Poland today that there was continuing unrest at the port of Gdansk between the army and union members on the anniversary of the . . .

Gdansk. *Danzig*! Of course.

Danzig! Give him bloody Danzig!

He remembered the tense faces round the radio, Aunt Edith waving aside the smoke from Grandad's pipe.

What's it to us, Danzig? If Hitler wants it, give him it!

What if he wants Manchester, sooner or later?

Who'd want bloody Manchester?
Who'd want bloody Danzig?
Mum smoothing his hair back from his forehead.
Come on sparrow, time for bed.

2235: Jill and Andrew leaned in and glanced at the screen.

'Dad? Can we switch over? They're doing a new video by Barking Eye. About angel dust. It's on Channel Twenty.'

'Yes. All right.'

Their own sets could not receive Channel Twenty. Andrew switched programmes, waved his hand over the light dimmer dial on the wall, and sat in front of the telescreen holding a glass of synthetic orange juice dyed as bright as his hair.

No lights. He remembered they couldn't switch the lights on because there was no blackout over the windows. The air-raid sirens were howling and moaning like frightened machines, droning down then wailing and howling loud again.

He was being lifted from the warm bed and wrapped in a blanket, held close to Grandad's tobacco scent and stubble face.

Come on, old lad, we're going downstairs.

People were trying to shout in whispers, as if the Germans might hear them. Feet thudded on stairs.

Harry? Have you got him?

Yes, go on, mind the door.

Oh God whatever's going to happen –

Edith. Come on.

Whatever shall we do –

The cellar was damp stone, clammy with laundry. The candle waved shadows over the zinc washtub, copper boiler, stone sink, enamel basins, shelves with dolly blue, Colemans starch, bleach, Oxydol, blocks of green soap. Monday-smells.

The sirens had faded. The rumbling a long way off was like when it got dark and thundered in the summer. But this came through the earth, as if there was a storm deep in the ground. It came closer.

So dark I couldn't find my slippers, said Edith.

Plaster shook from the cracks in the ceiling. Heavy thuds rattled glass and crockery upstairs.

Bloody Danzig, she said.

2240: The shaven-skulled man leaned back, the blue light catching the swastika tattooed on his forehead, then glinting on the sweat on his bare chest between the fragments of leather jacket looped with steel chain. He swung the electric guitar like a machine-gun at the camera, baring his teeth. The sound howled across the speakers and amplifiers in feedback shriek.

The children stared, expressionless.

Denny lifted the Newsfax Paper. In the dimmed light there were only headlines:

SOVIETS REJECT ARMS PLAN

WARSAW PACT FIRM ON POLISH CRISIS

He folded the paper and dropped it by the armchair. Beneath the paper, the carpet. Below that, floorboards. Below the floor, a space of half a metre, then the earth. Nothing else. No cellars.

Next time, he thought, *it will be quick.*

No memories.

Won't meet again. No old familiar places, or bluebirds over the white cliffs of Dover tomorrow, just you wait and see.

The camera tracked long shot across the screaming crowd, a mass of fists jabbing up in rhythmic response. Leaning forward, cut to close-up, the skull man contorted his face and spat.

Andrew arched his arm towards the telescreen, fist clenched, the light from the screen seeming to press his skin closer to the bone beneath the epidermis.

Once, Denny had asked his children why they watched this stuff. And Jill had stared at the screen and said: because they're *alive*.

In the cellar he had sensed fear far beyond his understanding. The thundering got closer like the maddened stamping of a huge animal furiously searching for them. His mother said, *let me hold him*, and her arms were cold and he had thought she was shivering with the damp cold of the cellar but of course it must have been fear. Don't get dust in your eyes, she had said when he looked up. She pulled the blanket over his head. The stamping animal screeched down with a wild bang, suddenly, right above, sucking the air into a throat-broken roar, shuddering the cellar full of sour dust. His mother made whimpering noises; Edith cried, 'Oh, the house! Stop it, stop it!' over and over again. But the shaking and banging went on and on through the night as though the sky itself had turned to heavy stone and steel and was dropping down over the world and nobody could stop it.

The worst fear, most frightening, came from realising the helplessness of these people he'd always trusted, who'd always been in control of the small world he knew. *Let me hold him*? What good would that do? Who was it supposed to help? He was amazed at its uselessness. It did nothing but push him against a shivering panic.

The world changed from then. The landmarks crumbled, nothing could be relied upon; just as daylight showed the familiar fractured into strangeness: cupboards opened on to the street, chimneys rested on beds, the sun shone inside wardrobes, curtains were impaled on railings, a bus had been thrown into a church. All this for him was a distraction, stunning images of a deeper, unrecognisable dislocation. He felt he'd found out something he shouldn't know and didn't want to know, and been changed in ways hidden even from himself.

Years later, at his grandfather's funeral, Edith looked at him across a roomful of relatives and said: our Denny was a brave lad in the air raids, didn't cry once.

I did afterwards, he said.

But she was deaf; and he was lying.

He thought, much later, that his dry eyes at the funeral must have been noticed, and she had responded. Why? Was it just her usual vague kindness, or was she trying to help him remember something he needed? If only, an explanation?

On the far side of the earth, his mind went back all the time. The dust of the cellar was in his throat again. Nobody held him now. Brave lad. Grown up. Face unstained.

2252: IntelSat confirmation of hologram booking for 1200 GMT, 2400 NZST.

He went out to the turbo car, sat behind the wheel and clipped on the seatbelt, activating the servodrive. The engine would not begin to function until he had pressed his hand on to the analyser panel on the wheel rim. The computer identified his handprint and ran a chemical check on his stress level. If it detected alcohol, it would not switch on the engine. If it detected ADN (adrenaline) above 2.5 microns per mg it would not permit speeds above 30 kph.

The engine came on, the dashboard flicking a warning light of a stress level of 2.1 microns. A valiol tablet clicked down from the panes. He leaned forward, then decided not to take it. The hologram booth wasn't far away; there was no hurry.

In fact it took half an hour to get there. The autoscan beamed a police radio warning through his quadraphonic speakers advising drivers to avoid Fenton and Bewick streets. No reason was given. Annoyed, he stopped the turbo, got out, and listened. There was the sound of sporadic gunfire in the distance. Flashing lights raked the darkness. Possibly a drug raid. Or more Polynesian trouble. His car, of course, was bullet-proof; but the police cordon would stop him. His safety would be irrelevant; they merely wanted to keep witnesses away from the district. *Damn*.

Then, when he got back in the turbo, his ADN rating had gone up to 2.5 and the car locked itself into its lowspeed mode.

The Telecom office was next to the supermarket, so there was no danger from muggers. The whole area was floodlit and patrolled by security men with Dobermans. He parked the turbo and entered a hologram booth by pressing his credit disk on the lock panel. Once inside he punched his database number and call number into the IntelSat terminal and sat down on the swivel armchair facing an identical chair about a metre away. The room was otherwise bare except for the screen behind him, on which had appeared (he knew without looking) a three-dimensional moving image of a beautiful sunlit New Zealand landscape. It was shown as if through a window to give the illusion that it really existed outside the booth.

But the booth was windowless and scented faintly of disinfectant.

At 2355, panels opened in the ceiling; a transmitter panel above his chair, and a projector panel above the empty chair opposite. The same would be happening in an exactly identical hologram room in Manchester on the other side of the earth.

The IntelSat chimed its transmission note and almost immediately a complete, apparently solid, three-dimensional hologram image of his Aunt Edith appeared sitting opposite him. His own hologram image, appearing equally real, would be sitting opposite her in Manchester.

'Hello Edith,' he said. She looked flustered.

'Oh, Denny,' she said; 'I can't get used to these things . . .'

Her hand, clutching a handkerchief, wavered in the air; 'poor Alice . . . it was just . . . it was so sudden really, but they looked after her at Terminal Centre, she wasn't in any pain or anything . . .'

No, he thought; pain was illegal at those places. Well, prevented, at least. And why not? Great advances had been made. Pain, cancer, accidents, war; almost everything was preventable. Except death, which ironically they encouraged, because a high percentage of elderly people placed a strain on the social services.

Edith went on talking. Behind her it seemed as if a window opened up on a 3-D image of central Manchester. Every time he had seen it, it looked less familiar, though it was probably the same picture.

And she spoke of the picture on the screen behind him, taking it for reality, as usual.

'It always looks lovely out there,' she rambled. 'It reminds me of that speech of Churchill's.'

'Churchill?'

'You wouldn't remember. During the war. I often think of it. He said, after it's over, we'll all live in broad sunlit uplands.'

The absurdly poetic phrase sounded odd in her Lancashire accent. But it seemed to mean something to her. He smiled.

'It's only – ' He was going to say, *only a picture*; but he stopped. 'Yes. It's very . . . nice, here,' he said fatuously, unable to locate any other words. Perhaps there *were* no other words.

'It never happened for us, though, did it?' she replied. There was a pause, and they looked past each other's images. He felt uneasy about the remark; she always spoke her mind, always had. But on IntelSat you never knew who might be listening. He hurried to fill the silence which was too expensive at the hologram rate of $100 a minute to waste.

'How are you keeping?'

'Oh, not so bad.' She gestured at her hearing aid. 'Can hear everything that goes on with this new thing they've given me.'

'Good.'

'Can't understand most of it, but I can hear it clear as a bell.'

'You'll see us all out yet, Edith,' he smiled. It was a stock phrase; but he admired her resilience. She had come unscathed through the twentieth century, the worst of times, the wreckage of wars and depressions and betrayals, and she was undefeated. He always felt reassured when he saw and heard her. Her endurance was the answer to the sense of helplessness. Perhaps you were powerless to stop the most terrible of events. You could only hope to survive undefeated. In a deep cellar, his mind said.

'You'll see us all out yet,' he repeated.

'Nay. I'm not . . . I don't have owt to live for, Denny. I don't see the point. Now Alice is gone . . .'

She fell silent. His voice choked. She looked straight at him.

'They have these courses, on the national health. Kubler something-or-other . . .'

'Kubler-Ross?'

'That's it.'

He stared back. Self-termination was illegal in New Zealand, freely available in England. Her image seemed to blur in his eyes.

'You know what it means?' he asked.

'Oh yes.' Another pause. 'It's all right, Denny. Don't fret, love.'

But he could already feel the tears, to his total astonishment, itching down his face. And he could see Edith, resembling his mother, her sister, forgetful again, reaching out towards him in the most natural gesture of comfort, in perfect futility. Because as the illusion of her hand, cabled with veins across its paleness, came closer, it could only vanish into empty light ghosting the surface of his face. He sensed nothing, but he realised he himself had instinctively leaned towards her gesture, and that, to her, his solidity must have dissolved into equal nothingness.

'I forget,' she whispered. Her hand stayed in mid-air, inches and half a planet away. 'Denny,' she said, 'don't take on so. You've got everything to live for. Nice home. Your family.' Her eyes glittered. 'Go on out into that sunshine.'

CROCODILE

ALBERT WENDT

Miss Susan Sharon Willersey, known to all her students as Crocodile Willersey, was our House Mistress for the five years I was at boarding school. I recall, from reading a brief history of our school, that she had been born in 1908 in a small Waikato farming town and, at the age of ten, had enrolled at our Preparatory School, had then survived (brilliantly) our high school, had attended university and graduated MA (Honours in Latin), and had returned to our school to teach and be a dormitory mistress, and, a few years later, was put in charge of Beyle House, our House.

So when I started in 1953, Crocodile was in her fit mid-forties, already a school institution more myth than bone, more goddess than human (and she tended to behave that way!).

Certain stories, concerning the derivation of her illustrious nickname, prevailed (and were added to) during my time at school.

One story, in line with the motto of our school (which is: Perseverance is the Way to Knowledge), had it that Miss Willersey's first students called her Crocodile because she was a model of perseverance and fortitude, which they believed were the moral virtues of a crocodile.

Another story claimed that because Miss Willersey was a devout Anglican, possessing spiritual purity beyond blemish (is that correct?), an Anglican missionary, who had visited our school after spending twenty invigorating years in the Dark Continent (his description), had described Miss Willersey in our school assembly as a saint with the courage and purity and powers of the African crocodile (which was sacred to many tribes). Proof of her steadfastness and purity, so this story went, was her kind refusal to marry the widowed missionary because, as she reasoned (and he was extremely understanding), she was already married to her church, to her school and students, and to her profession.

The most unkindly story attributed her nickname to her appearance: Miss Willersey looked and behaved like a crocodile – she was long, long-teethed, long-eared, long-fingered, long-arsed, long-everythinged. Others also argued she had skin like crocodile hide, and that her behaviour was slippery, always spyful, decisively cruel and sadistic and unforgiving, like a crocodile's.

As a new third-former and a naive Samoan who had been reared to obey her elders without question, I refused to believe the unfavourable stories about Miss Willersey's nickname. Miss Willersey was always kind and helpful (though distant, as was her manner with all us) to me in our House and during her Latin classes. (Because I was in the top third form I *had* to take Latin though I was really struggling with another foreign language, English, and New Zealand English at that!) We felt (and liked it) that she was also treating all her 'Island girls' (there were six of us) in a specially protective way. 'You must always be proud of your race!' she kept reminding us. (She made it a point to slow down her English when speaking to us so we could understand her.)

During her Latin classes, I didn't suffer her verbal and physical (the swift ruler) chastisements, though I was a dumb, bumbling student. Not for ten months anyway.

However, in November, during that magical third-form year, I *had* to accept the negative interpretations of Miss Willersey's nickname.

I can't remember what aspect of Latin we were revising orally in class that summer day. All I remember well were: Croc's mounting anger as student after student (even her brightest) kept making errors; my loudly beating heart as her questioning came closer and closer to me; the stale smell of cardigans and shoes; Croc's long physique stretching longer, more threateningly; and some of my classmates snivelling into their handkerchiefs as Croc lacerated them verbally for errors (sins) committed.

'Life!' she called coldly, gazing at her feet. Silence. I didn't realize she was calling me. (My name is Olamaiileoti Monroe. Everyone at school called me Ola and *translated* it as Life which became my nickname.) 'Life!'

she repeated, this time her blazing eyes were boring into me. (I was almost wetting my pants, and this was contrary to Miss Willersey's constant exhortation to us: ladies learn early how to control their bladders!)

I wanted desperately to say, 'Yes, Miss Willersey?' but I found I couldn't, I was too scared.

'Life?' She was now advancing towards me, filling me with her frightening lengthening. 'You *are* called Life, aren't you, Monroe? That *is* your nickname?'

Nodding my head, I muttered, 'Yes – yes!' A squeaking. My heart was struggling like a trapped bird in my throat. 'Yes, yes, Miss Willersey!'

'And your name is Life, isn't it?'

'Yes!' I was almost in tears. (Leaking everywhere I was!)

'What does Ola mean exactly?'

'Life, Miss Willersey.'

'But Ola is not a noun is it?' she asked.

Utterly confused, leaking every which way, and thoroughly shit-scared, I just shook my head furiously.

'Ola doesn't mean Life, it is a verb, it means "to live", "to grow", doesn't it?' I nodded furiously.

'Don't you know even your own language, young lady?' I bowed my head (in shame); my trembling hands were clutching the desk-top. 'Speak up, young lady!'

'No Miss Willersey!' I swallowed back my tears.

'Now, Miss Life, or, should I say, Miss To-Live, let's see if you know Latin a little better than you know your own language!' Measuredly, she marched back to the front of our class. Shit, shit, shit! I cursed myself (and my fear) silently. Her footsteps stopped. Silence. She was turning to face me. Save me, someone!

'Excuse me, Miss Willersey?' the saving voice intruded.

'Yes, what is it?'

'I think I heard someone knocking on the door, Miss Willersey.' It was Gill, the ever-aware, always courageous Gill. The room sighed. Miss Willersey had lost the initiative. 'Shall I go and see who it is, Miss Willersey?' Gill asked, standing up and gazing unwaveringly at Miss Willersey. We all focused our eyes on her too. A collective defiance and courage. For a faltering moment I thought she wasn't going to give in.

Then she looked away from Gill and said, 'Well, all right and be quick about it!'

'You all right, Miss To-Live?' Gill asked me after class when all my friends crowded round me in the corridor.

'Yes!' I thanked her.

'Croc's a bloody bitch!' someone said.

'Yeah!' the others echoed.

So for the remainder of my third-form year and most of my fourth year I *looked* on Miss Susan Sharon Willersey as the Crocodile to be wary of, to pretend good behaviour with, to watch all the time in case she struck out at me. Not that she ever again treated me unreasonably in class despite my getting dumber and dumber in Latin (and less and less afraid of her).

In those two years, Gill topped our class in Latin, with little effort and in courageously clever defiance of Crocodile. Gill also helped me to get the magical 50% I needed to pass and stay out of Crocodile's wrath.

Winter was almost over, the days were getting warmer, our swimming pool was filled and the more adventurous (foolhardy?) used it regularly. Gill and I (and the rest of Miss Rashly's cross-country team) began to rise before light and run the four miles through the school farm. Some mornings, on our sweaty way back, we would meet a silent Crocodile in grey woollen skirt and thick sweater and boots, striding briskly through the cold.

'Morning, girls!' she would greet us.

'Morning, Miss Willersey!' we would reply.

'Exercise, regular exercise, that's the way, girls!'

In our fourth-form dormitory, my bed was nearest the main door that opened out to the lounge opposite which was the front door to Crocodile's apartment, forbidden domain unless we were summoned to it to be questioned (and punished) for a misdemeanour, or invited to it for hot cocoa and biscuits (prefects were the usual invitees!). Because it *was* forbidden territory we were curious about what went on in there: how Croc lived, what she looked like without her formidably thick make-up and stern outfits, and so on. As a Samoan I wasn't familiar with how papalagi (and especially Crocodile) lived out their private lives. I tried but I couldn't picture Miss Willersey in her apartment in her bed or in her bath in nothing else (not even her skin) but in her make-up, immaculately coiffured hair and severe suits. (I couldn't even imagine her using the toilet! Pardon the indiscretion which is unbecoming of one of Miss Willersey's girls!)

The self-styled realists and sophisticates among us – and they were mainly seniors who had to pretend to such status – whispered involved and terribly upsetting (exciting) tales about Crocodile's men (and lack of men), who visited (and didn't visit) her in the dead of night. We, the gullible juniors, inexperienced in the ways of men and sex, found these lurid tales erotically exciting (upsetting) but never admitted publicly we *were* excited. We all feigned disgust and disbelief. And quite frankly I couldn't imagine Miss Willersey (in her virgin skin) with a man (in his experienced skin) in her bed in the wildly lustful embrace of *knowing each other* (our Methodist Bible-class teacher's description of the art of fucking!). No, I really tried, but couldn't put Crocodile into that forbidden but feverishly exciting position. At the time I *did* believe in Miss Willersey's strict moral standards concerning the relationship between the sexes. (I was a virgin, and that's what Miss Willersey and my other elders wanted me to retain and give to the man I married.)

One sophisticate, the precociously pretentious and overweight daughter of a Wellington surgeon and one of Crocodile's pet prefects, suggested the Croc's nightly visitors *weren't* men. That immediately put more disgustingly exciting possibilities into our wantonly frustrated (and virgin) imaginations.

'Who then?' an innocent junior asked.

'What then?' another junior asked.

'Impossible. Bloody filthy!' the wise Gill countered.

'It happens!' the fat sophisticate argued.

'How do you know?' someone asked.

'I just know, that's all!'

'Because your mother is a lesbian!' Gill, the honest, socked it to her. We had to break up the fight between Gill and the Wellington sophisticate.

'Bugger her!' Gill swore as we led her out of the locker room. 'She sucks up to Miss Willersey and then says Croc's a les!'

'What's – what's a les . . . lesbian?' I forced myself to ask Gill at prep that evening. She looked surprised, concluded with a shrug that I didn't really know, printed something on a piece of paper and, after handing it to me, watched me read it.

A FEMALE WHO IS ATTRACTED TO OTHER FEMALES!!!

'What do you mean?' I whispered. (We weren't allowed to talk during prep.)

She wrote on the paper. '*You Islanders are supposed to know a lot more about sex than us poor pakehas. A les is a female who does it with other females. Savvy?*'

'*Up you too!*' I wrote back. We started giggling.

'Gill, stand up!' the prefect on duty called.

'Oh, shit!' Gill whispered under her breath.

'Were you talking?'

'Life just wanted me to spell a word for her!' Gill replied.

'What word?'

'Les–,' Gill started to say. My heard nearly stopped. 'Life wanted to know how to spell "lesson"!' Relief.

'Well, spell it out aloud for all of us!' And Gill did so, crisply, all the time behind her back giving the prefect the up-you sign.

After this incident, I noticed myself observing the Crocodile's domain more closely for unusual sounds, voices, visitors, and, though I refused to think of the possibility of her being a lesbian, I tried to discern a pattern in her female visitors (students included), but no pattern emerged. Also, there were no unusual sounds. (Croc didn't even sing in the bath!)

Some creature, almost human, was trapped in the centre of my head, sobbing pitifully, mourning an enormous loss. It was wrapping its pain around my dreaming and I struggled to break away from its tentacles. I couldn't. I woke to find myself awake (and relieved I wasn't strangling in the weeping) in the dark of our dormitory. Everyone else was fast asleep.

Then I knew it was Miss Willersey. I knew it and tried not to panic, not to give in to the feeling I wasn't going to be able to cope. I wrapped the blankets round my head. It was none of my business! But I couldn't escape.

I found myself standing with my ear to Miss Willersey's door. Shivering. Her light was on, I could tell from the slit of light under the door. The sobbing was more audible but it sounded muffled, as if she was crying into a pillow or cushion. Uncontrolled. Emerging from the depths of a fathomless grief. Drawing me into its depths.

My hand opened the door before I could stop it. Warily I peered into the blinding light. My eyes adjusted quickly to the glare. The neat and orderly arrangement of furniture, wall pictures, ornaments, and bookcases came into focus. Miss Willersey was enthroned in an armchair against the far wall, unaware of my presence, unaware of where she was and who she was, having relinquished in her grief all that was the Crocodile. She was dressed in a shabby dressing-gown, brown slippers, hair in wild disarray, tears melting away her thick make-up in streaks down her face, her long-fingered hands clasped to her mouth trying to block back the sound.

Shutting the door behind me quietly, I edged closer to her, hoping she would see me and order me out of her room and then I wouldn't have to cope with the new, fragile, vulnerable Miss Willersey. I didn't want to.

All around us (and in me) her grief was like the incessant buzzing of a swarm of bees, around and around, spiralling up out of the hollow hive of her being and weaving round and round in my head, driving me towards her and her sorrow which had gone beyond her courage to measure and bear.

And I moved into her measure and, lost for whatever else to do, wrapped my arms around her head, and immediately her arms were around me tightly and my body was the cushion for her grief.

At once she became my comfort, the mother I'd never had but had always yearned for, and I cried silently into her pain. Mother and daughter, daughter and mother. A revelation I hoped would hold true for as long as

I was to know her.

Her weeping eased. Her arms relaxed around me. She turned her face away. 'Please!' she murmured. I looked away. Got the box of tissues on the table and put it in her shaking hands. I looked away. Tearing out a handful of tissues, she wiped her eyes and face.

I started to leave. 'It is Ola, isn't it?' she asked, face still turned away. In her voice was a gentleness I have never heard in it before.

'Yes.'

'Thank you. I'm . . . I'm sorry you've had to see me like this.' She was ripping out more tissues.

'Is there anything else I can do?' I asked.

'No, thank you.' She started straightening her dressing-gown and hair. The Crocodile was returning. I walked to the door. 'Ola!' she stopped me. I didn't look back at her. 'This is our secret. Please don't tell the others?'

'I won't, Miss Willersey. Good-night!'

'Good-night, Ola!'

I shut the door behind me, quietly, and on *our* secret.

Next morning there was a short article in the newspaper about her mother's death in Hamilton, in an old people's home. Miss Willersey left on the bus for Hamilton that afternoon.

'That Croc's mother's crocked!' some girls joked at our table at dinner that evening.

Yes. Crocodile Willersey remained married to her school and students until she died in 1982. By becoming a school tradition and a mythical being in the memories of all her students (generations of them) she has lived on, and we will bequeath her to our children.

Miss Susan Sharon Willersey, the Crocodile, I will always think of you with genuine alofa. (And forgive me – I've forgotten nearly all the Latin you taught me!) By the way, you were wrong about the meaning of Ola; it can also be a noun, Life.

'I really can't place you at all,' said Mona Carmichael and Humphrey noticed she drew the high arches of her eyebrows with grey pencil now, not the black his memory supplied.

'Aren't I a mess?' she used to say, sketching wildly on her forehead. 'Well, they're done now,' and flinging the pencil into the disorder of tangled beads, empty perfume bottles and spilt lotions on her dressing-table, strode away again in her big brown brogues. 'Get a wriggle on, you little beasts.' Babysitter Humphrey would have been left to grapple with James and Teresa.

'You do not,' she said now, 'ring any sort of bell.' There was a long pause. Always a large woman, she stood at the front door with a sagging ebullience that heralded the approach of a deflated but aggressive old age. 'Not any sort of bell at all.'

He noted that a marked little yellow growth had begun to creep across each of her eyes, had nearly reached the left iris. Sun damage, he thought, quite a painful operation to have them removed. He smiled at her suddenly. Never fatal, of course, never blinding, not unusual. Painful, though, and inconvenient. His smile broadened.

She had always been fond of sunbathing.

'Just take the little beasts for another walk, will you, Humphrey – I want to do my back for half an hour.' They were at the beach again for the day.

'Not right along to the old wreck again? But we've been there twice already,' said little James and placed a sandy hand in Humphrey's.

'It's miles and miles and I know it off by heart,' was Teresa's contribution. 'I can draw it without even looking.'

'Drawing's after lunch,' their mother hooted. 'Now, all run along. Mummy's tired.'

When they returned she rolled lazily over.

'Now, wasn't that fun?'

'No, it wasn't.' The children were almost demented with fatigue. 'What's for lunch?'

'It's a big adventure today. Mummy's just thrown everything in the basket and you can pick out whatever you like and make it yourselves. Humphrey can look after you.'

'I suppose you'd better come in,' she said now. 'I'll give Toby a yell. He might be able to place you.'

As they passed the old clock in the hall it struck a quarter-to-three. 'How time does fly,' she said. 'And what' – he seated himself carefully between piles of newspapers on the sofa, green now and not the familiar pink of his boyhood – 'do you do for a living?'

'I'm a surgeon,' said Humphrey and as she flopped into a chair on the opposite side of the room he saw the knots of veins in her calves. Varicose veins. Another painful one.

'I must say you've got a nice bright smile,' she said. 'It must cheer your patients up. What made you decide on surgery?'

'The only way you get out of the mud and the muck in this old world is to study,' she had said all those years ago, 'that's if you haven't got any pull and you haven't got any pull, have you Humphrey-Bumphrey?' He said he had no pull. 'You'll have to study, Humphrey-Bumphrey, won't you? Nose to the grindstone, burning the midnight oil? Better you than me.' Her large smooth face, turned towards him like an inattentive boiled egg, broke open with her shrieks of laughter. He thought her wonderfully wise. 'Just put some more oil on my back, Humphrey, and then you can take my purse and get the little beasts an ice cream, and have one yourself if a great big boy like you still has ice creams.'

'I've forgotten what decided me on it,' he said now as a violent blowfly attacked a figurine on the mantelpiece.

She stood up to check the time on the hall clock.

'It's ten to three,' she said as a door slammed at the back of the house. 'Here comes Toby.' The voice rose to a desperate cry. 'Toby, Toby, do hurry. I'm in the sitting room. This young man says he knows us, but aren't I a silly child? I can't place him at all.'

Advancing footsteps seemed to stop in the hall, near the clock.

'It's nearly five to,' said a man's voice. 'It's nearly time to turn it on.' In a moment Toby stood in the doorway, blinking over the top of his spectacles. 'What's all the noise about?' he said. She explained a second time.

'I wouldn't know you from a bar of soap,' said Toby at last. 'What was the name again?'

'He's a Dr Henry Girdlestone, Toby.' Mona smiled at him brightly and he saw that her dentures were unevenly worn, favouring the right side which could mean long-term ulceration of the left inner cheek.

'Humphrey,' said Humphrey. 'Humphrey Huddlestone. Mr.'

'Well, you've got a lovely smile anyway, hasn't he Toby?'

Toby was looking at the clock again.

'It's after five-to-three,' he said. 'You've usually got it turned on by now, Mon.' He coughed, a rich sound that Humphrey thought could mean a serious congestion in the upper thoracic cavity leading to later sporadic infection. 'By jove,' said Toby, 'you have got a big bright smile, haven't you? Shame we can't place you. You just don't ring a bell.'

'Just a private visit, is it, sir?' The receptionist at the hotel seemed a bright friendly girl and there was a genuine interest in her eyes, he thought, when he checked in an hour ago.

'Business, actually. I'm on a lecture tour,' Humphrey told her, 'but I have friends here. I'll be visiting friends.'

He had pictured it all. Mona and Toby would come running out to meet him.

'It's dear old Humphrey, after all these years.'

'Was there anything more, sir? Is there anything else you require?' the receptionist asked as the telephone began to ring again and as he walked away to the carpark he heard her say, with that same false concern, 'Yes, sir. Certainly, sir. Now, is that Johnson with a "t"?'

'I do hope you don't mind my asking,' said Mona now as the blowfly exchanged the figurine for a stain on the mat, 'but you weren't thinking of staying long, were you? It wouldn't be worthwhile putting the kettle on would it? You probably have to rush away.'

Humphrey thought of his articles on invisible sutures (received with some acclaim in the most reticent medical circles), his papers on the partial anaesthesia of digits, how he had laboriously learned to foxtrot, then mambo and samba. He had looked forward to being fussed over in his old home town.

'It's right on three,' said Toby. 'It's going to strike three any minute now. We're usually sitting there by now,' he said, 'all set up with the trays and the red thermos.'

'No, no.' Humphrey stood up. 'I just popped in for a moment. I've stayed far too long already.'

'What a shame you have to dash off.' Mona Carmichael's steady march towards the front door was as inexorable as a fugue or the line of grey blobs, possibly old porridge, that advanced across the seat of the sofa. 'We really mustn't delay you, Dr Girdlestone.' She paused with her hand on the door knob. 'It's a terribly funny thing that neither of us can place you. I had masses of people helping, as you might remember. Housework just wasn't my thing.'

'As I might remember,' said Humphrey.

'I always found,' she said, 'that the boys were much more willing than the girls.'

He knew that very well.

'Just whack up some of those Boy Scouts pikelets of yours, will you, Humphrey?' She used to shout. 'Just bash around a bit with the cleaner, will you, Humphrey, before all the girls come for bridge. I say, Humphrey-Bumphrey? This dress isn't too lowcut is it, for the afternoon? Do you think it's more evening?'

When he wheeled in the tea trolley she would say, 'Girls, I want you to meet Humphrey, my right-hand man.' He would find himself regarded by three pairs of eyes, all vividly outlined in blue or green, lipstick bleeding gently through the lines forming round those little mouths and all the scarlet-tipped nails almost glued to winning flushes. The Town Clerk's wife, in oyster artificial silk, sat like a draped and welcoming deity amidst the redolent cigarette smoke.

'We know all about you and your right-hand men, Mona,' she cackled.

'What part of town did you say you were from?' asked Toby as he stepped out on to the veranda.

'Over there.' Humphrey's right arm sketched a wide mysterious arc that could have encompassed the universe.

'I honestly don't think we ever knew anyone from over that way,' said Mona. 'It seems very odd. I mean, you remember everything so well.' She glanced at the clock again. It was two minutes past three.

'I'll just run and turn it on. I'll get everything ready.' Toby wheeled round and marched down the hall.

'Do you watch television at all?' Mona asked now. 'Have you ever seen *Now Beats the Heart*?'

'That's not really my field,' said Humphrey. 'I'm more . . .' How could he describe his gynaecological work? She might ask him questions about her own insides. They often did. 'I'm more further down,' he said at last.

'Silly man.' She tapped his shoulder. 'It's a drama. The clothes are out of this world. Mind you, I'm not glued to the thing, like some people.'

'It's got quite an appeal for people in all walks of life,' shouted Toby from the inner reaches of the house, 'even men.'

Humphrey looked back into the hall.

'Is that a picture of Teresa I see there?' he asked. 'Do you remember when she cut up her golliwog and put it in the teapot?'

'We don't seem to see much of Miss Teresa these days. They grow away, you know. Everybody says so.' Her wide mouth snapped shut.

'I remember Jamie,' said Humphrey. It seemed wise to change the subject.

'We don't mention Master James,' she said.

'Nobody of that name here,' shouted Toby.

'I simply do not know,' said Mona. 'Those children even had music lessons with the nuns.'

Humphrey took a giant stride to the sanctuary of his car. His wife, formerly his theatre sister, kept air-freshening canisters in the glove compartment and the soothing smell of lavender and verbena settled round him. The throbbing of the motor was hardly louder than the sound of his own pulse beating in his ears.

'I say, come back, come back.' Mona had been joined on the front lawn by Toby, carrying a newspaper. 'I say, you're on the front page of the old rag.'

'The old girl's going to put the kettle on.' Toby picked his way carefully through the dandelions and thistles.

'There's absolutely not a skerrick of anything in the tins. You know me.' She gave a barking laugh. 'But what's that between friends. I'll whack up a bit of toast and I've got some cinnamon,' she said, 'somewhere. I'll whack up cinnamon toast.'

Humphrey's immaculately shod foot prepared to caress the accelerator. He pressed the button that locked the windows. The Carmichaels, approaching at a fast trot, seemed about to tap upon them.

He noticed an uneven rhythm to the gait though, each favouring one particular leg. Hip replacements for them both, he thought, within five years. Quite an excruciating procedure and then all those months of hobbling about.

'I see your great big smile, you naughty boy.' Mona's face loomed beside his. 'I remember you – you're that quaint boy from the children's home. You can't imagine what a quaint soul you were.'

He could though, very clearly now.

Toby waved the newspaper at him and drew closer, hopping along through the weeds in that odd pecking way, legs apart. Possibly, thought Humphrey, incipient trouble with the prostate culminating in another painful piece of surgery, embarrassing too. There would be the devastating rubber draining tube snaking from under the bedclothes to the bottle strung up beside the mattress.

'And what colour is the bottle today, nurse?' the surgeon would ask.

'Rose, a deep rose.'

'Well, I think we'll have to leave it in another day.'

In his wards he insisted the bottles should be covered with tartan bags during visiting hours.

'You're quite the crème de la crème,' Toby shouted from the front gate.

'I don't want to interfere with this little job of yours, Humphrey,' Matron told him. 'Humphrey, you're nearly seventeen years old – you're far too old to kick the leg of the chair like that.'

He remembered sulking, and staring out the window. What could Matron possibly know and understand of the multiple fascinations at the Carmichael's house? Arthur Rubinstein playing Chopin, all those big long-playing records stored under the gramophone with the mahogany case? And Mona Carmichael throwing on her fur coat with that jolly laugh?

'Whizz out to the kitchen, will you, Humphrey? I seem to have made the most God-awful mess out there in the history of the world. Be a dear and clean it up. And Humphrey? Humphrey? Will I wear sparkly earrings or not?'

It was the noise and the mess that drew him, the carelessness of it all. Twenty-eight, twenty-nine. That was Matron counting the potatoes. If you have butter on your bread you can't have jam and vice versa. That was Mrs Jamieson who looked after the dining room. Elbows in. Eat your greens. If you eat crusts your hair will curl.

'You do look super, Humphrey.' Mona's big face still shone through the car window. 'You do look well. Frightfully Hardy Amies, if I may say so. Humphrey, I can't seem to get this window down. What a super car. I say, stop.'

'They keep you so late,' Matron said. 'You've missed tea again and I'm going to have to open up the kitchen and find something for you, Humphrey. I do stress that I know the money you've got saved up.' She looked after all their bankbooks, her kind, bluff face often furrowed as she checked the addition and the interest. 'I do know you've got nearly fifty pounds saved up, Humphrey, and you're going to need all that, aren't you?'

He agreed with her.

'And I'll have to work very hard,' he said, 'as well, because I haven't got any pull.'

'I beg your pardon,' said Matron, and he explained about pull.

'Oh really, Humphrey,' she said, 'sometimes I think I'd like to strangle that woman,' and they went off down the hall, feet squeaking on the old green linoleum, to the kitchen where she boiled him two nice brown eggs.

'And you might as well have some toast soldiers,' she said and thumped a plate of buttered toast fingers down beside him, 'though you're much too old, you silly great ass.'

The car glided forward, increased speed. Now he was at the corner. In the rear vision mirror he could still see Mona Carmichael, her eyebrows as arched as they ever had been, and he wondered who did her odd jobs now.

FIONA KIDMAN

Like turning your hand over, things could go either way with the weather. Six a.m. and the bay is turbulent and green, but at that hour of the morning anything can happen. Standing at the window, just listening, the whole house is a heartbeat. Looking at the bay, the water, the clouds. I think I can hear the busy clink and chatter of the rigging on the boats parked on the hard at the bay, but that can't be right, it's too far away. Oh you can hear anything, see anything on a morning like this, it's the day of the wedding. Our son's getting married.

There is a stirring in the back rooms; there is so much to do, I will never get done, it's crazy this, but the wedding's to be here, not at her place but mine. I am speaking now of the bride's mother and myself. Well, it's a long story, how the wedding comes to be here instead of there, but that's the way it is. She's bringing the food later in the morning, and there'll be crayfish and scallops like nobody ever had at their wedding before, and mussels of course. They are mussel farmers from the Sounds. They. Well I mean the bride's parents.

I love our daughter-in-law to be, I really do. You might think I don't mean that, mothers-in-law rarely do, but it's true. She's a good person. She's loyal. She's had to put up with a few things. Our son's on a win. I want to see him married.

Perhaps they know that. There are times when I think they haven't been so keen. Perhaps they think she could have done better. I don't know. It hasn't been easy, getting this wedding together. But if you knew him, our son, you'd know she wouldn't settle for anyone else. Anyone *less*. Now there's a mother talking, but I've fallen for it, that same old charm of his, and I'll go on forever, I guess. He puts his arms around me, and says, 'Love ya, Ma,' and I'd forgive him anything.

It's true. He brings out a softness in me. That, and rage. But the anger never lasts for long.

There is no time to go on reflecting about it this morning though. There's the smell of baked meats in the air, I need to open up the house and blow it through, I've got the food warmer to collect from the hire depot, and the tablecloths aren't ready, and I have to set up a place for the presents, and there's his mother, that's my husband's, to be got up, and there're relatives to be greeted, and oh God I am so tired. Why didn't anyone tell me I'd be so tired on our son's wedding day, it doesn't seem fair, because I want to enjoy it. Oh by that I mean, I want it all to be right, of course, and I want to do it graciously. We've been at each other a bit over this wedding. Them and us. But I want to make sure it goes all right today. They're bringing the food and the flagons of beer; we're providing the waiters and waitresses in starched uniforms, and the champagne. You have to cater for everyone at a wedding.

Eleven a.m. The food hasn't come. The flagons haven't come. She hasn't come. That's the bride's mother. The wedding is at two. I am striding around the house. The furniture is minimal. We've cleared everything back. There's hardly going to be standing room. That's if there ever is a wedding. There is nothing more I can do. Nothing and everything. If only we had another day. It would be better if we had held off another month. The weather would have been better. Not that it's bad but the breeze is cold. It'll be draughty in the church.

The church, ah, the church. It looks so beautiful. The flowers. They are just amazing. Carnations and irises, low bowls of stocks . . . there are the cars now, all the relatives bearing trays and pots and dishes, straggling up the stairs. The food looks wonderful. God, those crays, there're dozens of them. I'm glad they've done the food, I could never have done it so well. And the cake. Our daughter-in-law-to-be's auntie has made the cake and it's perfect too.

Everyone's exhausted, it's not just me, they've been up all night. Still, I wish they could have got here a bit sooner and we all have to get dressed yet. It's cutting things fine. I feel faint, even a little nauseous, as if lights are switching on and off inside my brain. She can't be as tired as I am, nobody could be that tired. How am I going to make it through the rest of the day?

'I'd better be getting along,' says the auntie to the bride's mother. 'I've still got to finish off your hat.' The aunt has a knack with things, clothes and cakes, she's the indispensable sort.

Inside me, something freezes. 'Hat,' I say, foolishly, and in a loud voice. 'You're wearing a hat?'

There is a silence in the kitchen.

'Well, it's just a little hat,' she says.

'You said you weren't going to wear a hat.' I hear my voice, without an ounce of grace in it, and I don't seem able to stop it.

There is ugliness in the air.

The auntie, her sister, says, 'She needed a hat to finish off the outfit. It wouldn't look right without it.'

'But we agreed,' I say. 'You said you couldn't afford a hat, and I said, well if you're not wearing one, I won't.'

The silence extends around the kitchen. She fumbles a lettuce leaf, suddenly awkward at my bench.

'It's all right,' I say, 'it's nothing.' My face is covered with tears. I walk out, leaving them to finish whipping the cream.

'Where are you going?' my husband says, following at my heels.

'Out. Away.'

'You can't go away.'

'I have to. I'm not going to the wedding.'

'No, stop, don't be silly.' He's really alarmed, I'm right on the edge, and he's right, I might go off at any moment and make things too awful for everyone to endure. At the rate I'm going there mightn't be any wedding.

'Come into the shed,' he says, speaking softly, like a zoo-keeper talking down a wild animal. 'Come on, it'll be all right. You're tired, just tired.'

I follow him. Inside the toolshed I start to cry properly. 'I want a hat,' I say. 'I wanted to wear a hat all along, but I promised her. I promised I wouldn't get a hat.'

'I'll get you a hat. Come along, we'll go into town and buy you a hat.'

'It's too late, the shops will be shut.'

'We could just make it to James Smith's,' he says. But it is too late, I can see that. Even if we broke the speed limit I'd only have five minutes, it being Saturday. The shops are due to close in half an hour.

'I can't go without a hat. What'll I do?'

'You'll think of something,' he says. 'You always do. Hey, we can do anything, can't we?' He pulls my fists out of my eyes. 'What can we do? We can . . .' He waits for me to join in the refrain with him.

'We can walk on water if we have to,' I chant.

But I'm not sure how I will.

Back in the kitchen everyone is tiptoeing around. 'It looks wonderful,' I say heartily. 'Just great. Don't you think you should be getting along. I mean, if you're going to get dressed?'

They nod. They are not deceived, but they are glad to be excused. They have been afraid to take their leave in my absence.

They are gone, and our son and his best man are dressed, preening in their three-piece suits. Oh they are so handsome. It calms me, just seeing them. As for him, I want to stroke and stroke him. My boy. In a suit. Oh I'm square. When it all comes down to it. But he's proud of himself too.

'Y'okay, Ma?'

He doesn't know what's been going on, but he sees I'm pale.

'Of course I'm okay,' I say, and for his sake I must be. I must also have a hat.

I ring our daughter. 'What about all those hats you bought when you were into hats?' I ask. I think of the op shops where she has collected feathered toques and funny little cloches. I have a feeling that none of them will suit me. She is so tall and elegant. 'I think they're in the baby's toybox,' she says.

'Have a look,' I command.

'God, I've got to get dressed too.'

'Have a look.'

I hold grimly on to the phone. She comes back. 'There's three, the black one with three feathers, and the sort of burgundy one, and the beige one with the wide brim.'

'That's it, the beige one. I'm sending Dad over for it right now.'

'But Mum.'

'It'll be all right. Well, look I can try it anyway.'

'But Mum.' This time she gets it out. 'The baby's been sick on it.

'How sick?'

'Really sick.'

No one is going to put me off now. I think she is conspiring with the odds to stop me making a fool of myself. I won't let her save me, though. 'Dad'll be right over,' I say.

But it's true. The baby has been very sick on the hat. I'm sure our daughter shouldn't have put it back in the toybox like that. I resolve to speak to her about it at some later date.

In the meantime there is work to be done. I fill the sink with hot soapy water and get out the scrubbing brush. In a few moments the sick has gone. I have a soggy felt hat dripping in my hands, but at least it is clean.

The husband and wife team, 'available for cocktail, waitressing and barman duties in the privacy of your own home', has arrived. 'Don't worry about a thing,' they say. 'You just enjoy yourselves and we'll take care of everything from now on.'

In the clothes drier, the hat whirls around.

Our son has left for the church. Soon we'll have to go too. My husband is resplendent. He wears his father's watch chain across his waistcoat. His father was a guard on the railways, back in the old days. That watch has started a thousand trains on country railway stations. Sometimes I remonstrate with my husband for wearing it; it doesn't seem appropriate. Today it is exactly right. The spring in the watch has given up long ago, but the watch will start the wedding on time. Sooner or later.

My hands shake so much he has to do up the pearl buttons on my Georgia Brown silk. 'It's time we were going,' he says tentatively. I know he's thinking about the hat, and wondering if he can get me away without it.

But it's dry. Dry, and softly drooping around the brim, so that it swoops low over my right eye when I put it on. I stare at myself in the mirror, entranced. I feel beautiful. I glow. I love hats. This hat is perfect.

Our son's wife-to-be is late, but then she usually is. Anyone is allowed one failing. I don't mind. It gives me time to relax, breathe deeply, smile and wave around the church. Across the aisle I see her, the mother of the bride. She is not wearing a hat.

Instinctively, I touch the brim of mine. I have shamed her into coming without her hat. I should feel jubilant but I don't. I feel bad, wonder how to take mine off without drawing attention to myself. But it's impossible. At the door to the church the priest has said, first thing when he sees me, 'Oh what a beautiful hat.'

I look away, embarrassed. I tell myself I must not think about it. The wedding is about to happen, and we can't repeat it when I'm feeling better, so I've just got to stop thinking about it, the hat on my head.

And then they're there, coming into the church together, which is what's been arranged, and it's not quite the same old responses, because some of that wouldn't be suitable, but they say some nice things to each other, making promises to do things as well as they can, and they're so young, so very young, and that's all you can expect from anybody, to do their best, isn't it?

The couple are facing the congregation now. This really is very modern. Our daughter stands up at the lectern and reads from the Book of Ecclesiastes, then some Keats, *O brightest! though too late for antique vows*, and she's pale and self-contained and not showing signs of things turning over inside of her, and so lovely; she and the boy, her brother, look at each other, and it's as if they're the only ones in the church for a moment, *Holy the air, the water, and the fire*, like a conversation just for the two of them, putting aside all their childish grievances, though a few people in the church who haven't done English Lit. look a trifle confused but it doesn't matter, these two know . . . *so let me be thy choir . . . thy voice, thy lute* . . . and then our son and his new wife's baby cries at the back of the church where he's being held by the auntie, and the spell's broken, as the two parents look anxiously after their child. The wind rises in the funnel where the church stands, and a plane roars overhead, and the light shines through the stained-glass window on to the same spot where my father's coffin stood last year, and with all the light and the sound I don't hear any more of the service, I just smile and smile.

It's over. We're forming up to leave. She and I look at each other across the church again. Suddenly it's all bustle and go, and what none of us have thought about is the way we get out of the church, but there it is, as old as the service itself, or so it seems, the rituals of teaming up, like finding your partner for a gavotte, step step step an arm offered and accepted she goes with my husband and I go with hers, that's the way it's done. Delicate, light as air, we prepare our entrance to the dance, to the music, but before we do, she and I afford each other one more look, one intimate glance. Hatted and hatless, that's us, blessed are the meek, it's all the same now. We're one, her and me. We're family.

BARBARA ANDERSON

Mr Levis invited them to call him Des. And this is Arnold he said.

Mr Kent said Hi Arnold.

Mrs Kent said that she was pleased to meet him.

Mrs Gallant said Hullo, Arnold.

Mr Gallant said Good Morning.

Mr Borges said nothing.

Des said that if they just liked to walk down to the landing stage Arnold would bring the boat down with the tractor.

Mrs Gallant said wasn't Mr Gallant going to leave the car in the shade.

Mr Gallant said that if Mrs Gallant was able to tell him where the shade from one tree was going to be for the next six hours he would be happy to.

Mr Kent said that he was going to give it a burl anyway and reparked the Falcon beneath the puriri.

Mrs Kent told Mrs Gallant that she and Stan were from Hamilton.

Mrs Gallant told Mrs Kent that she and Eric were from Rotorua.

Mrs Kent said that she had a second cousin in Rotorua. Esme. Esme. She would be forgetting her own head next.

And that she supposed she should wait for Stan but what the hell.

Mrs Gallant smiled at Mr Borges.

Mr Borges nodded.

At the landing stage Des said that he would like them to take turns sitting in the front and perhaps the ladies?

Mrs Kent remarked that the landing stage looked a bit ass over tip.

Arnold said that the landing stage was safe as houses and would the lady get into the boat.

Mrs Kent said Where was Stan.

Mr Kent said Here.

Mrs Kent asked Mr Kent where he had got to. She hopped across the landing stage, climbed onto the boat and into one of the front seats. She said that it wasn't too lady like but that she would be right.

Mrs Gallant followed.

Mr Kent and Mr Gallant climbed into the next row.

Des said that Arnold was on the Access Training Scheme and doing very well but it was difficult to fit in the hundred hours' river time in a business like this and that he hoped that the customers would have no objection if Arnold came with them and drove the boat back because of the hundred hours.

Mrs Kent said that she would be delighted anytime.

Mr Kent said Well.

Mr Gallant asked how many passengers the boat was licensed for.

Des said that it was licensed for seven passengers.

Mrs Gallant smiled.

Mr Borges said nothing.

Arnold said Good on them, climbed into the boat and sat in the back row with Mr Borges. Mr Borges smiled.

Des started the motor and picked up the microphone. He said that the river was approximately ninety miles long and had been called the Rhine Of New Zealand. It had been used as a waterway since the time of the first Maoris. Perhaps the busiest time on the river, he said, was the end of the nineteenth century and the beginning of the twentieth until the Main Trunk was completed. River boats plied, freight and passengers were transported in thousands and in all that time there were only two deaths which must be something of a record.

Mr Gallant said that he hoped that it would stay that way.

Des invited him to come again.

Mrs Kent said that Mr Gallant was only kidding.

Mr Gallant said No he wasn't.

Mrs Gallant said Eric.

Des said that he was born and brought up on the river. He had lived on the river all his life and he knew the river like the back of his hand and his aim was for every one of his passengers to learn more about this beautiful river which was steeped in history.

Mr Kent said that Des would do him.

Mrs Kent said Hear Hear.

Mr Borges, Mr Gallant and Arnold said nothing.

Mrs Gallant said that it was a lovely day.

Des said that she wasn't running as sweet as usual, probably a few stones up the grille.

Mrs Gallant asked What did that mean.

Des said Stones you know up the grille.

Mrs Gallant said that she realised that.

Mr Gallant smiled.

Mrs Kent said that they had a lovely day for it anyhow.

Des said they certainly had and to take a look at the flying fox across the river. He explained that the alignment of the posts was very important indeed.

Mr Gallant said that it would be.

Des said that otherwise she could come across but she wouldn't go back. On the other hand if it was wrong the other way she would go back but she wouldn't come across.

Mr Gallant said Exactly.

Mr Kent said it was all Dutch to him Ooh Pardon.

Mrs Kent said that the young man wasn't Dutch and that Stan needn't worry.

Mr Kent said Then what was he?

Mrs Kent said that yes the day certainly was a cracker.

Mrs Gallant smiled.

Des said that the cooling system wasn't operating as per usual either. Usually she stayed at twenty. That was what he liked her at. Twenty.

Mrs Gallant said that it was at seventy now was it not.

Des said Yes it was.

Mrs Gallant said Oh.

Mr Gallant laughed.

Des said that they certainly would like Pipiriki.

Mrs Kent said That was for sure.

Des moored the boat at the Pipiriki landing stage. Everyone climbed
out. Des put a large carton on an outdoor table and said they could help themselves to tea or coffee.

Mrs Gallant said that she and Eric would only need one teabag between them as they both took tea very weak without milk.

Des said that Mrs Gallant needn't worry as he had provided two tea bags each per person as usual.

Mr Gallant said that she was only trying to help.

Mrs Kent asked if there was a toilet.

Arnold pointed up the path.

Des said that after lunch they should go up and look at Pipiriki. Pipiriki House had once been a world famous hotel. It had burned down in 1959. He said to have a good look at the shelter and to go around the back as there were some flush toilets.

Mrs Kent said that now Des told her and they both laughed.

Mrs Gallant said What shelter.

Des said A shelter for tourists you know trampers, that sort of thing.

Everyone liked Pipiriki very much. After an hour they climbed back into the boat.

Mr Kent said that he wished some of those activists could see all those kids happy and swimming.

Mr Gallant said Why?

Mr Kent said to look at that one jumping there. That he hadn't a care in the world.

Mr Gallant said that that was hardly the point.

Mrs Gallant said Eric.

Mr Gallant said Hell's delight woman.

Mr Borges smiled.

Mrs Kent said that they used to live near Cambridge but that they had moved in to Hamilton when the boy took over.

Mrs Gallant said Was that right, and that she wished they had been able to land at Jerusalem.

Arnold said that he could go a swim.

Des said that he had been going to have a good look at her yesterday but that he hadn't had a break for so long and that he just hadn't felt like it.

No one said anything.

Des said that anyway he had had another booking in the end as things had turned out.

The boat leapt and bucked high in the air.

Mrs Kent said Ooops.

Des said that that showed you what happened if you let your concentration slip even for a second with a jet. She had hit a stump.

Mr Gallant laughed.

Arnold asked if the Boss would like him to take over.

Des and Arnold laughed.

Mrs Gallant said to look at that kingfisher.

Mrs Kent said Where.

Mrs Gallant said There. That Mrs Kent was too late. That it had gone.

Des pointed out many points of interest and said that no she certainly wasn't going too good.

Mrs Gallant said that hadn't the temperature gauge gone up to eighty or was she wrong.

Des said that no she was not wrong and that he had better give her a breather and stopped the boat. He said it was probably the temperature of the water, it being a hot day.

Nobody said anything. The boat rocked, silent on the trough of its own waves. The sun shone.

Des said that that should have cooled her down a bit and started the boat.

The temperature gauge climbed to seventy.

Des said that that was more like it and that there had been a Maori battle on that island between the Hau Hau supporters and the non-supporters.

Mr Gallant wondered why they had chosen an island.

Des said that Mr Gallant had him there and swung the boat into a shallow tributary of the river. He told Arnold that they had better check the grille and how would Arnold like a swim.

Arnold said that that would be no problem. He climbed around onto the bow of the boat and said that they would now see his beautiful body. He removed his shirt and told Mrs Gallant and Mrs Kent to control themselves.

Mrs Kent yelped.

Arnold faced the vertical cliff of the bank, presented his shorts clad buttocks and shook them.

Everyone laughed except Mr Gallant and Mr Borges.

Mr Borges stood up quickly, took a photograph of Arnold's back view, and sat down again.

Arnold jumped into the water and swam to the back of the boat. Des fumbled beneath his feet and handed the passengers various pieces of equipment for Arnold to poke up the grille. The male passengers handed the things on to Arnold with stern efficiency.

After some time Arnold said that he had found three stones up the grille.

Des said that that was good.

Arnold said that they were not big buggers though.

Des said Never mind.

Arnold handed the equipment back into the boat and did a honeypot jump from the shallow water into a deep pool.

Mr Kent said See?

Arnold swam to the bow of the boat and heaved himself into the boat.

Mr Borges took a photograph of Arnold's front view.

Mrs Gallant said that they were lucky that Arnold had come with them.

Mrs Kent said that Mrs Gallant could say that again and would the boat go better now that Arnold had removed the stones.

Des said that he hoped so.

Mr Gallant laughed.

They stopped several times on the return trip for the boat to cool down and as she was not going too well Des sometimes had to make several sweeps before she could pick up enough speed for her to lift up over the rapids. Des said that normally at this stage, when she was less than half full of gas he could fling her about all over the place no sweat.

Mr Gallant said that they must be thankful for small mercies.

Des swung the boat in a wide spraying circle and pulled into the jetty at the old flour mill. They climbed the hill, Des carrying the afternoon tea carton. After tea Des said that he would tell them about the old flour mill and the river in general. Everyone expressed interest. They trooped into the warm shadowy old building and Des began.

After half an hour Mrs Kent asked whether Des would mind if she sat down.

Des said that although perhaps it was technically more correct to call them river boats he still thought of them as steamers though strictly speaking they weren't steamers for long.

Mrs Kent sat down.

Mrs Gallant sat down.

Mr Kent looked as though he was going to cry.

Mr Gallant closed his eyes.

Arnold sat outside in the shade.

Mr Borges joined him.

After three quarters of an hour Des said that he hoped they had all learned something of the river.

They climbed down to the river in silence.

Des said that as she wasn't the best perhaps if Mrs Gallant and Mr Kent would like to sit in front.

Mr Gallant muttered something about sensible arrangement of ballast.

Mrs Kent asked Des why.

Arnold said it was because he liked the good-looking girls in the back with him.

Mrs Kent told Arnold to get away and climbed nimbly into the back seat.

Mrs Gallant said nothing.

They set off with Des at the wheel. The temperature gauge rose above eighty. Des asked the passengers to look around their feet for a tool which would enable Arnold to take another poke up the grille without getting out of the boat.

Mrs Gallant said that there was a pipe thing here if that was any help.

Mr Kent gave a startled cry and said What was that smoke.

Mr Gallant said that that was steam.

Mrs Kent said that it was red hot that pipe thing there.

Mr Gallant said that he was not at all surprised.

Arnold said that she would be right.

Des said that she had better have another cool off and stopped the boat.

The boat limped to the original landing jetty two hours later than planned. The passengers collected their belongings without comment and trailed up the hill.

Des told Arnold that he could bring the boat up.

Arnold said that Des was the Boss.

Mrs Gallant remarked that it had been a very interesting day and that wasn't the river beautiful.

Mrs Kent said that yes it was but that she had felt so sorry for the poor chap.

Mr Gallant said God in Heaven.

Mrs Gallant remarked that she saw that Mr Kent's car was in the shade.

Mr Gallant said that it probably had not been for the first six hours.

Mrs Gallant said that that remark was typical absolutely typical.

Mrs Kent said that they used to have Jerseys but the boy had switched to Friesians.

Mr Kent said that he had been happy enough in Jerseys but that there you were.

Mrs Kent said that they just want to be different and that it was quite understandable.

Mr Kent said that he had never said it wasn't.

Mr Borges said nothing.

Arnold appeared on the tractor, pulling the boat on its trailer. He parked it in the shed and appeared with a Visitors' Book. He invited the passengers to make their crosses.

Everyone laughed except Mr Gallant and Mr Borges.

Des said that he would give her an overhaul tomorrow that was for sure.

Mrs Kent signed the book and wrote Lovely day under Comments.

Mr Kent signed and wrote Ditto.

Mr Gallant signed his name only.

Mr Borges signed and wrote Sweden.

Mrs Gallant missed the signing. She stumped across the bleached grass and stood gazing at the river.

It said nothing.

I've just woken up, I'm already dressed in my gypsy costume – the striped musty dress, high heels, jacket. My face is painted mask-like to go with the dress, I'm beautiful this morning, like an aging doll. I feel like dancing along the street in full flower, I am so full of purpose, so highly strung. I give myself a smile in the mirror and then make a Diane Keaton face as I pat on some perfume. I'm in that kind of overwrought, clammy mood.

Looking around the scummy little kitchen, last night's glass upended on the draining board, I know I'm in no fit state. I talk out loud to myself for the reassurance.

'I'll clean up tonight.'

Unmade bed, the night's lone sleep fogging the windows, my nightdress lying in the hollow of the bed, still warm from my body.

It's very early for work, but the place is too depressing to stay in. I've been awake since dawn, counting my betrayals. There were quite a few.

All day yesterday crossing items off lists, sending files on, taking pulls at the flask of secret gin in my desk, saying goodbye to the lost children. No wonder I couldn't sleep.

I'm nervous, on my guard as I bang the door shut. It never shuts properly unless I kick it with all my might. I head down the quiet morning streets to the wharves for a bit of peace before the office. I always go there when things are getting rough. Seeing the real world grinding along is an antidote to the controlled hysteria of my job, it soothes me, puts me back on centre.

When I get down there, I'm comforted by its sameness. Nothing ever changes. Men watch me as I go past, the seagulls swoop over scraps of offal floating in the oily water. Rusting boats stinking of oil and fish, huge warehouses. Newspapers and grit flying up in my face. I go into the crummy café where fishermen, wharfies and the men working in the produce markets eat, and order a greasy delicious breakfast of bacon and eggs.

While I'm eating I play the jukebox. (*One heart, one love*, sings Bob Marley to the sullen waitresses with knowing eyes and the two young guys with tattoos, deep in conversation at the next table.) I sip my coffee, sleepy-eyed, watching the men work the wharves from out the open door of the café. There's the tang of other worlds drawing me, this place is so close to freedom, exotic territory. Cranes, sea, the aching fish smell, the barbaric and naked sinews of commerce, warehouses, concrete stacking bays, forklifts, high fences, the solid concentration-camp facades of long-established wharf factories (S. Perelman & Son Ltd. Est. 1890). The shabby little fishing boats rocking with the tide.

When I finally get to the office, late, my mouth still greasy, the place hits me like a blow. The lift stinks of aerosol, and my headache rises and spreads to my eyes. The air conditioner is suffocating, it makes me want to vomit. Every morning recently I've had to screw myself up to enter my room. It's no different today. My co-workers are both gabbling nonsense into the phone, around them the files are waiting, tattered after their long blind journeys through the departments. There's a big pile of them under the window, the women on the phone riffle through them absentmindedly as they speak. My own desk is swept clean. To all intents and purposes I've already left.

They have a surprise for me, a child to look after for a while. My colleagues want to give me a perk on my last day. It's an emergency, and there's been a hold-up on the papers so he's here all afternoon, this little fellow. They want to keep me quiet before they give me the coffee-and-cake farewell, so they hand over the child kindly. They can afford to be gracious now that I am really leaving.

I lift the passive body up onto my lap. His skin is slightly sour-smelling, though he's spanking clean, his eyes are as trapped and blank as a bird's. He smells unloved, antiseptic, like all the Welfare kids I've cuddled here. He is ugly with fear, his snotty baby nose has no one to wipe it, his eyes are blood-shot with grief. Sad-eyed children, their special clean unloved institutional smell. Even now his need can wrench me with pity. The file said he'd been found alone in a house in Kingsland. Police believed he'd been on his own for two days, with no electricity or food. Darkness, starvation, maybe rats – the child watches me dully, he is still stupid with shock. His body lies unresponsive against mine, his mind bombed out, corroded by all the indifference. An implosion has occurred and his fragile self has taken such a battering that he is already mangled beyond repair. Such a little boy to be alone in a hostile universe. A nice-smelling Pakeha social worker is about as much use to you as a chip of wood in a flooded river, my little fellow, however much I hug you. What will become of you? No one wants you, no one at all.

I take him into the private interview room to escape, just to sit there with him. In this box with its grey walls, its table and chair and tiny prison window, I realise I'm so strung up that I can hear the soundwaves from two years of anguished conversations hanging in the air or still zinging uselessly against the walls. The room is a dirty, atonal grey, shiny with black chair-leg marks, dents where people have bashed their heads against the walls in despair. All the words, the tears, the sobbing have been concentrated here into this cell. People sweated here, they watched me, the words they said stuck in my brain.

They all came here. They were overweight with tired skin, men with big hands, greying hair plastered back. Their miseries were real. Compared to them I was just fussing around with ephemera – clouds, rainbows. I had a desk, appointments, I was small, thin, pretty – I had absolutely no substance, no courage beside all these real people. They were so unfashionable, the people who came here to beg help – they mostly assumed that they would receive the justice due to them, though most never had. I knew their misery was a secret in this office, almost a sordid secret, and none of us really spoke of it.

I was Alice in Wonderland. I didn't believe that life was really like this. I turned the key, stepped into that huge labyrinth, those offices, that maze of human misery, and lo and behold! There was the dark side of the moon, there lay the real forces in people's lives – the powerful reigning, the powerless proliferating, their misery hidden as an underground river.

The women who came, sick with childbearing, beaten by their husbands, but still joking with a tired flash about the ironies of their lives. Big women with bad skin, children whining around them, trying to escape the blows, they came up to Welfare to beg – another humiliation.

'He pissed off, left me and the kids, we can't do nothing. I've got no money, no money.'

'There's no doctor where we live, eh, and we haven't got a car. No money, the day before benefit, the phone's a mile up the road. My mate Chrissie – she left the house locked up. I couldn't get in to use her phone. I stood in the middle of the road with her and cried. I bawled my heart out. Here, you bloody have her . . .'

And she slips the dead baby across the desk, it is tiny, cold, the mother watches me dry-eyed, her face is hard. I take the body and put it into a drawer.

'Next please!' I call out. I hear terrible crying, a woman is sobbing as if her heart would break . . .

It suddenly comes back to me, sitting here in my old work room, the child asleep in my lap. The dream I had last night about the dead baby. I'd woken with the feel of its rubbery doll body still fresh on my hands. It was nothing new, a savage dream like that, they go with the job. I keep dreaming of the lost children, night after night, and these begging, impotent murky struggles always leave me wrung out, aching with guilt. I dream of them being beaten to death, starving, being raped. They have shaven heads, they are homeless, unloved, begging to live. Their small hearts are thumping with fear. They have such tender bodies, my dream children, terrified eyes, they lift their helpless arms so innocently to ward off blows, they whimper as the bird bones crack. They are innocent, my lost children, small and trusting, their bodies are like flowers. My job, my dreams, my life are haunted by them, I am drowning in their lives, I have to escape before I go under.

Here at the interstices of the system, where everything becomes shadowy, ambivalent, where there are vague threatening shapes, where the din of shells is loudest, where nothing is certain – it is here that clean and safe people become most defensive. They evolve their own rules, their own jargon. They have their own loyalties.

The social workers, clerks, typists, the administrators all cope with the relentless avalanche of misery by shutting off, treating the poor, the battered, the oppressed, as people from another planet. I thought I'd never do that. I used to feel so coarse and alive and real beside them. I used to be so quietly superior.

But now I understand better. Me, the room I live in, the relentless machine of my brain, my weakness, are all too precarious. I'm no match for all this either. My pity and my rage are all swallowed up and I'm just like the others. The children can see no difference between us. It's all the same to them. They are so used to broken faith, the children I've met and loved here, people have always let them down. I can leave the job if I want, but they have no choice at all, nothing.

I sit there in the half-dark, the weight of the child anchoring me. His breathing fills the room. From where I am I can see a corner of the harbour out of the window. Far out, nearly towards Rangitoto, a fishing boat is heading out to the open sea. Stubby, determined, shabby from years of knocking around the coast, it ploughs steadily through the grey morning sea. I can almost smell the sour cooking and fish-guts, see the filthy oil-stained deck cluttered with fuel drums, the big fishermen who work her moving around in the chilly air. The sight of her tugs at my heartstrings.

The child snuffles into my arm and I look down at his small trapped head. He twitches like a dog, he is having bad drams, I realise it is nearly time for us to go.

NGAHUIA TE AWEKOTUKU

She felt like she weighed a ton, and she kept hearing Kuikui's voice, telling her she was getting too old for this stuff. Too old and too big. Too big, that was for sure. She shifted her right knee, wedged it along the other side of the tree's smooth trunk, balanced her bum on the very slightly swaying branch. If any of the old people saw her, that would be it. No excuses and no mercy. She'd get it for sure from Kuikui, who'd be the first to notice if even her little black rubber toe in its basketball boot slipped and dangled from the rimu tree's lush growth. Tahuri hoisted herself up further, into the branches. Bird's eye view, all right. She smiled to herself, brushed away the prickly tassel tickling her face. This was *worth* all the risk. And the shame, if she got caught. Or worse still, fell down.

Behind her, just beyond the corrugated red of Te Aomarama's roof, the wintry grey waters of the lake lapped and rolled. And below, all around, the marae was a mass of excited, milling, busy people, squashed together yet seething, like the steamy waters of the cooking ngawha, but with more colours than that, and everywhere a musty, familiar black. Raincoats and umbrellas, scarves and heavy skirts, thick socks, lace-up shoes, and heavy Black Watch tartan rugs. All excited, all looking in the same direction, up the road. On the wide pink concrete steps of Tamatekapua, near the bell, the koros sat in a neatly polished row, trouser legs creased sharp, and RSA badges winking even in the low bleak light of this overcast and chilly morning. Some talked to each other with smiles and scowls, one had his nose in a battered Best Bets, and another had his legs out straight in perfect line with his crustily carved tokotoko, his eyes shut while his lips seemed to be moving. A couple looked at the sky, firmed up their coat buttons. More just sat there, thinking about what they were going to say, who they were going to remember. And from his own chair, on big wheels like a pushbike, one koro held it over everyone, his rich, resonant voice bossing the women around, joking. They laughed back at him, tucking his woolly blanket snugly round his withered knees. They fussed about and were very busy, as if the rain, gathering above them, pressing down, just didn't seem to matter. And it didn't, really.

Tahuri moved her feet one more time. The black ripple soles of her boots gripped easily; she slid around, peered straight down. It was clear, almost completely clear. Soon, in maybe only a few minutes, the space would be just rows of empty forms; then they too would fill up, and the crowd be even tighter. Closer. She could hardly wait. Stretching her neck, she studied the entrance to the village. Most days it was just an ordinary street, lined with Maori Affairs weatherboard houses, dull green and cream and blue. Today, it was special. It was the gate into the village, the pathway to the marae, and little beads of steam delicately threaded into the air, telling the visitors that this marae, this village, was different.

She could hardly see them; they were bobbing around by their buses, packing themselves together, getting ready to come on. Then suddenly, quite suddenly, everything started to happen at once. And the ghosts began to move. While the softest, gentlest rain fell on their faces, the women's chant of karanga, of welcome, of mourning, of celebration, passed back and forth, then merged together, and the living and the dying and the dead were all as one. She sensed the weaving in the air around the tree, in the warmth rising from the ground, in the moving of the visitors, and the receiving of her own people, like they were all fitting together, fusing and fitting in to each other, slowly, easily. She switched off from the chant, and examined the oncoming ope, looking at them from the safety of her secret perch. And two faces – two figures – struck her, bolted right into her. She clutched the tree, rebalanced, concentrated on their faces, one, and then, the other.

The first was a middle-aged woman, wearing what looked like men's clothes. They had to be. Yet she was so strong, so confident – and so right. She looked great, and at first Tahuri couldn't take her eyes off her. There, second row from the front, just behind the chanting kuia. Compact and broad; the only man's hat amongst all the floppy ladies' felts and sober scarves. On a snazzy angle, and dark greyish brown, it was almost like the koros' – but more, well, up-to-date. Set just right, and though Tahuri couldn't be sure, the hair was really short too. Cut level with the turned-down collar of the big belted overcoat, hairy like a camel. Like the koros, but a much softer brown. Buttoned on the left side too, and the navy blue neck-scarf turned neatly in. 'Bet there's a shirt and tie underneath all that,' Tahuri said out loud to herself. 'I bet there is, and trousers, not sissy slacks. And the lace-up shoes . . .' The young girl was fascinated; it was all so right, so neat to see.

And then, right at the back, Tahuri noticed in the crowd coming on, a shining creamy-white guitar – and its carrier. Her face. The colour. The shape. The nose and the lips and the eyes. Most of all, the eyes.

The surging wave of visitors had paused; that chant gave way to snuffled weeping, the saddest sound of all; and then they fell back, as if blown by a silent wind, and the visitors' koros were sitting in the front, on the forms facing the huge carved house, while around them the visitors' kuia and other women settled down. Only a few people remained standing, the teenagers, some of the little kids, and most of the young boys. Tahuri looked at them all with interest, searching for that face. There she was, down there; Tahuri was transfixed again. She couldn't see that much, but the shoulders were mighty in the black peg jacket with big pockets. Funny-looking black pleated skirt, and that was all Tahuri could make out. The rest was behind the old Gibson guitar, half leaning, half carried against the young woman's body. Tahuri strained and stretched up in her hideout, wishing she could see those eyes again; the darked, roundest, biggest eyes she had ever seen.

As if she knew she was being watched, the visitor moved out of sight between two of the taller teenagers. Only the top of her head, wild glossy waves, shining and short, bright with the gems of freshly fallen rain, was visible. And bits of the guitar, spangled faintly with water.

Tahuri gave up for the moment, but determined to talk to her later.

She changed position, looked straight down, wondering who was on the form propped up against the rimu. She peered. Neat! The big woman in the hat and coat, there at the very end! Her knees were bent apart, and she was leaning on them, her elbows on her thighs, her head forward, listening to the first whaikorero.

She was absorbed, concentrating. Her back was massive, pulling the heavy coat across; the scarf had loosened, flopping casually over her collar. She adjusted her hat, pulled at the rim, lowering it in front, and Tahuri gasped at the fine black gloves, old leather wrinkled to her hand's shape, snug. The big woman continued to sit forward; and against her, someone else was leaning thoughtfully, too. She was a lady dressed in dark navy blue, her suit jacket expensively cut in three panels fitted on her narrow back. Flung across her shoulders, and pinned to one with a gold-rimmed oval of greenstone, was a thin shawl, night colours blending with the jacket, and on her head the daintiest hat. Over her knees was a rich mohair rug. She kept leaning against the big woman, snuggled. She must be cold, Tahuri thought. And still the big woman continued to watch the welcoming orator, to take in every word. He was winding down; he finished with a dramatic flourish, and a piercing female voice began an ancient song. The showering rain had stopped. Below her, the big woman leaned back.

She turned to the smaller one next to her. The lady looked around, jostled just a little, and was still. Her hands, pale and fragile, long fingers like the petals of pikiarero, were on her lap, twining and twisting thin fabric gloves. She wore no rings. She trembled and shivered in the cold. And in a flash, it happened. The big woman had taken her gloves off. Tahuri caught the gleam of gold links pushed through the cuff, turned back to reveal a man's watch. Frozen stiff with fascination, she gawked.

The big woman reached for the pale shivering hands, covered them with her own squareness, brownness. Covered them briefly, then slipped her forefinger and thumb around the small one's wrist, made a dark bronze ring, a playful bracelet of warmth. First on one, then the other, which she grasped, sliding her hands along the chilled flesh, caressing, lightly fondling, tracing the smoothly perfumed palm with callused tips. Tenderly.

Then she took one fragile hand and, with swift grace, touched it to her lips, pressed it to her face, returned it to the rug. So sudden, and so very very subtle.

No longer shivering, the lightly patterned shawl cuddled up against the thick brown coat. Their side – the visitors' first speaker – was on his feet, opening his responding speech with an echoing song poem. The big woman leaned forward, elbows on her knees. And again, she listened.

They were staying down the pa; Tahuri found out from her Auntie Tui as they sweated over the lunch dishes. Some were going out to Whaka, but the buses that came in that morning were going to sleep at Tamatekapua. If this wet weather didn't clear up, it was going to be one hell of a weekend; the haka groups would be performing inside the Ritz Hall instead of outside at the Soundshell, and a full house was guaranteed. Already the dining-room was overflowing, they'd had four sittings for lunch, and this was just the first lot of buses. Auntie Tui worried a lot, and no wonder. Tahuri moved across to the knives and forks and risked stabbing herself horribly; she jiggled them around in their tins while her younger cousins grizzled and snapped their tea-towels. With a bored sigh, she tipped the cutlery out, and set to drying it, cutting herself off from the clatter and chatter around her in the huge communal kitchen. She daydreamed about the big woman and the little one, and she wondered how she could get to talk to the teenage girl with the guitar. It was too early to go over to the meeting house – more buses were arriving, and more manuhiri were coming on, so they wouldn't start moving inside until all the welcomes and speeches were over. So now it was dishes and setting tables and doing the kai and hanging around helping out until then. Sighing, she got on with it.

Auntie Tui was shouting at her through the din. About getting the extra pillowcases from her shed, taking them inside now that the paepae had cleared for afternoon tea. This was her chance! She'd have to find the extra pillowcases first – there weren't that many, she could carry them herself – then she'd be free, in Tamatekapua and around the house, where she could look for those visitors, admiring one from a distance – and maybe getting to know the other.

The shed was a small wooden shack behind Auntie Tui and Uncle Jack's house which faced on to the marae. It was old, really old, and they reckoned it was probably one of the first pakeha-style places built in the pa. Layers and layers of paint marking years of time chipped into the weatherboards – blue, apricot-range, lime green, blue again, then dark green, and finally, Maori Affairs cream, which Tahuri would peel away at the corners, with an old pipi shell or pocketknife or whatever was at hand. She liked discovering the old colours – but even more, she liked going into the shed: it smelled old, and lavendery and interesting; of freshly washed and ironed linen, and mothballs; of kapok mattresses piled in a corner with pillows packed ceiling-tight on top, of firmly rolled whariki standing up in another, of kete full of pingao blades hanging yellow from the ceiling, of bundles of kiekie, of cut, scraped flax, of things ready for weaving. And against one wall, all the way along, there were shelves covered in wallpaper, nailed down flat, with cartons full of sheets, and two big washing baskets heaped with pillowcases. And on the lowest shelf, in a cedar glory box, the special linen, for special visitors.

This time, the shed was almost empty of its stored treasures. The whariki were covering the meeting house floor, every single one, and all the sheets were out. So were the kapoks, but three worn-out feather mattresses made a bouncy-looking bed just under the window, bundled together, puffed up and plump beneath a heavily patched sheet.

Tahuri quickly set about her job. The afternoon light was fading fast, and she wanted to do more than find the extra pillowcases. There they were, two dozen crisply cleaned and pressed, in the washing basket. She checked to see who was outside the door – no one – then had a sneaky look into the glory box; this temptation was always too much for her. The lid flipped open on its golden cords; the gentle scent of cedar drifted out; usually packed tight, it was less than half full because of the special visitors. But at the bottom, a few wonderful pieces lay flat, and Tahuri picked them up, one by one, letting them delicately unfold, spilling out their colours, and their patterns, and their rare, incredible beauty. They were like the pictures in library books and calendars, like the pictures pinned up in the art room at school. Except these were real, and they were made in the pa by all the old kuias, and they were wonderful. Much more than pillowcases, these. Embroidered and elegant – roses starting rich red on the inside and getting lighter and pinker as the petals moved from the middle, with bright leaves and thorny green-brown stems that twined around each other, making curves and corners; a spray of golden kowhai, threading shades of yellow and brown, with tiny emerald leaflets linked together. These two sets were too worn to be put out any more, so they stayed in the box. With the oldest pair of all, the set that Tahuri liked best. Respectfully, caringly, she lifted one high above her head, framing it in the mottled window. She gripped the fuzzy, fraying edges – and smiled at the design. Worked into the aged material was a carved face, splendidly shining eyes, with wide mouth and poking tongue, the cheeks curving outward and upward, meeting cleverly together, forming a circle of chainstitch, the colour of fading wine. Auntie Tui had confided that this set was a bit peculiar – the old people were very particular about who she put them out for, and they were really very old, the oldest in the cedar chest. So now, they were hardly ever used; and each year, each hui, the special visiting kuia and koro they were meant for were fading just like them; passing away, or ageing, becoming too frail and too old to go out any more. But when Tahuri looked at that design, she felt warmed and strengthened by the pattern, and all the faces that had ever rested on those pillowcases smiled back at her, sad, and happy, too. Pleased that she'd seen them, and more pleased that no one had caught her, she lovingly stroked their thin, silky lines, and folded them back into well-creased rectangles to be placed again inside the glory box. She took one more deep breath of cedar, stung this time with mothballs, and gathering the extra pillowcases under her arm, she set out. Evening was falling.

The girl was under the rimu tree, sitting on the damp form, tuning her guitar. Everyone else was in, or around, the dining-room, and Tahuri had just finished stuffing pillows. Her nose was full of kapok and sneezes and feathers, and she needed to stay outside for a while. Here was her big chance. She walked over and sat down, trying to be cool. Hoping not to sneeze.

'Kia ora.' Big cheesy smile. Charming. 'You had some kai?'

'Mmm. Ae. Yes thanks.' Continued to fiddle with guitar keys. Short fingernails, and tapered fingers. Calluses.

'Oh. That's good.' Smile not quite so cheesy, but still cool. 'Um. You settled in okay then?'

'Ae. Got me a nice warm bed next to my auntie, eh.' Turned to look at Tahuri, hands still. Grinned from ear to ear. 'This place is really neat, eh! Spooky, though, all the steam and boiling water and stuff, but I like it. You live here?'

Tahuri couldn't believe it. Heaven! It was so easy. She smiled the big cheesy one again, and was extra charming, extra cool.

'Ooh yeah, this is my home ground, my place. D'you want to have a look around? I'm a real good guide, know all the sights, where to go in the dark even!' She swallowed the last phrase. Her new friend looked at her, stood up – wow, she was big – slung the guitar over her hefty shoulder, gestured at it.

'I'd better take this inside first,' she said. 'Then – let's go! Oh yeah – my name's Mirimiri. Mills for short.' She laughed.

Tahuri laughed too; it was almost as if this manuhiri was the one in charge here; but no way, this was her place. She grinned back. 'I'm Tahuri,' she replied. 'Nothing for short. Eh, Mills, welcome to Ohinemutu, centre of the universe.'

Together they crossed the marae, and went into the big whare.

Mills had said their group was on at a quarter to nine. That meant Tahuri had to get to the Ritz by half past eight so she had to break out from the kitchen by eight. It wasn't raining as hard, and she looked forward to the long walk across town – if she could shake off the little kids. The clock said twenty past seven.

After what seemed another lifetime of dirty damn dishes in the dining-room kitchen, she asked Auntie Tui if she could go. The answer was 'Sure, wait for Uncle Jack and he'll take you and the kids.' Tahuri knew what that meant. She thanked her auntie, said she felt like walking, and was off out the door.

Masses and masses of people; smells of raincoats and damp Brylcreme and wet blankets and sharp perfume and roll-your-own cigarette smoke, all crushing around the doors, pushing to get in to the concert, out of the rain. Being not all that big, Tahuri squeezed through the side, popped out into another throng of big heaving bodies. She pretended she was looking for some important koro, and made her way along the wall, skipping from person to person, getting a kiss here and a pat there from relations dotted in the end seats or standing along the way. Close to the stage, she found the perfect spot, huge bunches of flax flower stalks and thick green blades were pushed into a sawn-down forty-gallon drum, edged with coloured paper and filled with sand. She wedged her bum on to it, taking care to keep the arrangement just right. She let out a long, happy breath, and waited, looking at the stage.

They came on. What an entrance! The crowd went crazy, yelling and stomping their feet and whistling enough to make your ears crack. It was fantastic! Two sets of performers, coming from both sides of the stage at the same time; voices strong and fabulous, their harmonies so rich and soaring, their karanga shrill, penetrating beyond the rowdy audience, lifting their greetings proud and high to the old people gathered in the crowd. And then the ranks joined together, and they were into their first action song, and everyone sitting down below went even more berserk, clapping and laughing and bellowing, and through it all, Tahuri heard the guitar.

The big woman was in the front row; their whole line-up was large and majestic, but she most of all. And her hair was very short, even mannish, and her teeth shone, and her hands quivered and her eyes flashed, and she became the song. Her stance was upright and muscular, but, like the others on either side of her, there was a softness too, in her firm large arms and bulging shoulders and rounded hips; there was laughter, there was grace. Piupiu superbly cut, a fanning arc of black and white, densely plaited, each strand fingernail fine, belted into taniko at the waist, swirling out to make its own music, to reveal ankles finely chiselled, and shapely, swelling calves. Even dressed up like all the other women she was exactly right.

Tahuri tried to spot Mirimiri. At the side, on the guitar, fingers moving, arms flexing, keeping pace. She was in full costume too, with something else; a short cloak trimmed with hukahuka, the black tassels shimmering as she strummed. On her head, clipped down but out of control, her taniko headband wobbled around uncomfortably, as if the elaborate red, white and black diamonds and triangles just weren't meant to be there. That, Tahuri considered, didn't matter all that much. The group was fantastic, just fantastic and she just couldn't wait to tell her new friend.

They didn't see each other again until the next day, Sunday, at lunchtime. Tahuri had got caught at the Ritz by Uncle Jack and one of those nosey little kids, so she had to go home with them; she was still too young to be walking the streets that late at night on her own, the family said. So home she went, with the magic of the concert lighting up her heart. And the rain started falling hard, again.

The manuhiri were leaving after lunch; boxes of food were being packed to take on the buses, and some had already left that morning, early. Mills had come into the kitchen to help; Tahuri was beaming. They worked away, cutting up scone bread, buttering it, the younger girl raving on and on about the fantastic entrance. And action song. And haka. And poi. And of course they had won the competitions. Mirimiri just smiled away to herself, muttering thank you, and kept on with her job. Tahuri went quiet, thinking about the bus leaving soon, and how they'd not had any time together at all. It made her feel sad, and also a bit frustrated. She chopped away at the scone. Around them, the other women, were busily cutting paper, stacking the bread, slicing the meat, wrapping the kai, and packing it up. Through the window, sheets of rain lashed across the marae, and thick clouds of steam rose rolling from the ngawha, blocking out the view.

Auntie Tui came in, looking as if she had something important to say.

She stood up straight, though she was very short and round, and, dramatically wiped her hands on her apron. This was her sign for everyone to pay attention; the women stopped working, and looked at her attentively.

'Well, girls,' she declared in a very loud voice. 'There have been major slips on the road out of town, the roads are all blocked up because of the rain. They're clearing it out, but the last buses won't be leaving until tomorrow lunchtime at the earliest. So! That's it!' Sighs and smiles from everyone; concern for the visitors and their families waiting for them at home; with murmurs of softer conversation, the women slipped back into the familiar routine. The boxes would have to be unpacked; more meat would have to be put on; someone would go for the milk. Auntie Tui went into action; everything was moving again.

Tahuri wanted to jump and shriek for joy. She looked across the bench at Mirimiri; they both stopped working. Something clattered to the floor. The butterknife. Swiftly, the older girl bent to pick it up; it had fallen by Tahuri's foot. She paused for not even a minute; softly, quickly, she linked her fingers into the top of Tahuri's boot, pressed her knuckles against the skin, pulled down the sock. Dug in with her fingernails, then hoisted herself up, staring directly into the other's wide gaping eyes. Challenging.

'Neat.' Mirimiri was smiling. 'That's really neat! Eh, Ta – who knows what the night will bring?'

Tahuri gulped. That spot on her ankle was electric, burning with excitement. Oh yes. Neat, all right. And she knew just the place, too, for the night to bring something.

Auntie Tui agreed Tahuri could sleep in the shed that night – if she moved the mattresses back in, the ones they weren't using any more, and packed the place up nice. She was glad, too; Uncle Jack had gone off with her key ring with the shed key on it, and she wasn't sure when he'd come back, and she didn't want the place open all night long. There might be drunks wandering around, looking for a warm place to sleep it off before they went home to face Mum.

'As long as you have a mate, lovey,' her eyes twinkled. 'Not a boy, mind you.' Not likely, her niece flashed in her head. Yuk.

'Ooh no Auntie, never, I'll tell Kui, then I'll ask Mirimiri – you know, their guitarist, eh.' Auntie Tui nodded, her head full of all the jobs she had to do, and walked off to do them. The old people had decided to make the most of so many people in the pa for another night – some of the koros were going to the club with the workers for a few spots, but most of the oldies and the young ones were going to stay on in the whare kai, have a bit of a social and some items, and maybe play cards later on. The home crowd was also gearing up to entertain, though they'd do their items in ordinary clothes, not dress up in concert gear. Tahuri was looking forward to it – she enjoyed the haka, knew she was useless at the poi, but would get up anyway and have a go. She was feeling a little bit funny, knowing she'd be up there in front of Mills – but fair enough, she'd seen her friend on stage the night before.

The bathhouse backed on to the lake; it was made up of rocks and mossy concrete and slippery old timber fencing that kept the pakeha tourists out during the day. Half of it was roofed over with tin sheets, but the pool itself gleamed under the clouds, the night, the stars. It was almost round, with one side squared off, and steps forming sunken seating just below the water level. As with most of the older baths in the village, sandy natural springs bubbled up from the bottom, and a narrow drain channelled the overflow down into the lake. Tahuri was too shy to light the candle in the corner – baths like this never had electric light. Massive clouds lolled across the moon, the steam rose like fat ballooning sails, and every now and then, the stars would twinkle through. Ha. It was enough that she and Mills were there, alone, together. Without saying anything, they undressed, hopped quickly in, not looking at each other. Water closed over them soothing, like a caress. They hardly talked at all – they were both tired out by the long day and running around between showers of rain, heaving mattresses back into the shed, stacking them up for Auntie Tui. She'd had them on the go all afternoon, and by night time they were stuffed. After the concert, they had both sneaked outside. Tahuri suggested they go for a bath, while everyone else was still in the dining-room. And off they went.

Mirimiri wasn't used to the mineral water, so they didn't sit in there for very long. They didn't touch much either – just kept thoughtfully apart, pulling on their clothes, tying their towels around their hips. Hands brushed very briefly as they passed through the door, stepped out into the swirling steam.

Some of the boys were sitting on the form under the rimu tree. They were talking and smoking and trying to be tough. One of them stood up. Hands deep down inside his crotch, he sauntered towards the young women. 'Gotta match Ta?'

'E hoa, you know I don't smoke, eh.' She kept her voice very even.

'Huh. Oh well. That's all right. You got some fire for me then, girl?' He moved towards her, pelvis first, cocky.

'No, I bloody haven't, you smartarse. Piss off or I'll tell Uncle Jack on you.' Her face was flaming. The boy laughed gruffly, swaggered around. He was getting the results he wanted. He wasn't too sure about the big dark one, though. She looked as if she was winding herself up for a scrap. And she was a big as him, maybe even bigger. She seemed to be sizing him up. Huh. He didn't care. The boys were there.

'You piss off, Miss Whakahihi Too Big For Her Boots. Don' wanchoo anyway. You're not what I call a real woman.' Guffaws and harsh laughter from the other boys. 'And as for your mate – haw haw haw. All a man can see is –' He stepped back into the safety of the pack, standing restless. 'All a man can see is your teeth . . . Moonshine.' Chortling with the strength of their numbers, their maleness, they blundered off, kicking at rocks on the road.

'Stupid little prick, I could've bitten his fucken head off, he'd get teeth all right,' Mirimiri swore, fists clenched hard. 'I could've wasted that little black shit. They make me sick. I can't stand the stupid bastards.' They watched the boys disappear towards town.

'Me too.' Tahuri scuffed along, embarrassed, humiliated. She was used to them razzing her, but she still hated it. And them. They thought she was pretty because she was short and had long straight hair and a fair complexion. But Mills was sort of the opposite, nothing half caste about her. Oh damn those creeps for spoiling the evening, damn them. She started talking to blot out her bad feelings.

'Do they really make you sick?' she asked. The older girl looked away, paused for a minute.

'Yep. In more ways than one. Let's say I'll put up with them and that's about it. I can't be bothered, you know. Can't figure out what it is about them that's meant to make us go silly – boy crazy, you know. Matetane! What!' she giggled to herself, it sounded rather strange. 'Anyway, darl. What about you?'

Tahuri started going red again, but fired ahead.

'Well. They make me sick, too. I don't like them much at all. And besides I think I'd sooner go with girls, if you know what I mean!'

She blurted the last bit out quickly, remembering how those fingers in her boot had cut her up with pleasure. Quickly, just in case Mills hadn't meant for it to be like that. The answer came back, soft and clear.

'Hey that's neat. Me too.'

But they kept on walking apart. Tahuri started up again. She was excited, and there was something she wanted to know.

'You know that big woman – your auntie – the one wearing the man's hat. Is she like that?'

'Well. Ah. We're not supposed to talk about it outside the family – you know what I mean. Ah. Ah. She could be. But it's not for me to say anything, eh . . . ' She trailed off. That subject was more or less finished. The younger girl went ahead and bounced on to a new one. They were close to the shed.

'I like your uniform,' she chattered on. 'Especially yours, with the little korowai and stuff. Did you have to make all the gear yourselves?'

'Yeah. Oh, my sisters helped me with mine, and all I had to do was put my name on everything, permanent like. And Auntie – the big one, you know, she gave me that dumb headband. I labelled that, too. Dumb. My hair's too thick and it's too short and I hate that headband. Can't seem to stick it on straight and it always comes off because I hate tight rings around my head squeezing out my brains and I wish I could lose the bloody thing!'

Tahuri recalled how funny and awkward it had looked; she touched

Mirimiri's arm, cautiously, on the shirt sleeve. The skin underneath felt warm, and promising.

'I reckon you'd look good in anything,' she whispered.

They were at the shed. Mills had said earlier that she'd sleep there too, help Tahuri keep the drunks out. Tahuri, whose blood was pounding, whose gut was creaking like the door. The two young women linked little fingers, and went inside. Bolted the shed shut. And wordlessly, curiously, hungrily, they fell into each other's arms.

Mirimiri had been in too much of a hurry to dry herself properly. Her skin was clammy from the bath; the faded black flannel shirt stuck to her in patches, she wanted to peel it off. Not yet. She pushed herself against Tahuri's body, they sank down on to the feather mattresses, cushioned and moulded, nesting their own hollows. Legs entwined, towels a sodden knot on the floor, dropped instantly the door had locked. Tahuri's jersey prickled at her neck and throat; the wool was damp and itchy, she didn't know whether to take it off or leave it on. So she left it on, and her underpants too, though they were soaking wet and not just from the bath. Mills leaned into her, hands found their own way up her jersey, dragging it off, bunching it at her armpits. She hauled it over her head; the other girl's came off too.

They looked at each other. Sat back, slightly away from each other, and they gazed and gaped at the ways they were so different, and yet so much the same. Mills was big; football shoulders and strong neck, and dusky shadows in her throat, dipping in to full breasts that sat up high and round, and jiggled slightly when she moved her arms. One was draped across her chest, covering its points, the elbow resting on her puku, a hard bed of muscle. Her other arm was up behind her head, supporting it on the squash of feathers. Tahuri noticed a hairless scoop of armpit, silken and completely bare. She instantly felt shy about her own hairs sprouting away up there — not that she had many, but all of her family and most of her girlfriend cousins had none at all, and she was the only one with them, like a pakeha, and it made her feel funny and different, but maybe with Mills that didn't matter. She hoped so. Still, she kept her arms down, and covered her front, too. God, they were so flat she looked like a bloody boy

– sometimes that was cool, but tonight she wasn't so sure, admiring Mills' big ones – and oh shit she was so *white*. Almost as white as the sheet, she realized with horror, as her foot found its way towards Mills, whose deep brown toes flexed and unflexed lazily. Like the paws of a huge black cat. Then Mills moved. She dropped her hands, kneeled forward across the piled bedding, and grabbed her, pulling her down.

Their bodies fitted together. Their mouths met, softly moist and flowering open, licking and leafing delicately, their fingers found their own way, probing, circling, kneading. Tracing the satin liquid smoothness of skin, teasing out the scatty scales of ticklishness, measuring the lines of magic-making pleasure. They hung on, and kissed and smooched and kissed.

Their underpants were tight and damp and tangled, a barrier. And the heat grew there, a strong, lustrous aching that seeped through the straining cotton, and tangled in their pubic curls. They throbbed and gasped and thrust into each other. Thighs scissored together, Mills' largeness overwhelming, she folded Tahuri right in to herself, they rocked around laughing between long heavy smooches, tumbling to the floor, as the feathers flattened. Tahuri was galvanized, moving herself up, moving into the other one's body, feeling her bone down there somehow sinking in to all that softness, feeling something else, too, pushing on her. Hard, it was, Mills' hip bone or front bone or whatever it was, it didn't matter, pushing and grinding and pushing her over the cliff, over the cliff –, but she hung on to the edge, she hung on, tight. Following Mills. Catching up. Or waiting for her.

Hands on her breasts, lips, too. Four breasts. All the same, all different. Small firm mounds, raspberry nipples, tiny dimpled rings, teeth rimming them, sinking in to the skin, or heavy ripe plum-purple swellings, juicy and eagerly plucked, their secret creases luscious, underneath and in between . . . The sameness and the differences; supple fingers spun and stroked, gently spidering their way about a shuddering surface of curves and flatness, bunched flesh, and taut skin. Pulsing; earlobes nipped and nuzzled, purring; and every bone along each back lovingly studied and stoked, with hands bold and calm and sure, counting, claiming. Going in, going home.

She groaned, her body arched and bucking gently, a melody of rippling muscles tingling all along her side, beneath her puku, along her flanks. Her eyes were shut, squeezed, her mouth so wide, swallowing the dark, and she clutched the hand, rolled on it, rolled over it, replaced it with her own, removed her own, let it find its way in to the other's place. For more, for more. Taking, giving, taking again. The underpants were beginning to be a bit of a damn nuisance.

'You know what?' They paused, cheekbone leaning against cheekbone, eyelashes almost woven together, breath mingling. Through the shed window, the moon sailed high, ringed with the eerie, haunting colours of more rain. Clouds wobbled across her face.

'I reckon we should take our underpants off.'

The next day started far too early for both of them. Auntie Tui had them up and helping with breakfast, then it was cutting and buttering more bread like they did the day before, for the boxes to go on the bus. They worked amidst the fuss of clearing up, stacking away, folding down, and generally getting ready to go. Tahuri and Mirimiri were quiet around each other, but staunch. They both knew that was probably going to be it, unless they saw each other at the next hui, and Mills wasn't very sure about that because she was thinking of going down south with her brother-in-law's shearing gang. But she'd try and get there; there was always someone coming up this way. And there was the holidays, too.

Too soon, it was time to go. Mills had the guitar under her arm again. She was leaning against the bus, and Tahuri was examining the rubble around her feet, tugging at the waistband of her jeans, or pulling restlessly at her plait. Just about everyone else had climbed aboard. The two young women look at each other; the dark one knew that she mustn't be the last one to get on the bus. She set her guitar up against the wheel, shoved her hands into her jacket pockets, half grinned at Tahuri, who smiled back. They embraced, hugged each other tight for as long as it was all right. They didn't cry. Just held each other, Mills' quick knowing hand sliding into Tahuri's back pocket, for the briefest second. She kissed her near the corner of her mouth, just missing it, and she whispered secretly, tenderly.

'Ka kite, darl. I mean it. We'll do it again, eh. Honest.' She grabbed the guitar, and was up the steps and out of sight.

Tahuri stood there, staring. She hated goodbyes, hated them. 'Ka kite, Mirimiri. Have a safe trip home. See you next year, eh? See you again!' I hope I hope I hope I hope I hope I hope, she muttered fiercely to herself as she turned her back on the bus and rushed back to the whare kai. There was heaps of work to do.

Before going in, she stopped at the rimu tree. The plank seat was still there. She sat down, trying to pull herself together, to stop the tears, to remember all the night's soft sweetness. Something dug into the left cheek of her bum – a hump in the back pocket. She pulled it out.

Black red white triangles and diamonds, patiki and nihotaniwha, the loveliness of a taniko headband shone in the dull winter sun. It was lined, too, neatly sewn in black cotton. And the name, boldly, beautifully embroidered in elaborate silk capitals. Chainstitched, in bright wine. MIRIMIRI. She squashed it hard against her nose, and breathed in deep. She wiped her tears on it, too, for they were coming now.

And with a bursting heart, she set off for the dining-room.

VINCENT O'SULLIVAN

It is usually assumed that if a man has two mistresses or two wives, then they must be physically quite contrary types. Perhaps literature has corrupted that part of our thinking irretrievably. There is always the 'dark she, fair she', as the gloomiest of English poets once wrote. Or what we drew from those books we were reared on. Walter Scott. Nathaniel Hawthorne. There is a blonde girl who embodies the domestic virtues, who wears a plaid shawl, looks after an aged father, and gazes at the hero with eyes so blue that ice floating in the coldest fjords is not to be compared. Truly. And there is a raven-haired woman who speaks directly from the blood. She is Mediterranean, and behind her we see the temples of forgotten faiths, a rage for existence which that blonde girl knows nothing of. She carries phials in her pocket, while the Anglo-Saxon angel has merely an address book in her reticule. Which is introductory to this simple fact: when Bob Roberts died, there were two women at his graveside. They were almost identical.

Helene, whose name had always enchanted him, said as they walked away from the dark gaping hole, 'We all get finally I suppose what we most deserve.'

The other woman was called Frith. She hated her name intensely because of that mucky story about the bird. She said, 'If only we did.'

Metaphor is something that Helene hates more than anything on earth. A plate is a plate. A fish is a fish. A plate can never be a fish, even if it is shaped with fins and painted with scales, and signed Picasso in the corner. Because there is always the irrefutable test. Give a hungry man a plate painted like a fish.

Frith does not think like that at all. To carry metaphor in one's emotional arsenal is to carry a thin stick that snaps open to a gorgeous fan. There is a semicircle of wonder as close as the palm of one's hand. Japan, as she once explained it to Bob, sits waiting in Dabtoe. There is holocaust in every match that is struck correctly.

At the graveside both women stepped forward simultaneously, to take a handful of clammy yellow earth. One had removed her glove while the other had kept hers on. The better dressed of the women reached out her right hand to the trowel which the undertaker offered them. The other woman took her handful from the left. Frith thinking of a cake offered on a cakeslice. Helene looking only at the clogged crumbs of earth.

When Helene threw that clutch of dirt into the grave, onto the polished wood and the freshly engraved metal plate, she knew quite absolutely she tossed dust to dust. So did Frith. But she was thinking how she knew beyond any disbelief in resurrection or anything else, that she was throwing eternity onto dear dead Bob. That all of us, walking or sleeping, wear bodies which are indeed the merest tip of the past, the arrowhead that shall then lie round for a million years. She thought, I am throwing the dust of today onto the ash of stars.

Bob had said to them separately, 'You cannot expect me to choose between you. You just can't.'

Each of them had said in her own way, which in fact was very similar, 'We're not cannibals, love. We don't believe for a minute that one has to devour the loved one.' Helene had spelled it out. 'Isn't that what we've been fighting against for millennia. That old *mine, mine* nonsense?' Frith put it like this. She said, 'If we could only think of sex as an aesthetic experience too, as well as a mere tingling of nerves.' (In her mind she saw the telephone exchange her mother worked at while she herself was a child. And on some days too many bells ringing in that small town for one operator to cope with. Until mummy's hands finally across her ears with the room ringing about her and the lights flashing on the switchboard and simply not enough hands for too many wires. With mummy crying *oh shit oh dear*.) What Frith in fact was saying: 'If you won a painting I mean. You don't turn it to the wall if someone else enjoys it too.'

At the graveside she wore a plain grey suit and Helene a black frock with a cut-away matching jacket. From not very far away they might have been sisters, one of them clearly richer than the other. They had both taken a taxi to the cemetery. Neither thought it important which of them had known the corpse the longer time.

Even now, if it came to the push, Bob would not have known what woman he preferred. Thank God though there had never been anything sneaky about the liaisons. He had told Helene quite openly. He had said, 'I don't consider myself a particularly randy sort of man but there's something I'd better tell you.' It was almost as if she had expected him to say it. She had stroked his hair as she leaned across him. He had thought, I'm buggered if I'd have taken the same thing from her. But another time when he had forgotten an appointment with her, Helene threw things at him when he next came into the house.

Frith was so much milder. Yet she wore exotic underthings and said the strongest words when her breath caught and her hands fluttered across his rump.

A point to be made here is that it's not at all the same thing as looking through a doorway, although it's easy enough for writers to imagine that it is, when the figures pull back from the sunlit and lovely oblong which is the top of a grave. To imagine it is like friends going from a room. As a matter of fact the legs are absurdly out of proportion to begin with. They are positive pillars. The heads too such disproportionate bumps above the big swinging handbags, the hands the women held together in their dark gloves rather like the mitts of boxers touching as they prance in their corners. Then when they drop those handfuls of dirt. Honestly, the way the clods came pouring in you'd think they had it in for you.

'I'm only a journo,' Bob used to tell them. 'Only run of the mill in the least elevated of callings.'

'It must be so marvellous to use words at all,' Frith said. 'With that freedom, I mean. That control. All I ever do, day after day, is hear children recite their grammar. Hear them conjugate, decline, fumble with sentences they will never know how to use. Languages!' she sighed. 'Those complicated and dreary ladders. Where do they expect them to reach?'

She liked it when he nuzzled close against her, ran his hand down her stomach and left it lying there. 'A man is like the *Zeitwort*, do you understand that? The verb. Women are so many nouns.'

When both of them stood back from the long bright space hanging there above him, he thought how lovely a patch of pure blue could seem.

The women turned away and walked for perhaps a minute in silence. Then Helene was saying to Frith, 'In the six funerals I've been to in this cemetery this is the first one it hasn't rained.'

They were cutting across the rows of the buried towards the road. A champion billiard-player's monument with its slate table, its marble cue, struck them as too absurd. 'God knows what Bradman will have. A whole oval made from brass.' They touched each other's arms in amusement. 'Imagine what Bob would think, us talking like this!' They remembered how he believed that women knew nothing about sport.

As it happened, he thought a great deal. He thought of Helene's knee on the side of his bed, her preparing to throw herself across him like the great Jim Pike across Phar Lap himself, and his telling her, 'You are lovelier than anything I know.' And her playfully putting her hand across his mouth so that he bit at that fleshy part just down from her little finger. Her saying to him. 'Never say *than*. Never say *like* or *as*. Do you hear?' Pressing with her strong knees against his sides. And his saying quite seriously, so that she roared with laughter, 'There's not a love poem I bet you in the whole of literature for that part of a woman's body. That little soft bit there on the side of your hand.' Helene would even laugh sometimes in the middle of their loving. With Frith there was either no talk at all, or those words she would never think of using anywhere else.

The first time he had ever seen them together. At an art opening he had to write up for his paper because the critic was down with the mumps. He was terrified at the thought of speaking to both of them at the same time. He leaned close to Frith as he came in and saw her by the table with the catalogues. 'There's an awful lot of people I have to nod to tonight. Or the paper does rather. Know what I mean?' He brought her a glass of wine and looked at some pictures with her. She knew the names of all of them without referring to her catalogue.

Helene said out very loudly, 'This is the most boring exhibition I have ever seen.' He had been shocked. He looked at the famous black figures against their ochrous background, the flashes of gums and flowers like gunshot in the violence of the light. She said, 'Introduce me to her anyway. She can't be worse than this.'

They had reminded him of a Moore exhibition as they peered down at him a few minutes ago. Their heads so small and distant, mere tufts on pyramids of flesh.

Helene, he had sometimes thought, liked to be with him so that she could *hone*. On anything. On politics or race or people they knew. 'Private money makes it so easy,' he would say to her. 'I could sneer at half the price.' She sat with her legs tucked under her, her glass of wine reflecting like a great coin. Folded on her knee was the paper with his column. 'What would you do if you actually had to look at something? Come into the open without your clichés? Your little images? Run like a nigger flushed from the cane-brakes, I wouldn't be surprised.' Her teeth when she teased him like that! So white and even and gleaming. She enraged him. And then so deliberately looking at her watch, declaring that her husband already had left his office, was stroking this very moment life into his Bentley. But the excitement never really wore off, because there was one lesson he learned very early. To root above one's station is the first step to the stars.

It is surprising how little it shocks one to hear that a friend is dead. It would surprise one more at times to hear that he had won a fortune or written a book or even that he had remarried. Death, when the chips are down, is a very ordinary thing to come to terms with. No sooner has one heard it than there are those meetings with other friends, the ceremonies that nudge it so easily, so gently, away from the warm place where we stand ourselves. To buy a hat, for example. How much of grief can be absorbed in that. To buy, as indeed Frith did, new black underwear for the funeral. Appreciating her own dark joke as she tried it on at home, for a moment there Bob was alive again, watching her from the bed, assuring her she was a bit of all right, bloody oath she was! That other time twenty years ago when she had surprised him with what she wore beneath her dress. The day she had opened the book that he gave her at the end of their first summer. In the tiled vestibule of the Seacliff Hotel! The dark pines on that space of lawn across the street, a solitary girl walking there in a white frock. *Munch!* Bob had said when he looked at her. One of his dreadful artistic puns. Just before he gave her the brown-paper wrapped present and told her to open it in the car. 'I'll open it now!' she had said, and they were tussling, fooling about, people giving them the oddest looks as they passed at the foot of the big staircase. She tore the brown paper and saw that marvellous gilded face. The thick black lines on the eyelids. The cheekbones of pure gold. All because she had said once, *wouldn't you love to go to Egypt?*

After the women withdrew, there were minutes in that oblong of brilliant light when almost nothing happened. A palm frond waved across bottom left. A flight of longnecked birds that could have flown from a Russian movie flicked over very high. Then a man sat there briefly with his feet dangling down as though he sat on a wharf, and smoked a cigarette. When he stood up again he hitched his belt and shouted across to another bloke to move his arse. And the earth started to rain in. Bob tried to remember something. Yes! That quick flowing across of girths and bellybands as ground-level cameras caught the jumpers at Beecher's Brook. The clods flying out from the impacting hooves. The clods now pouring down and the blades of the shovels flashing above there like aircraft in low flight.

And by Christ to hear them now you'd think they had been cobbers from way back.

Helene said, 'You must have known him as long as I did?'

'I suppose I must have,' Frith said. 'At least as.'

Helene said, 'Did he mention me much?'

'You know what men are,' Frith said.

Helene asked again, 'Did he ever mention me?'

'Only to denigrate,' Frith said. 'To say he was chained to a cunt the way men used to be tied to benches in galleys.'

Helene said,' Whenever he mentioned you it was like he spoke of a disease.'

Bob enjoyed their saying that. He thought how even here you could write your own column. But the women refused his script. They did not squabble as he had hoped. What Frith said in fact was this: 'He lied to both of us, of course.'

'He was a liar all right,' Helene said. 'And he wasn't even that bright, either.'

But there are ways the dead unsettle the living. There are casual remarks made long ago in the warm rooms of the flesh which become weapons in neatly-cuffed and buried hands. Bob thought, it is the least I can do for them now.

'Metaphor is shit,' Helene had said to him once, putting down his paper. His livelihood and his skill dismissed just like that. He had told her you have to be well off to say that. Only the rich were content to be exactly where they were. All very well for her with her fat books of philosophy she could read all day, her picture of Bertrand Russell on her desk like a boiled chook.

'If it wasn't for imagery life would be one long walk along a gutter.' That was to Frith. Her blue pencil in her hand, saying that to be able to put 9 out of 10 on a schoolgirl's work was indeed *délice*; *10* out of *10* was *jouissance*. They had a silly game in which she came to bed only after a pupil had scored the top mark. While Bob lay thinking then as now, that for a heavy smoker life indeed could be worse than keeping a gutter eye out for what his old man had called derbs. 'For every ten drowned butts there is one that lies there dry enough to light.' Not every father has that much wisdom to give a son.

He thought very hard about cigarettes, and the room where the women were talking.

In the large quiet room above the park Helene saw the walls flare sharply at her, then return to their tasteful white. It frightened her because she knew there had been no alteration in the light. She said to Frith, 'What were you thinking just now?'

Her dead lover's anterior and it seems always concurrent mistress said, 'I was thinking how life is like a rainbow when we come to think of it.' Strangely, for a moment there Frith had felt as though she bent back on space, her head and heels drawn towards each other, the ether as the poets call it so sparkling about her. *Arc-en-ciel – c'est moi*. Her eyelashes had seemed like the spokes of an iridescent wheel. She wondered if Bob was trying to get through to her. While Helene, because she was the cleverer of the two, thought: if that dead bastard is coming at this one . . . Talk of things like telepathy made her want to throw up. I am a single and finite mind, she told herself. I am not a bloody button in some cosmic jukebox.

From her chair on the other side of the comfortable lounge, Frith watched how her friend's hands met and laced and moved in the silvery light, the point of her cigarette so alive across there, so brilliant. *Alive*, she thought. As the dusk rinsed and dipped in the long low mirror that ran the length of the far wall.

He had quite expected the first night to pass slowly. The light coming up across the surrounding rows made him think of arriving at Kennedy airport in New York, one morning when it was very early, on a dawn flight from the West. Manhattan's blocks, its tall secular angels above their strips of narrow street, had made him think it was like a cemetery.

He thought, given time I suppose I shall remember everything. I shall get bored I suppose with this outlook as I have with every other until I remember this one is for keeps. And oddly, that quite comforted him. There would be the chance at last to find one experience that was inexhaustible. He would want to remember precisely what this sensation was like, the first light breaking of the first day. To recall it would be to continue it, to extend it and to know how this day differed from the second. And through memory living those two days as the third was added, and so on. The hundredth. The ten thousandth. To discriminate each moment, as he had liked to quote when he was a student, 'on that day of frost and sun' or whatever it was. Six crosses ranged to the right, then. A stone child dropping a stone rose. Those bloody Italian inscriptions he could never read! Then the college tower far over there beyond the fence, across petrol stench and the trees. There were some positions as he knew that had a damned sight less than this to pass the time. And in the distance there a corner of a building with the dawn smearing its upper windows behind which, had one turned directly about and walked through the lounge with its morbid mirror and its Aubusson birds, one would come to a passageway as they called it when he was a child in which a fumed oak stand protruded antlers for one's hat and a painted Victorian can waited for the winter months to receive one's umbrella, past which one proceeded clothed as a rule or dishevelled at times or on some few occasions starkers towards a bedroom where a woman now lay looking at the light which broke not only there for her but across a city, and given time, a country; a dawn into which she might walk from her own front steps with their small ornamental lions and along an empty street to the locked iron gates which suppose they were opened, she might then pass through and walk on between and beneath the elaborately cut stones and the marble figures, the religious confectionery which made her think if not of the bread of life at least the cake of eternity, and so come to the mound where the flowers already wilted although some of them this time yesterday had not been cut, their binding ribbons straggling damp, the handwritten consolations already dribbled ink. From a point equidistant, say, that mound of the grave, the shape of the bed in this greyish light, were not so fancifully unalike. Only Helene tugging her covers close, hoping for further sleep before she had to rise and take her bath and dress. At which moment, Frith: that quite as loved but much less wealthy woman lay with the fingers of one hand spanning the wrist of the other and thinking of how at Père Lachaise she had stood at the graves of so many famous of Oscar of Abelard of Alphonsine Plessais Chopin Daudet it could have been of Colette too so she heard later but had missed her at the time. *The grave's a sad and lonely place*, who said? It is a bed it is a bed, she thought. I am running out of what-it's-likes!

When the women met at the Jewish cake-shop at St Kilda Helene said the moment her gloves were removed and lay like something skilfully skinned beside her, 'That old sod's been on my mind practically non-stop all week.' Stabbing the golden arse of a *pêche* concoction. 'Don't tell me he hasn't been on yours?'

'My mind becomes blank whenever I try to think of him.'

'I wake,' Helene said, 'in the early hours and my mind's as full of nonsense as that glass counter there of European gut-rot.'

'You go over the past?' Frith said. She peeled the paper from the *torte* she had chosen.

'Sometimes I remember the past like it's the present.' Both women noticed the unexpected word that established itself in Helene's sentence.

Frith's cheek bulged horribly as in children's caricatures of toothache. She swallowed the wad of sweetness away. 'I used to dream for a bit but now it's pure bareness. *Le néant*.'

Helene said, 'Every morning when I do get round to waking all I smell is earth.' She laughed. 'I'm starting to think like you!'

Bob remembered a cake shaped like a ship with white frosted lines of rigging at a Sea Scout Christmas Party in 1938. He thought of four meringues that sounded like a gravel path when he crunched them and he had wolfed them down one after the other at the wedding of a cousin who wore a military uniform. He recalled in no particular order seedcake with aunts on Sunday afternoons, kisscakes with his mother measling down icing-sugar from a flour-mill lamingtons soggy as a rained out oval *Kuchentorten* and *Schlagsahnetorten* during his time abroad. Those aerated squares of pure dryness Frith dipped in her tea while she went on about Proust. He could think of every cake he had ever eaten. No two had been alike. No mouthful was identical with a following or preceding mouthful.

'I'm so sick of this already.' Helene slapped her tiny fork down on her plate. One cheek of her *pêche* remained untouched.

Frith dabbed at her lips with a paper napkin.

Back with their brandies they began to talk of God.

Helene said that when she was a child there had been a crucifix on her grandmother's wall. Two narrow strips of black wood and a grey contorted figure like a deep-freeze lizard.

Frith said she could still sing hymns quite seriously. At weddings or funerals for example. She never gave it a thought between times, mind.

Helene said she would have shot priests if she had been a Spaniard in the old days. 'I see those bastards in black I want to reach for my branding irons.' Which was not really so strong an image and certainly not a metaphor, when used by a woman who was a grazier's wife.

Bob used to joke that in any case a Christian was only a lapsed atheist.

He had known so many anti-clerical jokes that he couldn't keep up with invitations to speak at Catholic men's dinners.

But Frith had perched on him once, *in flagrante*, and quoted some lines of John Donne about tuning his instrument here at the door. He had turned on her and told her not to be so bloody disrespectful.

The two women now sat in the lounge and looked over the massed trees to the black iron fence and its acres of remembrance.

'You do wonder though what becomes of one. Gauguin's great painting, *Who are we?* etcetera. Cliché that it is.'

Helene reached irritably for her cigarettes. 'Anything worth saying is a cliché.'

'Aquinas, wasn't it, thought that you couldn't use any predicate at all of God? That any statement at all was pure tautology?'

'He fucking would,' Helene said. She had hated the Angelic Doctor since her childhood, when she heard that story about a semicircle being cut in the refectory table for his bulk to sit down to meals.

The women sat in silence for several minutes. Then Frith said, 'If He is there, it makes every moment so infinitely of value.' She was slightly embarrassed that she had said it.

'If he isn't of course,' Helene said, 'every moment must be more valuable still.'

'What?' Frith sounded surprised.

'Because there is only a straight line and not a circle. There is no redeeming time, I mean. Each act stands as itself forever.'

Bob thought, 'What if you're both wrong, you smart bitches?'

A picnic in the You-Yangs. The only time he had been with them both together, apart from that art show. A busload of them during a weekend seminar on 'Responsibilities of the Press'. Frith there because she believed such questions mattered, Helene — although she would not even know the word — because she was by nature a groupie. For opera. For *The Tree of Man* during its first year out. For existentialism in its time and then for Vietnam. Only a rich woman could have afforded to care for so much. So at least Bob thought while he sat behind them in the bus, listening to an academic who had been on the same panel with him that morning. He watched the heads of his mistresses sway and bounce.

That outcrop of ancient rocks gave him the creeps. He detested people who used words like numinous, or a few years later spoke of 'the vibes'. He looked at the group about him. Thirty minutes standing in prehistory, as they liked to think, then haring back to the free piss at the cocktail party. The thought of those great grey boulders, the sudden abutments and leaps of rock, depressed him enough to make him consider staying on the bus. Which of course a good journo would never do, because he would not seem one of the team. So he walked with the sociologist whom he suspected could not have written a convincing cheque, while the two women he slept with followed some distance behind. Frith said, looking up at the pure blue that hazed off towards the city, 'It's like being inside a jewel on a day like this.' Helene told her she had read how you saw further at this time of year than at any other. 'You can see a candle burning at night three miles away.' That in fact was no more true than the bit about the jewel.

Someone in the group had snapped photographs as they walked along. Eighteen years later Helene handed a print across the coffee table to her recent good friend. She said, 'Remember that afternoon do you?' Bob was some little way ahead. He was turned in profile, laughing. He looked young and happy. The collar of his sports jacket, so typically, was turned up at the back. In the distance far beyond him was the thin strip of the Geelong road. A woman's head was blurred beside him, but her hair was dark and long. Frith took her glasses from her purse. 'Which one of us is that – next to Bob there?'

Helene gave that laugh which sounded so butch Bob used to tell her it reminded him of rugby changing sheds. 'I'm damned if I remember,' she said. Her quieter friend began to laugh as well. The photograph fell as it passed back between them. 'Easy on it,' Frith said. 'One of us is being dropped.' That struck them both as very funny. Helene rubbed at her eyes as though smoke was stinging them.

The women went on to speak of something else, then something else again. While the sky either clouded over or grew dark, Bob was not sure which. It may have been a week later or a month. The two furthest crosses, and the rose-dropping child, were no longer clear in any case. The lawnmower that sometimes charged past like those bloody speedboats that used to irritate him so much the summer when he and Helene lay on that perfect beach on the Tasman Peninsula, that didn't seem to bother him too much at all. He was beginning to forget the names of horses, and football players, and the meals he had once eaten. He was not quite sure any more if *Mille feuilles à la crème* was a cake or a sprinter.

They were leaving the expensive restaurant where Helene had taken Frith to lunch. The afternoon was late as they passed the proprietor who swung back the door for them. They could see the gold tooth near the back of his head. If they wished to sit on with another coffee, he was assuring them, until five, five-thirty, what did it matter? They were not customers, but friends. Frith thought how that would sound so epigrammatic in Latin. While Helene leaned forward in front of her. She heard her friend's face scrape against the man's. She thought how the dangling palm there above the two embracing humans was like a great green hoof. *I hear an army charging*, she thought. What nonsense comes into one's mind!

Helene stood in the street with her car keys fretting in her glove, looking to right and to left.

'You left it up near Parliament,' Frith offered. 'Didn't you?'

'Of course,' Helene said, 'near that little lane where the press boys play about.' Old darling Bob! she thought.

Frith felt her eyes prickle suddenly with tears. Very aware, even now in the diminishing light and the sated aftermath of food and drink and her friend's expensive brooch not turned merely but *flashing* at her, aware of the lovely drifting of the past through the present's glint and whirl, knowing there was something on the tip of her tongue, in the back of her mind, an image just dissolved: with Helene turning as they walked up the slope to the sticks of traffic lights playing their brightness against the massive building, turning and saying with a smile, 'Do you realise we went a whole meal and never mentioned him?' People were walking between them, separating them, allowing them again to come together.

'Remember this same light that time the same at where was it, do you?'

'Dreamed it,' Helene said.

A man saying 'sorry' as he nudged against them.

'Wit then,' Frith laughing, knowing she was a trifle drunk. 'Would you believe I can't get my mouth round his name?'

'Wittgenstein?' They had talked about him at lunch.

'He sounds like a capital.'

'A brand of cigars.'

'*Prestige ist eine Zigarre namens Wittgenstein.*'

'Stop it!'

Oh their voices high, high and happy, happy and so thin and distant. Voices remotely clapping can one say that? Impacting anyhow softly. Like gloves say meeting hush so softly above there in the greying distance that first far day that afternoon, the praying over, the hands of the women palming like a singer's is it, her hands clasping under the notes, the most silent clapping?

On the pedestrian crossing Frith remembering, 'Was it Wittgenstein said can *to dream* have a present tense?'

LLOYD JONES

We were living in Napier at the time. My father pulled the keys down from the hook in the kitchen and my mother asked where he was headed.

'Up the coast,' he said, and my mother went on slicing the ends off the beans for the meal she now knew he wouldn't be around to eat.

'Allie,' my father said by the kitchen door. 'I feel like being alone for a while.'

My mother quietly emptied the colander of beans into the sink. She turned around to face us both.

'Just say where it is you are going.'

My father looked at the keys in his hand, and turned down the challenge. He crossed the lawn to the Hunter parked in the driveway. My mother followed as far as the porch. There she stopped, as if the lawn was a slippery area she would rather not cross, and yelled out: 'Why can't you say it, you lousy stinking coward!' My father settled behind the wheel and backed down the driveway. My mother raised her hands to her face. Then she noticed me; and that seemed to be last straw.

'What are you looking at . . . goddammit!'

From being hurt, she wanted to be forgiven. It was a confusing moment. Her face screwed up with anger, and she drew me over and said, 'Hug your mother, Charlie.' I was happy to, of course, but when I looked I noticed she had drawn herself into two parts: one I hugged, and the other – her proud face – had already turned with a thought to something inside the house.

I followed her inside, through to the living room. She walked directly to the bookcase, where she pulled out a thick book on flora. Most of our books were on plants, lichen and mosses. My father worked in the ecology division of the DSIR.

The book fell open, and the photo of my father fell out. It was taken near the snowline. There was no snow in the photo but you could tell from the rocks and the lichen grown over them that snow was not far off. My father had on his hiking boots. His arm was draped around a woman, an Australian. She was a plant illustrator, who had come here for dinner one night, a long time ago.

My mother studied the photo. She seemed to be trying to prise a bit more from it than the contents were prepared to tell. I couldn't say what she found. Perhaps it was because the photo was deliberately vague that she got so angry. She tore the photo into quarters and watched them settle over the carpet. My father's head was now severed; his whiskery smile even more a mystery.

My mother stepped back and almost fell over. She had forgotten I was there. She swore, then, she smiled bravely. 'Know what we're going to do, Charlie? No. Second thoughts I'm not going to tell you. Let's make it a surprise.'

Our town held few surprises, although it was useful to pretend otherwise. I was just as happy not knowing in any case, because we ended up at Chee's.

Some of the pub crowd had wandered across the road and were trying to chat up the Chinese girl behind the counter. The girl blushed and smiled out of politeness, but you could see she didn't know what the men were on about, and I thought it just as well.

We took the table by the window. Cars were leaving spaces outside the hotel. One of the men at the counter came over and sat at our table. 'Hello beautiful,' he said.

My mother turned and looked straight into his face the way it is said to be cruel to do with dogs. The man said 'Jeeeesus' and got up as quickly as he had sat down. Our meals arrived. My mother hardly touched her fillet.

She counted out the money on the table. She had enough, clearly more than she had thought, because she appeared to be relieved.

'Now is the real surprise,' she said, and we started toward the beach.

The sea breeze was on the way out and the leaves in the trees along the esplanade had stopped rustling. It was growing dark, and sure enough the storm clouds were bunched inland over the ranges.

'I feel like dancing,' my mother announced. She looked at me, then burst out laughing. We walked briskly. The music from the roller skating rink grew louder, and my mother pulled the sides of her cardigan to cover her chest. We could hear Cadillac Jack trying to hustle the crowd onto the rink. He spoke in rhyming couplets — so my mother said, and word had it he was brother of a famous American DJ. My mother always said, it was worth believing anything so long as it wasn't harmful. So little happened around here, anyway.

My mother fussed over the skates like they were vegetables from the cheap bin.

She glided out onto the rink. She did a lap. Her lips were pursed, kind of hard-looking without lipstick. She usually wore lipstick when she went out. Her eyes were concentrated, as if trying to find a way back to some partially lost feeling. She came down off the high shoulder at the beach end and overtook a bunch of kids from the high school. You could easily be fooled, but if you forgot the rest of her and watched the skates you saw she was in complete control. The third or fourth lap she came soaring down and picked me off the rail.

'Push off your toes, Charlie. Push. Push. Push. You're much too stiff.'

She glided out ahead, and started to do skater's goose-step, holding one skate out front about knee height and alternating with the other. She came past the crowd and turned the heads on half a dozen cowboys. Her face glowed. She knew what she had done. She took off her white cardigan and tied it about her waist. Some of the slower skaters moved out of her way and found the sides as she barrelled down the straight past the hot dog stand. Cadillac inside his glass dome let go a gi-normous hooooeeeee. My mother went into a speed crouch and shot up high on the end bend.

Just short of the cowboys, a guy in black jeans and a bush shirt tied at the throat with a length of string pushed off the wall. There were twenty metres in which to decide whether she would go around him. He held his hand out like a ballroom dancer. My mother dug in the toe of her back skate. The stranger's hand collected her around the waist; she spun round once, then again, this time under her own steam to show she enjoyed it.

They pushed off together. The cowboy holding her hand, and my mother bothered by a strand of damp hair that kept falling across her face.

I had stopped trying to skate. I leant against the rail in front of some spectators. I was wondering where my father was right this moment. What he was doing. And what kind of person the Australian woman might be getting to know. I suppose I had taken over my mother's thoughts for the time being – caretaking while she skated.

My mother and her partner seemed none the wiser that a lot of attention was on them. The people behind me had begun to mutter. Something about the 'prison escaper'. Cadillac had gone quiet.

At the town end of the rink they rose together up the shoulder; the escaper hoisted my mother into the air. She threw her head back and used one leg to clamp his shoulder; the other leg she clasped behind the knee and held it straight out front. In this formation they swept down off the bend. By the hot dog stand some of the pub crowd began to clap. I caught a glimpse of the escaper's face: it appeared caught halfway between a big loony grin and serious concern.

'I thought he had gone bush forever and a day,' a voice said behind me.

Somebody else said he had slipped out of the bush this morning.

'Robbie Hale seen him sniffing on the edge of town at daybreak.'

This time as the skaters came barrelling down the straight before the crowd my mother threw her head all the way back until her skates were over the escaper's head, which brought a gasp from the crowd. Then she brought her skates overtop, as if she were doing a backward roll. Over she went until her skates touched the rink. The escaper reached between his legs and drew her through until my mother was the lead skater. She turned to face him, now, and he lifted her so she had her legs splayed either side of him and they were joined at the waist. People had stopped talking and were just staring. My mother's head was well tossed back and she held onto the escaper's shoulders. She started to move up and down with her hips. Neither of them seemed concerned for skate speed. The escaper managed to steer them both up the end shoulder to see them down the straight. On the far side of the rink they moved through the pool of light from the overhead lamps, into shadows, then light again. My mother's face turned a fluorescent colour; now the escaper's head fell back. They were locked together with another movement that had nothing to do with skating.

I heard Cadillac come on over the sound to get more skaters onto the rink. But no one was listening. And there was no heart in the message because Cadillac did not repeat it.

What happened next had nothing to do with Cadillac, or the crowd looking on. From the esplanade a police siren could be heard. The escaper's head turned a fraction. I believe it was the only intervention he would have heeded. He and my mother had virtually come to a standstill in a shadow at the end of the rink. Some of the crowd had moved there to get a better look. The sirens were close, now. My mother was lowered on to her skates. She and the escaper stood straight and near to each other, like lovers in a park.

He kissed her once – on the cheek. Then he split. He pushed off and was nearly in a speed crouch when he passed me.

I heard someone bitch that the escaper hadn't returned his skates. 'Typical' from someone else.

He leapt the turnstile for the esplanade and skated through the first set of lights. One violation after another, cast behind like discarded clothing.

My mother was buttoning her cardigan, as if it was the most important thing in the world. Her cheeks were still flushed. She knew I was nearby, but she looked up in her own good time. She said, 'You enjoying yourself, Charlie? Not too much I hope because I feel like going home now.'

The drunks near the hot dog stand called out things, but she took no notice. 'Look at that, Charlie,' she said, and very deliberately she pointed over the heads of the cowboys, to a fairly ordinary sunset.

While we were getting out of our skates Cadillac came out of his glass dome. I had never actually seen him. He had a pointed beard – like the famous record-spinner – but he only just cleared the top of my head. He looked frightened, and in a quiet voice I never imagined might be his, he said the police had sent through word that they wished to speak with my mother.

He mentioned the man being an escaper, and my mother, still cool as a cucumber, said, 'What, you mean that nice young man?'

Two blocks away from the skating rink she permitted herself to say something, and I realised she was shaking life a leaf.

'I feel like singing,' she said to the trees. Then she stole a quick look at me. 'Charlie, you're not angry with me. Are you, Charlie? Don't be. I haven't skated like that for years.'

We came to our street and from here we should have been able to see the house lights. The car wasn't in the driveway, and I worried that it would have some effect. But she didn't appear to notice. Or, if she did, she didn't care. At the door she said she thought she might have a bath. As it happened we pushed through to the living room, where her eyes went straight to the torn quarters of the photograph. She crossed her arms, and thought.

'Charlie,' she said. 'Go get that glue from the top of the fridge. Let's not disappoint your father.'

OWEN MARSHALL

The heavy moonlight gave it all the appearance of quality linen, flattering the exposed walls of the Totara Eventide Home, and the lines of stainless steel trolleys and wheel chairs by the windows glinted like cutlery upon that linen. The moon was more forgiving than the sun, allowing a variety of interpretations for what it revealed. The shadowed places were soft feathered with blue and grey, like a pigeon's breast.

The only sound was Crealy pissing onto Matron's herb garden. The white cord of his striped pyjamas hung down one leg, and his bald head was made linen in the moonlight. 'Had enough?' Crealy asked the sage, basil and thyme. Residents were not supposed to come out and treat the Matron's herbs to such abuse. Crealy felt his life stir as ever at the defiance of rules. He could see the trim, summer lawn and the garden which paralleled the side path to the slope of the front grounds. The moonlight lay over it all as a linen snowfall.

Crealy had never before lived in a place so pleasant to the eye, or so well organised – and he hated it. Always a big man, he had never done anything with it; lacking the will, the resolution, the brains and the luck. At eighty-one and in Totara Home, he found that time had awarded him a superiority which he had been unable to earn any other way. He had given little; and lasted well.

Crealy's bladder was empty, so he put a large hand over his face to massage his cheeks, while he waited for an idea as to what to do next. Even in the moonlight the kidney spots on the backs of his hands showed clearly. He could think of nothing novel to do so decided to persecute Garfield. He went back through the staff door of the kitchen, and bolted it carefully behind him. Before seeking out Garfield, Crealy wanted to be sure that Brisson was settled in the duty room. He went slowly through the kitchen and the dining room, through the corridors which were tunnels in the Totara of all their past lives.

Crealy stood in the shadow of the last doorway, and looked into the corridor which led past the duty room. He was like a bear which pauses instinctively at the edge of a forest clearing to assess possibilities of gain or loss. He walked slowly down the corridor of mottled, yellow lino, his breathing louder than the regular shuffle of his slippers. Before the duty room he slowed even further as a caution, but his breathing was as loud as ever. The door was ajar, and Crealy looked in to see Brisson at leisure.

The duty room had a sofa, a chair, a log book with a biro on a string, a coffee pot, a telephone, a typed copy of the fire drill on the wall. It had the worn, impersonal look common to all such rooms in institutions, whether hospitals or boarding schools, army depots or fire brigades. Brisson lay on the sofa, and held up a paperback as if shielding himself from the light. His head was round and firm like a well grown onion, and light brown with the sheen a good onion has too. He wore no socks, just yellow sneakers on his neat feet. Crealy was surprised yet again to see how young some people were. He'll lie there all night and do nothing, thought Crealy.

'Who's that huffing and puffing outside my door?' said Brisson without moving, and Crealy pushed the door and took a step into the doorway. 'Ah, so it's you, Mr Crealy,' said Brisson. He swung the book down and his legs onto the floor in one easy movement. 'Why are you wandering the baronial halls?'

In reply Crealy made a gesture with his large hands which seemed more resignation than explanation. Brisson was lazy, arrogant, shrewd – and young. He took in Crealy: the awkward size of him, the sourness of his worn, bald face, the striped pyjamas, and between them and slippers, Crealy's bare ankles with the veins swollen. Brisson gave a slight shiver of joy and horror at his amazing youth and Crealy's old age.

'Mrs Vennermann said you squeezed the blossom off her bedside flowers,' he said. Crealy itched his neck; his fingers sounded as if they worked on sand paper, and the grey stubble was clear in the light of the room. 'She said you pick on people. Is that right?'

'She took my Milo,' said Crealy. Brisson picked up the exercise book that served as the log for duty shifts.

'Shall I put that in here then? Shall I? Mr Crealy deprived of his Milo by Mrs Vennermann. For Christ's sake. And someone said that you have been making Mrs Halliday all flustered. Aye?'

'It's just all fuss,' said Crealy. He began to think how he could get back at Mrs Vennermann.

Brisson smiled at his own performance, looking at old Crealy, at the mottled lino like a puddle behind him, at the exercise book with the cover doodled upon and the biro on a string from it. He considered himself incongruous in such surroundings. He had such different things planned for himself. 'I won't have a bully on my shift, Mr Crealy. If I have to come down to the rooms then look out. And don't you or the others come up here bothering me.' Brisson hoped to be with Nurse McMillan. What time was it?

'I don't do anything,' said Crealy in his husky voice. 'It's Jenny Pen.'

'What's that?'

'Eh?' said Crealy.

'Go to bed,' said Brisson, and saw the old man turn back onto the puddle lino, heard the shuffle and breath of him as he went back to the rooms of the east wing. Brisson did an abrupt shoulder stand on the sofa to prove age is not contagious, then relaxed again with his book and thoughts of Nurse McMillan.

When Crealy reached the room he shared with Garfield, Mortenson and Popanovich he was ready for a little action. Jenny Pen time. Jenny Pen was a hand puppet that Garfield's grand-daughter had made at intermediate school. Although christened Jenny Pencarrow it looked more like Punch, or the witch from Snow White, for its papier mâché nose and chin strove to complete a circle. Jenny Pen had a skirt of red velvet, and balanced all day on the left hand knob of Garfield's bed. At night, ah torment, she became the fasces of Nero's power, the cloven hoof, the dark knight's snouted emblem, the sign of Modu and Mahu, the dancing partner of a trivial Lucifer, a tender facsimile of things gone wrong.

Crealy lifted Jenny Pen from the bed end, and thrust his hand beneath the velvet skirt. He held her aloft, and turned her painted head until all the room had been held in her regard. Garfield began to cry; Mortenson turned the better side of his face aside, and wished his stroke had been more complete. Popanovich was just a shoulder beneath his blankets. Crealy walked Jenny Pen on her hands up Garfield's chest, and she seemed of her own volition to rap Garfield's face. 'Who rules?' said Crealy.

'Jenny Pen,' said Garfield. Garfield had played seventeen games for Wellington as fullback, and later been general manager for Hentlings. It was all too far away to offer any protection.

'Lick her arse then,' said Crealy hoarsely, and Garfield did, and felt Crealy's hand on his tongue. 'You're on Jenny Pen's side, aren't you?' said Crealy.

'Yes.' Garfield's voice barely quivered, although the tears ran down his cheeks. He could scarcely conceive the life he was forced to lead: his soul peeped out from a body which had betrayed him in the end.

Crealy's eyes glittered, and he looked about to share his triumph with others. 'What about you, Judge; want to do a little kissing?' Mortenson gave his half smile.

'It's difficult for me,' he said slowly.

'Bloody difficult with only half of everything working.' Crealy walked over to the last bed, and shook Popanovich's shoulder. There was no reaction. 'What sort of a name is that for a New Zealander,' he said. 'Bloody Popanovich!' he banged his knee into Popanovich's back, but there was no defence of the name. It put Crealy in an ill humour again, and he went back to Garfield with Jenny Pen. He began to go through Garfield's locker. 'It's share and share alike here, Garbunkle.'

'Communism has the greatest attraction to those with the least,' said Mortenson in his slurred voice, knowing Crealy was not bright enough to follow.

'Shut up,' said Crealy. He placed a bag of barley sugars and a box of shortbread biscuits on the top of Garfield's locker. 'Is that all you useless bugger,' he said. He looked at Garfield for a time, letting Jenny Pen rest on the covers, almost basking in the knowledge shared between them of Garfield's weakness and his strength. And even more, the mutual knowledge of Garfield's former strength and superiority, Garfield's achievements and complacency, now worthless currency before Crealy who had achieved nothing except the accidental husbandry of physical strength into old age.

'What else have you got hidden after all them visitors?' Crealy slid his free hand slowly under Garfield's pillow, and withdrew it empty. 'Come on now you bugger,' he said.

'Just leave me alone.'

'Make Jenny Pen sing a song,' said Mortenson. Sometimes Crealy would have Jenny Pen sing 'Knick Knack Paddy Wack Give A Dog A Bone', or 'Knees Up Mother Brown'. It was an awful sound, but better than the beatings.

Crealy listened a while, to make sure that no one was coming who could take Garfield's part, then he pulled the near side of the mattress up and found a packet of figs. 'That's more like it,' he said. He sat on the bed as if he were a friend of Garfield. 'You selfish old bugger,' he said mildly. 'How many figs do you reckon there are here?'

Garfield didn't answer, and Crealy took hold of his near ear and shook his head by means of it until Garfield cried out. 'Don't you start calling out, or you'll get more,' said Crealy. He opened the packet and began to eat. 'For every one you're going to get a hurry up,' he said, and gave Garfield one right away.

So it began. Popanovich remained in hibernation beneath his blankets, Mortenson watched, but tried to keep the true side of his face as expressionless as the other, even though his good leg was rigid. Garfield covered his ears, and Crealy ate the figs, hitting Garfield's face with each new mouthful. 'Figs make you shit, Garfield old son,' he said, 'but I'll make you shit without them. That's rich isn't it. I said that's rich isn't it, Judge?'

'Exactly,' said Mortenson carefully. What time was it? He tried to remember some of the letters of Cicero he had been reading.

The one light from Garfield's locker cast a swooping shadow each time Crealy leant forward solicitously to hit Garfield, and when Crealy held Jenny Pen up in triumph she was manifest as a monstrous Viking prow upon the wall. Mortenson had to accept the realisation that there were underworlds which he had been able until recently to ignore; now he was part of one, suffering and observing, powerless through reduced capacity and fear.

When he saw a little, shining blood beneath Garfield's nose he could contain his opposition no longer. Yet stress undid his recent progress and Stefan Albee Mortenson, barrister, solicitor, notary public could produce before the court of Jenny Pen, only, 'Crealy youb narlous narl stapp awus nee.'

'Careful, Judge. I don't need your squark. I might come across and give you more than just this feathering Garfield's enjoying. I'll do the side of you not already dead, you pinstripe squirt.'

Mortenson had nothing more to say, and Garfield sat with his chin on his chest as if in a trance. 'Had enough?' Crealy asked him. 'You're gutless the lot of you.' Crealy was bored with his immediate subjects, and with Jenny Pen still on his hand as his familiar he went to wander the night corridors of the Home. No conversation began in the room he left. Popanovich feigned the sleep of death, Garfield remained slumped in his bed and Mortenson had no way of travelling the distance between them to offer comfort.

Mrs Munro knew nothing of Totara's netherworld. She had her own room in the separate block before the cottages, and the sun was laid on the polish of several pieces of her own furniture which had accompanied her. Mrs Munro could never understand those who complained of time dragging. She herself delighted in time to spare for all those indulgences a busy life had denied her; all those intellectual and emotional considerations that the slog of a seven-day dairy had prevented her from enjoying. She wore the track suit which she had insisted on for a Christmas present. She liked the comfort, the lack of constriction, the zippers at ankle and chest which made it easy to get off. She liked the two bright blue stripes and the motif of crossed racquets, even though she had never played sport.

Despite something of a problem with head nodding, and a hip operation on the way, Mrs Munro was quietly proud that although she was an old woman, she was not a fat, old woman. She didn't complain about the food, and she drew more large-print library books in a week than anyone else in the Home. She rejoiced in an hour to while away over a cup of tea, or in writing to Bessie Hambinder, or in putting drops in her ear, or measuring her room with the tape from the sewing basket. Miss Hails from the main block did visit too often it was true, and her repetitions tended to start Mrs Munro's head nodding, but there was always the bedding store-room as a sanctuary, and Mrs Munro had built a little dug-out in the blanket piles where she could rest in her track suit after lunch until Miss Hails had given up looking for her, and gone visiting elsewhere.

For the present though she counted the spots of a ladybird on her window sill, and watched sour, old Crealy smoking on a bench by the secure recreation area. Crealy was not compulsive viewing, and when Mrs Munro finished her computations concerning the ladybird she decided she would begin her next romance of the British Raj.

Crealy's cigarette was the last in the packet he had stolen from Popanovich, who was sleeping again. The days were not as enjoyable as the nights for Crealy, because he was too much under the eye of authority, and the spirit of his fellows was not as easily daunted when the sun shone. He wondered if Mrs Halliday was by the goldfish pond, but couldn't see her, and so he went back indoors to check Mortenson's locker before lunch. In the main corridor he came across Mrs Joyce, who had her blood changed quite regularly at the clinic. Her forearms and elbows seemed forever to have the yellows, purples and blues of ageing bruises. Mrs Joyce had made binoculars of her hands and stood with them pressed to the glass doors, staring out. 'What's out there?' she asked Crealy.

'Herbs and spices, sycamores and young people. And bloody work.'

'I can't see it,' said Mrs Joyce.

'You've gone daft in there.' Crealy rapped on her head with his knuckles, but she kept peering out into the sunshine through the tunnels of her fingers.

'Let me join Jesus,' she said. Crealy looked down at her pink scalp beneath the white hair. Because there was no resistance whatsoever that she could make, because she was not even aware of his malice, Crealy couldn't be bothered hurting her.

'Dozy old tart.'

'Let me come to thee sweet Jesus,' said Mrs Joyce. Crealy had a chuckle at that, and at how Mrs Joyce was peering through her hands and the glass, although everything outside was perfectly clear to him.

Matron Frew heard the chuckle from the office, and it reminded her that she wanted words with Crealy. She first of all took Mrs Joyce's arm in hers, and walked with her down to the dayroom. She was back before Crealy could quite disappear from sight down the corridor however, and she told him with some bluntness of the indirect complaints she'd been receiving, particularly from staff who had noticed Crealy pestering Mrs Halliday and Mr Garfield.

'Mark my words,' said Matron Frew. 'I will be watching, and also I'm making mention of things in my report to the board this month. You show an unwillingness at times to be a reasonable member of our community.'

As she spoke Crealy hung his head, but not from meekness or contrition. He was counting the number of useable butts in the sandbox by the office door, and when he had done that he imagined himself in the mild, summer night standing over Matron's herb garden, and pissing on the chives, parsley, mint, fennel and thyme. A lifetime in the indifferent, hostile or contemptuous regard of others had rendered Crealy immune to all three. He recognised no value or interest other than his own.

On Wednesday evenings Matron Frew turned off the television in the east wing lounge and organised communal singing. It was not compulsory as such, but absence meant no chocolate biscuits at the supper which followed. As a professionally trained person, Matron knew that a variety of stimulus for the elderly was important.

The committed, the egotistical and the hard of hearing stood close around the piano, the infirm or less enthusiastic were rims at a greater distance. Golden oldies they sang, to Matron's accompaniment. 'The Kerry

Pipers', 'Auld Lang Syne', 'The Biggest Aspidistra In The World', 'On Top Of Old Smokey'.

Matron had begun her career as a physiotherapist and it showed in her playing; the keys kneaded like a string of vertebrae; each tune well gone over and the kinks removed. 'Waltzing Matilda', 'Home On The Range,' 'The White Cliffs Of Dover', 'Some Enchanted Evening', 'Polly Wolly Doodle'. Matron Frew allowed her charges to respond in their own way and order, but she always had Nurse Glenn or Nurse McMillan guide Mr Oliphant to the uncarpeted area by the door because the pathos of any Irish tune made him incontinent.

A refrain, particularly with high notes, would sometimes trigger Miss Hails' weakness and she would begin the incessant repetition of a word. It happened sure enough during 'Riding Down From Bangor', and for several minutes Miss Hails sang only 'May'. Crealy was present not just for the chocolate biscuits, but because it gave him perverse satisfaction, after the Matron's rebuke, to exercise intimidation almost under her gaze.

He stood on Mrs Dellow's toe during 'Annie Laurie', and stared into her face, daring her to respond. Her thin voice assumed even greater vibrato and her eyes misted. Crealy then leant in comradeship over blind Mr Lewin and sprayed saliva into his face as 'Christopher Robin Went Down With Alice'.

When the chocolate biscuits came at last, Crealy kept himself between them and George Oliphant until they were all gone, then he said, 'Now isn't that a bugger, George, they seem all gone.'

'Silver Threads Among The Gold', they sang, and 'Swing Low Sweet Chariot'. 'Home, home, home, home, home, home,' Miss Hails continued, until Matron Frew told her to suck her thumb until the cycle was broken. 'Knees Up Mother Brown' Crealy liked, but because it was his favourite, the others found no pleasure in joining in.

Mortenson enjoyed the association the songs bore, even if not the singing itself. He preferred to be at some remove from the piano and his fellows, for then he could imagine other company and past days: his mouth would twitch and his good hand move to the melodies. 'Some Enchanted Evening' – he would sing it with Deborah as they drove back from ski-ing, ready for court work during the week. He hadn't realised then, that all roads led to this. 'Roo, roo, roo, roo, roo,' began Miss Hails.

Before midnight, aware of an odd, sighing wind around the Home, Crealy made a patrol of his domain; only his harsh breathing and shuffle gave him away. In his own room everything was as it should be – Garfield was weeping, Popanovich sleeping, and Mortenson in his snores fell every few minutes into a choking death rattle which woke him briefly, then he slept and it all began again.

Further down the corridor Mrs Doone was talking to herself as she strung up non-existent Christmas decorations. Every night was Christmas Eve for Mrs Doone, and the wonder and *frisson* of it were freshly felt night after night. 'Compliments of the season, Mr Ah – ah,' she said as Crealy slippered by. Around the corner, Crealy paused outside the room Mrs Oliffe and Miss Hails shared. Miss Hails was doing her thing of course; for almost an hour she had been repeating the sound tee, while Mrs Oliffe was trying to find nineteen across which was Breton Gaelic for divine harbinger.

'Oh, stop going tee, tee, tee, tee,' Mrs Oliffe said, but the simple satisfaction of it set her off also, and she joined in. Outside, Crealy could hear them in unison, tee, tee, tee. He found his own head nodding and his mouth formed the sound. One night it might spread through all of Totara, and capture them in a transport of repetitive senility.

Crealy put his hand to his face to stop himself. He looked carefully down the corridor. 'Mad old tarts,' he said. He considered opening their door and frightening them into silence, but the chance of being caught up in their chant and left nodding with them indefinitely was too great. He went on, still with one hand to his face. Tee, tee, tee, tee, faded behind him.

Outside the Matron's office were chairs for visitors, and a varnished box with a sand tray in it for smokers amongst the visitors. Crealy was able to find several butts worth using again, before he noticed Mrs Joyce standing by the main doors once more. 'Jesus loves me this I know,' she said. She had two overcoats on, and stood with her hand on the catch of the locked door. 'I'm going home,' she said. 'I've been here nearly a fortnight and they are expecting me back now.'

'You've been here for years,' said Crealy.

'Oh no, just a fortnight, and I need to be at home for every special occasion. We've always been a very close family you see.' Crealy went through her double set of pockets as she talked, but all he could find was a small book of stamps.

'They may well send a car for me,' she said. They both looked through the glass doors for a moment, but there was only empty wind and moonlight: no car was parked on the linen of the drive.

'You can go home this way,' said Crealy, taking Mrs Joyce by the lapel and leading her towards the kitchens.

'Has the car come then?' she said, and 'God will provide, you know. Even Solomon in all his glory.' Crealy led her through the dining room laid for breakfast, and the kitchens, where worn, steel surfaces glinted like new bone. He unbolted the service door and set Mrs Joyce in the gap. 'There you are then,' he said. 'The main drive's just around the corner.'

'It's a clear path to home, thank Jesus.' The blue second coat would barely fit over the first, and pulled her arms back like the flippers of a penguin. Rather like a penguin she began walking, struck her head on a pruned plum branch, and reeled past the herb garden.

'What's your name again?' said Crealy, but Mrs Joyce didn't answer, and still unsteady from the blow made the best pace she could around the side path. She had the scent of freedom; she had a promise of home.

Crealy waited until Mrs Joyce was well gone and there was no sound of pursuit or return, then he went out himself and stood in the summer night, sniffing the aromatic air of Matron Frew's herb garden. He hung out his cock, and waited patiently for his prostate to relax its grip so that he could enjoy the physical relief and pleasurable malice of watering the herbs. He had both in good time, then he stood under the sycamore by the old garages and had one of the visitor's cigarette ends, after nipping off the filter.

The sycamore creaked and murmured in the night breeze which blew out from the land to the sea. Despite the ache in his joints, Crealy enjoyed being by himself there beneath the branches, and higher the summer sky, for he knew that he had always been unloved. Even though old age at Totara had given him a mirror image power and significance while always before he had been subjugated, he liked still to be alone, to have no sources of action or response other than himself. So he stood beneath the sycamore, and enjoyed his cigarette ends guardedly, shading the glow with a palm, and looking out to the better lit parts of the grounds. 'No bastard can see me,' he said. 'No bastard knows I'm here.'

Even a summer's night grows cold for old bones, and Crealy came in and bolted the door behind him. 'Had enough?' he had asked the mint and parsley as he went by them. He inspected Mrs Joyce's stamps in the dim light. He wanted to search her room but had forgotten her name. Crealy had never been an intellectual, and at eighty-one he found it difficult to move and think at the same time. So he remained stooped in the semi-light between kitchen and dining room, and he tried to remember what he had been going to do before he met Mrs Joyce.

He went into the pantry beyond the stainless steel moonlight of the kitchen, and lifted out a large tin of golden syrup. He took a thick crust from the toast drawer and with his fingers as a ladle spread golden syrup on it. The syrup lay dark in the tin, but silver in glints as it twined from his fingers.

Crealy replaced the tin, and stood with the bread and syrup in his clean hand, sucking his other fingers. He looked into the shadowed dining room: the identical tables, evenly spaced, and an oblong of light across them from the corridor. The golden syrup was rich and energy giving. Crealy began to wonder if Mrs Halliday was having one of her spells in the Home. He made such demands on his old mind that his chewing slowly stopped, and his hand no longer held the bread level. He stood in the kitchen doorway as a Neanderthal at the entrance to his cave. The syrup made a silver necklace to the floor. Crealy couldn't remember: couldn't remember at all.

'Bugger me,' he said at last. He was unable to come up with anything, so he stopped thinking, allowed the motor-sensory centres priority again, and moved into the lino tubes which were the Totara corridors.

At the duty room, Crealy decided to check on Brisson in case he was doing the unexpected thing and actually making a round. There was no key for the duty room door, but when Crealy pushed lightly against it, he found that Brisson had set the end of the sofa hard to it. Then he heard voices. Nurse McMillan talked as she and Brisson made love, but her topic was dissatisfaction with conditions of service, not romance. Lovemaking altered the normal rhythm of her words so that odd, accentuated syllables were driven out of her. 'GOD we've all thought OF handing in our resigNATIONS,' she said.

'There's nothing in all the world to match it,' Brisson said.

The palm of one of Crealy's large hands still rested on the door, though he pressed no more. He listened to a tune which mocked him, and his arthritis drove him on, shuffling and disgruntled; missing out as usual. Mrs Doone had finished putting up her Christmas decorations for the night, and the corridor was as bare as when she first began. Even Miss Hails was silent, but as Crealy passed Mr Lewin's room he heard a talking clock. 'It is twelve o'clock, midnight,' said the talking clock. Like a fox at a burrow entrance, Crealy stood before the door, but the clock didn't speak again, and blind Mr Lewin who must have activated it made no sound either.

As he neared his own room, Crealy could near Mortenson's stricken breathing, and remembered with sudden vividness a time more than thirty years before when he had been a cleaner at the Nazareth Hall and Mortenson had been president of a group that banqueted there. Crealy had looked out from the serving hatch, waiting to begin clearing up, and S.A. Mortenson CBE, barrister, solicitor, notary public, city councillor and party chairman, had been standing at the top table; standing in his dinner jacket to give an erudite speech which was buoyed up constantly by delighted applause and laughter from the other tables. The recollection had such strength that Crealy felt again the flat ache of his own incon- sequence, but it passed and he was aware of the cream Totara walls again, and the struggle Mortenson had to breathe.

Crealy laid Popanovich's open bottle of lemonade on the bed so that it would wet the sleeping man's feet, and plucked Jenny Pen from Garfield's bed end and held her briefly aloft. 'Wake up, Judge,' he said, and took Mortenson's nose between Jenny Pen's hands.

Mortenson's good side woke with horror. What time was it? 'Let's have poetry tonight,' said Crealy. He made himself comfortable on the bed with his room-mate. 'And I want to see you enjoying it, Judge; getting into the swing of it,' he said.

> And where the silk-shoed lovers ran
> with dust of diamonds in their hair,
> he opens now his silent wing

began Mortenson indistinctly.

Crealy put one of Jenny Pen's fingers into the slack side of Mortenson's mouth and pulled it into the image of a smile. 'Let's not be half-hearted about this. Try something else,' said Crealy. Mortenson wished to disregard the setting his senses made for him, and the only escape was through the words. He did his best with a bit of 'The Herne's Egg'.

> Strong sinew and soft flesh
> Are foliage round the shaft
> Before the arrowsmith
> Has stripped it, and I pray
> That I, all foliage gone,
> May shoot into my joy.

'Eh?' said Crealy. He tired quickly of poetry, even when seasoned with humiliation. 'Had enough,' he said. His thoughts turned to Garfield. There were hours to go, years maybe, before it would be day again.

Blind Mr Lewin was guided by Mrs Munro to the sunroom in the east wing the next afternoon. Mr Lewin loved the warmth, and found that he could sleep easily during the day in full sunlight. Mrs Munro kindly led him down, and Lewin could feel the warmth even as they approached the end of the corridor. Mrs Munro's head nodded companionably as she pulled a cane chair close to the large window; so close that Lewin was able to put out his hands and feel the glass while sitting comfortably, and she gave him his talking clock to cradle so that he would not be anxious about his meals.

Mr Lewin thanked her, and listened to the departing footsteps.

He had never seen the sunroom, and instead of the meek, faded place that it was, looking out over the crocodile paving and lawns in front of the cottages, he imagined it cantilevered high into the sun's eye and with only the yellow, benevolent furnace of the sun to be seen from the window. Lewin had known far worse times.

While Mr Lewin slept, Crealy elsewhere watched Mrs Halliday. Mrs Halliday was only in her sixties, but subject to Huntington's chorea in recurring spells during which she often came into the Totara Home to relieve her family. Crealy always took a considerable interest in her visits, for her breasts were large, she still had firm flesh, and caught at the right moment she could be used without much recollection of it.

Towards the end of the long afternoon she was at her most confused, and Crealy watched from outside the television lounge until he saw her talking to herself and constantly folding and unfolding her cardigan. He went in and firmly led her along the trail of mottled lino to the sunroom, which visitors or clergymen sometimes used to have their talks. 'Has the family come? Has Elaine?' said Mrs Halliday. Crealy was quite pleased to see blind Lewin there, close to the window, for he could pass as a chaperone at a distance, but not act as one on the spot. Crealy sat Mrs Halliday with her back to the window.

'Your family are coming soon,' he said, and opened the front of her dress.

'Is that you, Mrs Munro?' asked Lewin.

'Shut up,' said Crealy.

'The family you say,' said Mrs Halliday. She allowed Crealy to unclip her bra at the back, and he scooped out her breasts so they made two full fish heads in the flounce of her dress.

Lewin was still groggy from his sleep, but he didn't wish to seem discourteous. 'Where would we be without families,' he said gallantly, and fingered his talking clock for reassurance. Crealy stroked Mrs Halliday's breasts, and clumsily rolled the nipples between thumb and forefinger so that she pursed her lips and put her hands on his wrists.

'You need to get changed for your family,' said Crealy absently.

'What time is it then?' asked Mrs Halliday. Lewin pressed his clock.

'The time is 4.42 pm,' it said.

Crealy took another minute of satisfaction in the sun, then refilled Mrs Halliday's bra, and with some difficulty fastened it across her back. Matron Frew might come looking for her soon. 'Stay here and talk to Lewin,' he said.

'Am I changed for my family?'

'Good enough,' said Crealy.

'Who is that?' said Lewin, turning an ear rather than an eye for better comprehension.

'Jenny Pen rules,' said Crealy as he left.

The impartial sun which Mr Lewin blindly enjoyed, shone on Mortenson who sat in his wheel chair on a landscaped hillock which looked over the SRA – the safe recreation area. Within it the bewildered or fretful, the complacent and serene could be left in security. Only the staff could manage the latch. Crealy called it the zoo, but it was pleasant enough, more like a kindergarten. There were seats with foam cushions for thin flesh, and raised garden plots which keen Totarans could work on without stooping or kneeling.

The SRA was overlooked by the wide windows of the dining room on one side, but to the warm north side there was a view across the grass and gardens towards the cottages and the spires of the great world. Mortenson could see the goldfish pond in the zoo, and George Oliphant dolefully shaking the back of his trousers because he was in trouble again.

The Matron and Dr Sullivan stopped beside Mortenson on their round, but finished their conversation before greeting him. 'I've no idea how Mrs Joyce managed to leave the block in the first place,' said Matron.

'It can't be helped.'

'It's a puzzle though.'

'I haven't told her family the actual circumstances of the death: to minimise the trauma you see. And how are you, Mr Mortenson?'

'Mr Mortenson is brighter every day,' replied Matron. Mortenson gave his half smile. He could see the exquisite glow on the sunlit tulips, feel their sun's good will on his faithful side, and hear Miss Hails practising her word for the day. The word was Nell, or perhaps Knell; how was anyone to know but her.

'Nell, nell, nell, nell,' said Miss Hails. Like a prayer wheel she gave a benediction over all the zoo, the lawn, the cottages, the totality of Totara and beyond. 'Nell, nell, nell, nell, knell.'

'Well, nice talking to you,' said Dr Sullivan, and they went on their way. Mortenson felt an itching tic begin at the corner of his eye. In all that ground of apparent pleasure he wondered what Crealy was up to. What time was it? It came to Mortenson that his karma had been assessed; that from the best of lives he was in a spiral descent of reincarnation from which he would emerge perhaps a six-spot ladybird, as counted by Mrs Munro, and would clamp the stem beneath the wine glow of the sunlit tulip blooms.

What time was it? Dr Sullivan and Matron were trying to wake Popanovich. 'It's always the same. Ah, well, he seems healthy enough and sleep can't hurt him.' Dr Sullivan smiled at the other three in the end room, while Matron moved Popanovich in the bed. The doctor was not a dour person; he believed in good spirits and optimism. He looked about for something that would provide an occasion for light-heartedness and rapport.

Matron sensed that the mood had abruptly changed, though at first she didn't see that behind her Dr Sullivan had taken Jenny Pen from Garfield's bed and mounted her on his hand. Garfield began to shiver, and put his hands out, palms uppermost, as if to play patter-cake. Crealy hung his head to one side like an old dog, while the whites of his eyes showed as he kept things in his view. Mortenson felt a sweat break out on his good thigh beneath the rug, and his smile was slow to form and slow to fade. He smiled as a Christian might smile who catches the Devil out walking in the daytime.

'What a good life we lead at Totara,' said Dr Sullivan in falsetto for Jenny Pen, and he jiggled her to emphasise his humour. The only responses were those of Matron Frew's crepe soles on the lino, and at a distance Miss Hails saying her catechism for the day. It drifted to them down the corridor.

'Mi, mi, mi, mi, mi, mi.'

'Perhaps puppeteer isn't my calling,' said Dr Sullivan. He was disappointed by his reception and withdrew into professionalism. Matron knew how to keep that patter going.

Crealy's arthritis was giving him gyppo again. To appease it he walked the maze of corridors, and watched from window after window the sunshowers above the grounds. Dramatic clouds were towed across the sky, and when they met the sun they were lit with red and orange embers which glowed and shifted in the deep perspectives. From the dining room Crealy saw a travelling shower fracture the surface of the zoo pond, so that the goldfish lost their shape, and became just carrots in the shallow weeds.

On his second circuit Crealy noticed that Nurse McMillan had left the office, and that the morning's mail lay partly sorted on the counter. He eased in, and his stiff hands found envelopes addressed to Mortenson, to Oliphant and Garfield. He pocketed them, and was cheered by the petty malice even though he couldn't see Mrs Halliday in the TV room as he went past. For the life of him he could not remember when he last had a personal letter. Garfield on the other hand received far too much kind attention from outside, and Crealy decided to give him a hard time until the weather improved. He began a search for Garfield, but George Oliphant saw him checking the TV room, and afterwards went to the window which could be seen by Mortenson and gave a warning by semaphore, which Mortenson passed on to Garfield.

Garfield began his slow but urgent escape down the corridors of hours towards the bedding store-room. The door there had a plunger and cylinder to draw it closed without slamming. To Garfield the mechanism seemed to take an eternity to work, and the cylinder hissed as his view of the corridor and bathrooms narrowed. Garfield sat in semi-darkness, content with the little light entering from a glass strip above the door.

The broad shelves had stacks of sheets and pillowcases, and on the floor were piled blankets which rose like wool bales. Garfield sat on a half-bale to wait it out. He didn't trouble himself with the metaphysics of his situation: what he had come to. The former Wellington fullback and general manager for Hentlings sat grinding his teeth in the bedding store-room of Totara Eventide Home, and listening to the perpetual echoing orchestration which his tinnitus inflicted on him.

Crealy found him there.

It was nearly four. The showers had become less frequent, and a rainbow stood clearly behind the cottages, fading up towards the sun. Yet Mortenson couldn't concentrate on his history of Rome; he felt a helpless consideration for Garfield, and a fear of Crealy. He knew that where there are no lions then hyenas rule.

His chair was very low-geared, and despite the busy noise of its motor, Mortenson moved only slowly along the corridors towards the bedding room. At alternate windows the day's strange weather was displayed as sunlit promise, then skirts of rain from fiery clouds, then blue sky once again. The door took all the thrust his chair could manage, and sank closed behind him so that the failing light and hiss half hid Crealy's torture of his friend.

'Hello, Judge,' said Crealy. Once he found that Mortenson had come alone, he was pleased. He had become almost bored with Garfield. Yet an advantage can be gained or lost quite unexpectedly and with such an absence of drama that it is easy to miss the significance. Crealy moved to get a better leverage, overbalanced on the soft surface and fell backwards just a couple of feet into the comfortable crevasse fashioned by Mrs Munro between the banded blankets. His old arms and legs moved silently in the shadows, as if he were a beetle on his back there. He was too stiff to turn easily.

Mortenson took a pillow with his better arm and pushed it across Crealy's face.

'Come on,' he said to Garfield. It was more a delaying tactic at first, with neither of them having much hope of success; even Crealy gave a sort of grin whenever he managed to free his face, as if he recognised his temporary difficulty, but would soon pay them back all right.

But the more Garfield and Mortenson pushed, and the more Crealy twisted, the deeper his shoulders sank between the blankets. He began to pant and jerk; the others saw a chance indeed and their lips drew back in the dark and they pressed for all their lives. Crealy's big arms and legs fell in harmless thuds against the embracing blankets. Mortenson felt strength and justice in his good arm even though it trembled with exertion, and Garfield was on his knees to use his body weight upon the pillow.

'Had enough. Had enough, Crealy old son,' he kept whispering. The competitive urge in Garfield revived one last time. Crealy's arms and legs moved less, but his body bucked.

'Now let us play Othello,' slurred Mortenson.

'Had enough,' sobbed Garfield.

For a good time after Crealy was still, they continued to hold the pillow over his face. Accustomed to such full tyranny as his, they could hardly believe that they had beaten him so completely. Even when they heard his sphincter muscles relax, and had the smell of him, they held the pillow down. 'Had enough?' said Garfield tenderly.

'Put the pillow back,' said Mortenson finally, and he wiped the tears from Garfield's face. They didn't look again at Dave Crealy, who was a big, stupid man lying well down amongst piles of blankets. Garfield opened the door a little, and when he saw that there was no one outside he held it back for Mortenson's chair, and the snake hissed behind them in the dark.

As they went home they met Mrs Munro guiding Mr Lewin to the sunroom. Mrs Munro delighted in being useful, and was thinking also of a nice cup of tea. 'There's a rainbow,' she said, nodding. Mortenson and Garfield could see its thick, childish bands behind the cottages; at the same time the sun was strong enough to cast shadows from the benches in the grounds. Who knows what Lewin saw, but he could hear with them the piping of Miss Hails at a distance.

'Na, na, na, na, na, na, na, na.'

Mr Lewin pushed the button on his clock.

'The time is 4.19 pm,' the clock said.

VIVIENNE PLUMB

In the winter the nights become long and cold. In Honey Tarbox's house all is hushed on a frosty midwinter night.

Then slowly, slowly, Honey rolls over in her bed and starts to wake. She is speaking Japanese.

'Kyoo wa samui desu ne.'

'What . . .?' she thinks.

'Ohayo gozaimasu,' she says out loud. The words echo around the cold, still bedroom.

Her husband groans, 'Huh, wozzat?'

She stops speaking but her mind keeps turning, rolling around. 'What did I say,' she thinks. She doesn't know it was Japanese. She's the wife who spoke Japanese in her sleep.

At first she didn't speak much Japanese.

Her husband, Howard, stayed awake one night and described what he saw happen. He watched her go to bed. Gradually she fell asleep, then after an hour she started speaking in another language. She spoke for a little time.

When she woke in the morning, Honey was amazed to hear Howard's description.

She never felt tired. She was always rested, relaxed. But Howard often looked exhausted.

'The talking keeps me awake,' he said.

At first they couldn't understand which language it was. Neither of them had ever spoken any language themselves other than English. Honey had once gone on a holiday to Fiji but Howard had never travelled.

So one night Howard said he would tape Honey talking in her

sleep. The next day they took the tape to the School of Languages which was very close by. They asked to see a teacher. While they sat waiting, they watched six goldfish swimming in a large tank.

'Mr and Mrs Tarbox?' said the teacher. She wore spectacles and a maroon cardigan. Her hair was pulled back into a bun. To Honey and Howard she looked very educated.

'How can I help? What would you like to learn? Arabic? Spanish? Lithuanian? Mandarin? We offer them all.'

'Please listen to our tape,' said Howard, his face slightly flushed. He switched on his pocked machine.

'Nan desu ka,' said the voice on the tape. It didn't sound like Honey at all.

'What language is that?' asked Howard. The teacher listened.

'Why it's Japanese,' she said. She listened some more, then laughed. 'Good grief,' she said.

'What is it?' asked Honey.

'Well it's rather rude,' said the teacher. 'I don't think I could give you a direct translation. Where did you get this from?' Howard and Honey looked at each other.

'Umm . . .' they both said. Honey looked at her shoes, and Howard looked at the ceiling.

'Wait a minute,' said the teacher. 'Now what's she saying?' She leaned forward, concentrating on the tape recording.

'Wow, incredible. Who is this woman? I'd love to meet her. What a wonderful woman she is, she seems to know so much.'

'Why, what did she say?' said Howard. He wriggled on his chair. Honey watched the fish flipping around the tank and waited to hear what the teacher would say next.

'Well, it's a kind of speech, about mankind,' said the teacher. 'Sort of prophecies . . . it's hard to describe.'

They all stood staring at each other. The voice on the tape had stopped.

'She says things. She's like a kind of . . . oracle,' said the teacher. 'I'd really like to meet her. Is she a friend of yours?'

Howard giggled. Honey looked at the fish. One really big goldfish swam right up to the glass, its mouth opening and shutting at Honey. 'Oh! Oh! Oh!' it looked like it was saying.

'It's me,' said Honey in a flat voice. 'That tape recording is me.'

'You?' said the teacher. She was obviously surprised. She took her spectacles off and polished them and put them back on again.

'I don't understand,' said the teacher. 'If you speak Japanese, why don't you know what you're saying? Also, excuse me if I appear rude, but that voice doesn't sound like you at all. Hajimemashite. Watashi wa Florica desu. Doozo yoroshiku.' She bowed low towards Honey.

'No, no!' whispered Honey. She backed away. 'I don't understand you! . . . Tell her, Howard. Tell her what happens.'

Howard moved closer to Miss Florica and lowered his voice.

'When Honey goes to sleep at night, she speaks like that.' He nodded his head towards the tape recorder. Miss Florica gasped.

'She speaks in her sleep?' Howard nodded.

'And in a language she doesn't understand?'

'Yes,' said Howard. 'We don't know what to do.'

'But do you realise what she's saying?' asked Miss Florica.

'This voice on the tape is making prophecies. On the tape she made some predictions about the government of our country.'

'No!' said Howard. Honey looked away. She was feeling so embarrassed. She wished they'd never come.

'You must have a very special power,' said Miss Florica, 'to be able to perceive things that we cannot. A clairvoyant power.' She smiled at Honey.

But Honey said to Howard, 'Howard, let's leave, I just remembered I left the heater on at home.'

Howard came straight away. He'd never encouraged large electricity bills. Was in fact quite a penny pincher when it came down to it.

'Which heater?' he kept asking all the way back. 'The big one or the little one?'

'Oh, Howard, shut up,' said Honey. She withdrew to the bathroom where she ran a long hot bath. She didn't come out until she heard Howard leave for his afternoon class at the Community Institute. (He was learning how to make patchwork.) Now he was retired he had nothing else to do with his time. As for herself, the children had all grown up long ago. She had no hobbies, no pastimes, no job, but now she had this.

She looked at herself in the bedroom mirror. She saw a short, stocky woman, with blonde hair. A fleshy, plump body. She pinched the flesh on her face. When she pulled her fingers away, a white mark was left on the sagging pink skin.

She thought she knew what a clairvoyant was.

It was a woman, dressed with a scarf on her head, and wearing rings and jewellery. She had a rich plummy voice, and she waved her hands around in an artistic manner. She'd seen them in old Sherlock Holmes movies. The lights would be dimmed and then, the spirits would come. They would fill the room, knocking over lamps and tables in an effort to make their presence known.

Was she a clairvoyant?

She laughed. She shook her head and her blonde hair fluffed around her head like a halo. What a preposterous idea!

Or in the newspaper. Sometimes she'd seen them in the newspaper. A woman would be called in to assist the police in finding a dead body. CLAIRVOYANT HELPS POLICE it would shout across the front page. And there'd be a photo of her, hand outstretched, eyes shut. Could that be Honey?

Or at school, many years ago. She remembered they had learnt about the Oracle at Delphi. A woman had sat on a sacred tripod over a deep fissure in the earth. The mists of the inner earth would rise and send her into a trance. Then she'd speak, tell everyone all manner of things. She might talk for hours, then collapse exhausted. A priest interpreted her messages. People would come from everywhere to ask her questions. And often her answers were correct.

Honey considers herself. Looks at her hands, not artistic, but capable. She glances at her bed, smoothly made, her fuchsia pink nightdress rolled up and slipped under the pillow. And she wonders what the night will bring.

At nine o'clock that night there is a knock at the door. Howard answers it.

Miss Florica is standing on the step, her eyes shining.

'Good evening, Mr Tarbox,' she says. She has someone else with her, a friend, another woman. She introduces her as Mrs Brunt.

'Mrs Brunt knows a little of these matters,' says Miss Florica. 'She once had a psychic experience herself.'

Mrs Brunt wears short, black rubber boots, and a thick woollen coat. A black beret is balanced on her large square head.

Honey enters the lighted hall. Howard is excited. He is gabbling to the two ladies. It is apparent to Honey that Howard skipped his patchwork class and went instead to ask Miss Florica here tonight. Honey's shadow falls across the rose patterned carpet. All three stop talking and turn quietly towards her. Howard clears his throat.

'Honey, I know you won't mind if Miss Florica and Mrs Brunt stay and listen to you. It's in the interest of Science, I'm sure you'd agree.'

The two woman smile and nod their heads. Their heads look strangely loose on top of their wooden necks. Honey stays quiet, she doesn't smile back.

Please themselves, she thinks. She feels in control. All her life she's had nothing. But now, she has this. And this is becoming important, making her important.

'Have they brought me anything?' asks Honey.

'Brought you anything?' says Howard.

'Yes, a gift, a present. They must have something.'

The hall light hangs behind her, lighting up her body in silhouette, but they cannot see her face.

'I did bring something,' says Mrs Brunt. She pulls a rectangular object out of her crocheted shopping bag.

'A box of chocs.' She beams.

'That's good,' says Honey. 'If any more people come, Howard, you must ask them for their gift.' She turns away. 'I'll go and make a pot of tea.'

Howard is embarrassed.

'Really, she's never acted like this before . . . Come in. Come in.' He leads the two visitors into the lounge.

The fringed lamp shines a soft glow over the room. The television is on with the sound turned down and Honey's knitting lies on the sofa. It isn't long before Honey brings the tea.

'I'll get ready while you all have a drink,' she says. She goes into the bedroom and changes into her nightdress. She sits waiting on the edge of the bed. Howard comes in. He says,

'You go to bed, Honey. I won't ask anyone in until you're asleep.'

'Howard,' says Honey, 'what do they want?'

'I think they want to ask you some questions,' he says.

Howard, Miss Florica, and Mrs Brunt, stay waiting in the lounge. The clock ticks on. They make small talk. Mrs Brunt examines Honey's knitting.

'She's dropped a stitch ten rows back,' she says.

Suddenly they hear a voice talking in the bedroom. Miss Florica is on her feet straight away.

'That's Japanese!' she says. Howard leads them at a trot down to the back bedroom. He turns on a bedside lamp.

Honey is lying on her back in the bed. Her arms are folded across her chest. Her face is smooth, wiped of all expression. She is apparently fast asleep.

'Komban wa,' says Miss Florica. She bows towards the bed.

'Komban wa,' replies Honey. And a torrent of Japanese follows. She still looks like Honey but she doesn't sound like Honey. The voice is higher, more penetrating.

Miss Florica introduces Mrs Brunt. She presents the box of chocolates and says,

'Tsumaranai mono desu ga, doozo.'

Mrs Brunt smiles.

'Now she'll explain my problem,' she whispers to Howard. Howard pulls over another chair and they both sit down. There is a pause, then Honey says,

'Doomo arigatoo gozaimasu. Watashi wa ureshu desu.' Miss Florica smiles. She talks to Honey for about five minutes explaining Mrs Brunt's problem.

Honey replies, she talks on and on, hardly stopping for breath. The Japanese syllables sound strange to Howard. He crosses and recrosses his legs.

Finally Miss Florica turns back to them both.

'It's wonderful,' she says. 'It's all so clear. Her answer is simple.'

'What did you ask?' says Howard. Miss Florica and Mrs Brunt exchange looks.

'I don't mind if you tell,' says Mrs Brunt. 'I think we can trust Mr Tarbox.' Miss Florica explains:

'Mrs Brunt has a lovely miniature poodle, only three years old. His name is Schnookie. Schnookie is suffering terribly from arthritis and he may have to have plastic ligaments inserted in his front legs. Mrs Brunt was worried about the pain this operation may cause Schnookie, but now I have the answer.'

'And what is that?' asks Howard.

'It has been suggested Mrs Brunt finds a hypnotherapist.'

Mrs Brunt grins. 'What a terrific idea!'

'I'm so glad Honey helped you find the answer to your problem,' Howard says. Miss Florica and Mrs Brunt prepare to leave.

'Do you think Honey could help other people this way?' asks Howard. Miss Florica's face shines. She comes forward and places her hand on Howard's arm in a warm, caring way.

'Without doubt,' she says. 'Without doubt, I think I could say that Honey's advice and predictions could be the light at the end of the tunnel for many people. And I would make myself available any night to trans-late . . . for a small donation. Think about it, Mr Tarbox, and let us keep in touch.' She squeezes his arm. He opens the front door for them and says goodbye.

The sound of their footsteps fades away into the still, deep night.

The stars hang, glittering fiercely in the cold midnight sky. Howard hears a noise and swings around. It's Honey. She's wearing her fluffy lilac dressing gown.

'Did I do it?' she asks.

'Yes,' says Howard. His voice is low. 'They were very pleased. You were very successful. Miss Florica thinks you could help even more people.'

'I see,' says Honey. 'Tell her she can have thirty percent.' She turns and goes back to the bedroom. Howard comes inside. He's surprised. Honey seems so different, so business-minded, it's not like her. He frowns at the lock, pulls the chain across and slips it into its tiny slot. Tomorrow he'll ring Miss Florica and make her an offer.

During the next few months the Tarbox home becomes famous. Word gets around, and every night many people arrive at Honey's with a little hope in their hearts. Some have simple questions written on a tiny scrap of paper. Others come escorted by note-taking secretaries who read their questions out for them.

They ask so many things. How to become rich, how to look more beautiful, how to become loved, and how to love. How to be good, to be received into heaven, to die happy. Honey answers them all.

Now Honey wears a beautiful peach pink nightie. She has her hair styled during the day so she will look her best every night. Reporters come and go. Honey is a popular personality to interview. They adore her combination of mystery and modesty. They ask her opinion on everything, her favourite colour (peach), and her favourite food (watermelon). She's even been on daytime chat shows, and has been photographed with many of the famous and well known people who now pass through the portals of her house in search of advice and predictions.

Her predictions are often correct. Her advice, politely and kindly offered, is always well accepted.

The Japanese ambassador has visited several times. The last time he came they talked at length about the future of Japan.

'Are wa sakura desu ka,' he'd said, peering out of Honey's windows into the dark night.

'Hai,' Honey had answered. 'Haru desu.'

Waiting outside the door in the shadows, Howard had thought to himself how much Honey had changed.

To Howard, she now appears controlled, never flustered. She's always well dressed, her make-up well applied. She offers her opinions even when they've not been asked for. And she expects Howard to keep accounts that add up.

Howard thinks he liked the old Honey better. She pottered around the house in her fluffy dressing gown. She always looked to Howard for advice about the way to dress, besides everything else. She was warm, caring, and she looked after me, thinks Howard. Now he thinks she's a Dragon Woman.

The business of the accounts upsets him the most. Maths was never his forte and he often makes mistakes. Sometimes, when it all gets too much for him, he seeks Miss Florica's help. In her old cardie and smudgy pink lipstick and her dishevelled bun and glasses, she reminds Howard of the old Honey.

She is pleased to help Howard. She pats his hand and sometimes makes him a pot of tea. She calls him Howard now, not Mr Tarbox.

During the day Honey often likes to sit in the garden. Howard used to look after it. He would mow a flat square in the middle and clip back the rest.

But it's all different now. A young Japanese man, Kenta Yamashita, has offered to build a real Japanese garden for Honey. Honey's advice to Kenta about his problems with his mother has so touched him that he comes back all the time just to visit. Now he has offered to build the Japanese garden.

He has planted a cherry tree and wants to pull up all the grass and replace it with raked gravel.

He is setting three large stones in their geomantic positions. The large stones are covered with lichen. They are the mountains, says Kenta. The gravel will be the water. All the elements of life. Honey loves watching the transformation of the garden. She sees it somewhat representative of what has happened to herself. She's looking forward to the complete removal of Howard's dusty geraniums and proteas and the installation of the raked sand. Smooth, flowing, meditative.

One Monday morning Honey wakes earlier than usual. She walks up the hall and into the kitchen.

Howard and Miss Florica are pushed against the sink bench grappling with each other's bodies. Howard's hands are up Miss Florica's blouse. Miss Florica's hands are down Howard's trousers. Their mouths are squashed against each other's. It makes Honey remember the goldfish.

She coughs gently and they both spring apart. Miss Florica blushes.

'I don't know what came over me,' she says.

Howard looks smug. He says nothing. Instead, he leans across Miss Florica and takes two pieces of toast out of the toaster. He butters them evenly and eats them straight away. Miss Florica excuses herself and hurries out of the kitchen.

'Would you like some toast?' asks Howard.

'No,' says Honey. She prefers to eat fish for breakfast these days.

'You're so different now,' says Howard. It's the first time he's ever talked to Honey about the changes in their lives.

'You're not the same Honey I married.'

'We all change,' says Honey. 'From decay grows new life. From the old is born the new.'

'How poetic,' says Howard. Honey pauses, she then replies.

'I must now take this opportunity to thank you for starting me on this path.'

'No worries,' mutters Howard.

That night Honey dons a white sateen nightie. She pins her hair up, adding a flower or two to the arrangement. She applies a little lipstick to her mouth and climbs into bed. She lies still, waiting for Miss Florica to arrive. This is the way they always do it. When Miss Florica comes, she sits over near the window and Honey slowly falls asleep.

Tonight Honey is more voluble than ever. She is funny and witty, and very likeable in this mood. Her *joie de vivre* breaks the language barrier. When her visitors leave they are smiling and laughing. Miss Florica is kept busy. Honey talks at such a rate, she can hardly keep up.

Then suddenly Honey sits up in her sleep. She has never done this before. Everyone stops what they're doing.

'Howardsan wa doko desu ka,' she says.

'Quick! Call Howard!' shouts Miss Florica. 'This is for him!'

'Watashi wa megami desu. Me ga mienai. Kiri ga mieru. Howardsan ga kiete iku!'

'I can't see. I see a mist,' translates Miss Florica quickly. Her face flushes. 'A disappearance!'

Honey falls exhausted onto her pillows and goes into a deep sleep. Howard cannot be found until the next morning. (He was down at the all-night service station talking to his friend.)

The next week Howard disappears.

No one sees him leave, nor can anyone remember for sure what happened. One day he was there, the next day – zilch! No one had ever taken much notice of him anyway (except Miss Florica).

She is allowed to move into his old room. She touches the razor on his dresser and carefully runs her finger along the blade. The terylene curtains wave in the breeze coming through the open window. Miss Florica opens the drawers and wonders why Howard never took any spare underwear with him when he left.

Kenta Yamashita has finished Honey's Japanese garden. Ten tons of white gravel and sand were delivered and raked into uniform patterns. Only Miss Florica can remember the particular day that the gravel arrived.

Yes, she can remember the day, the month, and the year (in case she's ever asked). It was the day before Howard disappeared.

'Why is fate always so fucking inscrutable?' queried Perrin McDougal as Eric knelt at his feet, guiding his dead toes into his shoes.

'I suspect,' said Eric rather too tartly, because he hadn't actually thought he'd be acting as nursemaid, 'it means, that way, the old fraud is never quite caught out.'

They were in Perrin's exquisitely muted bedroom, with its frosty Viennese chandelier reflected in perpetuity in the floor-to-ceiling mirror. This now returned an image of themselves, ironically, in poses of almost biblical simplicity. Though Eric thought he caught a faint ammoniacal pong from Perrin's socks.

'Isn't it time, darling, these putrescent articles were, well,' Eric tried to sound noncommittal, '*substituted* for something more savoury?'

They used the telegraphese of old friends, accentuated by the frequently sharp, sometimes hilarious, even acid appendage of '*dear*'. Though in the present situation, with Perrin so ill, the *dears* had taken on a warmer, more amber hue.

'Can you find me my walking-stick?'

Perrin had phoned up that afternoon and commanded Eric – the tone was properly regal and brooked no contradiction – to take him off to the Remuera Garden Centre. Eric thought ironically – though fondly too, because in the contradiction lay the quintessence of his character – that here was Eric almost certainly going to be absent in the flooding spring yet he, Perrin, was planning a lavish bouquet for his 'spring' garden.

'What I see,' Perrin had announced over the phone in that way that had the faint edge of the visionary to it, 'is a mixture of marigolds, blue violas and delphiniums. Don't you remember . . . ?'

Eric didn't, but it didn't matter.

'Don't you remember how Aunt Priscilla down in Te Awamutu always had a daphne bush by her front steps and the way it always used to *invite* you – yes, *invite* is the right word – '

Perrin kept his legal precision intact, a careful weapon against the unknown, 'so that as you ascended the stairs into her hall, the scent was *incroyable*!'

Perrin now rose to his feet unsteadily. His once fleshy form had been stripped by the disease to a frightening gauntness. His stylish garments – once bought in Melbourne or 'inexpensively' run up in distant Bangkok – clothed his skeleton in a simulacrum of 'health'. To the outside world – that crowd of on-lookers who instantly became extras in the cinema reel of Perrin's declining life – he probably looked only frail, possibly suffering from cancer.

Eric clung to these illusions as he handed Perrin his elegant malacca cane. He was still getting used to the shock of being seen with Perrin in public.

He had told himself as he drove over to Perrin's Epsom bungalow (a clever pastiche of Frank Lloyd Wright, via his Napier disciple, Louis Hay) that the public gaze simply didn't matter, that it was more important to simply help Perrin, that this accompanying him a little along the road was the very least he could do. But the truth was he had gone into a state of near shock when he thought he'd left his sunglasses behind.

He realised when his fingers touched bakelite – they connected with the impact of a lodestone – that he was sweating uncomfortably, not even watching the road. His heart was banging away, in a mocking Judas dance.

'Give us your arm, dear.' Perrin now stood at the brow of his front steps whose very sweep and height had once signalled power. Now they simply spoke danger: Perrin's grasp of Eric's arm was surprisingly tight. Eric registered Perrin's frailty as he leant into him.

He watched the almost random – yet hesitant, hesitant – fall of Perrin's numbed feet.

Suddenly Perrin lurched to a halt. 'This!' he cried in a voice full of emotion.

Shit, thought Eric, stopping back his alarm, *the bugger's going to cry*.

'This is where I want to have a whole *flowery mecca*,' Perrin waved his wand towards a dug circle of dirt. Even though he was facing financial ruin he'd hired a student to create a new flowerbed. 'When people come to see me, I want them – to – feel *welcomed*.' The last in a breathless rush. Then Perrin took off suddenly, as if blown along on the coat-tails of his inspiration. Eric hurriedly shadowed his movement, getting ready to catch, hold, balance. But Perrin had miraculously connected with gravity.

'The scent of marigolds!' he cried out in something like rage.

'This is the whole fucking trouble,' Eric said to himself in an aggrieved way. You can never tell with Perrin what tangent he's going to hare off on next. He thought of the long somnolent telephone conversations they had each night while Perrin waited for his sleeping pills to take effect. Eric would sit in his armchair, armed with a glass of gin, half watching the televisual fantasy of reality while Perrin's voice purred away in his ear – sometimes thin as cellophane, occasionally close as a voice in a dream: his needs, emotional, physical; his dreams; his plans for the future. To sell the house and go to Venice. A week later to offer the house to people with the disease. Another week and he is planning to repaint the hall a Polynesian shade of blue. 'Sea-blue, just that shade of light at dusk – the moment before the sun sinks.'

Shit, and I'm only one of his friends. Eric often said to himself. Not even his oldest. What about his *family*? But Perrin's family in faraway Te Awamutu were in disarray. They were busy tending to their own emotional wounds; they would leave Perrin alone to attend to his actual torment.

Yet, if Eric was honest with himself – and he occasionally was, by dint of necessity rather than pleasure (he was old enough now to realise that honesty, though cruel, was the best policy in the end) – Eric's truth was, silently and subtly, he himself had come almost to depend on Perrin's presence: his closeness. The fact of the matter was Perrin's reality had become the ballast in Eric's somewhat unsteady life.

Ahead of them, as if a testimony, lay Eric's blue, shockingly dented Renault.

Eric's boyfriend was 14 years younger than him. He was a student of architecture who had never heard, thankfully, of aversion therapy as a 'cure' for homosexuality. He could not imagine a city in which there were no bars, saunas or nightclubs. Matthew, handsome, athletic like a basketball player, with an engaging sweep of hair that never quite managed to stay down, had pranged Eric's car in fury one night because, as he yelled out for the whole street to hear, 'You care more about Perrin's dying than *loving* me.'

It was unfair, it was emotional blackmail: it was true.

Eric needed Matthew, his beautiful boyfriend, for the warmth of his flesh, the passion of his kisses: the way he connected him back to life. In the middle of the night he could reach out and let his hand just roll down Matthew's flank and find that softly sweating crease in his knee. This soothed away the phantoms which hid in the dark: Matthew's body was so tangibly real.

Yet for Eric his experiences with Perrin – Perrin sick, Perrin dying – were almost like a pre-vision into the future, a kind of warding off of evil spells so that he would at least know the path of the disease if it should ever strike near him. This was his private truth. And Perrin, who never for one moment doubted Eric's presence by his side, communicated the full phalanx of his illness to him so that Eric's daily equanimity was conditioned by Perrin's. They moved in uneasy duality, two friends linked like horses on a circus merry-go-round, ceaselessly rising and falling together till that final moment when one horse would rise alone.

'Now my funeral,' Perrin took up as the car moved along the streets.

This is what is so odd, thought Eric, as he drove along. When he was with Perrin it was as if that became the centre of reality in the world. Even driving along it was as if the streets of Epsom outside, with their casual realities – a father pushing his babycart into the drycleaners, a woman ducking into the wineshop in broad daylight – became like a moving cyclorama which streamed past them: Eric and Perrin were at the storm-centre, stilled.

'For my funeral,' Perrin was saying in the matter-of-fact, 'now take note of this' voice he used for the important formality of his funeral. He was planning it as he had planned his famous dinner parties, with the exquisite silver, linen and flowers acting as courtiers, nervously anticipating the throwing back of the gilded doors, the regal entrance of the food. Now the unpalatable truth was that Perrin's body would be the main course: and Eric, as a friend who had come forward – and for who came forward and who fell back there were no rules – was to act as courtier, arbiter of Perrin's final feast.

'I only want flowers picked from people's gardens. I don't want one – one!' Perrin tapped the floor with his stick vehemently, 'of those embalmed creations dreamt up by florists! And fruit should be whatever is freshest in the shops. Vegetables of the season – organic. And definitely kai moana. That shop in K Road, you know the one. Only the freshest. Can I rely on you for that?'

'You can rely on me for that.'

A slight pause. Eric turned and looked at his old friend. 'Your Celestial Highness,' he said.

Perrin smiled but did not laugh.

Going through the Domain, they were suddenly accompanied by a flock of graceful runners. Eric slowed down in appreciation. There was one man, sweating in the silent chiaroscuro of sport which echoes so closely the fury of sex. They both watched him silently.

Suddenly Perrin wound down his window. 'You beautiful man!' he yelled out in the voice of a healthy male. 'You're the most beautiful flower in the whole fucking Domain today!'

Eric blessed the presence of his sunglasses while inwardly shrieking.

Fortunately the runner turned towards them and, in his endorphin bliss, showered an appreciative smile at them. The other men pulled away. They passed in a blur of sequined sweat on muscular flesh, with frolicsome cocks beating to and fro like agitated metronomes inside their tiny shorts.

Swiftly the runners became manikins in the rear vision mirror.

'Thanks, darling,' said Perrin in a small voice of exhaustion. 'I really appreciated that.'

Eric felt a surge of exhilaration as he moved closely behind Perrin through the gates of the garden centre. Already queues were forming, with well-heeled Aucklanders guarding trundlers full of merchandise. Eric realised he hadn't felt so good – dangerous would be the wrong word to use – since the very early days of Gay Liberation, when to hold hands in public with another man was a consummate – if inevitably provocative act.

Now time had shifted the emphasis somewhat – but Eric felt a shiver of pride at Perrin who, once so socially nuanced and named, could now lurch – almost like a toddler in reverse, Eric thought with a saving sense of hilarity. He was completely oblivious to the reactions of people around him. Indeed, as he stopped to pass a cheery word with the middle-aged housewife acting as a trundler-guard, he was actively engaging everyone in his act of dying.

Behind his shades, Eric was aware of people staring. They looked on silently, hit by the stilled impact of thought.

'Perrin!' Eric called out, because it suddenly seemed imperative to keep up contact, 'it's marigolds you're looking for, isn't it?'

He moved over to Perrin and, in a movement he himself had not contemplated, hooked his arm through Perrin's frail, bird-like bones and clung on. That was the mystery: it was he who was clinging to Perrin, not the other way round. But Perrin was off, putting all his suddenly furious energy into pushing the cart along. He was calling out the names of the plants as he went, voice full of glee: 'Pittosporum! Helleborus! Antirrhinum! Cotoneaster!'

Now people *were* staring.

But Perrin was unstoppable. It was as if he were gathering in energy from the presence of so many plant forms which, embedded in earth, nourished, watered and weeded, would continue the chain of life: just as his dust would one day, soon, oh soon, too soon, be added to the earth, composting.

Eric felt an uneasy yet piercing sense of happiness, a lyrical rapture in which he conceived the reality of how much he loved Perrin: of how Perrin was, at that very moment, leading him on a voyage of discovery so that they were, as in the dream, two circus horses together rising, leaping wonderfully high, almost far enough above the world, so that for one moment it was as if Perrin and he were experiencing in advance that exhilarating blast of freedom as they surged away from the globe on which all of life was contained, and beyond which there lay nothing – at least nothing known.

The plants were loaded into the boot. Eric had, at the last moment, tried to modulate Perrin's buying frenzy but, as if in testimony to his mood-swing, Perrin had impetuously bought too much, ordered Eric to shut up, and had sailed past the cash register issuing a cheque which Eric felt sure, with a lowering degree of certainty, would bounce. But Perrin, like a small child now, exhausted, almost turning nasty, threatened to throw a tantrum in front of the entire queue. 'I must have what I want,' he had cried. 'You don't *understand*. I *must*.'

And now, thankfully safe inside the car, Eric began breathing a little easier. He shook off his sunglasses, which now weighed heavy on his nose. He felt the beginning pincers of a headache. Perrin was saying to him that he wanted – he needed – to take Eric's car for a drive. He needed to be on his own. He could drive still. Did Eric doubt him? Why was Eric always doubting him?

'Trust me,' said Perrin in a small voice, like a caress.

Eric looked at his old friend. How much longer would he have him with him, to trust, not to trust, to doubt – to be astonished by. He did not know. So, doubting everything, doubting his own instincts to be firm, to say no, Eric allowed himself to be dropped off outside a mutual friend's townhouse, a refugee, and, standing on the pavement, about to go in, he watched Perrin drive away in his car, faltering out into the middle of the road, hugging the centre line. And seeing Perrin move off, odd, slow and cumbersome, trying so hard to control his own fate, Eric watched his dear love, his friend, turn the corner, with as much grace as possible, attempting to execute his own exit.

C.K. STEAD

He was 52 and had that London look – dry hair (he ran his fingers through it, glancing at himself in the lift mirror), tired eyes, something unhealthy about the skin; the suggestion of less than perfect cleanliness, which, like Lady Macbeth's 'damned spot', no amount of washing would quite remove. Was there a word for it? 'Careworn' sounded too Victorian and virtuous. 'Stressed' was its modern and equally self-serving equivalent.

Within himself he felt little of this – only allowed the recognition to run through his mind, thinking it was how she, a 26-year-old fresh from New Zealand, would see him. As the lift doors opened he caught sight of her sitting in Reception. It was her knees that registered first, primly side by side, in dark stockings, with neat knee-caps and a fine curve away from each side, cut off by the line of the skirt. Good strong Kiwi legs, he thought; and then remembered how when he'd first come to England it had seemed to him that young Englishwomen had no calf muscles. It wasn't true any longer. In the intervening decades Europe had become athletic.

She looked in his direction and must have guessed he was the man she was to meet, but he went first to the desk and said he would be out until three.

'James Barrett,' he said taking the hand she held out to him. 'And you're Angela McIlroy.'

Out in the street she'd lost her bearings. He pointed down Farringdon Street to where the figure of Justice over the Old Bailey lifted sword and scales against the dome of St Paul's. The sun glared down through the haze, casting no decisive shadows. The thump of a 24-hour disco came up through a basement grating.

Believing he knew how dingy and confusing these streets must seem to her, he hailed a taxi and gave directions.

They were settled at a table under a tree in a pub yard near the British Museum and had made their choices before he took the little tape machine from his pocket and propped it between the pepper and salt.

'You won't mind, will you?' he asked, and she shook her head. She was unassertive, making no attempt to impress him. Shy, he decided; slightly apprehensive, but self-contained – and he made a mental note of these descriptions.

No need to turn on the machine yet; no need to begin at once with her novel, which was the purpose of the interview. Better to begin – where else? – at their common beginning. She knew he'd grown up in New Zealand? – left as a young man intending to return, but had married an Englishwoman and . . .

Yes, she knew all that. She'd been told. 'Interesting,' she added, nodding and smiling – but he could see it was something other than interest she felt. Disapproval, perhaps? Or was it just indifference?

'I've been back, of course, but only for short stays – three weeks at most. There were eighteen years I never set foot in the place. By then it was too late.'

She'd ordered a salad niçoise. He watched her struggling to cut the lettuce in its bowl. Her drink was mineral water.

'Quite sure?' he asked, lifting his bottle of Italian white.

She held up one hand, like a policeman. Her mouth was full of salad. He filled his glass.

'Oh dammit,' she said, draining the mineral water and holding out her glass. 'Why not?'

'Why not?' he agreed, filling her glass.

'I'm not abstemious,' she said. 'Not especially. But jet-lag and wine . . .'

He nodded. 'Here's to A Short History of New Zealand.'

They touched glasses and drank, but the naming of her novel seemed to bring back that wariness which just for a moment he'd thought was about to be cast aside. She fell silent, waiting for him to lead their conversation.

'I read a large part of it coming down on the train this morning. It's quite a grim picture.' She inclined her head.

'And a true one, so far as I can judge.' And then, almost without meaning to, he began to talk as the expatriate. Once started, it was hard to stop. Some part of his mind was detached. Was this the way to go about it? But then, why not? Somehow he had to get a response out of her.

His view of New Zealand was almost entirely negative, and at first, from the way she met his eyes, nodded, murmured assent, he could see he was taking her with him. But then he went too far. He felt it himself, and saw it in her eyes. Even New Zealand's weather, it seemed, was now inferior. This was London's third good summer in succession. She put her hand over her mouth, and her eyes were smiling.

He looked down at the tablecloth and thought for a moment. 'I'm a journalist,' he said firmly. 'Sometimes when I get a twinge of the old nostalgia I just let myself think what it would have been like working on the *Herald* or the *Dom* or the *Press*, or the *ODT* for God's sake – just imagine it! – dealing with local cow and sheep stories, while all the world stuff was coming in on the wire, written by someone else.'

She nodded, but with such a blank face he began to feel irritation. Did she want him to write about her book? Did she understand that he was doing her a favour? 'My paper has a million readers,' he said.

Her face softened, as if there was something she understood. 'You've done well,' she said.

Her novel, *A Short History of New Zealand*, began with these sentences:

'One's name is Brent and the other is Hemi. One is white and one brown, and they are running under the moon. Ahead and behind and in all directions stretches away the landscape of the plains. You could say they are the cop and the robber. You could say they are the colonist and the colonised. You could say they are the Pakeha and the Maori.

'They are running through most of a long night. Sometimes they stop for breath. Sometimes Hemi reaches the end of this tether and turns on Brent. Pursuer is pursued, back over the same ground. But then it resumes, the other way. They run and keep running.'

The novel is set in a very small town – what used to be called a settlement – in the North Island. It has one cop, a young man who belongs to the local rugby club and takes long training runs with his team-mates. One night he's taking a last look around when he hears something in a storage shed. He goes looking. There are some tense moments in the silence and darkness of the shed – he's sure someone's there but can't find him – and then the burglar, a Maori, makes a break for it, straight out and down the wide main street, the cop in pursuit. In a couple of minutes they've left the town behind. They're out on the open road, running under the moon through that empty landscape, sometimes on the road, sometimes across ploughed fields, through bush, along stream-beds, back to the road again.

The Pakeha sprints. So does the Maori. They slow to jogging, recovering breath. The Maori sprints and the Pakeha almost loses him – but not for long. Sometimes the pursuit slows to a walk, or stops. They talk back and forth across a safe gap, reason with one another, threaten, shout insults.

Then they run again.

With the Sunday papers tucked under one arm he walked back from the village, over ploughed fields, skirting the wood where pheasants, bred for the annual shoot, scuttled away into the undergrowth. The gamekeeper had set snares for foxes, simple loops of fine wire along the edges of pathways. James tripped them as he went. He liked the sight of foxes appearing on his lawn. Why shouldn't those handsome predators, as well as the tweedy kind for whose sport it was intended, have game for supper?

Anne was waiting for him on the gravel outside the front door. He could see by the way she held her hands, and then by her anxious expression, that something was wrong. There had been a phone call from New Zealand. It was bad news. His mother . . .

He flew non-stop. There was no choice if he was to be there for the funeral. It meant eleven hours in the air to Los Angeles, a stop of two hours, and then on again – another twelve to Auckland. His grief was confused with jet-lag and a dread of finding himself among relatives with whom he believed he could have nothing in common. But after the service, when they gathered at his sister's Mt Eden house, drinking and eating and talking on the verandah and out on the back lawn, it came over him how much he was enjoying himself. The hugs of cousins he didn't at first recognise brought surges of old affection. Trivial reminiscences gave him pleasure. It even pleased him to be called Jamie. He'd expected to find himself behaving in a way that would be judged aloof, unfriendly, superior, but it wasn't like that at all. In his strange, jet-lagged state it was as though he saw it all from the outside – saw a different self emerge and take over – warm, outgoing, filial, fraternal, avuncular.

Once or twice in his life a death and funeral had had this effect. He hadn't wept. He'd become an actor on a public stage. But this time it was different – something to do with these people, and with the green of the plum tree in new leaf, and the white of pear-blossom, and the freshness of air and light and water. How long was it since he'd felt such uncomplicated happiness?

He remembered that when he was a boy he would meet his mother unexpectedly in a room or in the garden and they would smile – not anxiously, just with the pleasure each felt at seeing the other. The sadness of that thought didn't spoil his happiness. It was part of it.

Late in the day he was asked the inevitable question: how was he finding New Zealand? It would have been easy to evade – to say it was only hours since he'd stepped off the plane. But what came out was 'great' and 'super' and 'wonderful to be home'. He knew it was the right answer; but it was as if, at least for that moment, it was true.

His questioner smiled, glad to hear it, but then shook his head. 'This country's a mess, Jamie. I don't like to say it, but the fact is *you're better off where you are*.'

That night he crashed asleep while the others were still drinking and talking, then woke in the early hours of the morning. He was in the back room of his sister's house, with wide windows looking out on the garden that was overhung with pongas and cabbage trees. The silence was so complete he strained for something that would prove he hadn't lost his hearing. A floorboard creaked – that was all. These wooden houses shifted with the changes in temperature.

A light shower began to fall, whispering on the iron roof. In childhood rain on the roof had always brought sleep, but now he lay listening, soothed but wide awake, his body still on London time.

He turned on the bedside lamp and looked in his bag for Angela McIlroy's novel, and beside it his tape recorder. He put the machine close to his ear, switched it on, and put out the light.

'The framework of your novel's the chase, but in alternating chapters you go back into the lives of the two men – family history, childhood, schooling . . . Did you feel you could do that equally – I mean with confidence . . .'

'I don't think I felt confident about any of it. I just jumped in and hoped I wouldn't sink.'

'Well, clearly you didn't sink. It's rather unusual, from a woman novelist. Not about . . . Not the usual sub . . .'

'They have mothers and sisters.'

'Yes, but the central characters . . .'

'You don't find them convincing?'

'Oh yes, I think so. Sure. As for the, ah – the Maori background . . . Well, I guess – who knows? I think only a Maori could say.'

'I'm not sure . . . I don't think I agree with that. I mean anyone, Maori or Pakeha, could say they felt it was right. Or they felt it was wrong. If you're talking about feeling, that is. Of course if facts are wrong, that's different. But no one . . .'

'No, I'm not suggesting that.'

There was a break. In the background could be heard the clatter of plates, the murmur of other conversations, a burst of loud laughter.

'Look, I don't know how to put this – I'm just feeling my way towards something. It's certainly not a criticism of your novel which I think is well written and well shaped. But the way it's done touches on something . . .'

'Delicate?'

'Delicate – yes. But I think I mean . . . big. I'm not making myself clear, am I?'

'Keep going.'

'It's there in the title – a short history of New Zealand. That's quite a claim. Quite an indictment.'

'Oh, an indictment. Is that what it is?' There was the sound of her laughter. 'I think I plead the fifth.'

It was no longer a matter of law and order, or crime and punishment. It had become a question of who was fitter, stronger, cleverer; who would out-run, or out-fox, the other; who would win.

Those roads are long and straight, and when Brent saw headlights in the far distance he thought here was his chance. He would flag down the driver and tell him to call in help. But even while he was thinking this there was the twanging of fence wire and the Maori was off overland. He got a bit of a break on there, and quite soon, after crossing a couple of paddocks, he was in a field of corn. Something had happened to the crop. It was head-high but it seemed to be dried out, dead on the stalk and unpicked. The Maori plunged into it and disappeared. Brent hunted and then stopped. It was such a still night you couldn't move in there and not be heard. If there'd been a wind the Maori could have moved under cover of the rustling, but there was none. And the moon was bright. So Brent waited and rested. When the Maori made a break for it the chase was on again.

They ran through empty fields, through flocks of sheep, through cow-paddocks, through stubble, through crops of swedes and potatoes and cabbages, always well clear of farmhouses. Dogs barked in the distance. A nightbird sounded as they ran through the edges of a swamp. They came back to a road and ran on it. Then there was again the twanging of fence-wire and they were off over a field of onions. The onions had been turned up by a mechanical digger – they were lying on top of the soil, waiting to be collected, and they made it hard going. The Maori seemed to go over on one. It must have rolled under his foot, his ankle twisted, and for just a moment he went down.

Now you bastard, Brent thought. And then he wondered, What the fuck am I going to do with him? How'm I going to bring him in?

When he got to him the Maori was up on one knee, holding a knife. 'Come and get it, Dog-breath,' he said.

On the tape they sounded at first hesitant with one another, wary. He'd known it was because she distrusted him as an expatriate, expected him to be patronising. It had made it hard for him to get to the more difficult, and therefore more interesting, questions. But as the lunch went on, and she shared his wine, the exchanges had become more frank, less hesitant.

He ran the tape forward, and listened again.

'I keep coming back to your title . . .'

'Yes, it's bold, I know.'

'And it makes how the thing ends important.'

'Don't tell me about it. Terribly important. I spent so many months agonising over all that. Then I'd give away the title – look for something more modest. But that seemed the easy way out. The cowardly . . . You see I'd had the title in mind right from the start – before I'd written a word. That, and the basic story of the all-night chase, which was something that happened. I read about it in the paper, and straight away I thought this is a short history of New Zealand. But it had such symbolic force – too much. Pakeha chases Maori through his own land to enforce British law. Every now and then Maori rebels and turns on Pakeha, but then it's back to the old chase. That was okay in a way – as a story – because it was real. It happened, and it was believable. But if it was to carry that symbolic load . . .'

'That's why the end . . .'

'Yes, because it's not finished, is it? I mean the history's not. It goes on . . . So the end of the novel has to be – what's the word?'

'Tentative? Not definitive?'

'Yes, that's right, but . . . *Provisional*. That's the word. I had it on a piece of paper pinned over my desk. The ending had to be provisional. The first version ended with an arrest. They ran all night and then early in the morning Hemi just lost heart and gave up. Well, that might be how it would happen – but as symbol . . .'

'No good. I can see that. They haven't given up.'

'And then I had him get away. No good again, you see. Too easy. Sentimental. Because the real history . . .'

'Yes, it's tougher than that.'

'Then I had them fight it out. But how does that end? Pakeha kills Maori? Maori kills Pakeha? They're both killed? They make friends and walk off hand in hand into the sunrise? You see? Nothing seemed to fit.'

'Not as things are right now. But they're all possible, aren't they?'

'You mean in reality.'

'I mean – what do I mean? They're possible ends, most of them, if you think just of the two men. Maybe the problem is there's too much conflict, d'you think? The story sets them too much in opposition. After all, it hasn't always been like that. If you think of our history . . .'

'Our?'

'Yes . . . Oh, I see. You think as an expatriate it's not mine any more.'

And then the tape ran out.

'Come and get it,' the Maori repeated, holding the knife out in front of him. And then suddenly he was up and running, not away this time, but straight at his pursuer. Brent turned and ran.

The sprint didn't last long. They had run too many miles; but when they stopped the Maori must have felt he was on top.

'Okay', he said. 'Just fuck off and I'll let you keep your balls.'

He turned and walked in the opposite direction. It can't have been long before he heard footsteps coming after him, keeping a safe distance. Brent wasn't going to give up now. If he couldn't arrest the bugger, he'd stick with him until daylight.

It took a few runs this way and that before the new rules were established. When the Maori chased, Brent ran. Once it was so close he felt his shirt slashed, and a strange sensation – not pain, a sort of coldness – down his back. He didn't think the knife had cut him, but later he felt a trickle of blood. After that he kept his distance, but as the Maori turned and headed off, he followed.

Now the Maori ran again, effortlessly, as if he was doing it to suit himself. He didn't look back. They came to a stopbank – it loomed up high and straight above the plain on one side and the river on the other, with a flat grassy path along the top. They went up on to it and kept running, heading down-river towards the sea.

After half an hour they ran off the stopbank and down a road, and there, opening out in front of them, was the coast – dunes and sand all scattered over with huge white logs and driftwood that had come down the river over the years and gone out to sea only to be washed back by the westerlies. Under the moon it looked like a huge boneyard, with the sea thundering against it.

The Maori seemed to know where he was going now. He stopped short of the dunes and headed north over fields until he came to another road. It was there he went into a pine grove. Brent lost him briefly, and for the first time thought he should give up. He was now a long way from home, and nobody would know where. He might be ambushed and knifed. You could bury a body in the piles of needles and it might not be found for years.

But he kept going, relying on his ears and on the stillness of the night. He stood with his back against a pine trunk and listened. When the Maori moved, Brent went after him.

They came to a clearing and stopped. They were on either side of it, the moon coming through so they could see one another. They rested, sizing one another up. After a while the Maori said, 'You got a wife and kids?'

Brent told him he had a wife, no kids yet.

The Maori turned the knife-blade this way and that on his palm, as if his hand were a razor strop.

'What about you?' Brent asked.

The Maori said, 'Soon I'll introduce you to my mates. They're Rastas.'

Brent didn't reply.

'Where I'm taking you,' the Maori said, 'we got a big hole in the ground, like a cave, eh. We call it a tomo. You ever seen a tomo, Dog-breath? They drop dead calves down there. Sometimes a whole cow. Not even the stink comes up.'

He turned, out of the clearing, and began walking through the pines. He came to a fence and climbed over it. Over his shoulder he called, 'Come on Pakeha. Let's get there before the sun comes up.'

She'd solved her problem by adding a second layer – the story of the writer writing the story. It was what James had liked least about her novel, but he could see why she'd done it. There could be no end, so there had to be many ends – many possibilities, all left open. It was called 'meta-fiction' these days and it was very fashionable, but how could you get around the basic human appetite that every story should have a beginning, a middle and an end, and that to be enjoyed it had to be believed?

The rain was getting heavier. The whisper on the roof became rustling, and briefly a roar. There was the sound of water rushing along gutterings and through down-spouts, and dripping from ponga fronds on to the lawn. Then it died away again to a gentle hissing.

He thought of his Northamptonshire garden, the roses and hollyhocks, the woods across fields with crows circling and crying. At last drowsiness returned, and sleep.

He dreamed that he was talking to Angela McIlroy over lunch, or rather, listening while she talked. She spoke in fluent Maori, though words like niçoise and frascati were mixed up in it. Now and then she paused in her monologue to turn the blade of her knife back and forth across her open palm.

He strained to catch what it was she was telling him, certain that he did understand – that he was capable of it – but never quite making sense of it. It was like something just beyond reach, or a word on the tip of the tongue.

The two men in the kitchen fight on.

Nigel, the taller one, has rolled up the sleeves of his business shirt to reveal how the hair of his arms has been worn thin by the acrylic fibre brushing against his skin, day in, day out. His glasses wait folded on the table. The fight continues upside-down across their lenses, the light bulb burning in the middle of the spotless white floor.

Nigel's not broad. Warren – wider, squat – has the definite advantage, you'd think, except Warren wasn't expecting this – he was expecting to go into his bedroom, play some records and fall asleep. And now Warren's nose is bloodied, to the satisfaction of his adversary.

Nigel's satisfaction stems from a number of things. He's relieved, because he put the same odds on the fight as you or I would: he'd put Warren first. Nigel is not a fighter. It's not in his nature to lash out or stomp or even complain. Normally he puts up with things until his feelings are worn as bare as the skin on his arms. Also, he feels a sense of achievement. He decided several hours prior that when Warren walked through the door he would jump on him like a wild dog, and he's done it.

And thirdly, Nigel is satisfied because he is feeling something, and for a time there he was looking back – on the evening, the week, his life – and wondering if he could feel anything at all.

Warren goes to stand up and gets hit again.

It's quite a fracas, and downstairs the neighbours are wondering – as neighbours are apt to do – what the hell it's all about. As are you, probably. What is it between two men, eh? Why do they get so het up? It's over a woman, you're thinking, they're in love with the same one – but no, it's nothing as romantic as that. Then they're in love with each other, you say: and that's why they're fighting. Well it isn't that either. So what is it? you ask. *What's going on in Nigel's head?*

Let's take a look.

It's a routine. Which started . . . some night, sometime. He simply turned up and it all started. He attracts them. Like unlidded honey.

I remember it all. It's unfair of me, I know, but I do. I listen. I notice things, and maybe they mean something and maybe they don't. The most meaningful thing I can tell you is that I don't sleep very well, and so if my flatmate does come home trailing someone or other then obviously I'm going to hear. And it's a small place – you know the sort of thing. City apartments. Before I entered the lobby I looked up at the stars and saw all eight floors of window lights were off. And I thought: I bet everyone in the building has gone to town to the movies – in fact, I bet they're all at the *same* movie.

I was lying in the pillows counting the faces in the wallpaper with one eye when I heard him coming up the lift. Whatever he was doing, he was clumsy with it. There was the noise of feet on the floor and the chime and crash of the criss-crossed metal gate being opened and closed. Then the *thruuuummm* of the lift descending and his key scraping the door lock. I heard him offer someone a drink. I lay in the darkness thinking, right, Warren's brought someone home.

Interestingly (I realised later), all of them say yes to a drink, even if they're drunk already. You can hear them stumbling with the glass in hand, and the clatter after he suggests they remove their shoes. Then one of them drops something else – always, you can set your watch by it – and then there's the incredible noise of people going SHH SHH YOU'LL WAKE HIM.

He started with music. He always does. Like I said, it's a routine. You know, getting her in the mood. I worked that out. What I couldn't work out was which mood he was trying to get her into. Because instead of playing one record he was playing a whole lot of tracks from different albums, and none of them had anything to do with each other. None of the styles were the same, and none of the bands. Like tuning into some crazy radio.

He plays nineteen songs. Always nineteen. Same tracks, same order. I admit that after nights of this – weeks – the collection has begun to sound more natural, but hearing them for the first time I couldn't for the life of me work out how they came to be together. Each began with the clunk of the needle being dropped, and ended with the scratch of it being lifted again. Someone was poised over the turntable, painstakingly tracing the playlist.

After the last song came the sound of the record clicking in the groove. And then the pause. Then a little laughter, and the squeaking of the bed. Okay, so the usual thing, I thought, right? Wrong. Because then I heard it for the first time.

The whipping.

It seemed wet. Slick. A strop on bare flesh. Leather. Whacking. Three strokes, each four seconds apart. Then came a pause, and then another three strokes, then another pause . . . and so on.

Each night he brings them. And every night I hear it. It lasts for nearly an hour, and the speed of the strokes never varies. There is no quickening, no fever to it. And no reply: no crying out, or laughter, or words. It passes as unexplained as the songs beforehand and their crooked order of play.

When I left the next morning his bedroom door was shut. The apartment was empty when I got home that afternoon. I never saw the woman. In fact, I have never seen any of them. I do *know* they're women – the walls concede that much. After each beating the plasterboard lets slip voices and still later, the hobbled vocabulary of grunts and moans. That, and the whippings, is all there is.

Which is strangest of all. You'd think, wouldn't you (I know I do) that different people would, well, *react* differently. Old, young, short, tall, professional, amateur. They come to him from different homes, with different ways of speaking, different smells – nothing in common. The whipping is what joins them together. It threads them like beads on a string.

After weeks of this I was losing sleep. I took a night off, stayed at a friend's. Mischa, her name is. And yes, I did. We were sharing a bed and at 2 am I rolled over on top of her and she was waiting, tugging down her pants. And when her arms were up and her lips were hot against my ear I thought about – just for a second, a hot flash of a second I thought . . . and my hand pressed against her thigh and I thought . . . nothing. No, nothing at all really.

The next morning she went to work, and I wandered the streets. I looked in shops, my reflection unshaven in the counter tops. I purchased nothing. I mounted the lobby steps with my shirt-tail hanging out. Someone was watching me from another apartment: I saw curtains fall.

Warren was out. I showered and went to bed, expecting to be woken by his usual medley. But there was no performance that night. No Warren, not the next day, either. Then came a call from his work: apparently he'd skipped town. Unplanned holiday.

I lay on the couch in the sun. I watched *Sale of the Century*. I thought of looking in his room . . . and then sense got the better of me, and I pulled his bedroom door shut. The lock clicked, sounding loud in the hallway. Outside someone was talking on the landing, a shadow behind frosted glass.

The good weather did not last. It never does in this town – it changes from sun to rain to cloud to sun as if higher beings are flicking channels. It wasn't until the following night that they found something worth watching. At least, I hope they found it. I hope someone was amused.

It was late. I switched off the TV. In the silence I heard the lift stop and the gate swing open and then footsteps. The gate clanged shut again and the lift descended. There was a knock on the door. I opened it and she was waiting there on the landing. I didn't know her.

'Is Warren in?' she said.

'He's out,' I said. Her face fell.

And I realised: she was one of them. I thought, she isn't what I expected, and then I thought, no. I hadn't expected anything at all. She wasn't rough trade, she was clean. Small. Wearing a long black raincoat that dripped water on the floor, and a ludicrous hat – a plastic polka-dot bonnet, the sort grandmothers wear in discount supermarkets.

'Yes,' I went on. 'He's out of town. Holiday or something.'

'Shit.' She caught herself. 'Pardon me.'

We were three storeys beneath the roof but you could still hear the rain drumming on the metal.

'You had plans,' I said.

'Yes.'

She stood on the landing without anything further to say. She was unprepared for this. Unprepared in a way that went beyond the merely practical. She had been expecting him to greet her in the same way that she expected the rain to be wet. She tried to cover up for it by glancing over her shoulder, and I covered up for it by inviting her inside.

'He promised he'd be here.' She looked around. 'Are you sure you don't know where he is?'

'I've just come back to the flat myself.'

'Did he leave a message?'

'No. Are you cold? Let me take your coat.'

'My coat?' She looked puzzled.

'You're inside now.'

'Oh.' She almost smiled. Almost. 'Hang on – take it. Pardon me.' The coat was a huge fisherman's oilskin. The sleeve cuffs hung over her knuckles. 'If you roll them they catch the water,' she explained. 'Like gutters.' I held the coat as she took off her hat and stuffed it in one of the pockets. 'Thank you,' she said. The coat weighed a ton. I asked if she did a lot of walking in the rain. 'I used to live in Malaysia,' she said. 'It rains there all the time.' And I thought that was a good answer because it gave us something to talk about.

'Malaysia,' I began. 'That's interesting.'

'I used to strip there,' she said.

I hung the coat in the laundry. The cloth was so thick with oil it smelled like sardines. I walked down the hall, past the door to Warren's room. When I came back into the kitchen she was standing with her arms folded, asking for her coat back and saying she wanted to leave now, saying sorry for what she'd said. I'd thought she'd made the remark to shake me but now I wasn't so sure, and she didn't seem to know either. I looked at her and she looked at me. We were looking into each other's eyes. I coughed, breaking the stare. She looked down at the floor.

'You can't go out in that,' I told her. 'It's pissing down. I was making some tea. Have a cup. And then I'll call you a taxi.'

She looked up. 'I drove here,' she said. She was trying to be sarcastic, but it still came out as nerves. I pulled out the chair for her. She sat down.

She didn't speak as she watched me warm the butter on the jug. Her inertness was worse than fidgeting. There was a loaf of frozen-sliced in the freezer and it broke like a pack of cards.

We ate listening to the sound of chewing, and when finished she stood once more.

'My coat,' she said. 'I'm really sorry. I can't do this. I should go.'

'Warren might come back.'

'I doubt it.'

'You're different,' I blurted.

'Different from what?'

'From what Warren said,' I lied.

That slowed her down. 'What did he say?'

'He – said you were coming.'

'He did?'

'Yes.'

'Oh.' A silent thought fell from her round mouth. 'He said – to expect me?'

'Yes.'

'Well.' She straightened herself like someone taking bad news. Instinctively she ran her hands down the front of her skirt, pressing the material flat. For the first time I noticed her clothes. The shirt was navy, pleated. Splattered in black where the rain had touched. Her blouse was grey. Her shoes were flat. She wasn't wearing make-up. She looked up as if she had come straight from the office. If offices closed at one in the morning.

'Well,' she said again. 'I didn't realise.'

'I should have said.'

'No no. Not your job.' She sat down again. 'It's his place to do that.'

'Is it?' I nodded.

'That's the rule.' And now she did smile. It was small and resigned, but it was a smile.

'Why don't you have some more tea?'

'I'd like something stronger.'

'I don't know if there is anything.'

She hesitated. 'Warren has some scotch.'

'In his room?'

She nodded. 'On the dresser.'

'Do you want to get it?'

'Oh no.' She looked shocked. 'I couldn't.'

'I'm sure Warren wouldn't – '

'He would. That's just not allowed.' She crossed her hands in her lap. 'You have to get it.'

'I just thought, you know where it is . . .' She looked at me as if I was an idiot. I shrugged and went down the hall. 'Okay.'

'On the dresser,' she called.

At first the door wouldn't open: the handle was stiff. I went inside. Somehow it seemed more polite to search with the lights off, working in the glow thrown from the hallway. I couldn't see the bottle. Looking around, it wasn't on the bed or any of the shelves. I finally found it in the top drawer, and I was glad when I did. I shut the drawer and the handles rattled. And then I stopped. There was something else on the dresser. A coiled whip. The leather gleamed in the low light. I touched the handle and it slithered undone, spilling off the edge. It made a slapping noise as it hit the floor.

I took the scotch back to the kitchen. Her brow furrowed.

'Where is it?' she said.

I held up the bottle. 'Here.'

'Not that.' She stood. 'The whip.'

Now I stopped.

'You're going to use your hand?' she asked.

'I hadn't thought about it.'

She sighed. 'You'll get sore. Long before I do.'

I stood the bottle on the table.

'Warren uses his hand sometimes, and it's not as good.'

A bug was circling the light bulb, its shadow dancing on the walls.

'You don't understand,' I said. 'You've made a mistake.'

'Have I?'

'What do you think −' I couldn't say it. 'You used to do this stuff, right? When you were overseas?'

'Sometimes.' She considered telling me, weighed it up. 'Yes. Did it a lot.'

'And it makes you happy?'

'Delirious.' She watched my face. 'Oh, sometimes it's a downer. But you have to feel bad sometimes. Because we are bad and we do bad things. You do bad things, don't you? Don't you feel − wrong? You must.'

'Then you shouldn't do it,' I said.

'No. But,' she shrugged. 'It's not that simple.'

'He threatened you?'

She laughed. 'No.'

'I couldn't do anything that made me that depressed.'

'You couldn't?' She looked up.

I shook my head. 'I don't think so. I don't know how you can.'

'Because it's the only thing that matters to me. I have spent the whole day working up to this. I was thinking about it when I was doing the dishes and when I was in the shower this morning. I thought about it at work, I thought about it walking to my car in the car park. I chose my perfume because of what was going to happen tonight and when I go home I will talk about it to myself, remind myself what I have done, over and over, for hours. Can't you see?'

Her eyes were as wet as the streets outside.

'You've been drinking,' I said.

'Yes,' she said. 'Quite a bit.'

'Have another.'

There were shot glasses in the lounge cabinet. I took them back into the kitchen, rinsing them at the sink. She stood and waited. I stood the glasses on the table and poured. She sank it straight and cleared her throat.

'Would you like some music?' I asked.

'Music?'

'I hear it.'

'You do?'

'The walls are spit and paper – I can't not hear it.'

'You listen through the walls.' She was combing her eyebrows with the tips of her fingers. 'Do you listen to me?'

'I must have done.'

'Do you jerk off?'

I poured another shot.

'You're trying to get me drunk,' she said.

'You are drunk.'

'Then you want to be drunk.'

'Maybe. Yes.' I held the glass to the light. 'Yes. I think that I do.'

She turned and bent over the table, hiking up her skirt. 'Do you want my pants on or off?' she asked.

I sniffed the alcohol. 'You decide.'

'No. You have to say.'

'On.'

'Okay then.' She took a breath. 'Hurry.'

She was so blasé about it, and so determined. She was impressive and pathetic at the same time – exotic and a traveller and she couldn't find her house-keys.

I finished my drink and put down the glass and walked over and stood next to her. She was breathing fast, her face against the tabletop. Eyes closed. I put my left hand on her waist. No, she said and guided it higher, to the base of her neck. I didn't know how high to raise my arm, how far to draw back. She was holding her bottom lip in her teeth.

The bug was still flying around the light. It was dark outside. Raining so hard the windows looked as if they were melting. There was the noise of the traffic, noise from the bus stop downstairs. Once I heard the police helicopter. And music, I heard music. She was humming to herself. One of nineteen tunes.

I tried to count seconds between the strokes but, I don't know, I stopped counting. I don't know how long it took. She was right about my hand. It got sore before she did.

'Use the other one.' She rolled her head around, her hair flicking wet across her cheek.

'No.' I let go of her neck. My fingers were twitching. A nerve had become strained and tugged against the top of the hand. It felt as if my whole arm was piano wire, scraping and echoing, rumbling.

'Use the left,' she said.

'That's enough.'

'Why not?'

'That's enough.'

I stood in Warren's room for a time. It still seemed polite to leave the lights off. She stood in the kitchen and waited for me to finish. When I got back she stood up straight.

'I would really like my coat now,' she said. I got it for her. She put it on by herself.

She had one foot out of the doorway when I stopped her.

'Would you like to go for coffee sometime?' I asked.

'A coffee and what?'

'Just a coffee.'

For the first time, she looked tired.

'You don't understand,' she said. 'I want it. I really want it.'

'I have never wanted anything that much.'

'That's sad.' She shook her head. 'That's a real shame.'

Her coat was like her skin. I wanted to fuck her in her coat. I wanted to roll over and press against her, her pink flesh. It embodied her. She was beautiful in it, wrapped. She straightened the collar with her thumbs.

'Are you dead?' she asked.

'No.'

'How can you tell?'

She took the stairs. The lobby door clanged shut and she stepped out into the rain.

It is still pouring when Warren arrives. He comes through the door shaking his head like a dog, the water dripping from his coat. He starts to say something but stops when he sees his open bedroom, and the whip on the floor. His face wears the expression of a man suddenly remembering something. Then his face becomes dark. Dark and hard.

And I forget exactly who takes the first swing.

EMILY PERKINS

Your fingers are crossed because you've seen a white horse and until you see a black dog you have to keep them crossed.

> White horse white horse give me good luck
> Onetwothreefourfivesixseveneightnineten.

Sometimes you cross the fingers on both hands because this means double luck. Also it means one hand can keep crossed if the other one gets tired, or has to reach out and pinch your sister, who is sitting squashed against the car door as far away from you as she can because (she says) you stink.

This is not fair because last week at school you punched a boy who was mean to her. He wasn't mean on purpose but he threw a basketball across the quad and she was standing in the way and it hit her in the face. You saw her small and crying and you went up to him and you punched him. You also did it because he's Jeremy Lovegrove's younger brother and you like Jeremy Lovegrove but he doesn't like you. 'He doesn't even know I'm alive,' is what you sometimes say to your reflection in the mirror. It is a phrase you read in a book. 'He doesn't even know I exist.' But the truth is he does know, he just doesn't care that much, and he has brown hair and sandy limbs and you are a bit weird. Punching his brother who is younger than you is not a good way to make Jeremy Lovegrove like you. But you don't understand this collision of aggression and love, and besides it makes you feel better. You hit Jeremy Lovegrove's younger brother because you are afraid of the power Jeremy Lovegrove has over you by not liking you when you like him, and this makes you angry. You are angry with yourself and with Jeremy Lovegrove and also with his younger brother, partly because he looks like him and partly because he threw a basketball at your sister's head.

Your sister who is sitting with hair curled around her thumb and her thumb shoved in her mouth, sucking it even though she's not a baby any more. She looks at you and pushes her nose up with her finger and then looks away. You hate her. You will torture her later. She's a scaredy-cat and when you get to the camping ground it will be no sweat to catch her off her guard and give her a fright. Be a nasty monster, Dracula or Werewolf-Man. Stalk her slowly, put a pillow up the back of your jersey like a hunchback, reach your hands out for her neck with their fingers all stretched and pointy. Wolfie's here. She will scream and scream. She is frightened of you. She doesn't know how to fight against these sorts of games. She doesn't even know that she could.

Your mother passes peaches back from the front seat. You uncross the fingers of your left hand so you can hold the peach. She tells you not to get juice everywhere. You don't see how you're going to be able not to. The peach is over-ripe and squashy and as soon as you bite into it juice dribbles down your chin. It will be sticky later. The squeaking of the furry peach skin gives you shivers. You bite around a bruise. You unwind the window and throw the bruise bit out. It doesn't go out properly and slides down the door of the car. You hope your father didn't see. You stick your face out the window to feel the air rushing over it. You stick your tongue out to be dried by the air and then put it to the peach flesh and feel the spit rushing back into your mouth. Saliva. You hate that word.

You are driving past pine trees. It is a forest. Wolves probably live there. The sun is bright on the road and the shadows of the pine trees sit blackly on top of the shiny tar. For a while you count the telegraph poles. Then you breathe in and out by them. In as you pass one, hold it, out as you pass the next one, then in again. It makes you breathe slower than normal and you don't like it so you stop. Your fingers are tacky and sore from being crossed. You swap the peach stone over to your right hand and cross the fingers of your left. You bring the stone up to your mouth to suck the last bit of fruit from it and it splits in your fingers and as it drops in your lap you see two earwigs crawl out. You scream. Your father slams on the brakes. You jerk forward. You squirm around in your seat trying to see where the earwigs have landed. Your father pulls the car over. He shouts at you. It isn't fair because you can't help it if there were insects inside your peach and now they're on the car floor somewhere and going to crawl up your leg. When he's finished telling you off he pulls back out onto the road. Your face is hot. You stick it out the window again. You're not going to look at your mother and you're specially not going to look at your sister. You don't have to anyway.

You're looking at the pine trees and your castle is in behind there somewhere and it's big and made of stone and you live there and do magic. You can talk without moving your lips. It's called telepathy. You and the knights at your castle can hear each other's thoughts. Only the ones you want them to. And you've got ESP and you can move objects just by looking at them. That's called telekinesis. You've got that, like right now you could make a telegraph pole fall over or make your sister's own hand fly up and slap her on the cheek. All you have to do is concentrate hard enough. The telegraph poles are no good at the moment because the car's moving past them too fast. Later when you get to the camping ground you'll do it. Make the tent fall over or something. Make the billy boil by itself.

The pine forest ends and you're driving through a small town. You don't like this. You don't like the small town houses with their curtains pulled closed. They look like they're blind. You imagine people living behind those curtains as only being shadows moving. The flat footpaths scare you. The flat skies scare you. It's all so big and so small at the same time. You drive up to some shops. Your sister's saying, Icecream icecream icecream. Your dad stops the car and gets out. Stopped in this small town. He gets out and walks up to the dairy. He pauses in the doorway to pull up his socks and then he disappears into the blackness of the shop. Two boys are leaning, squinting, against the wall outside. One of them has a bike. He holds onto it lightly with just one hand resting on the handle. It's a chopper with a flag on the back. Him and his friend have got jeans on. You're not allowed to wear jeans. The boys see you looking at them and they try to stare you down. You win the staring competition. You always do, even if it makes your eyes water. The boy without the bike has got freckles. They're big and blotchy on his face, like tea-leaves. You can almost count them. Your dad comes out of the dairy holding Tip-Tops. He gets in the car and hands them out. Your mum says, Eat it before it melts. You peel off the wrapper with your teeth and suck the cold hard chocolate coating. The boys are watching. You've got an icecream and they haven't. You bite into it, closing your eyes and going mmm like in the ads as the chocolate cracks in your mouth and you taste the creamy middle bit. You curl your lips up and smile your mean smile at them, waving the icecream back and forth and moving your head from side to side. Your dad starts the car. The boys give you the fingers. You can't do them back because you've got one hand full of icecream and stick and one hand with the fingers glued together with peach juice. All you can do is poke out your tongue in the back windscreen while they wave their arms up and down, straight out in front of them, fingers held up in Vs. Fuck shit bugger damn, you say in your head. Then you say, Sorry God please God I'll never say it or think it again God, never ever as long as I live, sorry God sorry.

You twist back in your seat to face front again. And your bloody shit damn sister's eating her icecream slowly, tiny baby bites so she'll have heaps left when you're finished and she can gloat about it. You don't really care because you feel sick anyway, icecream and peach and marmite and lettuce sandwich and a hard-boiled egg all churning round inside. The heat outside. The road, starting to wind now over a hill. You think you might chuck. You tell your mum you have a headache. She goes Tch and sighs. Close your eyes, she says. You do and it makes the swinging of the car worse. Rolling back and forward, swinging, going up and down over dips and little bumpy bits. Mum, you say, Mum. She turns and looks at you. She's green, says your sister. She's all green. Your mum reaches her hand back and squeezes your knee. You'll be all right, she says. Not long now. How long, how lo-ong, says your sister. Shhh, says your mum, looking in the glove box for something. She hands you a barley sugar. Suck this.

Dad, says your sister, Dad, do A for horses. He doesn't hear her. Your mother nudges him. She murmurs something. He glances quickly round at you and your sister. He smiles A for 'orses, he says slowly, B for mutton – You join in. C for yourself, D for dumb. You know this game. Your dad knows it from when he was a little boy. Most of the things in it are from the olden days. From that time when your dad was running round in shorts and playing marbles and the war was on. The marbles are still at your gran's place. G for police. I for Novello. L for leather. That's a good one, getting to hear your Dad say 'hell' even though he's not really saying. O for the wings of a dove. You look up in the sky and see a hawk circling. They swoop down and eat the eyes out of baby lambs. At your castle you keep them tame and they carry messages for you. Z for breezes, your dad says, and your sister says, Again again. But your mum starts singing her favourite car song, in her low and whispery voice. I know – a dark – secluded place – a place – where no one knows your face – a glass – of wine – a fast embrace – it's called – Hernando's Hideaway. You imagine the room, lit with low yellow light and filled with Spanish music. Ladies like on the back of your playing cards, with big spotty dresses on, frills and flowers in their hair. Just knock – three times – and whisper low – that you – and I – were sent by Joe. You will be free – to gaze at me and talk – of – lo-ove. Your mum goes to that place. Well, she did before you were born maybe. She spent nights in Hernando's Hideaway, smoking cigarettes with a man in a hat and dancing to castanets. Your mother sings, looking every now and then at her own reflection in the window. There's a funny twist to her mouth when the song is over.

I want a barley sugar, says your sister, I want one too. Grow up, you say. Yours is gone and you don't feel sick any more. You glare at her. Your mum passes a barley sugar over to her. See, I got one, she says to you. Grow up, you say again. She pretends she can't hear you. The car goes over a really big bump. Your sister yelps. I swallowed mine, Mum, I swallowed mine. Shhh, says your mother. You mimic your sister under your breath. You make your voice whiny and high. I thwallowed mine. Shut up, she says. Thut up, you say. Stop it, she says. Thtop it. Mum, she says. Mu-um. Make her stop. Make her thtop. Shut your face. Thut your fathe. You can see your mother in the front with her sunglasses on and her eyes shut, humming. Your dad is frowning at the road. Your sister pinches your leg. You slap her hand. Ow, she says. Ow, you echo. She tries to dead-arm you. You rap her knee with your knuckles. She scratches your hand. You grab her wrist and say, Want a Chinese burn? She tries to pull away but you are stronger than her. Do you? No. Say please. No. Say please most beautiful sister. You start to twist the skin a little bit. She looks as if she might start bawling. You don't like the way you feel. You feel like a big fat giant. You throw her wrist back into her lap. Crybaby, you say, turning to the window again. She sits and rubs her wrist for a minute. Then she leans over and pinches your arm really hard. You let her do it. If you two don't stop you can get out here, says your dad. You roll your eyes. Dick, you whisper. You glance at your sister. He's a dick, you whisper to her. She giggles. You rub your arm. He eats turds for breakfast, you say. Big fat smelly ones. She giggles again. You say, What's red and gets smaller and smaller and smaller? What? she says. A baby combing its hair with a potato peeler, you say. She laughs even though you can tell she doesn't really get it. Hey, Mum and Dad, listen to this. What's red and gets smaller and smaller and smaller? What, dear? says your mother. A baby combing its hair with a potato peeler. You and your sister force big laughs out, ha ha ha. Oh, that's dreadful, says your mother. Really.

It's so hot in the car. Even with the window open it's boiling. You're driving past dry brown paddocks. Cows look at you when you go past. Sheep don't. You wonder if black sheep know they're different. Sheep look nice from far off but when you get up close they smell of dags and things. Their wool looks soft but it's not really. It's greasy and thick. You drive past a sign that says, One Way Jesus. Dumb. That doesn't even make sense. You feel sleepy. There's nowhere comfortable to put your head. You curl up as little as you can and close your eyes, listen to the car engine, the wheels on the road.

When you wake up your legs have got pins and needles. You were dribbling, says your sister. Was not, you say, wiping the wet seat, grumpy from sleep. So thirsty. The countryside smells. Silage is what it's called. And there's bits of paddocks covered with black plastic that's held down by old tyres. You wish you could read your book in the car without feeling sick. In your book the countryside is full of robins and pussywillow and little stone cottages. Ramshackle. There's a twinkly old farmer, and winding lanes and streams and primroses. The car bounces again and your stomach lurches. The road's bumpy and dusty, loose shingle. You must be getting closer to the camping ground. There's that funny red clay you never see anywhere else. In your book the kids have boarding school and tuck boxes. They eat sandwiches with the crusts cut off them. Pony club and gymkhanas. At the camping ground last year, they had a horse race along the beach on New Year's Day. You imagine winning it this year, the kids' race, miles ahead of everyone on your beautiful white horse that lives at the castle. And at the end of the race everyone just about falls over because you say the magic words to your horse and it starts to fly. It's got wings and you can fly as far as you like, high above the beach, over the bush and the hills and into another world where there are stone cottages and pussywillow and winding magic lanes.

You close your eyes again. Somewhere out of your dreams the car stops. Are we there? you say, stretching your neck. It's cooler now and the sun's not so bright. Soon, says your mum. Dad's getting fish and chips. Can I have L&P? you say. Go in and ask him. You open the door and almost fall out. Your feet feel strange on the ground. Put your jandals on, says your mother. You slip them on and stand swaying a bit outside the car. Your legs are all wobbly. You see your dad in the fish and chip shop. It's bright inside and you blink. You ask your dad if you can have L&P. He says yes. You lean against his leg. He puts his arm round your shoulder. The fish and chip shop smells of hot fat and sausages. You look out the glass door to the car. Your mother's leaning against it smoking a cigarette and looking down the road. Your sister's got her feet up on the seat and her knees up to her chin, sucking her thumb. You feel grown up. There's a purple electric light along the back wall. What's that, Dad? It's for killing flies, he says. They fly into it and get electrocuted. That's dreadful, you say. Really. The fish and chip shop man hands you a potato fritter in a white paperbag and see-through spots of grease on it. The fat fish and chip shop lady comes in through the plastic curtain strips that hang in the doorway to the other room. Long drive? she asks your father. We came from Wellington, he says, and she nods, waves fat fingers at you. The man shakes salt on everything and wraps it in newspaper and gives it to your dad.

The four of you sit in the car as it's getting dark eating your fish and chips. There's flies in there, you tell your sister, pointing to her chips. Are not, she says. Your fingers are salty. The car smells of food. You let your sister have a drink of your L&P. We'll be pitching the tent in the dark again, your mum says to your dad. Don't worry, you say, I can put it up by myself. You'll do telepathy on it and it will all go in the right place. You look out the window at the dirty street and think of your big stone castle. Even though you're sitting in the car with your mum and dad and your sister you feel as if you're all alone.

You take everyone's chip paper to the rubbish bin across the road. A black dog runs past. You forgot.

SUE McCAULEY

You ring work and tell them you have a temperature, you think it's a bug. Your son – the one who is doing a small business course and therefore still living at home – overhears on his way back from the bathroom, and tells you he also feels crook; he almost barfed in the handbasin. The way he says it you know he holds you responsible for wanton contagion.

You don't tell him you're just taking a sickie; you've always tried to lead by example. Besides he would want to know why.

There are brown marks in the toilet bowl, no bigger than fly spots but harder to shift. You wonder why you are the only person in the household who is capable of lifting a brush to slosh the bowl clean at the time. And you wonder if it was the pork pieces, since you couldn't remember how long they had been in the fridge. Your own bowels are fine – but now you remember that all you ate that particular night was a couple of cheese-flavoured crackers. You've had no appetite since *that* Friday.

Odd how, in one brief moment, a life can be tossed into the air and then land in a barely recognisable form; whisky and cask wine are now your primary caregivers; you can't imagine how you might get through the day without them. Food is an addiction you once had but certainly don't miss. You haven't yet tried, but it's very likely that already you would fit into the last pair of jeans you ever bought. From a factory shop in Marshlands Road – a pair for you and a pair for the youngest son, who still had a plaster cast on his leg, so he would have been eleven. Nine years ago.

There is always, you think as you run a wet cloth around the plastic seat, a plus, a silver lining.

You straighten the duvet on your bed and marvel at how smooth the sheets have remained, at how little impression is made when you sleep alone. Then you remember that you were only in bed for, at most, four hours. Unable to sleep, or read, or watch television, you got up and cleaned the pantry shelves. An exceptionally clean house is, surely, another plus. Not a large one.

You sit for a time on the bedroom chair that normally never gets used. Your mind drifts into a kind of sluggish backwater where nothing is going on, but outside time is passing at speed. This is a state your former self was unfamiliar with. From time to time you glance across at the mirror, hoping to catch your reflection unawares and see yourself as he sees you. You're waiting for your at-home son to leave for his course, so you can go out and humiliate yourself in a public street.

Of course you may not actually go, you may just intend to and leave it at that. But now you have a whole day for yourself and your home, like the food in your pantry, has lost all its attractions. Being there fills you with impatience.

Your son's door is closed. You knock and go in. The smell of unaired sheets and unwashed socks seems, suddenly, more stimulating, more *real*, than your own rituals with picked jasmine and old-fashioned roses. Your son is in bed with a comic book at the end of his nose. He is, surely, too old to be reading comic books. You tell him he'll ruin his eyesight. You're only aware that you've said this when you see him sigh and roll his eyes. Critical observations, you have to suppose, dribble constantly from your mouth without you knowing. You resemble a tap with a faulty washer.

'Your course,' you remind him.

'I told you. I've caught your bug.'

'I could give you a lift in.'

'I thought you were sick?'

'I am,' you say, 'but I've got things to do.'

You notice the way his shoulderblades jut and the creamy skin of his inner arm. You notice how even his freckles look brand new.

He is almost the same age as her. Crumpled sheet over pliant, peach-ripe flesh. That thought ignites inside you and explodes like a Double Happy.

Quickly – but not indifferently – you get yourself dressed. Leggings and the lemon shirt that covers your thighs. You decided on these last night before you gave up on trying to sleep and began on the pantry. You're aiming for a look that doesn't shout middle-aged yet is nonchalant. She must not have the satisfaction of thinking that you have been driven to a tragic attempt to compete with her at this level.

You're standing in front of a Christian bookshop. Directly across the road is the National School of Beauty Therapy. You look at the titles in the bookshop window – *Go the Distance, Timeless Treasures, Soul Management* – and wonder if she is a reader of books and, if so, what kind. You've never met a beauty therapist, let alone a beauty therapy student. When Greer heard what she did and sniggered it made you feel much better, but Greer, as your friend, is obliged to be totally unobjective.

The school opens at 10 a.m., but students are required to be there ten minutes before. You know all this because you rang the School of Beauty Therapy for details of their course, claiming a daughter with an interest in the field. Their brochure, when it arrived, made you glad that you had not, in your own youth, desired to be a beauty therapist. Students were required to wear uniforms, and the school rules took up two whole pages.

The brochure contained grievous grammatical errors, a fact that gave you unreasonable satisfaction.

You cross the road to stand just outside the entrance to the building that houses the beauty school. You are looking out for a young woman with blonde hair, neither short nor long. Shoulder length, you imagine. She is tall – exactly his height, which is five eleven – and slender and (naturally) beautiful. She may or may not be called Emily; your husband is protective of her. The less you know, the safer she is. Just what is it he imagines you might do to her?

You're not even certain about the National School of Beauty Therapy, except that Greer remembered seeing him one afternoon around four standing almost where you are standing now. Driving past, she'd tooted, but he'd failed to look her way. In retrospect, she found that significant.

You put this together with the one piece of information you felt certain of – the beautician training – and consulted the Yellow Pages. Bingo.

Twenty is the age you were when you got married. Twenty-two years and three sons ago. You weren't sure, at the time, if it was love or just fantastic sex. Only time, you thought, could tell.

Time said love. Emphatically. You only had to look at the relationships that other people put up with. At social events you would still gaze around with available eyes and choose him over everyone present. After twenty-two years and three sons the sex was perhaps less consuming than the need to have the lawn mowed, but there were compensations suited to your stage in life. Children, companionship, stability, affection.

You were lucky; you felt it in your bones, and other people told you so. Lucky, but not complacent. How could you be, when every year it got harder to think of anyone who hadn't split up and found someone new (not necessarily in that order). And then maybe split up again. In the midst of so much wreckage and turmoil how could anyone not know they were sailing in dangerous times, treacherous waters?

Perhaps that was why you'd got to feeling a little benumbed. Sometimes things in the books you read and the movies you saw (and you had more time to pursue these independent pleasures now that you and he were past the obsessional inter-dependency of earlier years) made you tremble, yearn or weep. Other people's passion would blow a draught of air on the charcoal embers of your own, causing a glow and a flicker, but never a great leaping explosion of flame. Yet you would remember, would *seem* to remember, holocaust, incandescence.

Sometimes you found yourself wanting to know how it would feel to split up.

Two young women cross the street, heading towards you. They wear tailored dark blue skirts and jackets. Air hostess uniforms, you think disparagingly; out-of-date, conservative, dreary. You wonder why and by whom they were chosen.

Both young women have dark hair. They enter the building, and wait in the foyer for the lift. You also enter the foyer and study the list of occupants on the marbled wall. The National School of Beauty Therapy is on the seventh floor, between a solicitor and the Alzheimers Society.

Four young women come in together, just in time to catch the lift. You barely get to look them over. Two are Asian, one is Maori or at least Polynesian, but the other is blonde – you try not to stare. She is no taller than you, and plump. They're holding the lift, waiting for you. Flustered, you smile and gesture them on their way.

You will watch the numbers for where the lift stops, just to be sure. Seven.

Classes at the National School of Beauty Therapy are, they told you, small, with twelve students at most.

A man in a suit enters; cell phone, briefcase, the works. You look towards the street as if you're expecting someone – which of course you are. You don't want a repeat of the lift-holding business.

Three more trainee beauty therapists scamper in giggling and rolling their eyes. For an irrational second you think that somehow they know who you are and why you are there, but as they jiggle and groan over the lift's slow arrival you realise that their laughter is the nervous kind, and concerns the repercussions of being late. A strawberry blonde, her hair in a ponytail. But she can't, surely, be twenty? And you couldn't say, even in kindness, that she was beautiful.

You walk back out the glass door and onto the street. The clock above the watch shop shows three minutes to ten. Either she arrives at class very early or she's running late. If she is late, why is she late? What has kept her?

Your husband has moved into Minka and Tom's sleepout in order to think things through. In other words, *to choose*. For the last eight days and nights, you conjecture, he has been writing out lists of pros and cons, comparing the demands of conscience and libido, and unsettling Tom with the irrepressible note of prize-winner pride that sneaks into his voice whenever he talks of her. So young. So lovely. So eager to please.

Is she, too, appalled by his indecision? He knows what he wants – he wants you both. An option she's grown accustomed to and is content to accept. You are the problem. Your refusal to be as accommodating.

You, too, have decisions to make and feel incapable of making them. You surely must understand, he pleads, that he is not in a state capable of thinking things through in a rational way. You concede the point – he looks exhausted. But when you consider what it is that has exhausted him you want to smash him around the head with something jagged and heavy. He was wise to move in with Minka and Tom. These rather exciting waves of insanity keep crashing upon you. You could be compelled to smother or strangle during the night.

You can't sleep, at most an hour here or there, yet you have an extraordinary supply of energy. He remarked, the day he moved out, on the amount of energy you had. He said that was his principal reason for going: he had a backlog of sleep to catch up on and you wouldn't leave him alone.

He told the resident son that he was taking a fishing trip up the Rakaia with Tom. You insisted the lie should come from his lips but, since you have to sustain the pretence, the lie is also yours. Yet you don't want to burden your son with something he may never need to know.

It feels necessary to keep this disaster contained, as if it's blood from a severed artery. The smaller the spread, the easier, quicker it is to mop up. At the same time you need to talk about it, because right now there is nothing else – absolutely nothing – that is of interest to you.

So Greer knows and has no doubt told Mick. And Tom and Minka, of course, know – have known, it seems, for quite some time. Which could mean that half your friends know, but are still pretending they don't. Minka has told you she felt terrible about it, but he was Tom's oldest friend and, well, these things happened. Had you noticed that she just couldn't look you in the face?

No, you hadn't. But you will never again see Minka's face without wanting to pummel it out of shape.

Fishing with Tom was what he'd claimed to have been doing on some of those nights. Then on Thursdays it was the Continuing Education class, Introduction to Western Philosophy. Turned out he'd only attended the first night and on the way home stopped off for a drink. That's when he met her, she was there with a friend. Outgoing, he's told you, and friendly the way that young women are nowadays.

That being so, you wish those young women would lavish some of their friendliness on your resident son, who seems in real need of it.

She said he had nice eyes. Or maybe that came later when she told him she liked married men: they were more together and didn't make too many demands. Also they had money. (He didn't tell you that bit; it's your own deduction made on a careful perusal of his credit card statement.)

'Don't blame her,' he said. 'She didn't *ask* me to spend money on her.'

That left you speechless. You could just see him sitting at that bar, a stupid ripe plum waiting to be picked.

She had a lifestyle to maintain. Her own flat and a late model car with eyelids. The beauty course was costing her twelve thousand dollars, and her wardrobe was full of fantastic clothes. She liked to have nice things, he said. You were trying to keep communications open, so you just bit down on your tongue.

She runs past you, late and breathless. The hair is pinned up with combs with a few strands trickled over her face so it's hard to gauge the length. You look at her face which has a wide-eyed Goldie Hawn prettiness, and you wait for some internal signal because after so many years you must surely know exactly what would attract him.

You can't be absolutely certain but she's probably the one. You follow her into the foyer and stand beside her, waiting for the lift. Your heart is crashing away in your chest. Is it possible that she knows what you look like? Who you are?

The lift doors open and you both step in. She presses button seven then looks at you questioningly, meets your eyes. The breath goes out of you and it takes several seconds before you realise she's waiting to know what floor.

'Eight,' you tell her. 'Thank you.' You recall that eight is the Alzheimers Society. Unusual encounters may be common-place in this elevator. *Talk to her*, you order yourself. *If it's not her you can gallop off in unrelated sentences*. But if it is?

Ask her anyway. *Are you Emily*? Go on, ask.

'You have nothing to say to her,' he's told you. 'I'm the one who betrayed you. It's me you should hate.'

But you don't hate him, how can you? You don't even hate this young woman standing beside you, not even when you consider what may have made her late for class and a six hundred-volt sensation, which three weeks ago you couldn't even have imagined, throws your heart into a higher gear.

At least, you tell yourself, she has good taste.

It's Minka you hate. Never, ever, will you forgive Minka.

You remind yourself about the credit statement – enough to have had the house repainted. This toughens you up.

You know exactly what you want to say to her, but there are only three floors to go.

What goes around comes around, you want to say. *Think about that. There's a kind of power in being young. All of us sense it at the time, though it's only in retrospect that we recognise it as power, and by then, of course, it has gone.*

Power has its responsibilities.

Let me paint you a picture. There's a man; he's attractive and flattered by your interest. You fancy each other. You discover he's also a great lover, kind to children and animals, and generous (you may wish to rearrange the order of importance). Despite your intentions you fall in love with him. He finds this irresistible and falls in love with you.

Everything is wonderful, except for his guilt. As I said before, this is a nice man. He felt bad enough when it was just an affair, but now that it's love he decides his wife must be told. Clearly there are decisions that need to be made. You discuss the options. He's besotted with you, ready to leave his home and family and move in with you. But that isn't quite what you had in mind. True, you'd like to spend more time with him, but not all your time. The advantage of married men is that they don't want to move in. You want the good times to continue and – you have eyes, you have parents, and you know there are lots of other women out there just like you – you know that co-habitation is a bad move.

You tell him to get a place of his own. It's a reasonable suggestion, but this is a man who likes to have a home and a garden and someone to feel his brow if he has a temperature. He hates the thought of living alone, or living with anyone other than you, or his wife and resident son, both of whom he is very fond of.

So, after much inner struggle in the sleepout, and drunken discussions with his best friend Tom, he decides he might stay with his wife, who these days has a rather exciting intensity.

So you and he have one last tragic, passionate night together, and he moves back home. And for a while it's like it was all those years ago, when they first got together. But as the wife's adrenalin level subsides and her husband sinks back, with a measure of relief, into normal life, they realise that things will never really be as they were all those years ago. Sour, unfamiliar emotions slide like bilge-water in her gut. Distrust, resentment, even dislike.

It takes maybe a couple of years. Possibly she meets someone else who has also been betrayed and they find they have much in common. The husband then goes looking for you, but you haven't even thought of him in months. You have someone else who may or may not be married.

Everything has fallen apart, you see. And maybe that's just life – or maybe it's a tragedy that could quite easily have been averted back on the day he first told you he was married.

You reach the seventh floor. The lift goes *ting* and the doors glide open. She walks out. You haven't said a word but it doesn't matter, at least now you have a face to hold in your mind.

You get out at the eighth floor, step straight into the reception area of the Alzheimers Society.

'Oops, wrong floor,' you mutter, embarrassed.

The lift is already on its way down. You can't wait here in the presence of this pleasant-faced woman who obviously has her life in order. You take the stairs – all the way down as penance for cowardliness. You almost run down those steps, suddenly light-headed, and part way down it comes to you that your life has reached a pinnacle. You are *up there* where the air is thin, and it's a heady, dizzy feeling. You're looking around and wondering which route will get you back down, and you suddenly realise you can't lose.

One route has you and him together and it's okay, it's better than okay and will stay that way despite her, or maybe even because of her. And the other route has you on your own, *starting again*. Which seems, all of a sudden, to be not so unthinkable. Even exciting. For you know now, having looked in her face – you can't explain it but you know – that he is the one who will be left with regrets.

It may not, of course, have been her at all. This thought returns just as you walk out of the building. At four o'clock you may have to come back and look again.

ROWAN METCALFE

The children's father came for them at 10.15.

'Are we going in Daddy's car today?' said the little one.

'Yes, c'mon, let's get your shoes on.'

'Are you coming, too?'

She was tying his laces. 'Not today,' she lied.

Not ever.

Charley said, 'Do you want to go up to the coast today?'

She looked out at the sky. 'Okay, let's,' she said. The clouds were stretching raggedly across the blue, thinning and shredding. She hung up the washing before they left, still the housewife. She took two chocolate bars from the fridge and two apples and let them roll around in the glove compartment. That apple will get bruised, said a voice. Fine, said another, I'll eat it bruised.

He put the radio on, she braced one leg comfortably against the dashboard. Charley's car had plenty of leg-room. And lie-back seats, for god's sake. She felt 17. Nobody in the back seat saying, 'Mum . . .' Charley took the narrow country roads with the happy abandon that men lose when their kids are strapped in the back. Her heart revved up as they approached the bends, her foot reached its own brake pedal before his did. The thick green foliage of May hung over the roadway, tall weeds and flowering grasses, the leaves fat in the hedges. Then they came out over the sea, its distant muddy dun tempered with a glimmer of verdigris, the North Sea. You could just make out a rig on the horizon. The square church towers of the coastal villages glimmered like ghosts on the pale air, like shadows, with no authority any more over the affairs of men, for whom Sunday is a drive in the car, a video from the hire shop. Soon they would start to crumble, the lovely towers and naves, they would sink into history like the temples of other ages, overgrown with ivy, and grasses, the collection plates finally empty.

Charley spotted the pub as they drove into the village. He always did. She'd started doing it, too. It was a pretty one, painted pink, up on a little green mound, with tables on the grass. The Bell. They took the potholed side road arrowed BEACH, passed the Pay and Display and parked on a littered stretch of verge near a sign that said PRIVATE PARKING. You could hear the sea roaring at the foot of the cliffs. She felt as light as a kite, the wind pulling at her excitedly. She'd liked the way it felt to walk beside a new man, finding out whether you could get comfortable or not, whether your strides were too out of synch, whether your arm would go neatly round his waist or hips. Charley wasn't really a new man any more. He was okay comfortable, he had a good feeling about him, solid, but vulnerable. He had a long, slightly bent stride like a cowboy, which matched the Cuban-heeled boots he wore and a motorcycle jacket a little too short for his long torso. He cut his own hair, short and brushed back on top, long at the back like an 18th-century rogue; it was soft and blond. He'd told her the other day that he'd originally wanted to be a patissier. A patissier. This information pierced her to the heart. A strange hot centre burned in her for a moment. She imagined him naked, dredged in icing sugar. Sweetie.

They went down the lifeboat slipway onto the beach. At the bottom there were long rows of sea defences made of great slabs of weathered grey wood. Her soles longed for them, and for the sand, silver blond, and she kicked off her sandals. They walked along the shore a way, pebbles stippled the damp sand under foot, there wasn't too much rubbish here, not too much plastic and oil. They broke contact and walked unconnected, in silence. She knew they were both thinking the same thoughts, heads down, jackets slung over their shoulders. You could just walk, nobody said, 'Mum . . .'

The sea poured onto the land, its swell and potency subdued by the long wooden groins that went out into the waves. Swells that promised breakers a hundred yards out were broken up and came in like lambs to her feet, a few white twists of spume leaping over their backs. Now and then she looked up at him again, thinking his name. Charley. It wasn't even his real name, he'd made it up for himself. She'd got used to it, it was easy to say now, in spite of its old-fashioned oddness. She couldn't think there'd ever be another Charley in her life. He'd be the only one. So she wanted to remember him, his profile against the clouds, the tender blond snarls of his hair across his shoulders. She could love him like that forever. The patissier. Cigarette smoke streaming back in the wind.

Her feet seemed so insubstantial in the sand, in its soft, tickling flesh. She realised how much she'd been wanting to walk on the sand. Ever since last summer, when she and the children and their father had still been a family. There was nobody much around today. Sunday dinner time, of course. She had the two chocolate bars in her bag. It was Charley who'd buy chocolate bars by the dozen and stash them in the fridge. And drink milk from the bottle standing by the open door. The sight of him drinking milk from the bottle brought her a deep, inexplicable satisfaction. She loved the way he went to her breasts, directly and greedily, without reverence, a famished angel. She longed to assuage his hunger, she had given herself generously, he had taken her without ceremony. Even Stevens. But it would not be enough. They both knew it would not be enough. Maybe it was the milk and the steak and chocolate bars and his taste for bottled salad cream, all food for growing boys, that told her it would not be enough. Not to mention the booze. She sensed his hunger was for something she was unable to supply.

He had been raised by his German grandmother. She was dead now, but she could feel his grandmother in him, the gifts she had given. Sometimes he looked at her with the mischievous blue eyes of a boy and she *was* his grandmother. She was grateful for that unknown woman's love, like a legacy passed from woman to woman for safekeeping. His grandmother had lived through two World Wars. He carried those things, too, the small dark shadows of events that happened long before he was born. She loved those things in him. But it still would not be enough.

They chose a spot under the cliffs, a bit sheltered from the wind that streamed ceaselessly along the shore. There was an ancient black trainer in the sand, swollen and distorted with its tongue protruding like the corpse of a minor sea monster. She picked it up and flung it as far as she could down the beach. A strip of weathered plastic, too, she tossed away on the wind, to get it out of her sight. He lit her a cigarette and they leaned up shoulder to shoulder, smoking. The longing and uncertainty made her heart ache. She sensed his restlessness, he knew he wasn't right for her. 'The sea's always so dirty here,' he said. 'It stinks.'

'It's the world's biggest sewer,' she said. Soon nobody would come to the beach to bathe, the children would be called back anxiously from the waves lest they catch the diseases that would teem in the brine. A dirty place.

Sometimes the world was too sad. Even sex, you couldn't do it any more without first purchasing a piece of rubber. The soft kiss of flesh to flesh was forbidden now.

But the clouds were finally tearing apart. She sighed and lay back on her jacket, feeling the gentle touch of the sun along her arms, grains of sand, strands of hair fanning across her cheek. If she let go and relaxed she could feel the lightness of it all, life bearing her up, holding her, the beach like the cool skin of the world letting her rest on it, as light as a thistle seed on a bubble. *If you let go, don't thrash around, don't panic, then life will hold you up,* she told herself.

He was restless beside her. 'Let's go and have a drink,' he said.

She felt the sun quietly holding her. 'No,' she said. 'I want to lie here a bit longer. It's nice, the sun's coming out.'

'Well I'm going for a drink.'

'You go. I'll wait here.'

She sensed his unwillingness. He wanted her with him, across the table or up against the bar, sharing the booze with him, companionable and easy. It was nice, calming, after the fraught tensions of her dissolving marriage. They'd been in a lot of bars together in the last few weeks, come out leaning on each other, hands all over each other. The drink always stirred her heart with the pleasure of him, the changing expressions of his blue eyes, the shape of his big hands, the texture of his hair, until the pleasures were almost pain. In bed his ferocious hunger came up like a wave to consume her. The boy in him vanished, with his body he would pay her back for every hurt women have ever inflicted on men. She loved him for it. But it would not be enough. The things you love can become the things you hate. She'd learnt that.

'You go,' she said again. 'Bring me a can of something. Cider.'

He got up to go but she knew he was still waiting for her to change her mind. He picked up a chunk of crumbled cliff face and broke it in his hands, his cigarette held between his lips, brow furrowed. She knew as a boy he'd looked for fossils. He wouldn't find any here. He picked up a few more pieces, tossed them back against the cliff, where they broke with a light thud. She closed her eyes again and waited for him to go.

He didn't ask her again, and she felt that pang of regret that accompanies every choice. When he was 20 yards away she called out, 'Don't be long.' A moment of weakness.

He looked back over his shoulder at her. 'As long as it takes,' he said.

She watched him for a while, until he was too far for her to catch up without losing her dignity. She saw him stop by an old World War II pillbox that had fallen down the cliff decades ago and landed upside down on the sand. She knew he'd go inside, like boys will.

When she opened her eyes again he was still in sight, his arms swinging loosely from his big shoulders, his back resolute. He wouldn't look back, she knew, but just in case she stayed lying down. Not until she judged he would be nearly at the slipway to the car park did she prop herself up on her elbows to watch him vanish. You could make out his tall figure, his distinctive gait, from miles away. She liked to be with a man you could see coming. And going. The air glimmered around him now, he seemed to be floating a little above the sand. A patissier. It was so unlikely, a man like him crimping pastry. It filled her with love. When he got halfway up the slipway, she saw him turn at last and look back. She raised her arm and waved. Had he expected to see her coming after him, she wondered, a woman following her man? Then he was gone.

She let herself float. The clouds passed and repassed overhead, split with afternoon sunlight. The waves ran along her spine like the long breathing of history, *sigh*, and she could hear the Vikings roaring in on the North Sea breakers, *sigh*, and the tumult of the battle crowds on bloodied fields coursing through her veins, *sigh*, and the song of the mother's blood, breathing in, breathing out, breathing in, breathing out.

She remembered the births of her babies, the girl first, then the boy, like mermaids sprouting from her body, the girl trussed in her red silken cord, as self-contained as a kewpie doll, the boy sticking his head out first, spouting water from his mouth, his red forehead screwed tight with an ancient concentration. The birth of a man. It amazed her that such a creature could come out of her, the next link in that unbroken chain of men, pursuing forever their dangerous dreams, generation after generation. To have come out of her. And so beautiful, a child as god would have intended, so utterly perfect that when she looked into his eyes, which were darker reflections of her own, she felt a pang of love for the man she had created, for the dangers he would draw down, for his reckless energy, for the great heart she knew he would have if she loved him enough.

The waves ran along her spine, tickling, like grass or young corn in the wind. She smelled her childhood, salt and sweet, the tingle of juicy sap in her shooting limbs, open space revelling in her presence, horizons lifting to welcome her. The world would be different for her children. The horizons full of houses and the distant glitter of traffic. The open spaces more polluted. The ordinary miracles cramped into a darker space. If only you could pull some cord, *halt here*. But there isn't one. You go on. Her marriage was gone now, well and truly gone. The promise was broken. So much the better. It was a hopeless promise.

She let the waves run along her spine. They touched her like lovers' hands. They were always there, they never ceased, day or night. They could roll over grief and heartache, grinding them like pebbles to sand, and over ecstasy, too, like foam flung up on the foreshore.

She wondered if he would really come back. Maybe he was the sort of man who could walk away like that, get in his car and go, if he felt he wasn't wanted. It was possible. Then she'd have to hitchhike home, she mused. If someone asked why, she'd say her boyfriend had left her at the beach. If they asked if they'd had a row, she'd say, No, it was a change of heart.

The sun warmed her, just enough; she arranged her jacket to protect her better from the wind. *If you let yourself float, life will hold you up.* She let the waves run along her spine. She could almost hope he wouldn't come back.

He said, 'Boo!' and laughed at the way she jumped and went for him. It was the blue-eyed boy she loved so much. She pushed him backwards into the sand, watching out for his long legs.

'Where's my cider?' she asked.

'I forgot,' he said. He wasn't at all contrite. She liked that. 'But I brought your apple,' he said, taking it out of his pocket.

'All right,' she said, accepting it.

He looked in her bag for the chocolate bars.

'I ate them both,' she teased him.

He grinned when he found them at the bottom and held one up in triumph. He sat down beside her and tore open the wrapper. With the same tear he employed on a condom packet, she couldn't help noticing.

She rolled the bruised apple in her hands, gently, as if she could heal it, round and round, over and over.

At last he said, 'I'm going to go back to Spain after all.'

She looked sideways at him. He meant it, she could see it on his forehead, his eyebrows. 'That's good,' she said. She felt a sigh run through her heart, she felt it break into the corners of her flesh, her fingers, her toes. He glanced at her and their eyes caught for just long enough. 'I'm glad.'

The tide of her gladness pressed at her every limit. She bit into the bruised apple and in a flood of gold the flavour burst on her palate.

At my father's funeral an old man in a crumpled black suit gets up to speak. He rises slowly on old man's legs from among the dark suits and neatly combed heads, murmuring apologies for flattened toes and kicked handbags.

For a moment I think that he is my father. The same old man's shuffling walk. But then I see that, no, they are different people. This man's nose is larger, more Roman.

It's a good turn out. Better than I would have thought for a man as quiet and solitary as my father.

I close my eyes and see him coming towards me, walking as he always did, stiffly, head down, shoulders hunched over as though moving into a strong wind. By the time I was 10 my father was already an old man, slow and careful in his movements. No cricket on the back lawn or kicks with the football down at the park.

I dread the awkward silence that always hovers near us. Soon I will begin to talk about the rugby or the latest rates increase although I don't care about either, and then inevitably, hating the cliché, I will work my way around to the rainy spell we've had lately. What does he think, will it be a hard winter?

I open my eyes and my father vanishes.

Someone has forgotten to turn the heating on. The church is a meat-locker despite the sunlight coming through the stained glass window behind the coffin. I stare at the colours on the pale carpet where the filtered light spreads like spilt fizzy drink – Fanta, Mellow-Yellow, Raspberry, Lemon-Lime.

Several people have already spoken. My father's boss from the insurance office said a few words. He took a piece of paper, smoothed it with fat, sweaty fingers and, head down, mumbled into the microphone. From the front row, I stared at his waist where the black suit bulged out over his belt.

'A sad day for family and friends sorely missed a diligent worker cared about his job in 30 years never a complaint punctual a good provider a great loss our condolences to Helen and Greg.'

The old man in the crumpled suit moves slowly across in front of me. He wades into the pool of spilt drink which splashes up over his black shoes and half-way up his legs, taps the microphone with a thin finger. From the front row I can see that there are dark spots on the back of his hands. Surprisingly, he seems to change his mind about the microphone and steps around in front of it.

'I hope you can hear me. Never liked these things much.' His voice is deeper and stronger than I had expected. It's an actor's voice or someone who's used to telling a good yarn. A younger man's voice.

Out of the corner of my eye I think that I see my father shuffling forward to listen, shoulders stooped. But when I turn my head there is nothing. A thick drape stirred by a draught in a shadowy corner.

'I don't expect many of you know me. My name's Reginald Black but Ray used to call me Blacky and after that most other people did too. I was Ray's best mate right through from when we were about 16 to when I moved up to Napier. That was when I was 25. A fair few years ago now. We used to play rugby together on a Saturday for Brighton and we'd go to the local afterwards for a few beers. On a Friday night we'd drive to the dances in town hoping to meet a couple of girls who wouldn't mind going for a ride in Ray's car after it was all over. Most weeks we'd find a couple who were game.'

And then, amazingly, he winks, a slow old man's wink and he's looking right at me when he does it. A few people laugh nervously, unsure if this is the type of talk suitable for a funeral. The old man's skin is very brown and I have a sudden image of him down on his knees digging in rich black soil, a tomato plant in his dirt-caked hand.

Out of the corner of my eye I noticed my father shuffle forward again. I don't turn to look this time and he remains there in the corner, listening.

'But what I mostly remember about Ray is the time he carried the dead boy home.' I look up, not sure if I have heard the old man correctly.

'We were both still living with our parents then. We must have been about 20 or so. We lived down by the beach and Ray was building a small sail-boat in the shed out the back. Nothing fancy. Just something to potter around in on weekends and sometimes I'd go over and give a hand. We'd take the frame out and put it on a couple of saw horses. It was good working outside like that. Ray's parents' house backed on to a reserve down by the estuary. Big pine trees kept the wind off and we could hear the surf as we worked if the wind was right.

'This particular day, I remember it was hot and Ray wasn't wearing a shirt. He was brown and covered in sweat and sawdust from the work. As we sanded down the hull, we'd seen a couple of kids playing in the reserve, running in and out of the trees, shouting and laughing, playing cops and robbers or such like. One of them was Trevor O'Brien. His mother lived two doors down from Ray. They had a dog with them.

'Then after a while we heard the dog barking. The barking went on and on and not like when the kids were playing near us either. The dog was pretty good then. It was a strange barking, all high and excited like it had treed a possum or maybe gotten itself tangled up in a fence. After a bit of that, Ray and me looked at each other and I remember Ray said something like, "Let's go and have a look, eh?"

'It was cold in the shade of the pines after being in the sun. There was no undergrowth, just a thick mat of brown pine needles on the ground. We walked at first, a good excuse for a break, but as the dog's barks got louder Ray started running. I don't know why. I never asked. He just started running. Ray went up a trail between the lupins and I lost sight of him in the sandhills. I followed and came to a clearing with walls of sand all around. Not the sloping, dry white sand that you get down by the water but a harder mixture of sand and earth and clay that made steeper walls. It had been raining a bit that week and the sand was wet and dark. All around the top, lupins blocked out the sun. It was like being in a pit. The dog was over in one corner whimpering and digging in the sand.

'By the time I arrived, Ray was down on his knees with his back to me and he was digging too. "What's happening? What's going on?" You see, even then, I still didn't understand. But when I got close enough to see properly I understood all right. Sticking out of the sand was a kid's foot and part of his leg. Trevor O'Brien and his cobber had gotten bored with cops and robbers so they'd dug a tunnel into the hard sand. They'd dug a pretty good tunnel too, big enough for them to both crawl inside. There was a good sized pile of sand where Ray was kneeling so I reckoned they'd dug back a fair ways. A great little tunnel. Until it collapsed in on top of them.

'Ray grabbed the kid's leg and pulled. He was a big bloke, big, broad shoulders and back. With Ray's pulling, that kid came out of the sand like a cork coming out of a bottle. It was Trevor's friend. Ray never even looked at him. He just handed him to me, like a sack of potatoes. "Get him to my place. Get a doctor." And then he was down on his knees again, digging.

'A 10 year old kid weighs a fair bit but I ran with him bouncing up and down on my shoulder all the way to the house. Ray's mum had been a nurse during the war and she knew what to do, although she got a hell of a surprise when I crashed through her kitchen door. I watched, sucking down air in great gulps, as she cleared the sand out of the kid's mouth and then she blew into him. He was lying on the kitchen table. I watched his chest rise up with every blow that Ray's mum put into him. When the doctor finally arrived I didn't wait to see what happened. I ran back through the trees to Ray.

'He was still digging. He'd had the idea of digging down from above on more of an angle. The sand was wetter higher up from the rain and didn't cave in so easy, plus the roots of the lupins held it together more. He'd dug enough so that only his legs from the knees down still showed. I hollered at him that I was there and he yelled back for me to help move the sand piling up in the entrance to his tunnel. He was pushing it back between his legs and I grabbed the sand and flung it away until my shoulders ached but no matter how much sand I moved Ray always pushed out more. After a while not even his feet showed and I had to lean right into the tunnel to scoop out the sand.

'A long time after, I heard Ray shout something I didn't understand and he pushed out more sand and then he began backing out of the hole.

I grabbed his legs and pulled. Ray was dragging the kid by the shoulders but as soon as I saw him, I knew that Trevor was dead. Mostly from his eyes. They were half open and the eyeballs were covered in sand and some ran out from his nose and the corners of his mouth.

'Ray was gasping from the digging, but he held the dead boy in front of him like a baby and began to run. I ran along behind but even with the kid, Ray was faster than me. He fair flew between the trees. I remember that his feet flicked up dry pine needles as he passed. The dog ran behind, barking.'

The old man pauses and looks out over the people. Out of the corner of my eye my father moves again, shuffling away. He's heard enough.

'I was right. Trevor O'Brien was dead. As near as I can figure it, he was under the sand for half an hour. We went to the funeral. Mrs O'Brien's husband had died of a heart attack a few years before and she only had the one child so she took it badly. Ray took it pretty hard too; that he hadn't saved them both.

'Well, I reckon that's all I want to say. After I moved to Napier we lost touch. Neither of us were great letter writers but Ray was a good mate, a good person. For years after, he'd visit Mrs O'Brien, help her with repairs around the house and gardening and such. And, you know, when he was digging that tunnel all I could think about was that it was going to cave in like the other one and then Ray would be dead too. But when I asked him about it after, he said he hadn't even thought about that. He was just thinking about the boy.'

Stepping off the carpet the old man begins the long walk up the aisle. His walking stick clicks and clatters on the stone floor. As he passes me he turns his head and nods. His eyes are the same shade of blue as my father's.

After the echo of the final hymn has faded from the rafters, I help to carry my father's coffin up the aisle. It slides easily into the waiting hearse. A small river runs by the church and as we wait for someone to bring around the car, I walk away over the lawn and down to the water.

Looking across to the opposite bank I see a young man with blond, wavy hair standing under a tree. He is not wearing a shirt and the reflection of the light off the water plays over his tanned body. He is sweating and damp sand clings to his skin in patches.

In his arms he holds a dead boy. He cradles him gently as though the boy weighs nothing, a baby. The young man looks at me for a long moment, and then smiles gently, happy to be alive and young.

Turning, he begins to run. He runs along the river bank, smooth and easy despite the boy in his arms. His feet kick up dry pine needles as he passes.

I watch until my father disappears between the tall trunks of the pine trees.

They lived in small wooden houses in the vast suburb that stretches from the harbour to the ocean. Their kitchens smelt of gas, of sheepmeat and of tea. They kept bowls of mutton fat in the meat safe with some curly bacon. Tea leaves accumulated in a colander in the sink. On the bench a dish cloth slept coiled like a small grey animal. Under the sink were shelves behind a curtain on a wire. There were mousetraps and a wire shaker with a piece of yellow soap.

The kitchen table was covered with patterned contact plastic, turning up at the corners. Cups hung on hooks and were stained with tea. There were biscuits in a Coronation tin, sometimes stale sandy cake with pink icing.

The front rooms were cold and cluttered with china ornaments. Surfaces were adorned with doilies and embroidered cloths. There was always a mirror above the mantelpiece, plastic flowers and wedding photos. A fire was blocked off but soot persisted. A two-bar heater sat in the hearth, awaiting illumination.

Their bedrooms were modest and smelt of face powder. Saintly faces looked down on their beds, where folded eiderdowns promised comfort. At the windows hung nylon curtains and roller blinds, as well as drapes. No expense was spared to exclude the light and the eyes of strangers.

The front gardens were minimal because the street en-croached. There were dahlias, hydrangeas and arum lilies. There was grass in the back yard, washing lines hung with cheesecloth and tea towels, a vegetable garden with silver beet and dead beans, tin fences, forty-four-gallon drums.

The streets received the northeasterly, a wind of the ocean, cold and salty. It drove before it a sheet of misty rain, sweeping away the discarded fish-and-chip parcels and cigarette packets, and the small piles of dust and leaf litter that They had brushed into the gutter.

At certain times of day the streets were busy. Children dawdled, picking the flowers that poked through fences and singing their times tables. The children never grew up. From time to time they would leave behind a small glove, which they did not retrieve in spite of its being impaled on a picket as a sign.

High-school boys walked five abreast, shouting fuck and pushing one another into the gutter. At any time of day they seemed drunk on their hormones. But they passed, always having somewhere else to go.

Mothers herded their children along the narrow footpath. Their voices rang out. Don't touch that, Jimmy. Dirty. Put it down. Ugh. Don't run. Wait. Jesus, they said to one another. It wasn't even morning-tea time.

Men passed at predictable times. Some were gentlemen and raised their hats. Others chewed on cigarettes and averted their eyes, concentrating on a short inventory of animal pleasures that could not be taken from them. They spat sometimes to show their contempt for the street, and the earth and their subjugation.

This was where They had lived all their lives. This suburb, this street, this house. From behind their net curtains They saw men spit and dogs urinate. Wind and rain would flush the street of body fluids and carry off the cries of mothers. They knew the futility of protest, the inevitability of conformity. Here death wrought the only changes.

On Friday They went up the street to get the messages. At the butcher's They got a lovely piece of hogget for Sunday. Mr Thomas gave them cheek. They called him a hard case. They met Mrs B. She said Doris was going into the Mater to have the operation. They said give our regards to Doris, tell her we were asking after her. They shook their heads. They didn't like the sound of it.

Whenever possible They went to funerals. They said he was a good age. They said he had a good send-off. It was a good turnout.

They went to church on Sunday. They were glad if it was Father Jack. They had a lot of time for Father Jack. They said he was a good sort, he was a godsend. God bless him. Father Culling was all right, but he was too young.

After church They made a pot of tea. They put on the tea cosy. They took milk. They took sugar. They had a smoke. They talked.

They said let her stew in her own juice. They said you can't have your cake and eat it. They said it would break your heart. Give them an inch, They said, and before you can say Jack Robinson . . .

They had had a good laugh. It did them good.

They had had a flutter. They liked a flutter. Now and again.

No harm done. No luck, though. They had no luck.

The talk stopped. They drew on their cigarettes. They looked past each other and the walls of the kitchen where rot was setting in. The calendar showed a kitten. It always did.

They drained their cups and picked the tea leaves off their tongues. They picked the strands of tobacco off their tongues. They felt their tongues for places where cancers might grow. They stubbed out their cigarettes, and nothing held Them any more. Their hands rested on the edges of the table. The pattern on the contact was of kitchen things: patty cakes, teapots and onions. It was curling up at the edges and there were toast crumbs sticking to it.

They were looking down on it, on the ashtray and the cups and the cosy teapot. They could see the fly-spotted light shade and the cobwebbed cord. They were lighter than air and They bobbed about under the ceiling. If the window or door had been open, They might have been drawn outside and floated away on the northeasterly, over the densely populated suburb and the racecourse, and out to sea, their frocks hugging their short thick bodies, their cardigans flapping.

Just as well.

They floated down. Their cigarettes still smouldered in the ashtray. Somehow their hands still rested on the tabletop.

Down to earth, They said.

Mind you, They said, it takes the weight off your feet.

But. Even so.

How heavy their legs seemed now, bloated with fluid. They were getting old. They took off their shoes and put on slippers.

No time like the present, They said.

He drove a Jeep Commando with 'Jeep' written on the driver's door in case he mistook it for one of his other three vehicles. He drove you to distraction. His wife drove an Alfa bought with family money. She drove over your Yamaha 50 when she reversed out of the drive one day and after that you had to bus everywhere so you had an excuse to hate her.

His name was Dante. Dante Zuckerman. Later Bruce would call him Schmuckerman but it was only you who thought of the Inferno. As the jeep scorched out of the cul-de-sac every morning, you felt your stomach burning. You pretended it was the hair-dryer that had made your face hot.

Bruce's name was Bruce. He drove a ute. You'd never understood why car yards were always so full on Sunday afternoons but now you realised. People were using their spare time to paw over their own identities. After this became clear, you secretly started calling Bruce's ute The Utility Vehicle. It seemed more appropriate, the way you were feeling about him.

Zuckerman hadn't talked to you until his wife added an hour's commuting time on to your day. So you had that to thank her for at least. He turned up on your landing at 7 pm and produced an American apology, ie his wallet. He gave you some dollars for a new tyre. Except he was American, so you guessed he thought it was for a 'tire'.

Linda hadn't realised until she saw the scratches on her paintwork, he told you.

Sure, you told him, though you'd seen her stick her head out the window, pull it back in, and Alfa away. She was his wife after all, you didn't want to alienate him right off, so you went back inside and calmed yourself by scoring imaginary scratches on her painted face.

Bruce despised both of them immediately. His disapproval of Americans was based on three hours in the transit lounge at LA airport. Dante and Linda didn't stand a chance. You saw his dislike stemming from the fact that Dante had self-made muscles and Linda had had cosmetic surgery.

He could see the scars joining her ear to her jaw, Bruce told you.

Welcome to the real world, you felt like telling him. You contented yourself with agreeing that Linda was a vain bitch but you looked at his trainers and homespun socks and felt like telling him that vanity wasn't always a bad thing.

They're all the same over there, he told you.

His stance seemed a bit hypocritical, you thought, since his entire career was founded on copying nature's methods. The only difference (as far as you could see) was that he did it with molecules instead of with a scalpel.

How had you ended up with a material scientist whose mission was to revolutionise the field of angioplasty? (You were a pharmacist, so you supposed you'd admired this ambition at one stage.) Sometimes he talked in the middle of the night about what he called a Roto-Rooter. The second or third time you heard this you realised it was nothing to do with sex, it was about planting some miniature robot into people's blood vessels, and so you rolled over and left him to it.

Bruce carried a photocopied scientific article with him at all times. Dante carried a cell phone. Linda carried an attitude. You carried heavy shopping bags home hoping that a jeep instead of a ute would stop and pick you up.

Your first break came two weeks after the Zuckermans arrived in your building. You looked out from behind the venetians and there was Dante in his running clothes, warming down, talking on his mobile, and listening to his walkman. You'd already observed that he'd imported the American compulsion to do three things at once. You'd observed that he ran like a god. Through your striped line of vision, you saw him power to the lobby door. You saw him try the door, hit the door, kick the door.

Linda had forgotten to leave the key out, he said.

Too bad, you said, thanking God for human inadequacy.

He bounded up the stairs to his apartment door. You waited, hardly breathing.

And she'd locked the apartment door too, he said.

He descended to your level like an angel. You didn't have to offer, he just assumed. He wasn't the type to hang around on landings.

Inside your apartment he wanted water but not when he found it was out of the tap. You had orange juice but it wasn't 100 per cent.

This wasn't America, he commented.

Sorry, you said, and you were.

He took a beer instead and talked about provincialism and parochialism. You couldn't think of any long words beginning with P so you were silent.

Thank God it was the age of air travel, he said.

You'd only ever been as far as Napier so didn't feel you could comment. All you could think of was that he looked like an ad for Budweiser but you didn't think you should say that.

Didn't you want to leave New Zealand? he said to you.

All you could think of was that you never wanted to leave the kitchen but you didn't think you should say that.

How long was he out here for? you managed.

Six months, he said.

How long had they been married? you tried.

Six months, he said.

And he lived at number sixty-six! you said inanely.

So? he said.

So many sixes, you babbled.

Huh? he said.

Nothing, you said.

When Bruce walked in with his article sticking out of his back pocket you were sweating. You needed a shower way more than Zuckerman, who wasn't sweating at all. Instead of making for the bathroom, you made introductions.

When Bruce heard that Dante was a scientist, his hand went to his back pocket in a friendly gesture. When he heard Dante was a seismologist, he abandoned his article and his arms folded. You'd been reading a body-language book lately but you'd known that one forever and it wasn't good.

Dante put his foot up on a chair, Bruce's shoulders went back. The atmosphere in the kitchen became less like a locker-room, more like a boxing ring.

Would Bruce join him in a beer? Dante said.

Dante happened to be drinking the last one, Bruce said.

You'd never been glad before to hear the Alfa engine. You'd never been so pissed off with Bruce as after Dante left.

Why the pit-bull impersonation, you asked him.

Seismology wasn't a science, Bruce told you. He put his safety glasses on which meant he wasn't going to talk any more.

You went and looked up seismology in the dictionary, just to be sure, and then you looked up fault lines on the Internet. You learned only good things.

You were happy that Wellington was on a major fault line. You were appalled that you were happy that your entire city could collapse any day now.

Now you realised why the earth moved when Dante walked.

After a month Dante and Linda asked you and Bruce to dinner. After the phone call you had to walk around the hall smoothing your hair and face before you could go and tell Bruce.

Actually you couldn't see why they'd invited you, unless they needed some diversion from New Zealand TV. Bruce couldn't see why either: why did he have to go. He sat in front of a documentary all afternoon and drew aggressive molecules on paper; you went upstairs and put an aubergine rinse through your hair.

Dante served aubergine. Linda wasn't helping with the cooking, she just sat and drank multiple Martinis. You thought she kept out of hot kitchens so her beauty wouldn't melt, but she said she was a caterer.

So she never cooked at home, she said.

Too tired? said Bruce.

Too boring, said Linda.

Too bad, said Dante, raising his eyebrows at you.

Everything about Linda was glossy. She looked as if she'd bought her exterior with one cheque, which corroborated Bruce's conspiracy theory about American cosmetic companies. She looked a lot better being a conspiracy victim than Bruce did knowing about it, though.

After the first course Bruce mounted his attack. He started so disarmingly that even you, experienced in Bruce tactics, didn't notice the launching of his stealth bomber from behind the Californian white.

So where exactly was Zuckerman from, he said.

UC Berkeley, Dante said.

You were extremely impressed. Bruce wasn't, though he guessed it was as good a place as any.

California, man, what better place for earthquake engineering? said Dante.

It didn't seem to matter with such a random 'science', Bruce said. His inverted commas were so masterful that you had to respect him in spite of your hatred for war-games.

Spoken like a true layperson, said Dante.

Millions of federal funding wasted every year, said Bruce.

Wasted? said Dante.

Just to reduce the 'potential' cost of 'possible' quakes! said Bruce.

What exactly was he getting at? said Dante.

At this point you tried for an intelligent placatory comment about the Richter scale. You were ignored.

Irony, said Bruce.

Care to illustrate? said Dante.

Bruce's eyes gleamed. You knew his belief that Americans were incapable of irony had just been confirmed.

Like the vulcanologists estimating a point-01 risk factor the day

Ruapehu erupted, he illustrated for Dante.

Maybe New Zealand scientists were crap, Dante said pleasantly.

Maybe he was using a local example to show up an internationally ludicrous discipline, said Bruce unpleasantly.

Did Bruce mean Dante's discipline was crap, Dante asked.

Yes, unfortunately he did, Bruce told Dante.

Well Bruce could go fuck himself, Dante told Bruce.

Bruce went silent, Linda went to the toilet. You went to the kitchen for water. Dante went after you.

Did he ever loosen up? Dante asked you.

You wanted to be honest and you wanted to please. For once your aims were compatible.

Not really, you said.

Dante put a cube of ice down your neck.

You needed a new scientist, he said.

Linda came in while you were groping down your back. You stopped and the ice slid to your arse.

Was her husband boring you with *New Scientist* talk? she asked.

Yes, issue number 666, Dante said.

Against the wall, his hair stood up in sexy horns. Linda yawned.

Bruce had gone home, she said, and she was going to bed because she had a cocktail party to cater the next day.

She catered for all his needs, Dante told her.

After she'd left the kitchen he stuck his tongue in your ear. Then he told you your hair looked great and walked you to the door. You reeled down the stairs to your flat and found Bruce in bed reading the packet for your hair dye.

Did you know what was in this, he asked you.

No, and you didn't care, you said.

It was unbelievable that corporations could charge people to poison themselves, he said.

Choosing a silent rebellion, you went to the bathroom and got out a packet of Dylon. When Bruce came in for a piss, you were lying against the bath painting your eyelashes blue velvet.

What the fuck? he said to you.

He snatched the packet up and read out a string of chemicals. You couldn't tell where one word ended and the next word started but to tell the truth you were more interested in getting an even coat.

Did you have any idea what this stuff could do to you? he asked.

Hopefully it would make you look a bit less myopic, you said.

Those chemicals were restricted in the lab, he told you.

Really, you said politely.

They could blind you, he said.

Yes but could he help you get the little corner lashes? you asked him.

That was it, you were fucked in the head, he told you.

He marched off to bed, you lay against the bath. You didn't know if you were fucked in the head but you knew you were headed for trouble. Also your eyes were stinging a bit.

After this you didn't see the Zuckermans for two weeks. You waved to Dante, you smiled distantly at Linda, you waved and smiled distantly at Bruce when you encountered him in bed. You were busy laying in earthquake supplies – candles, torches, tinned beetroot – though you wondered if you'd find them anyway in what would be the wreckage of your home.

Because your quake preparations were inspired by Dante, they seemed like a direct criticism of Bruce so you had to stop talking to him. Which seemed to be what he wanted anyway. Despite the widening gulf between you, the earth stayed reasonably steady.

The day it happened, you'd borrowed Bruce's bike because you were sick of sweaty bodies on the bus. Apart from wanting her car and her husband, you didn't particularly want to be like Linda, but riding your bike down the hill reminded you of the way she glided through life. And it wasn't bad.

You'd worked late (because of poverty rather than altruism), the street was empty, the sun was in your eyes. You took your hands off the handlebars to open your packet of pretzels. You ate, you glided, you enjoyed the combination of speed and carbohydrates. You hit the edge of the gutter.

You were lying there with crumbs smashed into your face when you heard an engine. Of course it was the jeep. You continued to lie, hoping you were covered by a lengthening shadow, but apparently you weren't.

Sesame seeds impeded your vision but you thought he was smiling.

Were you okay? he asked you.

You weren't, because he was there and you had pretzel ground into your chin. But you thought he'd probably witnessed quake victims with missing limbs so you said you were fine.

Should he call Bruce? he asked you.

You didn't want him to call, ring, or contact Bruce in any way, because every time you borrowed the bike Bruce told you not to ride with no hands.

Dante didn't look at all surprised that you didn't want Bruce. He loaded you into the Commando with one arm and threw the bike in the back with the other. You, he, and Bruce's bike went to the nearest pub, where he ordered vodkas and you ran to the toilet to exact damage control. There were still a million crumbs in your fringe but none in your blue-velvet eyelashes. When you got back to the bar you talked about nothing you could remember.

Dante bought two more rounds. Bruce always made a point of meticulously alternating. Dante ordered without asking you what you wanted. Bruce usually had trouble getting the barman's attention. You felt disloyal acknowledging it, but somewhere in the past few weeks you'd become tired of PC-ism. Suddenly you were revelling in being treated like an American cheerleader. You sat admiring Dante's chauvinism or did you mean chivalry, and swallowed your shame with your drink.

Hungry? asked Dante.

You were a bit, you said.

Pretzels? he offered, putting his hand up to your hair.

You didn't know if he was hitting on you or removing debris, but you knew you were ravenous and not for food.

It was dark when he pulled up outside the apartment block. The jeep sat high above the cul-de-sac like a tank and you felt invincible until you noticed it was 22.00 hours and Bruce was at base headquarters. The windows were blazing like guns. You dreaded going over the top, but you were forcing yourself to reach for the door-handle when Dante manoeuvred himself closer to you and took command.

At first you were too shell-shocked and then you were enjoying yourself too much to resist. Dante handled you like a general, hurling you deftly round the interior of the jeep. Your body turned traitor under his lips. You stayed locked in combat until you were hit in the face by the headlights of Linda's car.

Get down, Dante told you, and he started to issue instructions.

You plummeted to the floor, ejected from the passenger's side, and hit the ground running. You ran low over the grass, through no-man's land, to the side door. When you got inside Bruce was already entrenched in bed.

Had you been drinking, he wanted to know.

You didn't bother to answer because he was irrelevant territory now.

You could float a battleship on the vodka in your stomach so you crashed between the sheets too. As you plummeted into sleep you were aware that the bed was shaking, but you weren't sure if it was your heart or Bruce's.

You woke half an hour later. The ceiling was shaking. You jumped out of bed, ran for the doorway, ran back and grabbed your photo album in case it was the Big One, ran for the doorway.

It was the Big One! you shouted to Bruce.

It was the jerk upstairs locked out again, said Bruce. (This was more than he'd said to you in the last twenty-four hours.)

You went to the kitchen anyway. In retrospect, it wasn't surprising that the fallout happened in the kitchen – most of the emotional tremors had so far. Afterwards you had vague thoughts about Dante and Hell's Kitchen but you never followed them through.

You didn't find broken plates but you found you could hear the rumblings of the Zuckermans' private life exceptionally clearly if you rested your head on the inside of the pantry wall. You wished you'd discovered this much sooner, and soon you wished you hadn't discovered it at all.

Linda had to let him in! Dante was saying, hammering on the door. Linda said nothing.

He just wanted five minutes of her time, Dante said.

Linda refused.

Just sixty seconds of her life! said Dante. He sounded as if he was going to start begging. You started to sweat.

It wasn't his fault, cried Dante, he'd been trying to break free.

Linda said more like break someone's heart. You winced.

She'd thrown herself at his head, cried Dante. You grabbed the nearest thing to you which happened to be the Marmite jar, and squeezed it so hard your hand cracked. You winced.

Would Linda just talk to him, he was begging her, please, just thirty seconds face to face was all he needed to explain, cried Dante.

Silence. The ground stress increased. You leaned on the cornflake box watching the walls of your future crumbling.

Linda had to realise that the chick meant nothing! cried Dante.

Cracks appeared in your heart. The roaring in your ears grew.

Was less than nothing! cried Dante.

You'd heard enough, had enough. You wanted more silence and fewer words. You pushed off from the cereal shelf and made for the front door.

All exhibitionists, Americans, and arseholes were to vacate the building immediately! you shouted. You stormed back inside, slammed the door, caught your T-shirt in it, opened the door and saw Zuckerman's face.

No hard feelings, he said hopefully.

Feel this, you said, and you slammed the door again, making sure your T-shirt was with you all the way.

You strode through the kitchen and into the bedroom where Bruce was pretending to be asleep. You swept his arms and legs off your side of the bed and got in before you realised you were still holding the Marmite. You strode out of the bedroom and into the kitchen.

In the pantry you put the Marmite to rest and your ear to the wall. You listened briefly to the silence. Then you left your post, marched back to bed and fell backwards into sleep like a stone.

Bruce had often told you that ostriches don't actually bury their heads in the sand. This was what you really wanted to do. When ostriches are threatened, Bruce had told you, they crouch low to the ground until the danger's past. For the next few days you made like an ostrich.

Linda looked more beautiful than ever and flaunted herself like a peacock whenever you couldn't avoid her on the stairs. Dante hunched his head forward like a hen. You'd always thought of Bruce as a paradise duck but you weren't sure any more that he wanted to be mated for life. Even after the Zuckermans moved out, he continued to disappear into the desert of his fourteen-hour working days. When the alarm went off at 6:30 every morning you couldn't see him for dust.

No personal oasis appeared on the immediate horizon. You made yourself think of the great scientific advances presumably resulting from the breakdown of your relationship. You consoled yourself with the thought that the suffering of two was nothing compared to the well-being of many angioplasts. You ate a lot of cheese because you knew that victims of aftershock needed protein.

You had your head in the fridge searching for the Edam when Trevor called from the lab.

Had you noticed that Bruce had been a bit upset lately? he said to you.

Yes, you'd had a suspicion, you said.

He'd just had a bit of an accident with some benzene, said Trevor.

How bad? you asked.

He was a bit shaken up, said Trevor.

You knew that scientists were excessively wary of drama so you had no way of knowing if Bruce was blind or needed skin grafts. You stuffed the Edam wax into your mouth without noticing and called a taxi because it was an emergency and the bottom was falling out of the day. You waited in the car park outside the lab and kicked the tyres of the ute until the soles of your feet felt numb.

When you saw the safety officer exit in mask and boots, looking as if he'd cleared away the aftermath of chemical warfare, you had to sit on the bumper bar. A little bit later Bruce came out onto the steps in his homespun socks.

He saw you and waved, which you took to mean he wasn't blind. As far as you could see his face was still there, but you set off across the car park to reassure yourself. He started walking too, which was a good sign.

You reached him, he reached you.

They'd confiscated his boots, he told you.

Why? you asked.

Contaminated, he said, so he hoped you didn't mind driving him home.

You walked with him to the ute. Without his boots on he seemed more on your level. You told him you'd buy him a new pair of boots with your next pay packet. He started telling you about the resilience of artificial nerve-cells and you concentrated on driving.

BIBLIOGRAPHY/ ACKNOWLEDGEMENTS

All stories are copyrighted to the author/publisher except where indicated.

Anderson, Barbara, *I Think We Should Go into the Jungle: Short Stories*, Victoria University Press, Wellington, 1989.

Ballantyne, David, *And the Glory*, Whitcombe & Tombs, Christchurch, 1963, © the estate of David Ballantyne.

Bilbrough, Norman, *Man with Two Arms*, Vintage, Auckland, 1991.

Bridger, Bub, *Te Ao Marama 5*, Reed, Auckland, 1996.

Cowley, Joy, *New Zealand Listener Short Stories*, ed. Manhire, Methuen, Wellington, 1977.

Davin, Dan, *Selected Stories*, Victoria University Press, Wellington, 1977, © 1981 the estate of Dan Davin.

Duggan, Maurice, *New Zealand Writing Since 1945*, eds. Jackson & O'Sullivan, Oxford University Press, Auckland, 1983, © the estate of Maurice Duggan.

Else, Chris, *Dreams of Pythagoras: 10 stories*, Voice Press, Wellington, 1981.

Farrell, Fiona, *Women's Work: Contemporary Short Stories by New Zealand Women*, eds. McLeod & Wevers, Oxford University Press, Auckland, 1985.

Frame, Janet, *Women's Work: Contemporary Short Stories by New Zealand Women*, eds. McLeod & Wevers, Oxford University Press, Auckland, 1985.

Gaskell, A.P., *New Zealand Listener Short Stories*, ed. Manhire, Methuen, Wellington, 1977, © the estate of A.P. Gaskell.

Gee, Maurice, *A Glorious Morning, Comrade: stories*, Auckland University Press, Auckland, 1975.

Grace, Patricia, *Collected Stories*, Penguin, Auckland, 1987.

Grenfell, E.S., *Landfall Country; Work from Landfall 1947–61*, ed. Brasch, Caxton Press, Christchurch, 1961, © the estate of E.S. Grenfell.

Harrison, Craig, *I Have Seen the Future: New Zealand Science, Future, and Fantasy Fiction Stories*, ed. Gadd, Longman Paul, Auckland, 1986.

Henderson, Michael, *The Lie of the Land*, John McIndoe, Dunedin, 1991, © the estate of Michael Henderson.

Hulme, Keri, *Te Kaihau/The Windeater*, Victoria University Press, Wellington, 1986.

Ihimaera, Witi, *Pounamu, Pounamu*, Heinemann, Auckland, 1972.

Johnston, Christine, *The End of the Century and Other Stories*, Canterbury University Press, Christchurch, 1999.

Jones, Lloyd, *Swimming to Australia: and other stories*, Victoria University Press, Wellington, 1991.

Kidman, Fiona, *The Best of Fiona Kidman's Short Stories*, Vintage, Auckland, 1998.

Koea, Shonagh, *The Woman Who Never Went Home*, Penguin, Auckland, 1987.

Mansfield, Katherine, *The Best of Katherine Mansfield's Short Stories*, Vintage, Auckland, 1998.

Marshall, Owen, *The Best of Owen Marshall's Short Stories*, Vintage, Auckland, 1997.

McCauley, Sue, *It Could Be You*, Vintage, Auckland, 1997.

Metcalfe, Rowan, *New Zealand Listener*, 25 October 1997.

Middleton, O.E., *A Walk on the Beach*, Michael Joseph, London, 1964.

Mincher, Philip, *Short Stories by New Zealanders One*, ed. Meikle, Longman Paul, 1973, © the estate of Philip Mincher.

Morrieson, Ronald Hugh, *The Oxford Book of New Zealand Short Stories*, ed. O'Sullivan, Oxford University Press, Auckland, 1992, © the estate of R.H. Morrieson (Maurice Shadbolt).

Morrissey, Michael, *The Oxford Book of New Zealand Short Stories*, ed. O'Sullivan, Oxford University Press, Auckland, 1992.

Nixon, Carl, *Sunday Star Times*, December 1997.

O'Sullivan, Vincent, *Palms and Minarets: selected stories*, Victoria University Press, Wellington, 1992.

Perkins, Emily, *Not Her Real Name*, Victoria University Press, Wellington, 1996.

Plumb, Vivienne, *The Oxford Book of New Zealand Short Stories*, ed. O'Sullivan, Oxford University Press, Auckland, 1992.

Quigley, Sarah, *The Picnic Virgin*, ed. Perkins, Victoria University Press, Wellington, 1999.

Sargeson, Frank, *Collected Stories, 1935–1963*, Blackwood & Paul, Auckland, 1964, © the estate of Frank Sargeson.

Scott, Rosie, *Queen of Love and Other Stories*, Penguin, Auckland, 1989.

Shadbolt, Maurice, *The New Zealanders,* Victor Gollancz, London, 1959, © Maurice Shadbolt and David Ling Publishing, Auckland.

Stead, C.K., *Author's Choice: leading New Zealand writers choose their favourite stories and explain why*, ed. Marshall, Penguin, Auckland, 2001.

Taylor, Chad, *The NeXt Wave*, ed. Pirie, University of Otago Press, Dunedin, 1998.

Te Awekotuku, Ngahuia, from *New Zealand Love Stories: an Oxford Anthology*, ed. Kidman, Oxford University Press, Auckland, 1999.

Texidor, Greville, *In Fifteen Minutes You Can Say A Lot*, Victoria University Press, Wellington, 1987. First published in *New Zealand New Writing*, No. 1, Wellington, 1942, later published as 'Epilogue'.

Wedde, Ian, *The Oxford Book of New Zealand Short Stories*, ed. O'Sullivan, Oxford University Press, Auckland, 1992.

Wells, Peter, *Dangerous Desires*, Reed, Auckland, 1991.

Wendt, Albert, *The Oxford Book of New Zealand Short Stories*, ed. O'Sullivan, Oxford University Press, Auckland, 1992.